ARCTIC MELTDOWN

Geza Tatrallyay

A Black Opal Books Publication

GENRE: SPECULATIVE HISTORY/CLIMATE CHANGE/FANTASY

This is a work of fiction. Names, places, characters and incidents are either the product of the author's imagination or are used fictitiously, and any resemblance to any actual persons, living or dead, businesses, organizations, events or locales is entirely coincidental. All trademarks, service marks, registered trademarks, and registered service marks are the property of their respective owners and are used herein for identification purposes only. The publisher does not have any control over or assume any responsibility for author or third-party websites or their contents.

ARCTIC MELTDOWN
Copyright © 2021 by Geza Tatrallyay
Cover Design by Geza Tatrallyay
Cover photos used with permission
All cover art copyright ©2021
All Rights Reserved
Print ISBN: 9781644372975

Second Publication: AUGUST 2021
First Published in 2011 by Geza Tatrallyay

All rights reserved under the International and Pan-American Copyright Conventions. No part of this book may be reproduced or transmitted in any form or by any means, electronic or mechanical, including photocopying, recording, or by any information storage and retrieval system, without permission in writing from the publisher.

WARNING: The unauthorized reproduction or distribution of this copyrighted work is illegal. Criminal copyright infringement, including infringement without monetary gain, is investigated by the FBI and is punishable by up to 5 years in federal prison and a fine of $250,000. Anyone pirating our eBooks will be prosecuted to the fullest extent of the law and may be liable for each individual download resulting therefrom.

ABOUT THE PRINT VERSION: If you purchased a print version of this book without a cover, you should be aware that the book is stolen property. It was reported as "unsold and destroyed" to the publisher, and neither the author nor the publisher has received any payment for this "stripped book."

IF YOU FIND AN EBOOK OR PRINT VERSION OF THIS BOOK BEING SOLD OR SHARED ILLEGALLY, PLEASE REPORT IT TO:
skh@blackopalbooks.com

Published by Black Opal Books **http://www.blackopalbooks.com**

DEDICATION

For all the Inuit and other native peoples of the Arctic, especially those in Greenland and Northern Canada, who will be most affected by climate change and any ensuing conflict in the polar zone.

"The last great geographical prize the world has to offer adventurous men."

—*Robert Peary*

PROLOGUE

At the North Pole and subsequently around the world— Thursday, August 2, 2007

Mir 1 touched down on the seabed a few minutes past noon after a three-hour descent through the freezing waters of the Arctic Ocean, its bouncing impact causing the fine clay sediment to billow like smoke. As the dust settled around the specially adapted submersible, its headlights illuminated a world never before exposed to light, bringing to life myriads of glistening, minuscule, shrimp-like creatures. The depth gauge showed that *Mir 1* was 4261 meters below the surface.[1]

The three occupants of the submersible—two Russian politicians, and an accomplished scientist engineer, Dr. Anatoly Sagalevich, the chief pilot—stared out into the uninviting cold and darkness through the thick glass of the portholes. Some sea anemones were burrowing into the ancient sediment—several per square meter—and fish swam slowly above the flat seafloor, unperturbed by the invaders of their environment.

The chief pilot pushed a button to free up the submersible's robotic arm, then deftly maneuvered a series of levers to scoop up soil samples from the ocean bottom, vainly trying to minimize disturbance so as to preserve whatever visibility they had. After ascertaining that *Mir 1*'s systems were in good working order, Sagalevich glanced at the expedition leader, Dr. Artur Chilingarov, revved up the engines, and piloted the submersible north.

It was not long before *Mir 1*'s sophisticated compass indicated that they had reached the North Pole. The three men congratulated themselves on being the first human beings to attain the northernmost point of the earth's surface without intervening columns of water and ice, and on conquering a monumental engineering, logistical and scientific challenge.

Sagalevich undid the arm again, and used it to place a titanium Russian flag, as well as a time capsule containing a message to future generations and some symbols of United Russia—Vladimir Putin's and Chilingarov's party—spot on the true North Pole, commemorating the historic feat, and thereby claiming it and the entire Eurasian side of the Arctic for the Russian Federation.

Andrei Gruzdev, Chilingarov's fellow parliamentarian, popped open a bottle of Nazdorovya, the sweetish bubbly that masquerades as Russian champagne, and the three clinked glasses.

They explored the bottom of the ocean for well over an hour, the first humans to do so this far north. The chief pilot used the robotic arm to scoop up further samples, since the mission's primary objective was to gather proof that the Lomonosov Ridge, along which the North Pole was situated, was an extension of the Russian continental shelf, in support of its claim to a large chunk of the Arctic seabed and its resources.

Finally, Sagalevich, wanting to leave enough of a safety margin to find the hole in the ice through which they had entered the frigid Arctic Ocean, observed that it was time to ascend. After checking the submersible's systems again, he started to pump water out of the ballast tank, and *Mir 1* began to rise through the eerie void.

When it, and its companion, *Mir 2*—which followed roughly half an hour behind—reached the surface and were lifted back on board by the specially fitted crane of the *RV Akademik Fedorov*, Chilingarov declared the *Arktika 2007* expedition a huge success. The assembled sailors of the polar research icebreaker and the accompanying scientists cheered in jubilation and congratulated Chilingarov and his companions. Via the ship's radio, the message was relayed to President Putin, who personally commended the brave team, especially praising the installation of the Russian flag on the ocean bed.

෴

Reaction in foreign capitals was swift.

"We're not throwing flags around. I'm not sure whether they've—you know, put a metal flag, a rubber flag, or a bed sheet on the ocean floor. Either way, it doesn't have any legal standing or effect on this claim. We certainly are skeptical about the claims made," Tom Casey, deputy spokesman of the US Department of State, said right after the Russian press release on the *Arktika* expedition.[2]

Canada's then foreign minister, Peter McKay, expressed even stronger irritation: "This is posturing. This is the true north, strong and free, and they're fooling themselves if they think dropping a flag on the ocean floor is going to change anything. There is no question over Canadian sovereignty in the Arctic. We've made that very clear. We've established—a long time ago—that these are Canadian waters and this is Canadian property. You can't go around the world these days dropping a flag somewhere and say, 'We're claiming this territory'. This isn't the 14th or 15th century."[3]

The angry Russian response to MacKay, from the distinguished Dr. Chilingarov himself, was unequivocal: "If someone doesn't like this, let them go down themselves…the Arctic has always been Russian."[4]

Denmark claimed that the 1500 kilometer Lomonosov Ridge was its property, and Danish science minister Helge Sander told reporters: "The preliminary investigations done so far are very promising. There are things suggesting that Denmark could be given the North Pole."[5]

In September 2007, Russia's Natural Resources Ministry issued a statement in defense of its claim: "Preliminary results of an analysis of the earth crust model examined by the *Arktika 2007* expedition, obtained on September 20, have confirmed that the crust structure of the Lomonosov Ridge corresponds to the world analogues of the continental crust, and it is therefore part of the Russian Federation's adjacent continental shelf."[6]

The Russian press took the US Department of State's reaction, and the responses from other western capitals to the installation of the Russian flag at the North Pole, "nearly as a declaration of war for the Arctic Region," claiming that "the US wants to take up Moscow's gauntlet" and that "the Arctic front will become another field of competition between Russia and the West."[7]

In response to the increasingly aggressive attitude of Russia, one of the last acts of outgoing President George W. Bush in January 2009 was to sign a policy directive dealing with the Arctic, clearly enunciating that the "United States has broad and fundamental national security interests in the Arctic region and is prepared to operate either independently or in conjunction with other states to safeguard these interests." The directive goes on to say that "these interests include such matters as missile defense and early warning; deployment of sea and air systems for strategic sealift, strategic deterrence, maritime presence, and maritime security operations; and ensuring freedom of navigation and overflight."[8]

Matters heated up between Russia and Canada again early in April 2010, when Canada's Foreign Affairs Minister Lawrence Cannon blasted a Russian plan to drop a team of airborne parachute commandos right at the North Pole, saying: "It's another stunt like the flag planting some years ago. It doesn't affect Canada's sovereignty...People have been going to Mount Everest and planting flags on Mount Everest since Jesus wore short pants...Nobody owns the North Pole...The Russians' stunts and Russian propaganda or public relations...it doesn't impress me. What impresses me is the work that's being done here."[9]

China, too, did not hesitate to get into the fray. In March 2010, a Chinese admiral stated that "the current scramble for the sovereignty of the Arctic among some nations has encroached on many other countries' interests," and he added that China had to "make short and long term ocean strategic development plans to exploit the Arctic because it will become a future mission for the navy."[10]

China's economic, political and military interests in the Arctic were set out already in a 2009 article by Li Zhenfu, a prominent Chinese academic, when he wrote in a journal of the China Association for Science and Technology that "After the Northwest Passage is opened up it will become a new 'axial sea route' between Atlantic and Pacific...Whoever has control over the Arctic route will control the new passage of world economic and international strategies."

The Arctic, Li concluded, "has significant military value, a fact recognized by other countries."[11] Moreover, much to the consternation of Europe, the Chinese have been trying to buy land and concessions in both Greenland and Iceland—for example, the intention to purchase 158 square kilometers in Iceland was announced by industrialist Huang Nubo in September 2011, ostensibly to build an eco-resort. The Icelandic government did not give its approval partly because of concerns that the motivation may not just be economic but also geostrategic: the Chinese, in addition to gaining access to oil and gas and other resources, are, according to this line of reasoning, paving the way for the eventual establishment of deepwater ports in what they see as the logical end of the Northeast Passage in the North Atlantic.[12]

Norway's Rear Admiral Trond Grytting summed up the situation in the Arctic in a presentation at a conference in Tromsø (entitled "From the Cold War to the Hot Arctic"): "We have lots of natural resources, military personnel and disputed borders in the Arctic. This has never been a recipe for peace."[13] And he added: "The Russian doctrine is unmistakable. The army is supposed to advance the state's goals in the surrounding region."

൜൞൜

Jurisdictional issues over maritime claims are governed by the UN Convention on the Law of the Sea. Article 76 gives each coastal state the right to a 200 nautical mile Exclusive Economic Zone (EEZ), and establishes a series of precise geological and topographical criteria that govern claims to extensions of the continental shelf beyond the EEZ. A special body, the Commission on the Limits of the Continental Shelf (CLCS), was created in the UN to make recommendations to coastal states regarding the establishment of the outer limits of jurisdiction over the continental shelf where a state's claim extends beyond the EEZ. The Commission is made up of twenty-one geologists, geophysicists and hydrologists nominated and elected by the signatory countries of the Convention.

Article 76 permits additional claims to be made out to

a maximum of the greater of either 350 nautical miles from the "baseline" of the shore or 100 nautical miles from the 2500 meter isobath or depth contour line. States have to demonstrate that the subsea land they claim is a "natural prolongation" of their own territory with the same geological history. A country can claim out to the "edge" of the shallower area where the deep sea starts.

However, there are also complicated criteria in place to define the "edge" which permit interpretation to play a role. Thus, the "edge" can either be 60 nautical miles out from the "foot" of the slope, which is where the steep incline of the shelf edge meets the seabed, or where the thickness of the sediment on the ocean floor is "at least one percent" of the distance back to the foot of the slope.[14]

In one of its key provisions, the Law of the Sea clearly excludes the use of ridges for extension of continental shelves. However, another subsequent paragraph that delimits the maximum extension of continental shelf jurisdiction to 350 nautical miles, states that the paragraph "does not apply to submarine elevations that are natural components of the continental margin, such as its plateau, rises, caps, banks and spurs."[15] It is this uncertainty on how to define an oceanic versus a continental ridge or rise that is allowing Russia, Denmark and Canada to make claims regarding the Lomonosov and the Alpha-Mendeleev Ridges in the Arctic.[16,17,1]

The Law of the Sea does not provide for effective dispute resolution. The Commission's mandate is only to review the evidence and make recommendations, and there is no mechanism to enforce decisions. Claims are subject to counter-claims by other states, and the entire process could degenerate into posturing, unilateral extra-legal actions, and lengthy bilateral negotiations. It has been said that the weakness of Arctic international law during a crucial time in the region's development threatens to create "a cacophony of arguments that could keep lawyers and geographers busy for decades" and "potentially a return to the dangerous Realpolitik of a previous era, where possession enforceable by force usually amounted to nine-tenths of the law."[18]

൙൙൙

Russia first made a submission to the UN Commission in 2001 claiming an extension of its jurisdiction; Canada, the US, and Denmark made comments that challenged the basis on which the claim was made, signaling that the information provided in the Russian case was insufficient for them to take a definitive position. The Commission sent the Russian submission back for further clarifications and revisions. While the deliberations of the Commission are not made public, it has been surmised that Russia failed to prove that the Lomonosov Ridge was a "natural prolongation" of its continental shelf, and therefore a continental versus an oceanic ridge. Apparently, the Commission observed "morphological breaks" in the ridge suggesting that it was not historically linked to the Eurasian landmass.[19]

Since 2001, Russia has sent a number of missions to the Arctic to collect further data for a resubmission of its claim to the Lomonosov Ridge and an additional 1.2 million square kilometers (463,000 square miles) of sub-ocean territory, an area three times the size of Germany, which promises to yield immense natural resource earnings. The *Arktika* expedition's mission included the gathering of new material for this submission. In addition, throughout much of 2009 and 2010, the Russian "North Pole-37" floating station was gathering scientific evidence and the *RV Academic Fedorov* spent the summer of 2010 collecting information about the Lomonosov and Mendeleyev under water ridges.[20]

The formal deadline for consideration of Russia's claim passed in 2009, and it was not until February, 2016 that Russia finally made a second submission formally claiming the additional 1.2 million square kilometers of continental shelf. UNCLOS consideration started in August of that year and in April, 2019, Russia claimed that "UNCLOS declared that the outer limits of the Russian continental shelf submission are geologically similar to 'the structure of the continuation of the shelf and the continent of the Russian Federation.'"[21] However, experts are clear on the point that despite any political spin, definitive scientific and political definition of extended national jurisdiction will take years, possibly decades, to settle.[22] Final adjudication will certainly await the submissions of all other concerned states.

Canada and Denmark have also been diligently gathering data to advance their claims to subsea territory along the Lomonosov Ridge, which extends all the way across the North Pole to Ellesmere Island and Northern Greenland. This was the primary purpose of the *LORITA 1* and the two *LOMROG* expeditions in 2007 and 2009 led by the Danes.

The Kingdom of Denmark has submitted three partial submissions relating to subsea territory surrounding Greenland to the Commission in 2012, 2013 and 2014. The third such submission—regarding the area north of Greenland—was submitted on December 15th, 2014 and covered an area of 895,541 square kilometers. The two previous partial submissions for Greenland were, respectively, the area (about 114,929 km2) south of Greenland submitted in June 2012 and the area (about 61,913 km2) northeast of Greenland submitted in November 2013. In August, 2016 a joint delegation from Greenland

and Denmark made a presentation to UNCLOS to further detail the claim.[23]

Since 2004, Canada has budgeted close to $150 million to perform the necessary studies to back up its claim[24] which have included joint aerial mapping, sonar surveys and gravitational measurements with the Danes[25] as well as the deployment of Canada's first undersea drone—an Autonomous Underwater Vehicle (AUV) to gather data on the seabed with unprecedented efficiency.[26] In 2013, Canada filed a preliminary submission to the United Nations concerning the outer limits of its continental shelf in the Arctic Ocean.[27] It made its final submission to UNCLOS in May 2019 claiming "approximately 1.2 million square kilometers of the Arctic Ocean seabed and subsoil in an area that includes the North Pole"[28] and overlaps with the claims of the Danes and the Russians.[29]

This overlapping territory is likely to be in the order of 200,000 square miles and hold[30] up to 10 billion tons of hydrocarbon deposits. It will no doubt require a diplomatic solution to resolve these competing claims.

The extent of this overlap is shown in the map following the Prologue.

༺༻

UNCLOS states that if a country disagrees with the Commission's recommendation, it may make a revised submission "within a reasonable time."[31] However, since the Commission has no power explicitly to reject a country's claim, the situation has been compared to a game of "ping pong between the Commission and the coastal State," in which the State and Commission volley the proposal back and forth without any hope for resolution.[32] Moreover, Rule 5(a) of Annex I of the CLCS Rules of Procedure states that "…in cases where a land or maritime dispute exists the Commission shall not consider and qualify a submission made by any of the States concerned in the dispute…"

Given a legal regime that does not result in binding rulings from the Commission and indeed specifically forbids it to issue such rulings where there are known conflicts between states, it could become tempting for states to take unilateral action and resort to alternative justifications, legal or based on historical precedent, for such action.

If its jurisdictional claims are not agreed by the international community according to the legal framework established by UNCLOS and if there is no diplomatic resolution to any overlap, one possible course of action for a country like Russia, would be to revert to the "sector principle" originally used by the Soviet Union in its claim to half of the Arctic. In fact, there are at least three other well-documented precedents for such a sectoral division of territories along a line of latitude, and the more recent two related to the Arctic. The first was the Treaty of Tordesillas in 1494, whereby Spain and Portugal agreed a line of demarcation between their empires. The second was the 1825 treaty between Britain and Russia defining Canada's western border as a line of longitude, 141° West, which would extend to the north as far as "the Frozen Ocean". The most recent precedent was the 1867 Russo-American treaty that fixed the border between Alaska as a line of longitude running through the Bering Strait "due north, without limitation, into the same Frozen Ocean".[33]

In 1926, the Central Executive Committee of the USSR used the sector principle to declare that "All lands and islands both discovered and which may be discovered in the future, which do not comprise at the time of publication of the present decree the territory of any foreign state recognized by the Government of the USSR located in the northern Arctic Ocean, north of the shores of the Union of Soviet Socialist Republics up to the North Pole between the meridian 32°04'35" East from Greenwich...and the meridian 168°49'30" West from Greenwich...are proclaimed to be the territory of the USSR."[34]

Interestingly, it could serve Canada's interests as well to adopt the sector principle, since it would bolster its claim that the several variants of the Northwest Passage and all the channels among its northern islands are internal waterways. Indeed, in 1907, Senator Poirier, in a speech in Parliament, stated that Canada should lay claim "to all lands that are to be found in the waters between a line extending from its eastern extremity north and another line extending from the western extremity north" to the Pole.[35] In 1909, just a few months after Robert Peary reached the North Pole, Captain Joseph Bernier unveiled a plaque on Melville Island claiming for "...the Dominion of Canada...the whole Arctic Archipelago lying to the north of America from longitude 60°W to 141°W up to the latitude of 90°N."[36]

֎֍֎

The five Arctic coastal nations have, on several occasions, stated that they will not resort to conflict over jurisdictional issues in the Arctic, rather resolving them by peaceful means and with recourse to international law. As early as October, 1987, Mikhail Gorbachev, Secretary General of the Communist Party of the Soviet Union, in a visionary statement at Murmansk, called for the Arctic to be a nuclear-free "Zone of Peace," with the region's resources developed cooperatively by the Arctic nations, restrictions on naval activities and peaceful cooperation on such issues as environmental protection, science and the rights of native peoples.[37]

This sentiment was clearly picked up in the Ilulissat Declaration at the Arctic Ocean Conference in May 2008, where the five committed to the "legal framework" of the Law of the Sea and "the orderly settlement of any possible overlapping claims".[38] Government officials of all the countries have reiterated this stance on a number of occasions since then. In fact, at the International Arctic Forum in Moscow in September 2010, President Vladimir Putin himself stated that "...we should maintain the Arctic as a region for peace and co-operation...If you stand alone you can't survive in the Arctic. Nature makes people and states to help each other."[39]

The flurry of research activity by all five Arctic littoral countries nevertheless is clearly aimed at bolstering claims for extended continental shelf jurisdictions in front of the UN Commission on the Limits of the Continental Shelf. And, ominously, notwithstanding statements that it would prefer to have its territorial claim well-grounded in accepted international law and practice, Russian officials have also enunciated a different—and perhaps more fundamental—position at the highest levels of the government.

"If these rights are not recognized, Russia will withdraw from the UN Convention on the Law of the Sea." From no less a figure than Artur Chilingarov, Deputy Speaker of the Duma, the Russian Parliament, and the government's unofficial spokesman on the Arctic.[40]

Russian Security Council Secretary and former head of the FSB, the successor to the KGB, Yevgeni Patrushev was even stronger with his accusatory remarks: "The United States of America, Norway, Denmark and Canada are conducting a united and coordinated policy of barring Russia from the riches of the shelf. It is quite obvious that much of this doesn't coincide with the economic, geopolitical and defense interests of Russia, and constitutes a systemic threat to its national security."[41]

This perception at the highest levels of the Russian government and the determination to ensure that Russia's interests in the Arctic remain paramount has led to the unveiling in recent years of a new Arctic command along with four new Arctic brigade combat teams to be operational from fourteen new airfields and sixteen deep water ports and the addition of eleven new icebreakers to add to its existing flotilla of forty. (The United States has one working icebreaker for the Arctic and one that has been taken out of operation.)[42]

Russia's aggressive stance is understandable from an economic standpoint: A Council on Foreign Relations report in 2017 stated that products from the Arctic account for twenty percent of Russia's gross domestic product and twenty-two percent of its exports. More specifically, ninety-five percent of Russia's natural gas and seventy-five percent of its oil emanate from above the Arctic Circle.[43] Moreover, the Northern Route over the top of Siberia is at least forty percent shorter than the Suez Canal or Cape of Good Hope routes, so as the passage becomes free of ice year-round, this could lead to a major reshuffling of global oceanic transportation and substantial leverage for Moscow.

And so it continues…in September of 2018, Russia conducted *Vostok-2018*, the largest military exercises ever in Siberia, with over three hundred thousand Russian soldiers, thirty-six thousand military vehicles, eighty ships and a thousand aircraft, helicopters and drones, as well as three thousand five hundred Chinese troops.[44]

In response, NATO held its biggest exercise in the Arctic in October 2018 with fifty thousand soldiers, two hundred and fifty aircraft, sixty-five ships and ten thousand tanks and other ground vehicles from thirty-one countries in the Trident Juncture war games at locations from Iceland to Finland. The games are meant to test NATO's response to a fictitious attack on Norway by "Murinus" an aggressor state clearly meant to be Russia.[45]

The actions and statements by its top officials hint that there is a possibility that Russia may, as has been suggested above, resort to unilateral action with respect to its Arctic claims if it disagrees with the outcome of deliberations pursuant to the international legal framework. Conflicting statements by senior Russian officials in other contexts historically indicate that they are willing to work along more than one axis to secure their interests. The Arctic is too entwined with the Russian psyche, its culture, history and economy, for Russia to give up lightly on what it feels belongs to it.

❦❦❦

The above paints an impressionistic picture of the backdrop against which this novel is written. The story takes us on one possible, but hopefully not probable, apocalyptic path that these events may unfold along, and outlines what could be a feasible, peaceful and beneficial outcome to the serious, and unfortunately little appreciated issues that mankind faces in the Arctic.

If only our politicians would listen!

❦❦❦

People and events in the novel are fictitious, and any resemblance they bear to actual persons is purely coincidental to the story. Also, the consideration of the various submissions to UNCLOS has been collapsed into a much shorter time frame and is clearly my own imagined version.

Danish Claims Showing Overlaps with Neighboring States[46]

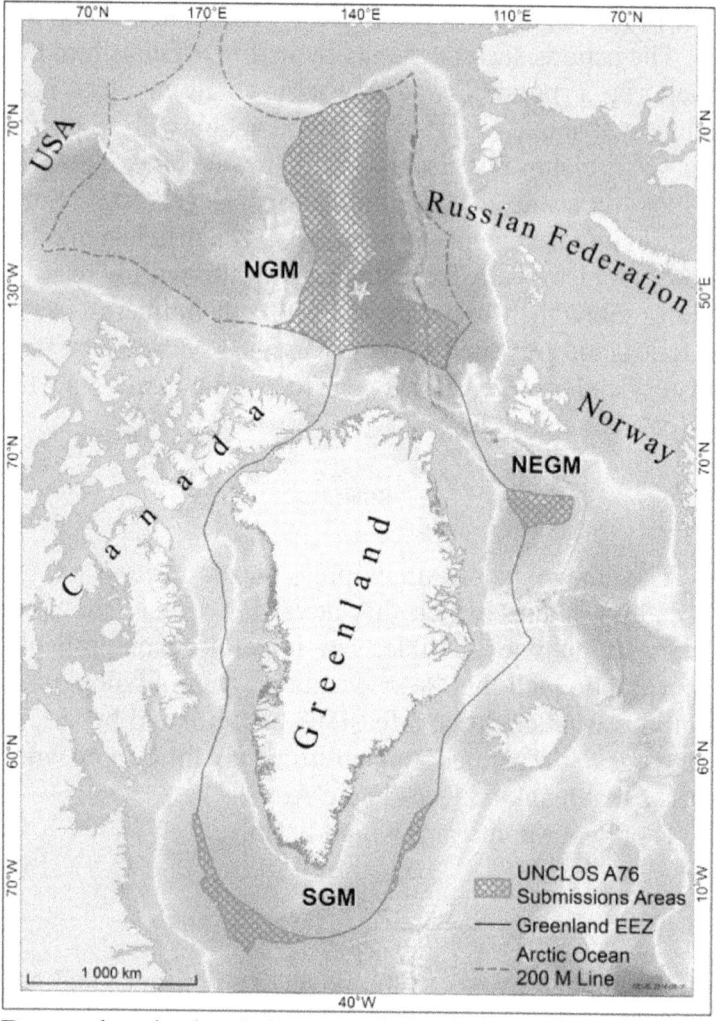

Denmark submitted three partial submissions relating to Greenland to UNCLOS in 2012, 2013 and 2014. The third partial submission—regarding the area north of Greenland (NGM)—was submitted on December 15th, 2014 and covered an area of 895,541 km2. This claim overlaps with Norway's submission from 2006 and Russia's submission from 2015, and also with Canada's most recent claim. The two previous partial submissions for Greenland were, respectively, the area (about 114,929 km2) south of Greenland from June 2012 and the area (about 61,913 km2) northeast of Greenland from November 2013.

What follows is fiction, but based on today's realities, it is one of several possible future histories.

Hanne's Arctic

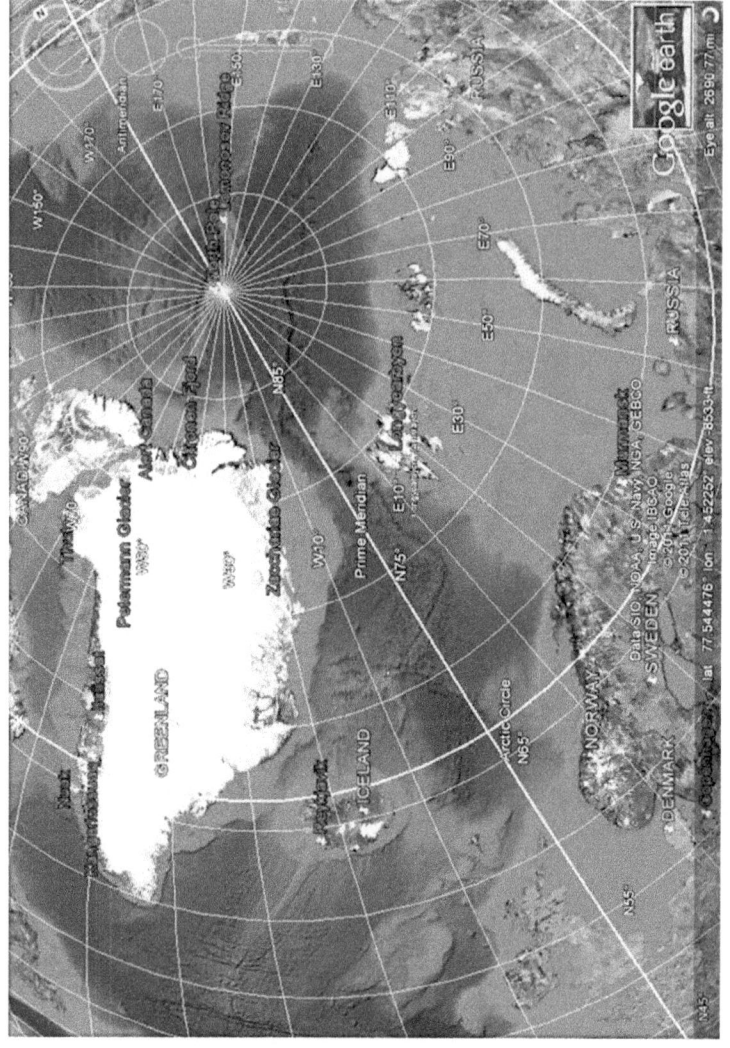

CHAPTER 1

Warming Land, Northern Greenland—Friday, August 12, twenty-twenty

It was the time of day, and the season, Hanne loved most in the Arctic. The astonishing warmth of the sun, the vivid colors of the sky and the sea, the brilliant white of the ice against the browns and grays and purples of the land, the blues and greens of the fjord, and the solitude.

Yes, above all, the solitude. Particularly when the men were away from their base camp at the sheltered end of this remote fjord, and she could strip to the buff and walk peacefully along the water's edge, while all her cells rejoiced in the rare heat of the sun.

Hanne performed the same routine on each of these very few, lovely Arctic summer days when she was alone: after a leisurely breakfast of instant coffee, rice cakes and freeze-dried strawberries, she would fill two buckets with the crystal clear, glacial water of the fjord, set them in the sun to heat up, and place, on a nearby boulder, a bar of soap, some shampoo and a thick towel. She would then take her sleeping bag out from the tent, and march it down to another big flat rock about fifty meters along the shore, where she would shake it well and spread it to air out. When the sun reached its zenith—or sometimes a little before, if she could not wait any longer—she would take off all her clothes, quickly wash her hair and scrub herself clean. Then, with blond hair and shapely body rapidly toweled down, she would walk along the shore of the protected inlet—allowing the cooling breeze coming off the water and the heat of the noonday sun to finish drying her—in the direction of the rock where she had spread her sleeping bag.

Today, for some reason, Hanne felt a happiness that she could not ascribe just to the summer warmth and the enjoyment of her routine. Maybe it was the fulfillment of having done a good job, of being close to completing the mission, and perhaps the prospect of going home to Copenhagen in a few days when the men returned. And there, to see her dear ones: her father and mother, her sister, and her nieces, Alise and Madja—Hanne loved the little girls—her best friend from school, Kristi, and, of course, her boyfriend, Jens. Although she was less sure of that, now that she had been geographically separated from him again for well over two months. Hanne was not fully convinced that Jens was the right partner for her: she found him too focused on his work with the Green Liberation Front, with little concern for anything else, sometimes even her. She had the sense that he held her back, and did not nourish her need to grow, to express her wild side. Her doubts about the relationship usually intensified during these periods when she was away from Copenhagen doing fieldwork.

No matter, Hanne was happy: she broke into a run, started to dance around and sing, waving the towel above her head, then erupted in the scintillating laugh that had made Jens fall in love with her. She slowed to a stroll, and coming to the rock, positioned her towel as a pillow and stretched her sleek body along the open sleeping bag to regale in the warmth of the full Arctic sun.

There were maybe only five days, perhaps seven now

that every summer the temperatures were higher and it stayed warm longer, when one—even a born Scandinavian—could think of frolicking around naked in Northern Greenland. It was ironic, Hanne had often thought to herself, that this, where they were, was called Warming Land—after the Danish botanist and ecologist Eugen Warming—and not because the land and the sea all around were heating up due to global warming. Hanne and the two younger men working under her were stationed in this remote part of the world to study the effect of climate change on the glaciers of Northern Greenland, particularly the Petermann Glacier, just west of the Warming Land Peninsula. Andreas Hansen and Bent Pederson had taken a five-day side trip to study the impact of climate change a year after a huge ice island had broken off from the glacier and to measure the overall shrinkage during the past year.

∽∾∽

Hanne's routine on these solitary, gorgeous Arctic summer days, lying there naked on the big gray rock slab, included allowing herself to drift into erotic imaginings. In the first several weeks at Warming Land, still inside her sleeping bag in the tent, she would conjure up some of the times she had made love with Jens. And, occasionally, the off-and-on relationship she continued to have with Kristi, who had been her very first sexual partner.

But now, here on the rock, these vivid thoughts—yes, they were like movies—were more generalized, with beautiful, muscled men she did not know. And perhaps because she had been away from Jens for so long, more urgent, more violent. On these occasions, she would close her eyes, and start to arouse herself by stroking her breasts; her hands would move lower to fondle her pubic area, eventually bringing herself to a crescendo of pleasure. What she enjoyed most though, was the involuntary trembling of her entire body after coital release, and then the drifting off into a euphoric state of half-sleep, half-wakefulness under the Arctic sun.

∞∞∞

This time, Hanne was brought back to consciousness by what she thought was the far away buzzing of an airplane engine. She opened her eyes to the glare of the sun and sat up quickly to search the sky. Noises carry far in the Arctic, and it was so rare to hear the otherwise familiar sound of an airplane engine here—only the odd AWACS plane high in the sky above the Kennedy Channel, or a Canadian transport supplying CFS Alert over on Ellesmere Island, or perhaps the twice weekly Danish Air Force flight monitoring Greenland's shores—that Hanne knew them all, and this definitely was different. This was the faint sound of the far-off motor of a smaller plane, a Beaver, or an Otter perhaps.

And then, just as Hanne stood up from her rock, still searching for the aircraft, the big clumsy looking bird suddenly appeared from the other side of the striated bluff bordering the fjord, and it loomed much, much larger and closer than Hanne had thought based on the engine drone. In fact, in a moment, it flew right over her, twice tipping its wings…It was only then that Hanne remembered that she stood there gazing at the sky with no clothes on.

As the Otter—yes, it was an Otter—flew low over the fjord to check for a path free of ice floes and underwater rocks, only to do a tight turn and scoot rapidly back towards her, finally skimming the surface with its pontoons, Hanne grabbed the towel and started running toward her tent. She was halfway there when the plane came to a stop in the shallows about fifty meters offshore, and the door was flung open by a tall, tanned man who yelled through cupped hands, "Ahoy there! We're coming ashore."

When Hanne reached the tent, a quick glance backwards told her that another two men had also climbed onto the pontoons and the three of them were laughing while they rapidly inflated a rubber dinghy. She could just imagine the lewd remarks and sexual allusions they were making, but decided she didn't care. She had a great body, and so what if they had seen her naked. Inside the tent, she quickly pulled on her jeans—she could not find her panties in the mess—and a turtleneck, and reemerged, pushing her hair out of her face, just as the men were paddling ashore. To her shore.

"Fancy meeting a gorgeous lady up here at the North Pole," the tall man started, walking toward her while the other two pulled the boat up on the rocks. "I thought only Santa Claus and sex-starved musk ox lived here." Hanne not only did not like the man's blatant sexism, but she also found his condescending attitude and Australian accent annoying.

"Hello. Hanne Kristensen. I'm Chief of the Glaciology and Oceanography Department of the Geological Survey of Denmark and Greenland," she said icily. "My two colleagues are due to come back from a field trip at any moment. Latest tomorrow." Hanne wanted to let these strangers know right up front that she was not alone in the high Arctic.

"Hanne, pleased to meet you. Although I think we've already been fortunate enough to be introduced to...most of you. But that was from afar," the tall man said with a smug little laugh. "My name is Lachlan McTierney. Lock's good enough. This is Jack Scott...And that one over there is Will O'Brian. We're exploring here for Greenland Earth Resources, an Australian mining company."

"Good to meet you…" But she still needed convincing.

"That was quite a show you put on for us as we came down…"

"Sorry…I didn't think anyone would be watching."

"No worries. It was a pleasure to see." Lock clearly delighted in making Hanne blush, but once he had, he was ready to get on with business.

"Would you mind if we set up camp alongside? This seems like an easy place to pitch our tents. Besides, we would enjoy some new company. I'm getting tired of talking to Will, Jack and myself."

⁂

In less than an hour, the Australians had their tents pitched: one to sleep in, and a bigger one to use as an office, kitchen, dining and living room. For the Arctic, this tent was quite spacious, and they even had four folding chairs and a camp table.

"We've got some work to catch up on now, but will you do us the honor of dining with us?" Lock strolled over and asked Hanne as the other two miners finished moving their stuff in from the Otter. "At six, does that work for you?"

"Thank you. That will give me time to finish my work for the day too."

⁂

The sun was still bright but lower in the sky at six ten when Hanne made her way over to the Aussies' tent, with mixed feelings of excitement and just a tinge of trepidation. She did like the idea of company—solitude was fine, but only when alleviated by the possibility of eventual interaction. And, she too, was getting a little bored with the silent meals she shared with Andreas and Bent. She was not sure though, about these Australian miners. They seemed a bit crass, sexist—and there were three of them and only one of her. Lock—he was a bit of a puzzle—seemed intelligent, and at times kind and pleasant, and sometimes, well, downright off-putting. But good looking, unlike Bent and Andreas, who were typical geeky scientists.

She knew she was at their mercy in this remote spot. But Hanne, at thirty-one, had seen a lot, and she was confident that she would be able to handle any situation.

She did not bother to change, only adding a tight baby-blue fleece over the navy cotton turtleneck, but did, of course, wash her hands and face and comb her shoulder-length blond hair. She had no makeup, but never used much anyway. She felt that the heat of the sun soaked up by her cells had fortified her, and with a confident flourish, she flipped open the flap of the Aussies' tent.

Inside, the camp table was set for four with real china and silverware, and wine glasses. An open bottle of red stood in the middle. The three men had already started drinking, and Will, the chef, had an apron on and was busying himself over a small gas camp stove with a large skillet on top that had an entire fish in it.

"Arctic char," Lock said, smiling as he handed Hanne a wine glass. "Fresh from the fjord. Here, let me pour you some vino. Hope you can handle an Aussie red with the fish. D'Arenberg McLaren Vale Shiraz 2007."

Hanne knew nothing about Australian wines, but was quite glad to have a drink. Even though she was used to white wine with fish. The last alcohol she had consumed was when she went out for a goodbye dinner with Jens at the end of June. She had never thought she would be served a fine vintage wine this far north of the Arctic Circle.

⁂

Dinner was delicious: the fresh char, caught by Will while the other two had settled in and started to work, accompanied by quinoa and freeze-dried broccoli, followed by vanilla pudding with a bilberry coulis, and, of course, several bottles of the D'Arenberg. It was a pleasant change from the rather vapid rations supplied by the Geological Survey of Denmark and Greenland, and Hanne found that she was thoroughly enjoying the evening, and changing her mind about the men, especially Lock.

When Jack referred to him as "Prof," Hanne took the occasion to enquire what their mission was in Northern Greenland. She had heard of Greenland Earth Resources—in fact, she had been briefed on all the mining, oil and gas companies doing business on the large island—but did not know they had any interests this far north.

"My specialty is the exploration and exploitation of underwater mineral deposits, especially on continental shelves. I teach geology at the University of Beijing. GER took me on as a consultant for the summer…You know, Hanne, based on what we know about the geological formations here and in the adjacent continental shelf area, and the geophysical data, we believe there could be significant rare earth deposits off the coast and extending along the eastern side of the Lomonosov Ridge. We're here on an exploratory mission."

"The Lomonosov Ridge! That is a sensitive topic…"
"Don't I know it!"

"I was part of the joint Danish-Canadian Expeditions, *LOMROG I* in 2007 and *LOMROG II* in 2009. Sorry, that's the acronym we use for the Lomonosov Ridge of Greenland project. I also spearheaded the Danish claims that we submitted in 2012, 13 and 14…and the presentation in 2016…"

"To UNCLOS? And *LOMROG II*? On the Swedish boat, the *Oden*? Very interesting!"

"It was…"

"We found the adaptations made for the collection of seismic information—the multi-beam echo sounder, with the integrated sub-bottom profiles—very innovative."

"Yes, it helped us gather some great data…"

"Hanne, I haven't seen all the material that you generated, but Denmark's claim is interesting from what I know about it. Your submission to the Commission on the Limits of the Continental Shelf…"

"You can rest assured that the case we put together is strong."

"Well, just so you know, my view is that the Lomonosov Ridge is clearly an oceanic elevation and not the extension of any continental shelf. I teach this stuff in Beijing in a crossover course to International Law."

"I'm glad you're not on the UN Commission then. Because our submission proves that it is. An extension of the shelf off Northern Greenland."

"Good luck defending it. With some of the geezers on that Commission, you might just be able to carry it off."

"What about the Russian claim?"

"Hanne, as I'm sure you know, the first Russian submission was thrown out by the Commission already in 2001."

"Yes, of course…"

"Since then, they've made a lot of noise—including planting that titanium flag at the North Pole some years ago. Then parachute dropping those commandos…"

"Some real showmanship that was."

"And then of course they created the new Northern Command and the four commando units…plus, they have been building all those bases and airfields up there."

"Yes, that is certainly all very intimidating…"

"And that Andrei Laptov fellow—you know, that famous Polar Explorer—he is also an elected politician, I think—has been quite outspoken too…They were working on another submission, and were supposed to resubmit in 2009, but only did so finally in February 2016. This second submission claimed the additional 1.2 million square kilometers of continental shelf, just as the first rejected one did. And there is significant overlap with ours. As well as the Canadian one, submitted in 2019."

"I suspect the Ruskis came up with some flaws in their original argumentation, hence the long time they needed to paper it over. The little I have looked at the Siberian side, the geology there looks quite complicated. For one, the contact between the Ridge and the Siberian shelf is severely faulted."

"Hmm. That is our view as well."

"In fact, there may very well be a break there that would eliminate any semblance of legitimacy for their claim to half the Arctic."

"Interesting…"

"They must have had to go pretty deep with their seismic soundings to try and prove otherwise and I suspect the deeper structure may not help them either. But it seems that they are now asserting that UNCLOS has essentially agreed their claim."

"Hmm. It couldn't be final until all the claims are considered. And perhaps they will even need to be taken together. In any case, we have made our submission and we are quite happy with it. Now we wait until we are called to defend it. Meantime though, any summer I can, I prefer to spend up here."

※※※

Lock proposed that they go for a walk while Jack and Will cleaned up. Hanne was glad to get out into the fresh evening air. The sun was lower in the sky, and an Arctic chill had descended on the land, so Hanne zipped her fleece up.

"Tell me about yourself, Hanne. What's a beautiful woman like you doing up here in the solitary north these days?"

"Right now, my team and I—we're studying the shrinking of the glaciers in Greenland. It's scary what is going on, as I'm sure you know. Two huge ice islands broke off Petermann in 2010 and 2012—the first one, two hundred and sixty square kilometers, four times the size of Manhattan, and the second one half that size— and that's after considerable degradation in the years before. Since then, there has been some growth, but in 2017 we saw a new rift develop and we are afraid that this may result in another huge chunk breaking off. Petermann has one of the longest tongues reaching into the sea and sooner or later we will see some of this calve. My colleagues are out there doing some monitoring and final measurements right now."

"I guess, in the long run the melting ice could be good for Greenland and bad for the rest of the world. Global warming will unlock some of Greenland's rich resource base and make it more habitable. But it'll cause drought and flooding in many other parts of the world. For example, my country."

"What is unbelievable is that the world's politicians

have not been able to agree on how to make a big enough dent in greenhouse gas emissions. Copenhagen in 2009 was a disaster. Cancun did not amount to much either. Durban, too, was a bust. At least some progress was made in Paris—but then the USA announced they are pulling out. COP 25, too, was disappointing. And America, China, India—the largest emitters in the world—are still at best only making token efforts and continuing to burn coal."

"Yeah. Not much good comes out of those big meetings. Other than hot air. Excuse the overworked pun…"

"At least we have the youth movement worldwide led by Greta Thunberg. But I'm afraid it's too late already. The repercussions globally—except for maybe a country like Greenland—will be terrible."

"Yes, the terrible fires in my country … and the floods in Indonesia and elsewhere…"

They walked in silence for a while, away from the camp. Their path along the shore of the fjord led them to the rock where Hanne had lain earlier in the day, and she sensed herself become intensely aware of the man beside her. She turned and looked at Lock and realized that she felt an attraction, an animal magnetism, draw her towards him. Maybe it was the particular spot—with her sleeping bag still spread out, ever so invitingly—and the erotic memory of lying there naked in the full sun, or the satisfied sensation of having drunk good wine and eaten a delicious dinner, or, for that matter, the feeling of desolation in the face of the enormous problems they had been talking about, but Hanne yearned for physical contact.

And Lock, seeing this in her eyes, and perhaps also conjuring up the image of her naked body on that rock, felt the Arctic fever he had heard about from the Inuit. He reached out to her, drew her to himself: his lips found hers, his tongue parted them, exploring the sensuous, soft inside. Before they knew it, she and he both tore at their clothes and threw them haphazardly on top of the sleeping bag left there by Hanne. Then, when they were both naked, Lock gently pulled Hanne down on top, and entered her. It did not take either of them long to climax, such was their hunger.

Afterwards, they lay on the rock in each other's arms, relishing the contact of skin to skin, lips to lips, body to body. Infinitely better, thought Hanne, than earlier, all by herself. Or, for that matter, with Jens, although that was a distant memory by now.

It was not long before the cooling Arctic evening imposed itself on the new lovers, bringing shivers: they got up from their rock, put their clothes on, and slowly walked back to the tents. When they reached Hanne's, she turned her face to Lock's for one last kiss and went inside.

Lock went down to the water's edge, picked up a few flat stones and skipped them over the surface.

Only much later did he go into the tent that he shared with the other men.

Chapter 2

North of Ellesmere Island, Arctic Ocean—Morning, Wednesday, August 3, a year later

Hanne was up front in the bow of the *Freyja*, the Swedish research icebreaker and, as the summer fog of the Arctic Ocean lifted for a moment revealing the sporadic ice floes floating on its surface, both she and her companion on the deck peered silently out into the unreal seascape.

The little warmth from the hazy sun that penetrated the gray mist was not enough to warm her up, and in spite of herself, she snuggled closer to Richard. She was glad that when she proposed they get some air, the handsome Canadian foreign affairs officer had agreed to accompany her on this short walk around the deck.

Richard Simpson had joined the mission at the last minute, introducing himself as the diplomat selected by the prime minister to lead the Canadian team structuring and negotiating Canada's stance on Arctic jurisdictional issues. Since the *Freyja* had left Longyearbyen seven days earlier, Hanne had grown fond of this competent and urbane bureaucrat, with his self-deprecating humor and quick wit. She was astonished at how easily he understood the geological and geophysical concepts thrown around in the daily briefing meetings, but then he did admit that he had excelled at the earth sciences courses he took as a minor at Harvard at the expense of his major in international relations.

Suddenly, less than a couple of hundred meters and dead ahead where the mist momentarily lifted, Hanne was stunned to make out the black hulk of a submarine floating lazily in the deep grey blue water.

"Look, look!" She pointed out the sleek metallic cigar to Richard, who had actually been admiring the ruddy, lightly freckled cheeks and aquamarine eyes of the pretty Danish scientist. And, just as she said this, Hanne saw another similar dark shape emerge through the haze about hundred meters to the left.

"What are those two doing here?" Richard asked, equally surprised.

"Out here, in the middle of nowhere…"

"They must be Russian, I think."

"It's far from home for them. We were at 88° North and 59° West or thereabouts this morning—way the other side of the Arctic from Russia."

"The new Graney class attack sub, I think, judging from the looks. Nuclear powered. State-of the-art. Armed with twenty-four cruise missiles. Virtually undetectable underwater when they use only passive sonar." Richard was not only versed in geology, but also in Arctic security issues.

"They must be trawling the Ridge."

"I think they've seen us. They're getting set to dive."

"Amazing," Hanne said, as first one sleek machine slid beneath the dark blue waters and then the other; within moments, the silence returned, and it was as if the two intruders had never been there.

॰॰॰

Hanne glanced up to the bridge to see if Captain

Teodor Arnstrom was there, and when she didn't see him, said: "Let's go below. We've got to tell the captain."

"Yes. I'd also like to radio Ottawa ASAP."

They found Arnstrom in the Swedish research icebreaker's conference room, which had been turned into a twenty-four hour data analysis center. He was discussing the next day's course and the points where they would take bathymetric and seismic readings with the respective Danish and Canadian expedition experts. Both teams were on the Swedish boat together to gather some additional data to use to defend their submissions for UNCLOS. Denmark and Canada had agreed to share data and coordinate their submissions as far as possible.

"Captain, we've just sighted what I think are two Russian Graney class subs," Richard broke the news.

"Yes, we've had reports that their submarine fleet was aggressively patrolling all over the Arctic," Captain Arnstrom replied. "To bolster their claim. I'll have Sodegren radio Copenhagen. Ottawa, too, if you'd like. And Thule, to let the Americans know. Thanks."

ల/సిల/స

The *Freyja* continued her voyage along the Lomonosov Ridge to the North Pole, and Hanne was thrilled that she was able to achieve a life-long wish of following in the footsteps of Peary and Amundsen. This trip though, was also a remarkable feat: it was the first time a surface vessel had reached the furthest point north on earth unencumbered by ice. Sure, they had encountered countless floes along the way, but the Arctic ice pack had broken up and melted this summer more so than ever before, and it was possible for a thick-hulled ship like the *Freyja* to make its way to the pole without using its icebreaker capabilities. This was certainly a first—although Hanne thought to herself, it had been made possible by the rapidly changing climatic conditions in the Arctic.

At the pole itself, the *Freyja* took some last bathymetric and seismic soundings, and having completed its scientific data collecting mission, turned its nose around and started heading back towards Longyearbyen, on Svalbard Island, Norway, its home base.

CHAPTER 3

Northeast of Greenland, Arctic Ocean—Night, Friday, August 5, a few days later

Marge was delighted. She and Ralph were well bundled up in the down parkas provided for the trip by North Pole Expeditions, the company that had organized the cruise. Arm-in-arm out on the deck of the *Akademik Kurchatov*, they were taking a brief stroll after a rather ordinary dinner which had been much improved with a bottle of very expensive Bordeaux she had sprung for. They, and some of the other passengers, were out braving the cold to view the stunning Zachariae Ice stream, one of the great glaciers of Northern Greenland, in the light of the late Arctic evening, before the *Kurchatov* headed due north to get as close to the North Pole as possible, now that ice conditions permitted.

A voyage to the North Pole had been Ralph's childhood dream, to follow in the footsteps of the great Polar explorers: Franklin, Nansen, Peary, Amundsen. And when Marge had given him the tickets for the cruise as his sixty-fifth birthday gift, bought with the money she had saved in her job as a part-time cashier at the Western Mall Safeway, the grin that lit up his face extended from one ear clear across his face to the other. Even though her joints now ached from the bitter cold, that smile had made it all worthwhile.

This was their third night out of Longyearbyen, where the cruise had originated. The *Akademik Kurchatov*, built in 1989, was a Russian registered ship with specially strengthened hulls and stabilizers to cope with the sea ice. Supposedly, its main purpose was research, but with its capacity to carry one hundred and ten passengers, its owners were clearly in a position to profit from the growing and lucrative tourist interest in the Arctic.

When Marge had booked the cruise, she was doubly assured by the company that the boat was totally safe. The professionalism that Captain Palinsky radiated at the champagne reception on the first evening at sea also went a long way to reassure her.

"Ralphie, I'm cold. Let's go downstairs," Marge said after a stolen kiss beside the lifeboat that for a moment blocked the rays of the sun still lingering in the sky and illuminating the eerie wall of ice looming a kilometer or so in front of them. The wind was picking up, and, as Marge glanced out to sea, she noticed that the floes the *Kurchatov* had been plowing through during the day seemed to have thickened and closed in all around them.

"Yeah. It's bloody cold out here. You're right, Marge. Maybe it's time to snuggle under the covers, and see what tomorrow brings," Ralph said, turning to face her. "And Marge, thank you. This is the best birthday ever. You don't know how much I'm enjoying it."

⁂

They went below, took their parkas off and hung them on the hooks by the door. Marge couldn't help shivering, and rubbed her hands to warm them up.

"Ralph, go ahead. You go to the bathroom first." Selfishly, Marge wanted to get undressed and put on her nightie and warm bathrobe before brushing her teeth. But she also wanted to give Ralph a chance to take his little blue pill; she was keen on rounding out a hitherto wonderful birthday for Ralph with the now rarer pleasure of sexual release. Indeed, she thought to herself, it had been a long time since she herself had experienced an orgasm.

It was when she was tying the belt of the robe that she heard the deafening noise.

"Ralph, are you…" But no, the unearthly loud crack had emanated from somewhere outside and it just went on and on.

Ralph opened the bathroom door, and putting his hearing aid back in his ear, asked, "What did you say, my dear?"

"Ralphie, what in God's name was that noise?"

"Ahh, dear, no idea…"

Another diabolical rumble, an extended thundering boom, all outside, and then a searing, swooshing sound that seemed to approach rapidly, the roar gathering intensity.

And then, all hell broke loose: the whole room seemed to move, the ship turned on its side. Marge was thrown against Ralph, and both rolled head over heels across the small space, hurled vehemently against the far wall, which now served as the floor below them. She felt pain as ribs cracked, saw a huge gash appear on her thigh, and blood streamed down her face, soiling her nightgown.

Oh no, what is happening? How could it end like this… was Marge's last thought as she passed out, with the limp and bleeding body of Ralph on top of her.

༄༅༄

Up on the bridge, when Captain Palinsky—whose eyes were constantly scanning the shadows of the seascape ahead, sipping on his mug of black tea—first heard the piercing crack, he knew from experience that the Zachariae must be calving.

"Good. That will be nice to show the tourists tomorrow," he muttered to himself. He stared out at the ice cliffs, and thought he saw some movement somewhere far ahead.

When the roar did not let up for several minutes and only got louder and deeper, Palinsky's danger sensors were triggered, and he jumped into action. He knew this was going to be a big one, a huge ice island probably, or several significant icebergs, and that there would be a tsunami-like effect, which, with all the loose ice around, could be particularly dangerous. He immediately got on the *Kurchatov*'s radio and started putting out an urgent mayday signal; then he concentrated on trying to maneuver the ship farther away from the glacier face. He continued frantically as he saw an enormous wave carrying threatening large ice floes bear down on, and tower over the bridge. The captain's "Save Our Souls" signal was only broken off when he was swept from his position at the wheel along with all the broken glass and twisted steel of the cabin, as the reinforced windows were smashed by the big blocks of ice thrown against them by the giant wave.

The *Akademik Kurchatov* had been bowled over on its side and, completely swamped, disappeared into the dark waters of the Arctic Ocean.

CHAPTER 4

Northwest of Svalbard, Arctic Ocean—Night, Friday, August 5, and Daytime, Saturday, August 6, the next day

Lars Sodegren was in the middle of an exciting paragraph on page 282 of his paperback copy of *Twisted Reasons*, which he was reading for the second time, when he first heard the faint crackling sound coming from the *Freyja*'s radio. He took his time to finish the sentence, then reluctantly put the book upside down, still open, on the table, and in a reflex action, leaned forward to get nearer the box in spite of the fact that he was wearing hi-tech earphones. He turned the volume up and concentrated all his senses and mental energies on trying to understand the message coming over the sound waves.

Yes, it was definitely an SOS signal he was hearing: he piqued his ears because it was hard to hear, but with much effort, he was finally able to decipher the coordinates. *78°N by 30°W*, he wrote on a slip of notepaper. Sodegren's familiarity with Arctic geography was good enough so he knew immediately that the location was somewhere off Northeastern Greenland. He nevertheless quickly brought it up on the computer screen beside him—yes, just off the coast. As he zoomed in, he saw that two major glaciers spilled into the ocean right there—the Zachariae, and the one just known by its latitude as 79 North.

☙❧

Captain Arnstrom was sitting in the boat's mess chatting to some of the mission members, including Hanne and Richard, over a light supper of smoked salmon on pumpernickel with sliced red onion and a Carlsberg beer when his mobile intercom bleeped.

"Arnstrom."

"Captain,"—Hanne could hear Sodegren's voice—"I just picked up what sounded like an SOS. Off the coast of Greenland. Seventy-eight north by thirty west. Did not read name of ship, the signal went dead. Nothing since from there. Position is roughly where two major glaciers empty into the sea."

"Hmm. Contact Danish Navy to see if they know what vessel might have been there. Thule too. And the Canadians. See if there is any traffic nearby. We may be the closest ship—I will be up on the bridge. Let me know what you find out."

"Roger."

"Captain," Hanne started, as Arnstrom pushed the off button on the intercom, "the position is at the foot of the Zachariae Glacier, one of the biggest in Greenland, and one which has seen considerable degradation recently. What may have happened is that a major ice island broke off—like at Petermann a few years ago. If there was a boat nearby, it could have been completely swamped."

"I sure hope it wasn't one of those cruise boats with gawking tourists trying to catch a glimpse of a glacier calving."

"Umm," Richard cleared his throat. "Yes, well, we in Canada have been advocating that all traffic coming into the Arctic be registered and closely monitored. And only boats with specially strengthened hulls be allowed. Also, of course, that cruise ships travel in pairs in case of problems with the ice."

"Richard, but if it *was* a large ice island breaking off from the glacier, having two boats there instead of only one could have just made the catastrophe a lot worse," Hanne countered.

"Let's go. Why don't you two come up with me to the bridge? We will head in that direction until we have confirmation that others can get there before us," Arnstrom said, standing up and leading the way. "Although the likelihood of any survivors is zero."

⊱⊰

Bolstered by many cups of coffee, Hanne and Richard stayed on the bridge with the captain through the entire night as the *Freyja* sped toward 78°N and 30°W. Early on, the Danish authorities did confirm that the *Freyja* was in fact the closest ship to the coordinates of the SOS signal. Thule airbase promised to send a reconnaissance plane in short order.

The American military also relayed a series of satellite images from several hours earlier that clearly showed an ice island five times the size of Manhattan shearing off from the Zachariae Glacier, and a few minutes later, a tsunami-like wave forming locally as the front-end of the immense new iceberg settled into the sea. One picture showed a lighter spot that could have been a boat, but in the visuals of the aftermath it was no longer there.

After several hours, an exhausted Sodegren came back on the intercom saying that a radio message from Murmansk had finally corroborated that the Russian research ship *Akademik Kurchatov*, with one hundred and seven tourists on board, was scheduled to be in the area at the time of the SOS.

"Not good," was all Arnstrom said as he clicked the intercom off and glanced glumly at his watch. "But we should be nearing the coast in an hour or so if we keep up this speed."

⁂

After dozing off for what seemed like just a few moments, Hanne finally caught sight of the glistening cliffs that towered over the floe-filled sea and that she at first thought formed the east coast of Northern Greenland. It was only when the powerful *Freyja* forced its way through the broken-up ice to get closer, that Richard observed that what was in front of them was, in fact, probably the new ice island.

Arnstrom ordered all hands out on deck, and armed as many as possible with binoculars and telescopes to search for any remnants of life or of the *Kurchatov* on the ice or in the water, knowing full well that this was a hopeless task. He was experienced enough to realize that no human being would survive in these waters beyond just a few minutes, and that the force of any tidal wave caused by such a significant calving event would have sunk the *Kurchatov* without a trace.

There was great surprise on the deck, therefore, when, after about twenty minutes of the difficult task of searching the blinding floes, Richard emitted a cry, "There, there, I see something!" and pointed excitedly with his free hand. He passed the binoculars to Hanne, who, at first, did not see anything, despite trying to adjust the glasses. Only when Richard touched her hand to correct the direction in which she was looking, did she finally catch sight of the bright orange ring shape of a life saver on top of an ice floe several hundred meters away, and with great difficulty, managed to read the last two letters of the inscription in black capital letters on the hoop: an O and a V.

"It is the *Kurchatov*," Hanne said solemnly as she handed the binoculars back to Richard. "Let's go tell the captain."

ಉಲೋ

The *Freyja* was already a good half day's journey on its way back to Longyearbyen when first Euronews, and then twelve minutes later, CNN International picked up the story. Captain Arnstrom had switched on the two big flat screen TVs on the bridge soon after he turned the boat around and notified the relevant capitals that the only sign of the *Akademik Kurchatov* they had found was the life saver.

Both these first news reports captured a late morning press conference hastily put together for Harald Sorensen, the Danish minister for transport, to announce that a Russian registered research ship, serving as a cruise boat with 107 tourists aboard, had disappeared off the coast of Greenland, with the only trace being a life saver on an ice floe.

"It is feared that the cruise ship and its passengers may have been the victims of a tsunami-like wave produced by the calving of one of the glaciers on the coast of Northeastern Greenland. Clearly, we are investigating further."

And, being an avid environmentalist, Sorensen added, "Sadly, these people may have been the latest human sacrifices of climate change"—for which, over the next few days, he would be lambasted by the conservative media around the world.

ಉಎಉ

A couple of hours later, as the *Freyja* sailed through the rough Arctic seas toward its home port with the TV screens still tuned to CNN International or Euronews or BBC, Hanne, who was trying to concentrate on writing up her report on the mission in one of the smaller meeting rooms, was interrupted by Richard who barged in and said, "Come, you gotta hear this."

She followed her friend to the ship's cafeteria, where the large LED screen was tuned to CNN, and quickly noted that they were doing a simultaneous interview of two experts on Arctic maritime affairs reacting to the recent disaster.

"Brewster is a good friend," Richard said as he pulled out a chair for Hanne. "He usually makes a lot of sense." Seth Brewster was identified on screen as a Professor at the University of British Columbia and an expert in international law and Arctic geopolitics.

"...The federal government, as long ago as July 1, 2010 introduced a mandatory registration system for all ships of more than three hundred tonnes traveling through any Arctic waters under Canada's jurisdiction. Which, of course, includes the Northwest Passage. The US, the International Maritime Organization, and the Baltic and International Maritime Council and countless others protested..."

"Sure, because this unilateral step by Canada clearly transgresses the right of innocent passage enshrined in the UN Convention on the Law of the Sea," the voice of Manuel Leader, BIMCO's chief international affairs officer, brought into the studio from Copenhagen by satellite, was heard to say. "And, of course, underlying this is the fact that Canada's jurisdiction over the Arctic waters it claims—particularly the Northwest Passage—is in question."

"But, Manuel, will you accept that the safety of human lives and preventing any more damage to the already endangered environment in the Arctic must take precedence over the right of innocent passage. Surely…"

"Yes, but any new regulations have to be devised and implemented through the right channels. The IMO…"[47]

"The IMO has lots of other concerns and is very slow moving. To get agreement there could take years. It is full of so many vested interests, including yours, I might add. It really is time that all the Arctic nations adopt regulations similar to Canada's. Perhaps in the Arctic Council…"

"Well, there you go," Richard said with a beaming smile, turning to Hanne, "that's Canada's position. Maybe this tragedy will wake up other countries and the Arctic Council enough for them to do something jointly."

"Yeah, but even if they do, how could those rules be enforced?" Hanne answered with a question, slightly put off by Richard's seeming smugness.

"Each Arctic country would have to police its own zone."

"That could get expensive for a little country like Denmark with a big Arctic exposure."

"Well, that's just the cost of having so much territory."

"Thanks, Richard. It's time for me to go finish my report," Hanne said. She was annoyed, not just because Richard had dragged her away from her work, but since she had landed in this silly argument with him. This was not her area of expertise, and she knew that Richard was right. Now, though, as she went back to the meeting room, she felt sorry. She did like Richard as a friend, and she should not be so sensitive to everything he says, Hanne told herself. It was not like her.

CHAPTER 5

Novo-Ogaryovo, Russia—Afternoon, Sunday, September 12, the next month

The president got up from the comfortable leather couch in his home office, stepping over Buko, his black Labrador retriever, and made his way over to the massive walnut table that served as his desk. He wanted to be sitting upright when he received his guest, seen to be working on some papers, even though they were on at least superficially friendly terms, built on mutual respect. He had asked Pavel Laptov to come to the luxurious government-owned dacha in Novo-Ogaryovo outside Moscow for a private chat on this particular Sunday, because he wanted to impress upon the famous polar explorer how important he considered his appointment to be to this special position in his administration.

On his way over to the desk, Andrei stopped for a moment to smile at his image in the mirror, stood at attention and put his thumb inside his shirt, like his hero, the equally diminutive Napoleon Bonaparte, once Emperor of France and the world.

Laptov was the last of the appointments he was making in this mid-term cabinet reshuffle. Or rather cabinet rethink. He would install him as one of the select few Inner Cabinet members, just to put the importance of the role more into focus. He had thought about it, long and hard. He had held off for a while, but was now convinced that this was definitely the right way to go.

The position he had in mind for Laptov was, in the current environment, perhaps the most important appointment he would make. For Andrei was about to elevate the respected parliamentarian and polar explorer to the post of Minister for the Arctic.

Laptov was the right man for the job, he was sure of that. More than anybody in the government, the old scientist adventurer knew the Arctic and how important it was. For Russia's future. Andrei admitted to himself, that it was, in fact, Laptov, with his relentless arguments, who had convinced him—and then they together the rest of United Russia—that it was essential for the party to be seen as a leader on the Arctic issue. The Russian people would love it, he had said, as indeed they did. The recent polls had borne that out. The Arctic belonged to them. It was part of their psyche: they had explored it, fought for it, toiled in it, lived in it, died in, and for it.

But more importantly, Laptov had emphasized that it was key from a strategic standpoint, for the future of Russia, to be strong in the Arctic. And, Andrei smiled at the thought, we will control it, because it was paramount for him personally as well, since his friends who ran Gazprom, Rosneft and the other natural resources companies that would benefit, would know how to reward him. The process was in place.

Laptov, the old arctic fox, had convinced him that the Arctic must become Russia's main strategic base for raw materials. Even though he insisted that development would have to be sensitive to environmental issues.

He had versed Andrei in the figures: Arctic Russia was already responsible for over twenty percent of the country's gross domestic product, and a similar percentage in terms of export earnings[48]. Those figures were several years old, and were now a few points higher already, he was sure.

With proper exploitation of the resources on the enlarged continental shelf that Russia was claiming and he was sure would be awarded, these numbers could easily double. After all, it was studies done by scientists at the US Geological Survey that showed that the Arctic seabed contained over twenty-five per cent of the world's oil and gas resources[49], and was also abundantly rich in, diamonds, gold, platinum, tin, manganese, nickel, lead and the rare earths. That most of this fell into the Russian half of the Arctic was a fortuitous gift of nature. Also, now that much of the Arctic Ocean was more or less free from ice—thanks to global warming—at least in the summer, seabed mineral resource extraction and transportation had become much easier and less costly.

It was Laptov who had led the research for, and writing of, Russia's submission to UNCLOS to gain all this additional subsea territory, so he really deserved the appointment. And it would have to be up to him as minister for the Arctic to lead its defense and do whatever was necessary for Russia to own half the Arctic, Andrei told himself as he signed one more document.

෴

A knock, and Andrei looked up from the papers he was pretending to be reading, pen poised in hand.

"*Da.* Come in."

The door opened and the president was once again struck, as he looked up, by how robust and healthy the polar explorer looked: tanned, rugged face, framed by the well-trimmed, but full, white moustache and beard, white mutton chops, sparse silver hair on top, wire-rimmed, tinted prescription glasses, the tall muscular build clad in a wrinkled olive green corduroy jacket and black pants, an open-necked shirt, and, despite his age, the sprightly walk over toward the desk.

"Thank you for coming on a Sunday, Pavel." Andrei got up from the desk and went over to greet the older man. "I wanted to talk to you privately, away from Moscow. But, you know, it is so nice outside…Why don't we go for a walk before lunch?"

‸‸‸

It was a gorgeous autumn day: the sun was shining, the water a shimmering blue, and the trees and bushes had just started to sprout leaves. Laptov took his jacket off and slung it over his shoulder, as Andrei followed Buko down the path to the Moscow River.

"Pavel, let me get to the point. You and I have talked a lot about the importance of the Arctic. For us. I don't think there is anyone in the party who knows this more than you."

"Thank you, Mr. President."

"I have decided that I will create a separate position in the government. I want you to be minister for the Arctic. You will be one of six senior ministers in the Inner Cabinet who report directly to me, and you will have all the resources necessary put at your disposal. Scientific, financial, legal, intelligence, military. Everything. You will see to it that we end up with jurisdiction over the half of the Arctic that falls on our side. Through legal means if possible, military if necessary. Do you understand?"

Pavel hesitated for a moment before saying, "Yes, sir." What else could he say? He had grown up in the Soviet Union, so he was aware of what the consequences of disagreement with the president might be.

"You know my objective: a Russia that is a strong

global power again. The dependence of the West—certainly of Europe—on us for energy and minerals is a key part of this strategy. For this, we need to lock up the Arctic. And I do not care if it upsets Washington, Brussels or London. Or Beijing, for that matter."

"Of course..."

"You led on the research for our submission to the United Nations to stake our claim to the Lomonosov and Mendeelev Ridges. The North Pole and, what is it—almost one and a quarter million square kilometers of the Arctic. I want you to continue to spearhead the defense of our claims in our submission. To hone and make the arguments so that they are crystal clear. Watertight."

"Thank you. We think we have presented a definitive case in our submission that gives us the Lomonosov Ridge up to the North Pole based on the science required by the Law of the Sea. Our position is founded on soil samples and the thickness of sediments, and our scientists are confident this will be strong enough. The Canadians and the Danes will, no doubt, make comments that will counter some of what we present. As you may know, Mr. President, both their submissions make claims that overlap with ours."

"So clearly there is more to come...."

"And, of course, the Americans will also be critical, even though they are not at the table since they never ratified the treaty. Nevertheless, they are advancing a different interpretation—that both the Lomonosov and the Mendeleev Ridges are oceanic ridges and not extensions of any continental shelf..."

"Yes, I am aware. But we have to overcome those and all objections."

"Of course, President Gusanov. We will do our best."

"You know, Pavel, I do think we have a fallback position. The sector principle. You know our history in the

Arctic. We are the successor state to the Soviet Union after all, which early on claimed the Arctic from both ends of Russia right up to the North Pole. At the time, this was not questioned by any of the western powers. Nor have we ever formally renounced the principle..."

"Canada still lays claim to the various versions of the Northwest Passage based on that concept, I think."

"There you go, Pavel. We could make a unilateral claim based on the old sector principle, which in fact, would give us a considerably bigger piece of the cake. And if the Commission rejects our argument, or other states quibble with our claims, we will not hesitate to upset them, you can be sure of that. It shouldn't matter then if we take a bigger slice of the Arctic."

"I see what you are driving at, sir."

"And, Pavel...you know, there is also the Greenland issue. They've had home rule for quite a few years now, and they are no longer part of the European Union since that referendum they held. When was it? Sometime in the eighties, no? The current prime minister there—Rorsen—wants full independence from Denmark."

"Yes. I met him at a conference two years ago."

"Well, I was thinking that we must have a word with this Rorsen. At the appropriate moment, of course. In case the UN awards Denmark and Greenland the North Pole and most of the Lomonosov Ridge. If this happens, we should encourage Greenland to declare independence right away..."

"I see your thinking, sir. An independent Greenland means that those resources are no longer owned by a European Union state."

"We could offer a guarantee of Greenland's independence and our help in resource extraction. Since they will have seceded from Denmark, their NATO membership will also be a question mark."

"Very clever of you, Mr. President. That way, not only will the EU lose the Greenland portion of the Arctic resources, but Russia will have a chance to control them."

But Pavel definitely did not like this approach.

☙❧

Riding back to Moscow after his private lunch with Gusanov—Beluga caviar, smoked salmon with *blinis*, sour cream and chives, accompanied by lots of vodka—Pavel had time to think. For a moment there, during the lunch, he had thought of saying no to Gusanov. Refusing the job he was being offered. That might have been the honorable thing to do. Although he would never show it, he did not like the man and the others he surrounded himself with. The *siloviki*. They were all just crooks in his view: lining their own pockets, while pretending to be doing everything good for Russia.

Well, hadn't he already compromised by joining the party, United Russia? And accepting the position as chairman of the Duma's Committee on Science and Technology? True, to a certain extent, but holding that largely ceremonial post was nothing compared with being an important member of the Inner Cabinet. He would be party potentially to all kinds of decisions he did not agree with…

And, more specifically, on the Arctic, he did not like the president's aggressive stance. For it could very easily provoke a similarly bellicose response in other countries' politicians—say, the US's—or perhaps even China's, who have also been agitating for a greater say in Arctic affairs.

But in the end, what had swayed Laptov to accept the offer was not so much the possible implications for him personally, but more so the consideration that…Well, what would happen if he didn't? That jerk Gusanov would put someone else in the position, someone who saw eye-to-eye with the president. A yes-man…So much for his beloved Arctic then!

Yes, better that he accepted the job, put the brakes on these criminals whenever and however he could, and saved what he could.

CHAPTER 6

Copenhagen, Denmark—Late Afternoon, Sunday, September 19, a week later

Hanne was exhausted, both physically and emotionally. She just did not know where this relationship would, or could go. She should have broken up with Jens when she came home from the Arctic. She had been telling herself that every summer: she was going to end it when she got back. And then, and then...she never had the heart. It was just so easy not to. After all, what would she have, if she didn't have Jens? Jens, with his save-the-world enthusiasm...

Hanne lay there in bed, sipping her glass of red wine, with the remnants of the late afternoon sun streaming in through the curtains, Jens in the bathroom. They had lunched at the BioM, the restaurant that billed itself as the only biodynamic restaurant in town, Jens's favorite, and then gone back to his apartment on Fredericiagade. To make love, as was expected whenever Jens was about to go off on a 'business' trip. But it had not been satisfying for Hanne: she found it too robotic, too selfish, lacking something. The sex with Lock that one time had been so superior...A memory that still aroused Hanne every time she let it surface.

Selfishly, Hanne felt relieved that Jens was leaving for a couple of weeks. Although she knew it would not be an easy trip for him. Dangerous even. He was an avid member of the Green Liberation Front, and he was joining a mission on their boat, the *Soldier of Gaia.*

They were off to somewhere near the Russian coast by Murmansk, where they intended to launch a fast rubber dinghy to film and protest the launch of yet another Russian nuclear submarine. Jens and his friends: Sven, the quiet film director, and Erik, the son of the wealthy industrialist, along with a handful of other crazy Green Liberation Front types.

But Jens would be gone for at least two weeks. Maybe she would have the courage to break up when he came back…

They had had an argument after making love. Hanne had dared show her enthusiasm at being involved in proving that the Lomonosov Ridge belonged to Denmark right up to the North Pole, and Jens had jumped on her. He, Mr. Righteous, was of the opinion that that was all baloney: the entire Arctic should be declared a world heritage site, a world nature reserve, with no resource extraction rights, and very stringent restrictions on maritime traffic.

At last she heard Jens flush the toilet, where he had annoyingly parked himself for an inordinately long time, and, in the middle of the swishing noise, the familiar music of her cell phone. Mozart, the *Turkish March*. It was coming from over by the window, where she had dropped her clothes on the floor the night before.

Hanne threw off the sheet, and naked, skipped two giant steps, retrieving her jeans, frantically searching for the rectangular shape in the pocket. Finally extracting it, she pressed the green button, and said, "*Hej*. Hanne Kristensen speaking."

"Hello, Hanne," a woman's voice spoke at the other end. "This is Lise. Lise Frondholm. I'm sorry…"

Hanne's mind suddenly switched gears as she realized she was talking to Denmark's minister of climate and energy, her boss's boss.

"Hello. Yes, I'm sorry to disturb you on a Sunday afternoon, but I'm wondering if you could come over to my office. I would like to have a talk with you, and I think it would be best if we could do it before my Monday morning cabinet meeting. Just you and me, over coffee. Would that be okay, Hanne?"

"Yes. Yes, of course. What time?" She barely knew Frondholm, having met her only a couple of times.

"Whenever you can get over here."

"I'll be there within half an hour."

༄༅༄༅

When Hanne arrived at the Ministry, behind the National Museum of Denmark, the weekend porter had been given her name, and she was directed straight to the minister's office on the top floor. There was no secretary parked outside, so Hanne knocked on the slightly ajar door.

"Come in," she heard from inside, and as she entered, "*Hej*, Hanne. Thanks for coming straight over." The office was sparse, with functional furniture.

"Hello. I'm glad you found me." Hanne was eager to find out what was so important that the minister would call her on a Sunday afternoon.

"Hanne, my predecessor and the director have both said very good things about you. I know you've been instrumental in the research for, and then ultimately in putting together our submission on the continental shelf extension. Up in Greenland, and the Lomonosov Ridge..."

"Yes. It's been interesting..."

"Your work has come to the attention of the prime

minister and the minister of foreign affairs."

"Thank you."

"Hanne, we need someone who can lead the defense of our claims in front of the Commission. We will no doubt be called to do so soon, to answer any questions, issues, concerns. We have to make sure that our case is unassailable. We need someone who has a quick mind, good capabilities both to analyze and to synthesize, and excellent presentation and diplomatic skills."

"Yes…"

"The prime minister has asked me to bring you to the cabinet meeting tomorrow. He and the foreign minister want to meet you personally. We would like you to be the one who takes this on. This is a huge role and the importance for Denmark and Greenland is tremendous. If our claim is agreed, we will gain access to very valuable oil, gas fields, and mineral resources. But you know all that better than I do."

"Yes, Minister."

"Please call me Lise. Hanne, will you do this? I cannot stress enough the importance for Denmark. And, of course, our department. Although you will be seconded to foreign affairs, and will work closely with the minister there and their officials."

"Of course. I'm honored that you have chosen me…Lise."

"Excellent. You will come to the cabinet meeting at nine, and then we will prepare a memorandum for the PM's signature to all the relevant parties with instructions to give you their full cooperation. Anything you need. If you don't get the support, come and tell me. This is our number one priority."

"Yes. Thank you!"

"Hanne, the Canadians have suggested that we coordinate the defense of our submissions in front of the

Commission. They have suggested that we have talks to that effect before we are called to any meetings. Their prime minister called ours—we jointly want to build as strong a case as possible against the Russians. So that means getting on a plane to Ottawa, Hanne. And by the way, you will have a special budget."

"Thank you, Lise."

ଔଔଔ

Hanne, elated, said "Wow!" to herself as she walked down the corridor to the stairs and then out the front door of the Ministry. She was sure she would do a great job: what the minister had asked her to do played to her strengths. Plus, it meant she would have to go to Canada, work with Richard, whom she rather liked. Then at some point to New York, to defend the submission to the UN Commission. It really could be good. And maybe this would give her the impetus to break up with Jens…

It could be a fun year or several—for Hanne was experienced enough to know that these things took time. And, of course, that what she was about to embark on was supremely important, as the minister had said: if she were able to convince the Commission to award Denmark the Lomonosov Ridge right to the North Pole, that could mean huge wealth for Denmark.

A lot was riding on her shoulders.

CHAPTER 7

Ottawa, Canada—Afternoon and Evening, Monday, February 11, the next year

Hanne was wondering what she was doing in Ottawa, in February, meeting with the Canadians. She looked out the window of the Lester B. Pearson Building housing Foreign Affairs and International Trade Canada, out into the northern winter darkness that had descended some time ago, out across the partially frozen Ottawa River toward the distant lights of Hull, Québec.

For a moment, she admired the carefree dance of the pristine snowflakes as they floated across the beams of car and streetlights before melting on the slushy surface of the road, or joining the millions of faceless others that now formed the white blanket covering the ground until April.

Traffic in front of the building was already stop and go: the bureaucrats were leaving to go home for the evening, and even though this was the fifth time they were meeting, they seemed to be going over the same material time and again. But—she tried to convince herself—perhaps that was the nature of the beast. If they were going to convince the Commission that the Russian case was weak, they had to have an argument unassailable from every angle. And they all had to buy into it, and know it down to the last geological detail.

"Look. First we need to present our key points and our breakthrough interpretation of the Lomonosov Ridge. We cannot forcefully argue against the generally accepted notion that the Ridge split off from the Eurasian landmass some sixty million years ago and then moved along some kind of transform fault to its current position. But what we will want to stress is that the Ridge was always connected to the North American landmass…And we have presented the facts to prove exactly this point. The magnetic and soil data so far all clearly suggest that the Lomonosov Ridge is an extension of the North American and Greenland continental shelves."

"Yes," Richard, who was now technically Hanne's counterpart heading up the Canadian team, acquiesced. "Whereas there is huge and deep faulting across the seabed where the Russians claim Lomonosov joins the Siberian shelf…"[50]

"That will certainly be a point in our favor," Frederik Hansen, Hanne's geologist colleague from Copenhagen voiced his support. "Against the Russians."

"But what about that eight hundred meter deep and thirty-five kilometer wide saddle between our continental shelf and the Ridge?"[51] Richard continued. "Surely, someone—on behalf of the Russians—might try to argue that that proves that it is not a natural prolongation of our shelf?" Not being a professional geologist, he was able to hone in on the critical issues more easily, Hanne thought to herself.

"On the contrary. We will need to emphasize the point that those physical features are just the scarring from the movement of the tectonic plates. The geological and geomagnetic data all prove our case…" Hanne was pleased with the way the argumentation was starting to stack up.

"Good." Richard liked her counter to the point he had

raised. "We want the Commission members to accept the interpretation both teams will stress in defense of our submissions. And, of course, along the way, we will pooh-pooh both the Russian case and the negatives. *Voilà!* That will do it for sure."

"In our case, after we have stated our position, we will back it up by addressing the similarity of the geological composition of the rocks and sediment on the Ridge and on Ellesmere Island and Northern Greenland. And, importantly, that this similarity is unbroken. Uninterrupted…" Hanne wanted to underline the detail of what she thought had to be addressed by both teams. "That is the first key block of evidence, and you should also touch on that."

"Excellent." This from Richard.

"Will you flesh that out, Frederik? With Richard?" Hanne looked first at her Danish colleague, knowing that she could trust him, and then at Richard. "So both teams are on the same page."

"Sure, Hanne."

"Then there is also the magnetic data, which clearly suggest that the Ridge is part of a Precambrian complex linking to the Canadian Shield. I'll work on that with Barry, if you agree."[52]

"Of course," came the reply from Barry Macdonald, the Canadian geophysicist she found to be technically excellent.

"And that leads very nicely into refuting the Russian claim, because, as we have seen, the magnetic profiles on the Eurasian side of the Ridge closely resemble those typical over both the Atlantic and Pacific oceans. So it seems that there is a gap of oceanic origin between their shelf and the rise. The profiles on the North American side of the Lomonosov Ridge, on the other hand, are completely unlike the oceanic data and show a striking similarity to typical profiles over the Precambrian rocks of the Canadian Shield."

"This is great." Richard liked the way the outline of the submission was emerging. "We will emphasize the similarity of the magnetic data with that of the Canadian Shield and then lead into a discussion where we present the resemblance of the profile on the Eurasian side to the oceanic ones, which underscores that there is a clear 'oceanic' break between Siberia and Lomonosov."

"Very good. And then we both need to pull out the *coup de grâce* for the Russian claim: the seismic studies showing that the Ridge becomes deeper as it approaches Siberia, with a lot of faulting in the deeper sediments. Which suggests that even if the Ridge is in some way now attached to the Siberian shelf, ten million years or so ago, it was probably not part of the shelf at all. And therefore, cannot be a natural prolongation."

"And what are the negatives they might level against us?" Barry asked. "In support of the Russian claim, that is…"

"Actually, there are two points, when I think about it," Hanne continued. "First—and I don't think this is serious—it is just that the sedimentation is not thick enough to build a case for extending jurisdiction under the UN-CLOS sediment thickness rules. Our submissions are strong enough without this. More important though, is the argument that the Lomonosov Ridge is a deep oceanic rise and that it originally came from a different part of the subsea environment, and has, over the last few million years, slid along a transform fault to its present location. But this is where the similarity to the Canadian Shield that you mention, Richard, is so important: we can argue that it was always a part or an extension of that at our end."

"Very good…"

"Okay. I think we are finally there with a pretty solid and coordinated defense for our submissions. Oh, *ja*—as we go through it again, let's note any holes in the data—some of our colleagues will be up there again this summer, and we can have them do some more specific digging, if need be. We'll pass anything new we discover on to you. But I really do think we are in pretty good shape…"

☙☙☙

Hanne bundled up and left the conference room with Richard at her side.

"Good job," he commented. "I think we made good progress."

"Well…in our case, we will have to make sure the prime minister and the cabinet are okay with all this. What about you?"

"No. Just our minister of foreign affairs. And the minister of natural resources."

"The politicians do have to have their say. Although I doubt that they would understand any of the science."

"Yeah. But it doesn't matter."

"I guess it's just that they all have to feel good about it."

"By the way, Hanne—not to change the subject—but would you like to join me for dinner? There is a nice little restaurant in the market I think you'll like…"

Hanne had been looking forward to a quiet evening and a good night's rest before catching her flight back to Copenhagen the next day. But maybe the distraction would be fun, she thought to herself. And she did like Richard. As a friend, at the very least.

"Sure, why not!" she answered on an impulse.

"I'll pick you up at your hotel at seven?"

"Make it seven-thirty," Hanne said glancing at her watch. "I wouldn't mind a little time to collect myself."

"Great. Seven-thirty it is. Come, I'll give you a ride to your hotel now."

☙❦❧

In mid-February, evenings in Ottawa are bitterly cold, with a biting wind blowing off the eponymous river and the Rideau Canal. As she came out of the Chateau Laurier on Richard's arm to jump into a taxi, Hanne nearly froze, even though she had worn a coat over her dress. Although it was a fur-lined wool coat, and the taxi driver had the heat on full blast during the short ride, she was still pleased when the *Maître d'* at the Stella Osteria placed them near the huge fireplace with a fire roaring in it. She looked stunning in the simple, low-cut red dress, her blond hair accentuating her long neck and tanned shoulders.

Once they had ordered—she a caprese salad, followed by a *fettuccine boscaiola*, he a minestrone and *osso bucco*, and pulling out all the stops with a bottle of Castello Banfi 1999 Brunello di Montalcino Reserva Poggio—they could not help but assess the success of their endeavor.

"Well, here's to us!" Richard led off, raising the glass of the Prosecco he had ordered as an *apéritif*.

"And to our submissions," Hanne added, laughing, clicking his glass with hers.

"Yes, well, I think they're both in pretty good shape, actually. Our arguments against the Russian position are quite strong."

"Well, we'll still have to address the overlap between our two submissions," Hanne mused. "Although I haven't yet seen your final claim."

"You will just have to yield to us in any negotiations," Richard said, laughing.

"The one thing that could be detrimental to us and the Russians is if the US view wins out. That the Ridge is of oceanic origin, and not linked to either continental shelf."

"Hmm…"

"Certainly, some of the evidence could be interpreted in that way."

"Let's not spoil the evening with negative thoughts, Hanne," Richard, said laughing.

After several bites of tomato and mozzarella, while her mind was clearly working, Hanne said: "Well, Richard, I am sorry, but here is another negative thought."

"Okay, if you really must."

"What if the Russians play the bad guys? If their claim isn't agreed. Didn't their minister for the Arctic, Laptov, announce that they would withdraw from the Convention?"

"That was just posturing, I'm sure."

"But if they unilaterally take control of the area…"

"It would be difficult for them to defend it."

"That goes for us too. If they wanted to start extracting resources along the Ridge in international waters. Or for the sake of argument, let's say in newly granted Canadian waters. What would you do? What could you do?"

"Well, I think we've created a number of reserve units—including one made up of native people—that are supposed to be the backbone of our Arctic defense. We have also been building several more icebreakers, and there are our bases at Alert and Eureka…"

"What will that accomplish?" Hanne asked, smiling. "The Russians have by far the strongest northern forces right now. They have put in place a new Arctic command structure, with four dedicated commando units and five air squadrons. There are fourteen new airfields and sixteen deep water ports spread out across the Russian north. They recently announced that they are adding eleven new icebreakers to their existing flotilla of forty. They have over thirty submarines in the Arctic—most nuclear powered, many with ballistic or cruise missiles, plus ten or so surface vessels. Probably more on the way too. That's not counting the more than forty plus icebreakers and other boats that could be called upon in case of conflict. There is very little you, we, or the Americans could do if they chose to impose their will unilaterally in the Arctic."

"Boy, Hanne, you're amazing. You know a lot about Russia's military might…"

"Well, it's something we in Denmark are very concerned about."

"But in any case, if they did something like that, they would become international pariahs, a rogue state. I doubt that they would risk that. No one would trade with them."

"On the contrary, they would be betting that we need them even more if they control the resources in the Arctic. Maybe not you in oil-rich Canada, but certainly we, in resource-poor Europe."

"Ugh…Okay, Hanne. Time's up. No more negativity. Now it's time you told me more about yourself."

છ્ય્છ

"Hanne, why don't you come by for a nightcap?" Richard mustered his courage to ask when they stepped outside the restaurant into the bitter cold Ottawa wind. "I'm just up here, a block and a half away."

Hanne had been revived by the sumptuous meal. The glass of bubbly, the Brunello and the after dinner Limoncello had put her in a good mood. She was not quite ready for the loneliness of the hotel room, and she did like this Canadian diplomat…She glanced at her watch, and seeing that it was still just after ten, said: "All right Richard, one drink. Just to see your place. And then I have to go pack."

೧೭೧

Richard took Hanne's coat, saying, "Please, make yourself at home. What would you like? I have all the usual after dinners—a Napoleon Cognac, Cointreau, some more Limoncello, or red or white wine. No Prosecco, but some nice Cava from Spain." He made his way over to the kitchen side of the counter that separated the cooking from the living area.

"Maybe a glass of red would be the best," Hanne answered, sitting down on the plush, wide, grey couch. "I don't like to mix too much."

"Coming up!" Richard reached above the counter to pull a bottle out from the suspended wine rack.

"You have a great apartment." Hanne eased her feet out of her high heels and pulled them up under her body on the couch.

"Well, I want it to be comfortable when I'm here," Richard said, laughing as he pulled up the levers on the rabbit corkscrew, "because, when we're out in the field, it's anything but…"

"Although, in my work, I love it out there, in nature, with no one around."

"Yeah. So do I…Here, this is not as good as the Brunello, but it's still not a bad wine from Tuscany. A Tenuta di Carmignano." Hanne took the glass, while Richard turned on the gas fireplace with the flick of a handle before coming around to sit down beside her on the sofa.

"*Salut*," Hanne said, clicking goblets with Richard.

"Thanks for the dinner…"

"It's nice to get to know you, Hanne." Richard paused after a sip, as if to get his courage revved up, then put his glass on the coffee table and continued. "You are an exceptional woman. Beautiful, intelligent, cultured…"

As Richard maneuvered closer to her, Hanne put her half-finished wine down, knowing what was coming next. But she realized she didn't mind, she was relaxed, and she did want to find someone other than Jens. So she responded when Richard touched her upper arm to draw her closer and sought her lips with his. In fact, she found it pleasant, even wonderfully different, and soon, the two were stretched out on the couch, Richard on top…

But she noticed that Richard was frantically tearing at her clothes and his.

"Richard, slow down! Relax. There's no need to hurry."

Richard was not to be slowed down though, and within moments, he had tugged her dress over her head and had unclasped her bra, at the same time undoing his belt and pulling his pants down over his ankles.

"Richard…"

And then he was inside her, and that was also a pleasant sensation since she was already quite moist, but within seconds, Hanne felt him release and she was nowhere near that point…

Richard went limp in her arms, and as she gently pulled him around to get on top to satisfy herself, he was limp inside her…He was spent, with nothing left, a deflated balloon.

"Hanne…I am sorry. I don't know—"

"Don't worry. It happens. Especially when you've not practiced for a while."

Hanne, though, was clearly disappointed, and started to gather her clothes, clasp her bra, pull up her panties. "I think I better get back to the hotel now," she said, before setting off for the bathroom.

Oh well, at least it had been a nice dinner...But it could have been great, like with Lock—you don't really know until you try, Hanne said to herself, smiling at the memory.

CHAPTER 8

Arctic Naval Base, Severemorsk, Murmansk Oblast, Russia—Afternoon, Friday, March 29, the next month

"Admiral, it's so nice to see you," Pavel Laptov greeted his host, as he stepped off the Ilyushin Il-96-300PU operated by the Russia State Transport Company for the exclusive use of the president and his special emissaries. The tarmac was covered with hard-packed snow, and it was clear that Vice Admiral Yevgeni Maslenkov was eager to get on with proceedings after standing in the howling wind and bitter cold while the plane landed and taxied to its position.

"Thank you, Minister, for coming," Maslenkov responded. "It is a great honor for us that you chose the Severemorsk Naval Base to visit."

"Yevgeni, old friend, let's cut the formalities," Laptov said smiling. "You and I have shared a bottle of vodka together many times. You know it is not by chance that I am here. You, and the forces you command, are critical to Russia's objective—as you well know—to control the Arctic. And that is the policy of this government I need you to help me implement."

Yevgeni was certainly pleased to hear that. He sensed his time had finally come and he would have a lot to thank this white-haired, sun-wrinkled polar explorer who had, almost single-handedly, brought the Arctic back into focus in Russia. And focus meant importance, money, attention, more activity—all of which was breathing life back into this, and the other naval bases in Russia's far north.

Maslenkov had seen the president, Andrei Gusanov,, on state television, holding a special press conference several months earlier to announce his friend Laptov's appointment, underscoring the importance his government placed on securing Russia's hegemony over the Arctic. He was savvy enough at interpreting Kremlin dynamics to know that the minister for the Arctic was now key to his future, and if he played his cards right, he could even achieve his life-long ambition and rise to the very pinnacle of the military. So much the better that their friendship went back to their youth, when Yevgeni was the naval representative on a mission in Antarctica led by Pavel, who was already then making a name for himself as a polar explorer.

The vice-admiral led the way into his office in the ugly Communist-era building that housed the military staff.

"May I take your coat, Pavel?"

"Thank you." *At least it's warm in here,* Laptov thought, rubbing his hands.

"Can I offer you some tea? Or better still, some vodka to fortify you against the cold?"

"Tea for now, thank you, Yevgeni. Vodka after I give my talk to your men." Pavel went over to the small sofa against the wall. While Maslenkov asked his orderly to bring tea for two, Laptov looked around the sparse office.

On the wall behind the desk was the official picture of the president—when he had served in that role the last time—and beside it smaller photos, presumably of Maslenkov with different dignitaries. Out the window opposite, he could just see the mast and bridge of what he knew was the *Pyotr Velikiy*, the heavy, nuclear-powered, guided missile cruiser, flagship of the Northern Fleet, loom above a series of low buildings.

"Well, I know the soldiers are all excited about your talk…"

"Yevgeni, before we go out there, I wanted to tell you that I have the agreement of the president to speed up the construction of the planned three new Yasen class attack submarines and more importantly, also three new Dolgorukiy class nuclear-powered ballistic missile submarines. They are to be built over the next three years. As you know, this will require a massive effort at Sevmash to finish all six on time. We will make sure that the work is properly funded, and you, Yevgeni, will be put in charge of bringing their construction to completion."

Maslenkov was delighted to hear this. He was not one to shirk from responsibility, and he was sure that with these added ones and the growing importance of the Northern Fleet, he would soon be a full admiral. And then he would be just a step away from being supreme commander of Russia's armed forces.

"And Yevgeni," Laptov continued, somewhat embarrassed to have to say this, "we do want to make sure that there is no glitch at the launch of these submarines…No problems like the last time."

Maslenkov blushed but did not answer: he knew his friend was sending him a coded message. He was referring to that incident with those hooligans from the Green Liberation Front at the commissioning of the last submarine for the Northern Fleet. With dismay, Maslenkov remembered that he then had to deploy two fast cruisers to force the *Soldier of Gaia* into port and have his GRU men arrest all nine of its crew. These radicals were then held in prison for ten days before being released after a major international crisis and the intervention of the Danish and

Dutch prime ministers, as well as officials from the European Union.

He regretted having allowed the matter to get out of hand, but then, he had no alternative: the Green Liberation Front had made sure the press was present. And, of course, that then had meant that military intelligence had to hand the prisoners over to the FSB—just as well, in some respects, because he himself did not relish handling such matters. But the messy situation did raise a cloud over his head—however, fortunately since then, it all seemed to have dissipated. Been forgotten. Until this little reminder, from someone who was, well…a friend.

☙❦❧

"Vice-Admiral Maslenkov, officers, soldiers of the heroic Northern Fleet, I salute you," Laptov's voice boomed through the loudspeakers. "You are the cream of Russia's youth, and your service to the country in these troubled times, is of paramount importance. With the opening up of the Arctic Ocean to maritime traffic, countless countries are showing interest in the north. Many of these are historical enemies of Russia. They want to exploit the rich resource base of the region. But we know that the Arctic belongs to us. We have shed blood, sweat and tears for many years to secure the north for ourselves, and we will not let anyone steal it now. You may be called upon by your country to defend what is rightfully ours. And defend it you will, because you are the bravest of the brave—you are Russian soldiers!"

The minister for the Arctic paused to clear his throat. He looked around and saw the men assembled on the deck of the *Pyotr Velikiy* and on-shore: he knew they would be cold, colder than he, because he was at least sheltered from the blustering Arctic wind and had a big fur coat and hat on. *Keep it short,* he told himself. *They know you are a man of action.*

"I have come here to tell you and your commander, that the president and I and the rest of the government are fully behind you. We will give the Northern Fleet whatever it needs to ensure that the Arctic is, and remains, Russian. I have just told Vice-Admiral Maslenkov that we are commissioning three new Yasen submarines and three new Dolgorukiys..." Pavel's speech was interrupted by a loud Russian hip-hip-hurrah from the men. "There will be promotions you can be sure, but in any case, I want you to know that I have brought the president's command to Vice-Admiral Maslenkov to give everyone in the Northern Fleet a ten-percent salary increase across the board as of the first of the coming month..."

Laptov stopped again as an even bigger cheer erupted. The sailors threw their hats high in the air, catching them on the way down. "Now enough said, men, and back to your battle stations."

Pavel turned towards Yevgeni, who complimented him with a smile. "Thank you, Minister...Pavel," before continuing. "That was an excellent speech. As you saw, the men are extremely happy."

"Brr. Now for some of that vodka..."

Chapter 9

Copenhagen, Denmark—Morning, Saturday, May 4, the same year

Saturday morning, and Hanne was relishing the long lie-in, with Jens on his stomach beside her. They had a late night, the wedding of Kristi, her school friend. And off-and-on lover, especially when she was still experimenting in college.

It had been good, really good, their relationship, before Jens and she paired up, but they had remained close since. And occasionally, all too rarely, still got together to share intimacies and have sex...They just could not give each other up.

Hanne was the maid of honor, and both she and Jens had indulged, perhaps a little too much. The waiters kept pouring the champagne and the wine, and the music was terrific for dancing. Mo-town, her favorite.

Then, to top it off, they had a wild night of making love...She was surprised—it was far better than usually with Jens: she will definitely need to comment on that. He had let himself go, and aroused her in a way he had never done before. Perhaps it was because she had finally told him about her relationship with Kristi, and that had turned him on...

Kristi had married Henrik, a university friend she started dating only fairly recently, after a troubled fling with Erik, one of Jens's Green Liberation Front friends. They seemed very happy together, and were planning a family. Two children at least—more, if possible. Henrik and Kristi both had good jobs, and their parents were supportive. Hanne looked over at Jens beside her, and tried to contemplate what it would be like to be married to him. But he was so…so…very Danish…

She told herself she needed someone more international, someone with more get up and go, with a broader perspective. Someone wilder, more spontaneous. And he was sort of…how should she describe it…too morose. Especially since his return from that Russian expedition that had gone all wrong. Or maybe it was the sullen Scandinavian character coming through. Yes, maybe that was it: Jens was just too Danish…He was too serious, too focused on saving the world, the Green Liberation Front way. Not that that was necessarily bad, but surely there was more to life…

That said, it would not be such a bad existence to have his children, right here in Copenhagen. She adored this city, even though she loved to travel and see the world. And the Danish state made raising children at home very easy. She was getting close to the age where she would have to take the plunge…Otherwise it might never happen.

As if out of penance for thinking negative thoughts about him, Hanne slid back under the sheet and moved into the spoon position behind Jens, causing him to stir.

"Hello, love," he said to her, as he turned around and pulled her to himself, kissing her.

"Good morning. Did you sleep well?" Yes, this is not that bad, Hanne thought to herself. She imagined Jens a loving husband, and if last night heralded a new Jens, the sex might even turn out to be good too.

The *Turkish March* began to sound from the chair, over in the corner, where she had dropped her purse with her mobile, in the inebriated rush last night to make love.

"Oh God, not now! Who could it be?" Hanne mumbled to herself, as she pulled her tongue out from Jens's mouth. But Jens kept kissing her, and the rousing music went on and on. Hanne kissed him back, and the score eventually stopped.

But only for a moment, as the marching tune annoyingly started up again.

"Oh damn, I better get it," Hanne said, suddenly remembering the call from the minister. She tore herself away from Jens's arms, throwing the sheet off as she jumped out of bed, naked and took two long strides to the chair, extricating the cell phone from the chaos inside her pocketbook.

"Hello?"

"It's Bent. *Hej*, Hanne. I hope I'm not disturbing..." Her colleague from the Survey, who was now helping prepare the material for the defense of their submission to the UN Commission.

"What's up?" She almost added: that couldn't wait until Monday."

"Did you see the announcement?"

"No, what announcement?" Hanne climbed back into bed beside Jens.

"From the United Nations, the Commission. Reporting the results of that special election for a new Australian member to replace—What's his name, the guy who died so bizarrely swimming off the Great Barrier Reef? You remember, in that shark incident..."

"Oh. You mean Ansell Murphy? The oceanographer."

"Yes, yes, of course."

"Who won the vote?" And then, in a flash, she finally understood why Bent was on the phone. "Someone who might support our case? Is that why you are calling?"

"Well, no…No. But Hanne, do you remember that Australian geologist? The one we met up in Warming Land two summers ago? He was there when Andreas and I came back to base camp…The professor in Beijing."

"You mean Lock McTierney?" Hanne sat up, and looked over at Jens. Yes, she did remember, how could she forget. And what fabulous memories she had of their short time together…

"Yes. That's the guy."

"Well…You don't mean he's the one? Who got elected?" Jens put a hand innocently on her leg.

"Yes, Hanne, he is the new Australian representative on the Commission."

"Hmmm. That's not good for us…"

"I thought you and he were friends."

"Well, sort of…" Jens's hand moved higher up and started caressing the soft inside of her thigh. "But his views on the Lomonosov Ridge are not helpful. He thinks it's clearly an oceanic ridge and not connected to a continental shelf at either end." The thumb and the index finger were now twisting her soft blond pubic hairs. "At least that's what he thought then."

"Ugh…"

"Maybe we won't get him. In the Sub-commission dealing with our case, I mean. Anyway, there is nothing we can do at this point. But thanks for letting me know. See you Monday." Hanne closed the phone and put it on the nightstand. Jens reached across and pulled her to him; his face moved up to hers, his lips kissing her cheeks, nose, eyes, lips.

But she had lost the desire thinking about Lock. The new Australian member of the UN Commission she and her colleagues would have to convince…

To please Jens, she went through the motions. And finally, she too, reached orgasm, with Jens thrusting inside her.

But it was Lock who was in her mind's eye the entire time.

CHAPTER 10

Beijing, China—Morning, Wednesday, June 12, the next month

Lock's Mandarin was good enough to decipher the big white Chinese characters gracing the two red placards on either side of the Xinhuamen—the "Gate of New China"—as the limousine the general secretary had sent for him pulled to a stop at the barricade. On one side, the slogan read "Long Live the Great Communist Party of China" and on the other "Long Live the Invincible Mao Tse-tung's Thought."

Lock's view through the entrance to Zhongnanhai, the central headquarters for the Communist Party of China adjacent to the Forbidden City—which indeed, foreigners were normally forbidden to enter—was shielded by a traditional screen wall with the slogan "Serve the People," written in Mao's handwriting.

The limo was instantly recognized, and after a brief exchange between the driver and the smart soldiers of the Central Guard Regiment, they were waved through. Once around the screen, Lock was surprised to see a vast body of water in front of him—he was later told it was known as the South Sea—surrounded by willow trees, with a beautiful pavilion used to entertain guests on an ornamental island on the other side of the tranquil waters.

The car skirted the lake, and after driving a few more

minutes along narrow roads past ancient buildings mixed with newly constructed grey offices, it pulled up in front of a more substantial edifice. Lock guessed that it was the Huairentang, the famous "Palace Steeped in Compassion," where party and government meetings traditionally were held.

A smart Central Guardsman ushered Lock inside and led him down a long hallway to a massive wooden door, where the soldier knocked and peeked in. Lock was told to enter and found himself in front of a man dressed somberly in a black suit and tie with a white shirt, sitting at an enormous mahogany table.

Wen Shaojing, the general secretary of the Communist Party, exchanged greetings with Lock.

"Congratulations, Professor McTierney. I see you have mastered our language. Please sit down."

"Sir, I am but a mere student, and would not presume to be fluent." Lock took the proffered seat opposite Shaojing.

"You speak it well enough to teach at our university."

"Much of my work is with Chinese graduate students who speak perfect English."

"Professor McTierney, let me get to the point," Shaojing said, clearing his throat. "We have watched your career with great interest, and China is honored that you have chosen to teach in our capital. We need men like you, with your expertise. We value your contribution greatly."

"Thank you," Lock muttered as he wondered who it was who had been watching his career.

"We noted with pleasure your recent appointment to the United Nations Commission on the Limits of the Continental Shelf. We know you are an expert on these important matters."

"My specialty is the mineralization of continental

shelves around the world..."

"Yes. And that is what interests China. We are very aware of the role the Commission plays in issues related to extensions of jurisdiction beyond the Exclusive Economic Zone of a country."

The general secretary was indeed well briefed, Lock observed.

"For one, we have been following closely the rising interest of many nations in the Arctic, with its huge resources. Of course, I cannot deny that China, too, is among those countries."

"Yes, indeed, it is an area of enormous economic potential but also of potentially devastating political and military conflict..."

"As you know, the developing world is essentially locked out of getting access to any of those resources. The rich old capitalist countries—the United States of America, Canada, Norway and Denmark—and one resource rich, and frighteningly unregulated newly capitalist country—Russia—stand to divide the spoils."

"Yes, sir. The countries with continental shelves reaching into the Arctic. That is, Greenland, for Denmark."

"Precisely the point I was getting to, Professor. As you know, Greenland is on a path to independence in a few years. It has already declined membership of the European Union, and, as a sovereign country, one could argue that it will be part of what the capitalist west has dubbed the Third World. It has a rich natural resource base, but that is all. No industries other than the extractive ones to speak of..."

"Yes, Greenland is very rich in minerals...and fossil fuels."

"As you know, China has become active with many countries as an investor in their resources. And as protector of their freedom. We intend to do the same for Greenland as soon as it is independent. With less than sixty thousand people, Greenland will need us."

"Yes, sir. I have noted that China has been spreading its wings internationally…"

"Professor McTierney, the reason I asked you to come today is not to discuss China's foreign policy, but to put to you a very specific deal."

"Oh?"

"We know you share our views…Especially on the so-called Third World."

Was Shaojing referring to his role in helping found the Socialist Alliance in Australia in 2001? Or to his participation in the three-day long blockade of a summit of the World Economic Forum in Melbourne to protest global capitalism the previous year? That was all such a long time ago and since then, he had not been active…

"Now that you are a member of the Commission—and even more so, if you will be part of the Sub-commission which will inevitably be appointed to adjudicate Arctic issues—when the time comes, you can help ensure that Denmark's submission to the Commission is upheld and that it—that is, Greenland—is awarded a large chunk of the Arctic."

So that's what this was all about…

"Our Politburo has approved an investment of up to twenty-five-billion US dollars in Greenland's extractive industries, once it is independent," Shaojing continued. "I trust you will keep this to yourself, since this is a confidential, internal decision, not yet made public."

"That is a lot of money…"

"And here is my proposal to you, Professor. If you help steer the decision of the Sub-commission—we will do everything in our power to make sure you are appointed to it—to agree to Denmark's full claim, we will pay you two million dollars in an account either in Hong Kong or Singapore, or of course, here. Plus one million each year thereafter to consult on developing an independent Greenland's expanded resources, especially the rare earths. Which, as you know, are very important for China."

Yes, indeed, Lock was aware that China was doing all it could to corner the market on the rare earths. But what an offer, shameless and incredibly rich! And could they really manipulate selection to the Sub-commission dealing with the Arctic? Of course, he had no doubt.

"You do not need to give me an answer now, Professor. But I would like to know before the end of the month—shall we say in two weeks—whether you are willing to work with us."

"Thank you, Mr. Chairman."

"And I am sure you understand that this is all highly confidential."

Lock was enough of a China hand to know that if so much as a whisper of this discussion got into the open, he was as good as dead.

༺༻

Lock did not sleep much that night, nor the next several nights. He had difficulty concentrating on his teaching, and after four anxious days of mulling over Shaojing's offer, he decided to leave Beijing and do something he had always wanted to: go on a hike along the Great Wall. Maybe the fresh air and stress free environment would help crystallize matters in his head.

It was on the last ten-kilometer stretch between the Jinshaling and Simatai sections that Lock finally came to a decision. He had spent the several days weighing the pros and cons of accepting the offer, and in the end, he found the tally coming down on the side of working with China. The appeal to help the poor countries of the world, the professional satisfaction of overseeing the development of the extractive industries of a huge new country, with a particular focus on the rare earths that were his specialty, and not least, the tremendous monetary rewards, all lined up in his mind against what, by then, seemed like a mere peccadillo: compromising his objectivity in the work of the UN Commission.

Plus, he said to himself, he could not turn the Chinese down, because they would then consider him an enemy of their country, and fear that he would divulge the conversation. He would not live much beyond saying no, he was sure.

And, in any case, the matters he would be ruling on were so subjective, that in the end, he probably wouldn't be compromising himself, he argued, as he waited in his tiny office for the colleague at the University who had originally set up the meeting with Shaojing to come collect the note with the Chinese characters saying above his signature "I accept".

A knock on the door, the professor of mineralogy entered, bowed and smiled as he took the envelope, lowering his head again before he retreated and closed the door behind him. Lock watched through the window as he jumped onto the saddle of his bicycle and pedaled in the direction of the Forbidden City to deliver the message that would seal Lock's fate.

CHAPTER 11

UN Headquarters, New York City, USA—Morning, Tuesday, April 1, the following spring

Lock glanced at his watch: he knew he was running late—the signing in and security at the UN's identification office had taken longer than he remembered from his first session as a member of the Commission last August.

He was looking along the corridor for Committee Room 9, and finally had to ask one of the staff, who hurriedly led him straight to it. When the good-looking brunette opened the door for him, Lock saw that the secretary general was already sitting at the chairman's place in the center of the horseshoe array of desks bearing placards with country names.

Everyone, including Sung Chi Park, the secretary general of the United Nations, looked over in his direction as he sought his place at the desk marked 'Australia'. Fortunately, it was close to the entrance and he sat down as inconspicuously as possible.

As the secretary general said his words of welcome, and underscored the importance and difficulty of the work ahead for the assembled members of the Commission, Lock sat back in his seat, looking around the room at the others. Yes, all males: they seemed so old, so serious. Which is what had struck him at the previous session.

God, this will be tough sailing again, so boring…

The secretary general got up to yield his place to the chairman of the Commission, the Argentine Juan Carlos Guido, who thanked him for his comments as they shook hands.

"I too, would like to extend my welcome to all of you once again, this time to this session of the Commission." Greg remembered that Guido was a respected geologist from the Servicio Geológico Minero Argentino—the Argentine Geological and Mineral Service—and actually not a bad guy. "Our work is not easy, especially this time around, as you would have already seen from the submissions sent to you for study during the summer. But, as the secretary general said, it is very, very important work."

Guido looked around and smiled at Lock as he recognized him, before continuing. "We have more than sixty submissions in the queue, some of them competing, many with comments from other UN member states. Exceptionally, we have prioritized the ones concerning the Arctic for this round, and we will be meeting tomorrow in plenary session with the teams responsible for the submissions. The Russians first, then the Danes followed by the Canadians. To make sure that our assessment is fair and even, we will appoint one Sub-commission for in-depth consideration of all three of these submissions. This will, as per our procedural rules, only include members from countries that have no competing interests with the concerned countries. And, as always, we will also want to make sure that we have a good mix of expertise on the Sub-commission. We will want to get started tomorrow bright and early, so please get some rest."[53]

Almost as an afterthought, the Argentine added: "There is some additional briefing material—mainly the comments on each submission by other states. You can pick this up as you leave the room."

The simultaneous translation ended with the exhortation of "Good work" which, translated from the Spanish exhortation "*Buen trabajo*" of the Argentine, seemed to Lock to be not quite right in the context. "Lots of work" would have been more appropriate, he told himself.

༺☙๛༻

"Professor McTierney?"

Lock turned around as he finished collecting the papers from the desk, and saw the Chinese delegate behind him. He recognized him from the last time—he had been quite critical about Bangladesh's submission that was under consideration in the previous session last August. Yes, Zheng Li, the Chinese representative on the Commission, a marine geophysicist from the Institute of Oceanography in Hangzhou—actually, Lock remembered him from China, where they had served on an advisory panel together several years earlier.

"Hello, Professor Li."

"Glad to see fellow professor from China. We make good team together, no?"

God—he had not thought much about the deal he had made with Wen Shaojing ten months earlier, and had vaguely hoped during the last session when nothing happened that the whole thing might have gone away. But it seemed Li was reminding him that now would be the time for him to do his part. That is, if he wanted to stay alive…

CHAPTER 12

Alex Hotel, New York City, USA—Afternoon and Evening, Tuesday, April 1, the same day

And then he saw her. Sipping a glass of red wine, talking to a man whose shirtsleeves were rolled up, jacket slung across the back of the chair next to him, sitting in the unseasonably warm, New York spring afternoon sun, outside the hotel in the sidewalk Riingo Café. It had been more than two years…

He walked straight up to her and said: "Hello, Hanne. Wow, you look terrific!"

She, surprised to see him, stood up—indeed looking fabulous in a sky-blue suit, hem just above the knees, white silk blouse—delight in her eyes.

"Lock! Wonderful to see you. I heard you had been appointed to the Commission. How fantastic…Congratulations!" She bent forward to exchange the double-cheeked kiss, not averse to contact. His smell brought back the sensations from that summer day in Northern Greenland.

"Lock…McTierney," she said, looking at a slightly perturbed Richard. "Lock, come sit down, sit here," and she slung Richard's jacket over an empty chair at the next table. "Come…This is Richard Simpson, on the Canadian team. Just discussing…you know what." She gave a little laugh. "We have very complementary submissions.

You'll find our case very, very compelling. Not even you will be able to resist, Lock. I remember you had very entrenched views on the subject of the Lomonosov Ridge…"

"I'm already completely enthralled and ready to give in. So you're here as part of the Danish team, defending your claims? Hanne, that is tremendous."

"You might say. Since I last saw you, I have become even more involved with our submission. And, I guess that's why I'm here—I am now the expert in Denmark on continental shelf extensions. And I have been asked to lead the Danish team to defend our submission. My friend Richard here is my Canadian counterpart."

It was not long before Richard was feeling superfluous as Lock and Hanne began the dance of catching up on the several years they had not seen each other. Richard finally managed to get a word wedged in the conversation to take his leave, but Lock interrupted: "You know, I've got a couple of hours of reading to do to prepare for tomorrow." He stood up, grabbed his briefcase and looked deep into Hanne' blue-green eyes. "But I'd love to have dinner with you tonight to continue our discussion. Call me. I'm just around the corner…" Lock pulled a card from the hotel out of his jacket pocket and gave it to her. "102 Brownstone. Boutique hotel, room 22." Then, glancing at Richard, he added, "I'm sure I'll see you around," leaving it to Hanne to sort out how to handle him.

⁂

Hanne glanced at her watch as she made her way to the elevators and determined that she had time for a good workout before dinner. She was happy that Lock had asked her out, though it was difficult not to include

Richard. But he had his chance in Ottawa. Now she wanted to be alone with Lock.

Back in her room, she changed into her Lululemon exercise wear and took the elevator to the exercise suite to do a vigorous workout. After a good hour of stretches and a session on the elliptical, still full of endorphins, perspiration covering her body, Hanne went back to her room and called Lock. They agreed to meet in the lobby of the Alex at eight. She showered, dressed and put on just the faintest hint of make-up to tone down her freckles. She took a last glance in the mirror, and, satisfied with what she saw, headed out the door.

෴

Lock was sitting on one of the David Rockwell armchairs when Hanne materialized from an elevator in an above the knee red A-line dress, carrying a light gray spring coat, looking gorgeous. He eagerly got up, gave her a quick kiss, and grabbed her lightly by the elbow, saying: "Let's get out of here before any of your friends show up. I reserved a corner table at Alcala."

It was not just Richard he wanted to avoid, but the other members of the Commission, some of whom he thought might be staying in the hotel. He had been given the choice, but had opted for the smaller 102 Brownstone. For a moment, Lock felt he was heaping conflict of interest on top of conflict of interest by going out to dinner with the beautiful leader of the team from one of the countries over whose jurisdictional and economic interests he would have to sit in judgment during the next few days. *But dammit,* he told himself, *our relationship goes back well before my appointment...*

After Hanne ordered a seafood salad, and Lock the fish of the day, with a bottle of a Rio Baixas Albariño

2019 from Spain, they continued the catching up on what they had been doing in their respective worlds. Lock told her that it had been difficult for him to rearrange his teaching schedule at the University of Beijing to make time for the work of the Commission, and that he especially missed the crossover course with the law faculty dealing with the Law of the Sea, and specifically Article 76.

Hanne told him that she had spent most of her time the last couple of years honing the research to back the Danish case for an extension of their EEZ off the coast of Northern Greenland, based on the view that the Lomonosov Ridge was a natural prolongation of the Greenland continental shelf.

"You're going to have a difficult job, Lock. To sort through Russia's submission versus ours and Canada's. Especially with Russia being so belligerent…"

Maybe not as difficult as you think, he thought to himself.

"And I do hope you're open minded, Lock. I remember you seemed to have a pretty set view that the Lomonosov Ridge was an oceanic feature. We have submitted proof showing that it links to the Greenland and Ellesmere Island continental shelf. Just give little old Denmark a chance…"

"Now, now, Hanne," Lock said, laughing as he reached for Hanne's hand. "You mustn't try to influence me!" But to himself, he thought, *boy, and how I will let you try!* Even though, with the Chinese, there was no need for any additional persuasion…

"Mustn't I?" Hanne reacted to Lock's touch, by rubbing her leg against his under the table.

"Although you know, I would do anything to get you back in bed with me…" Lock got straight to the point.

"That was on a rock the last time. The only time, may I remind you."

"The beds in the brownstone are much softer…"

"Well, then what are we waiting for?" Hanne relished being more forward than her attractive date.

Lock tried and finally caught the waiter's attention to ask for the bill. The tab paid, they walked the few blocks to Lock's hotel.

Alone in the elevator, they could not wait, and Lock took Hanne in an embrace, kissing her passionately. The elevator reached the sixth floor when they were just starting to explore each other's mouths with their tongues. Lock tugged Hanne down the hall, frantically searching for his key card in his pocket. He barely closed the door before he had her in his arms again, his right hand deftly working the zipper at the back of the dress. As she stepped back to shed the A-line, he kicked off his shoes, undid and stepped out of his pants, unbuttoned and took off his shirt. The rest of their clothing came off on the way to the bedroom.

Hanne pulled Lock onto the sumptuous duvet, and they explored each other's bodies with hands and tongues. But the urge was too great for extensive foreplay, and it was not long before Lock was inside Hanne. Her orgasm came first, taking Lock by surprise, but her release quickly brought on the same for him, and they collapsed in each other's arms, panting, fulfilled, ecstatic.

"I've dreamt of this almost every day for the last couple of years," Hanne said, clinging to Lock.

"I'm not ashamed to admit that I have too. And if this is the prize, then I will cast my vote in favor of Denmark's submission, for sure."

But Lock knew that this would not be the only reward waiting for him.

CHAPTER 13

UN Headquarters, New York City, USA—Daytime, Wednesday, April 2, the next day

Lock did not want to be late for the first working session of the Commission, but he had to scramble to get ready and skipped his breakfast—Hanne had not let him get out of bed without making love yet again in the morning, knowing that the Russians were to present first. Having sex with Hanne was one thing he was not going to miss out on, certainly not to be on time for any Russians.

When Lock arrived at Committee Room 9, Guido was just assembling some papers before sitting down at his desk in the center of the horseshoe arrangement.

"Let us begin. I believe our Russian friends will be here shortly, but there are a few issues we need to consider first. Critically, you will have no doubt noted that there is an overlap of the Russian claim made several years ago with both the Danish and the most recent Canadian claims. And a much smaller one between the two latter submissions." And then to the technical assistant manning the computer: "Could you please show the slide? Yes, right here…And here." A little red laser beam jumped around on the big screen on the wall as Guido moved the penlight around.

"Specifically, both Denmark and Russia are laying

claim to the North Pole, and as you see, there is a large area of overlap between the Canadian claim and Russia's, and a smaller one between the claims of Denmark and Russia. There have also been extensive comments by these nations on each other's submissions, which you have no doubt read. Moreover, as you have seen, the USA has offered *ex officio* dissenting comments on both Canada's and Russia's submissions—that is, on the Executive Summaries that were circulated to other states—and Norway has commented on Russia's claim as well."

Guido looked up to allow the interpreter to catch up and to see if he still had the attention of the other twenty scientists in the room. "I would like to remind you that our mandate does not extend to settling disputes regarding shelf boundaries between coastal states. We can only point out what does or does not comply with UNCLOS and comment on the underlying science, given our respective scientific backgrounds and all the facts at hand. If there are legitimate overlapping claims, the states will have to negotiate bilaterally to determine the boundaries of their jurisdiction."

Guido paused again, and looked around the room, as if to make sure that his words had been understood, before continuing. "It is time to get to work. Mademoiselle Givry," he addressed the good looking brunette at the back, dressed in the light blue uniform of the UN, "would you be kind enough to see if our Russian guests have arrived?"

⌘⌘⌘

Outside, in the halls of the UN headquarters, there was great commotion as the Russian minister for the Arctic, Pavel Laptov, arrived with his team. Accompanied by the ambassador to the UN, Sergei Mitkinov, and an army of security thugs, Laptov and his supporting cast of scientists and lawyers were shown to Committee Room 9. They were waiting impatiently outside when Mademoiselle Givry invited them in.

"Welcome, Minister Laptov. Welcome." Guido stood up to greet the minister, then looked toward Mitkinov, "Ambassador." Lock had never met Laptov, but had heard a lot about him, and the famous polar explorer exceeded all expectations in real life. "Please, please sit down." Guido pointed to the desk beside his, bearing a 'Russia' placard and with several chairs behind it.

"It is a great honor for us that you have come in person, Minister. We are ready to start, if you are. I will now call on the delegates from Russia to make their presentation." Guido seemed glad to cede the floor.

Laptov spoke to the bespectacled, balding, somewhat overweight man in an ill-fitting black suit behind him, who said something in Russian as he handed a memory stick to another one of the Russian delegates, and then sat in the seat Laptov vacated.

"My name is Dr. Novikov," the large man started his speech, "and I have been asked by the minister to give the presentation in defense of our submission, which you have had the chance to study for the last several years."

Lock sat back, hoping this would not be one of those typically wordy, overbuilt Russian presentations he had been subjected to on previous occasions. The simultaneous translation of course made the whole process all that much more laborious. He forced himself to concentrate, and told himself to try to keep an open mind, as the Russian continued.

"From the submission we made already in the summer of 2015, you can see that we are claiming the same maritime territory as an extension of our continental shelf that we laid claim to in our submission back in 2001. A block of 1.2 million square kilometers of undersea territory, stretching to the North Pole from one hundred seventy °West longitude to approximately one hundred nautical miles east of the Lomonosov Ridge, as shown on this map."

Dr. Novikov went on to construct the Russian case on principles similar to those forming the basis for their 2001 submission: that, for one, the Lomonosov Ridge was a "natural prolongation" of the continental shelf falling into the category of "submarine elevations that are natural components of the continental margin," and therefore the Ridge was not subject to the three hundred and fifty nautical mile limitation on claims for extensions of a country's continental shelf set forth in Article 76 paragraph 6 of UNCLOS.

"Thus, the 'outer constraint line' for the claim in this case should be determined by the rule that draws a line a hundred nautical miles seaward of the two thousand five hundred meter isobath," he stated.[54] So far the legal argumentation was sound; the case would stand or fall on the strength of the data provided to back up these claims, Lock thought to himself.

Dr. Novikov cleverly pointed out that the Russian position was similar to the one the US was advancing in its claim to the Chukchi plateau off the Alaskan north coast. Despite the fact that they had not yet signed or ratified the Convention on the Law of the Sea, the US argument, according to Novikov was that the plateau and its component elevations, situated to the north of Alaska, were covered by the 'submarine elevations' exemption of Article 76, and thus were similarly not subject to the three hundred fifty mile limitation. Dr. Novikov went on to reference the International Law Association Committee on the Continental Shelf, which made the point that the term 'submarine elevations' in Article 76 paragraph 6 qualified by the clause 'that are natural components of the continental margin', clearly indicated that while those elevations could be distinguished as separate features, they were, at the same time, closely linked to the continental margin.

"The Committee goes on to determine," Novikov took his glasses off to read from his notes, "that this also applies in the case of features which at some point in time may not have been a part of, or may have become detached from, the continental margin and have, through geological processes, become or stayed so closely linked to the continental margin as to become or remain a part of it."

Novikov stopped for a minute to allow the interpreters to catch up, before continuing the legalese: he asserted that this interpretation also applied to the Lomonosov Ridge, which, as some scientists have claimed, was ripped away from the outer part of the continental margin of Eurasia in geologic time, probably from north of Scandinavia and Russia, and "may in fact have slid for several hundred kilometers along a transform fault until it reached its current location on the Siberian shelf." He then paused again, obviously relieved to have gotten through the legalistic section of the presentation, and gave Guido a pained look, as if wanting to be done with the whole thing. "We have provided the necessary data to prove this in our submission…"

"Yes, yes, and that is something we will deal with first in the Sub-commission," Guido said, somewhat impatiently, after it was clear that Novikov had finished. "I thank the delegate from Russia for his presentation. Tomorrow, we would like to move to the Sub-commission meeting. It will start at nine am in Conference Room 7, and we will notify you later today of the composition of the Sub-commission. Please, be ready for in-depth discussion and defense of your submission—you will be requested to be present at nine-thirty."

☙❧

Lock used the long lunch break to finish reading the comments on the Danish submission's Executive Summary, and, as he hurried back to Conference Room 9, he saw that Hanne and the rest of her team were already waiting outside the door. He brushed Hanne as he went past, relishing her scent and whispering "Good luck," before he went to find his place inside.

Guido was a few moments late—Lock wondered whether he had had a glass or two of Malbec with his *ojo de bife* at lunch—and, as he sat down, announced that they would now hear the Danish presentation, and would Mademoiselle Givry kindly show the guests in.

Hanne led the troop, looking gorgeously professional, Lock thought, in her red above-the-knee suit, and Guido asked the three-person team to introduce themselves. Before he turned the floor over to Hanne, the Argentine could not help but make the sexist comment "that we should not be swayed by the fact that we have a very good-looking delegate making this case…"

Lock thought, *on the contrary, so much the better if these old geezers are bowled over by Hanne's looks—at least my duplicity might not show through as much.*

☙❧

Hanne was brilliant. She started by outlining the Danish claim, but focused her presentation on demonstrating that the Lomonosov Ridge was, and always had been part of the North American plate, and clearly a "natural prolongation" of the Greenland/Ellesmere Island continental shelves. She stated that Danish scientists accepted the notion that the Ridge may have—and she emphasized the 'may'—split off from the Eurasian landmass some fifty or sixty million years ago and then moved along a transform fault to its current position, but at the same time they firmly asserted that the other end of the Ridge must have always been connected to the North American landmass. She added that this is "as we understand it, also the position of our Canadian colleagues." And finished with the point that "the magnetic and soil data clearly suggest the Lomonosov Ridge is an extension of the North American and Greenland continental shelves, and we are happy to present and discuss this now or in Sub-commission."

Hanne turned the floor over to her colleague Bent, and Lock found interesting his contention that the relatively small saddle—eight hundred meters deep and thirty-five kilometers wide—between the Ridge and the Greenland/Ellesmere Island shelf was merely scarring due to tectonic plate activity, "and that essentially the magnetic, lithographic and seismic profiles showed virtually no break or anomaly." Lock's view had always been that there was oceanic seabed between the Ridge and the continental shelf. So much the better, though, if the Danes had sound proof to the contrary.

Hanne took over again to say that where there might be overlap with a legitimate Russian or Canadian—or indeed US claim—Denmark would be happy to negotiate a mutually agreeable resolution. And she threw out the challenge that Denmark was ready to subject its submission to rigorous examination by any Sub-commission that the Commission should choose to appoint.

〜〜〜

After Hanne and the Danish team left the room, Guido took the floor, saying, "That was an excellent presentation by the delegates from Denmark. We still have to hear the Canadians—and I propose we do that tomorrow morning—and then in the afternoon start the work of the Sub-commission. So let us now move on to selecting the Sub-commission members…"

Guido cleared his throat and looked around the room, his eyes settling on Lock, as he continued, "Now, as per Rule 40 of our Procedures, we ask for nominations of seven of you from the floor, taking into account that such nominations shall not be from the countries concerned—in this case, Russia, Denmark and Canada, which is not a problem since we do not have representatives of these countries in our midst—nor shall it be a delegate who has worked on any of the submissions, either directly or indirectly, as an advisor. The submissions did not indicate that this was the case, but if you are nominated and you are compromised in this manner, please declare your ineligibility. I, as Chairman, will also exercise my authority to ensure that the Sub-commission is balanced in terms of expertise and geographical spread. Now, nominations from the floor please."

Lock saw Li's hand shoot up, and Guido recognized the delegate from China. "Mr. Chairman, I nominate Professor Lachlan McTierney from Australia. He is very knowledgeable about the Law of the Sea, particularly continental shelves. He teaches several courses in Beijing and has worked in the Arctic many years."

"Anyone second that?"

Lock didn't realize he was so popular, as several hands went up in support of his nomination, and he was voted in unanimously. Maybe it was because he was relatively new, and hadn't made any controversial noises in his first session on the Commission…

But he soon came to the conclusion that the first seven to be nominated would be elected, unless there were too many geologists or hydrologists, or all the nominees were from Africa or Oceania. Group mentality though ensured a reasonable spread, and Guido did not have to exercise his self-proclaimed authority to guide the process.

Lock was dismayed when the third nomination, by Emori Naitini, the hydrologist from Fiji, as he ascertained from the briefing material, was Zheng Li. No doubt Li would have instructions on how to vote, perhaps even what to say during the deliberations of the Sub-commission. Did Naitini have instructions to put Li's name forward?

So now it was up to him, with the Chinese professor's help, to move the decision in favor of Denmark. No, of Greenland...and China. He had already seen that the submission was very strong, a well-presented case. It could be believable that he would be convinced by the science to move away from the position he had been espousing publicly up until then. It need not be evident that he had sold out to the Chinese, Lock rationalized.

But what kind of a scientist was he, if he went into these deliberations with his mind made up? Well, not totally made up, because, if the science was not there to support the Danish case, would he go along with it? How much would he stretch the limits of scientific credulity? But it would not get to that, Lock told himself.

Lock was pulled away from his anxious musings by Guido's sonorous voice. "Now the seven elected members need to choose a chairman, a vice-chairman and a rapporteur, so that the Sub-commission can start its work first thing tomorrow. First then, any nominations for chairman?"

While Lock was considering whether he should put

forward any one of the seven—if for no other reason than to prevent his own selection—he saw the hand of Paolo Kwemba, the pleasant oceanographer from Angola who had talked to him yesterday after the introductory meeting, shoot up, and Guido nodded to him.

"I nominate the distinguished delegate from Australia to chair our Sub-commission," Kwemba announced in a clear and sonorous voice. This was again seconded by Emori Naitini. No doubt, all at the behest of the Chinese.

So Lock was duly elected chairman, with Guido congratulating him and wishing him well as he drew the meeting to a close. Carlos Figuiera of Cuba was chosen vice-chairman and Kwemba rapporteur.

On the way out, Li came up behind him again, smiling. "Professor McTierney, I am very glad I am on Sub-commission chaired by you. We work together, make good team." He was starting to repeat himself, the Chinese professor was.

Lock answered with a curt, "Delighted."

Oh God, how could he sink so low?

೧೦೧

On his way back to the hotel, Lock thought of calling Shaojing to tell him the deal was off. He just couldn't go through with this. But then, he was quite sure the Chinese would not let him back out. And stay alive. On the plus side, too, there was the money. And all the other rationalizations he had already rehearsed millions of times…

CHAPTER 14

Alex Hotel, New York City, USA—Evening, Wednesday, April 2, the same day

Hanne, still panting from the session on the elliptical in the Alex's exercise facilities, opened the door to her room and immediately saw the red message light blinking on the phone next to the bed. She ran to the night table, confident it would be Lock.

"Hello, you sexy one." Hanne's disappointment at hearing Jens's voice came as a surprise to her. "Just wanting to know how things went today. Am up until midnight, so do call." She looked at the red numbers on the digital clock and saw with some relief—again surprising herself—that it was already 6:37pm, so well after Jens's bedtime in Copenhagen.

Why hadn't Lock called? The way he had looked at her all afternoon, undressing her with his eyes…Having him there had brought out the best of her presentation skills—she admitted that she had wanted to impress him. Pleased at how well it had all gone, Hanne pulled her exercise top over her head and threw it in the bottom of the closet. She was just stepping out of her body-hugging bottoms when the phone rang. Now, this had to be Lock…

Naked, she eagerly picked up the phone. "Hello, you sexy one." Hanne was surprised at the coincidence of the repeat salutation, but this time, she was right: Lock's deep voice could not be mistaken. "You were fabulous today."

"Thanks."

"But Denmark's case is not won yet. If you want to have any hope of your submission being approved, you have to have dinner...and ahem...the 'usuals' tonight with the chairman of the Sub-commission. Meet at eight, downstairs in the Alex?"

"So...you...?"

"Yes. You're in luck. I am the Chairman."

"Wow. Congratulations! How did you swing that?"

"Never you mind." That was a question he was not going to answer. "Just remember, if you want to win your case...the 'usuals'!"

"You sexist pig. See you at eight." Hanne hung up, laughing, and looking forward to another evening with Lock.

೧೨೦

Over dinner at Convivio, a one Michelin star restaurant just a few blocks away, they discussed the day. Relishing her starter—*Moleche*, semolina dusted soft shell crab on arugula, with a caper aioli—Hanne was elated as she listened to Lock's exuberant praise for her presentation.

"It was just right. Perfect. You made the case succinctly, and you had your colleague Bent tell them that you had the data to back it up and you finished off by stressing that Denmark was ready to negotiate bilaterally if there was overlap with any other country." Lock took a bite of his *Insalata di Frutti di Mare*. "This is sensational!"

"So is this. Care for a bite?" Hanne dipped a bit of the

crab in the aioli to pass to Lock. "But the hard part comes now: convincing the chairman of the Sub-commission whose entrenched view is that the Lomonosov Ridge is an oceanic ridge and not connected to any shelf..."

"Well, you're half way there, my dear. And the Russians still have a long way to go. In fact, they may never get there..." He passed his fork to her with a scallop and a leaf of arugula.

"What do you mean?"

"I don't think I would really like to get, you know...a blow job from Dr. Novikov. Not while you're around, anyway..."

"Stop it. Seriously, tell me."

"Hanne, I really can't talk about it. Shall we say, it seems that they may lack convincing data to show that there is no oceanic seabed between the Eurasian end of the Ridge and their shelf. But we'll see more tomorrow."

"Okay. Then, at least can you divulge who else is on the Sub-commission?" Hanne sipped the delicious Falanghina Sannio Feudi di San Gregorio 2018.

"Great body, no?" Lock chewed the wine, obviously enjoying it. "Just like you, my dear," he added, laughing.

"Come on. That's enough now. The names, Mr. Chairman..."

"Well, your friend Guido, for one. I don't know how he managed to get himself selected, but there you go. I think though, he is a pretty good geologist. Anyways, he has the hots for you, so no doubt he will be a pushover."

"Okay. That's it. Enough of that. I am not interested in that slimy old geezer with the Grecian formula black hair. And I am not just a sex object."

"No, I know. But you are fantastic in bed!"

"The names, Lock McTierney, concentrate on the names..."

"Well, then there is Zheng Li," Lock said hesitantly.

"Oh, yes. Isn't he a marine geophysicist? From some Chinese institute?"

"Yes. The Institute of Oceanography in Hangzhou. Strong reputation in the Far East. Lots of publications, some better than others."

"That's why his name is familiar. I've read a couple of his articles. On the changing melting properties of frozen sea ice. He's in your camp, no?"

"You might say that again…"

The waiter came to clear their plates and pour some more wine.

"Who else then?"

"There is the Angolan, Paolo Kwemba," Lock answered. Hanne felt a hand on her bare thigh inching up her skirt.

"You have a one-track mind…"

"Yes. With you sitting across from me…Kwemba was elected rapporteur."

"What?"

"Rapporteur. Don't you love these UN titles? He's the one who will have to pull together the Sub-commission's report."

"That will be a big job…"

"He is also an oceanographer. The other one on the Sub-commission. Actually a pretty good guy."

"Who else?"

"Then we have the Romanian, Nikolai Contanescu. A geophysicist at the University of Bucharest. He is relatively new on the Commission too. I don't know anything about him."

"Well, at least we have one European…"

"I wouldn't count on him siding with your position. He could be old school. Judging from his age, his formation was during the Ceaucescu era."

Lock put his hand back on the tablecloth as the waiter

placed in front of Hanne a plate of steaming pasta from which wafted a delicious bacon and cheese aroma—*Orechiette alla Carbonara* with pancetta, pecorino, scallions, egg and black pepper—and between Lock's fork and steak knife, an inch thick *Costoletto di Vitello*, *parmigiano* crusted veal chop, with spigarello hen of the woods mushrooms. He poured the previously opened Barolo Scanavino 2000 for Lock to taste, which he did with obvious pleasure.

"Delicious," Lock said, holding the glass up, as he swirled the contents around, studied them in the candlelight. "Superb legs..." He laughed and looked over at Hanne. "But don't worry, my dear, I like yours even better." He moved his roving hand to cover Hanne's. "Oh yes, the Sub-commission..."

"Yes, I was squeezing the names out of you one by one, but it is really hard work. Your hedonistic side seems to always get the better of you." Hanne paused for a sip of the Barolo, and then added, giving Lock a smile with her eyes, "I may just have to squeeze your testicles to get you to spew them out..."

"Well then, back to work... but just for a moment. We also have the Cuban marine geologist, Carlos Figueira. He was elected vice-chairman. And from Fiji, Emori Naitini, a hydrologist. Pretty eclectic group all in all."

"Hmm. I am not sure I like it..."

"Well, you can probably count on the Romanian and Cuban members to support the Russian cause. And likely vote against Canada and Denmark."

"You may be right."

"Then there is Guido, who I am sure will support you."

"That's at least one."

"Kwemba could go either way. Although he could take the view that we are talking about an oceanic elevation. So could Naitini."

"Hmm…What about Li?"

"I am sure he will go against the Russians. The Chinese do not want to see a Russia with more resources and a strengthened strategic position."

"So what you are saying is that two will side with us, two with the Russians, and the rest of you, the ridiculous hardliners, will vote us both down…"

"Well, there is still tonight back at the hotel for you to work your magic, love." And once again, Lock let loose with that sexist laughter of his that Hanne found so irritating and so irresistible at the same time, before continuing. "But as you know, Hanne, I am an easy lay. Kwemba and Naitini may be more difficult to get into bed with you."

Although they may, like I, already be…in bed with the Chinese, that is, Lock could not help thinking as he finished the last hen of the woods mushroom on his plate, washing it down with a huge gulp of the Barolo.

⁂

It was a pleasant walk back to the Alex, and Hanne could not help but think what a great day it had been so far. She had done her job well, and shared an excellent dinner and a wonderful time with this man she was…was she falling in love with him? If not love yet, then certainly becoming very, very keen on…

And there were still the pleasures of actually making love with Lock to look forward to.

"Good evening," the doorman greeted them as they walked through the Alex's doors, trying to look inconspicuous as they scurried through the lobby to the elevators. They made it without seeing any familiar faces from the UN or the various presenting teams.

The elevator doors opened, and, poised to quickly step

in, Lock did a double take. Figueira, holding an unlit cigar, emerged deep in conversation with Contanescu.

"Well, hello, gentlemen," Lock said, as he and Hanne got in. "See you tomorrow."

But there was no way they would have not noticed the beautiful Hanne at his side.

As the elevator doors closed behind them, for a brief moment Lock thought, *how stupid, we should have gone to the Brownstone.* Oh well, you gotta live dangerously, he told himself, as his mouth eagerly sought Hanne's.

CHAPTER 15

UN Headquarters, New York City, USA—Daytime, Thursday, April 3, the next day

Lock went to his seat at the center facing the horseshoe of desks in Committee Room 7, and extracted his papers from his briefcase. The six other members were there already: they too, found their places, spread out behind their country name placards.

Lock caught himself wondering whether he and Hanne had been right the evening before, trying to figure out who among these men was likely to be in the Russian camp, who would support the Danish and Canadian submissions, and who were the Chinese stooges. Or, would they all be truly objective? As scientists were supposed to be…

And who, if not he, would advance the view that the Lomonosov Ridge was not an extension of any continental shelf, and therefore no country should gain access to additional resources in the Arctic?

Paolo Kwemba? Not likely. Emori Naitini? Doubtful, given their performance yesterday. Yes, when he thought back on the nominations the day before, it had all been too slick, had happened too fast. China had clearly gotten its way, and these men had played a role. He had better watch them.

Once they had all settled into their seats, Lock cleared

his throat and clinked his water glass with his pen. The room turned quiet.

"Distinguished delegates..." He still found the UN jargon hard to get used to, but had thought long and hard about this moment as it would be critical in setting the stage for the outcome of the deliberations of the Sub-commission.

"We have the difficult task of looking at three submissions which have some overlap, as these claims all revolve around considerations of the Lomonosov Ridge being an extension of a continental shelf. There are, in my view, four possible outcomes, with some gradations. One, we reject all three, on the basis that the Ridge is oceanic in origin, and we agree to no extensions at this stage. The other extreme scenario is that we accept that the Ridge is connected to both the Eurasian and the North American continental shelves, and that therefore Russia, Canada and Denmark all have legitimate claims to extend their jurisdiction as permitted by Article 76. We will have to tread carefully on any overlap in the submissions, and ask the countries with conflicting claims to negotiate a mutually acceptable compromise. The other two possible outcomes are that we accept the claims of only the Russian or the other two submissions, which, as I understand it, provide very similar argumentation..."

Lock hesitated for a moment, as he was distracted by Guido, who had taken a huge handkerchief out of his pocket and ceremoniously blew his nose.

"...Having started to study the various papers submitted by the three teams, I would say that certainly the Danish and Canadian cases are backed up by very sound research, and Russia has also provided us with a lot of new material. But as you know, we need to keep an open mind and assess the submissions based on the merits of the science backing them up." He glanced sideways at Li, but the Chinese scientist was looking noisily through his papers.

"Once we are ready, we will have a preliminary presentation from the Russian team, which will go over the main aspects of the evidence to support their claim, and hopefully throw more light on the unresolved issues from the last time when their first submission was considered. Are there any questions before we bring in the presenters from Russia?"

✧✧✧

The Russian delegation, led by Minister Laptov, filed in and moved quickly to occupy the seats around, and behind, the desk next to the chairman's in the center. Dr. Novikov, at Laptov's bidding, again took the front seat, and signaled that he was ready. Lock noted with dismay that Li was not in the room.

"Distinguished delegates, members of the Sub-commission. Yesterday, I set out Russia's claim," Novikov began. "Today I will move straight to the supporting detail, if you permit. But if there are any questions regarding the claim itself at this point, I would be happy to address them." He looked around the table, then at Lock, who spoke up: "I guess not, Dr. Novikov, so please just continue."

"Thank you. You will see from this slide that the geology of the Ridge is analogous to formations on the Eurasian side in the Barents and Kara Sea regions. This supports our contention that the Ridge was ripped away from the outer part of the continental margin of Eurasia, north of Scandinavia and Russia—here and here—in probably the early Tertiary period—that is, fifty to sixty million years ago—and slid along a transform fault to its current position. Here."[55] Novikov used a little red beam to highlight the places on the map shown on the slide.

Li finally came into the room, looking stressed as he put his cell phone away, and mumbled a quick apology.

"You can see in this chart," Novikov continued, "that the known lithologies, ages, P-wave velocity structure, and thickness of the crust along the outer Barents and Kara continental shelves are similar to the values of these parameters we have recently measured over the Lomonosov Ridge. Especially the seismic, gravity and magnetic data demonstrate that the ridge basement is most likely formed of early Mesozoic or older sedimentary or low-grade meta-sedimentary rocks over a crystalline core that is intermediate to basic in composition. Magnetic anomaly highs at shorter wavelengths observed along the upper ridge flanks and crest may denote the presence of shallow igneous rock formations..." Novikov cleared his throat and Lock had to admit that he was starting to admire the dogged professionalism of the overweight Russian scientist.

"...And, as you see on this slide, our studies confirm the multichannel seismic reflection data acquired during the 1990s by Professor Jokat and his colleagues[56]. These results strongly support the interpretation that the Ridge is a continental...sliver...you would say, that tore away from the outer shelf of Eurasia, as they clearly indicate that the Ridge has an asymmetric internal architecture that consists of older pro-grading sequences on the Amerasia Basin side—here—and a fault-bounded and steep margin on the Eurasia Basin side—over here."[57] The little red beam skipped gaily around the map.

Hmm, when put like that, Lock thought to himself, *maybe the Russians did have a case.* Science was so, so subjective—it was all in the perspective from which you analyzed the data. But then he saw that Li was getting agitated in his seat, and surmised that he wanted to speak.

"I recognize the distinguished delegate from China."

"Yes, thank you, Mr. Chairman. Dr. Novikov. That is all well and good," the Chinese scientist squeaked impatiently in his high-pitched voice, "but what you make of seabed between Eurasian end of Ridge and foot of Siberian continental shelf?" Li looked down at his notes before continuing. "This is where we note the Ridge becomes much deeper as it approaches Siberia, with lots of faulting in the deeper sediments," he read from the papers in front of him.

Novikov, nonplussed by the intervention of the Chinese scientist, cleared his throat and looked over at Laptov.

"Yes, Dr. Novikov," Lock chimed in, "I must say, I have a similar concern to Dr. Li's. Particularly, as those faults suggest that although one can argue that the Ridge currently seems to be attached to the Siberian shelf, prior to say, ten million years ago, it may not have been part of it at all, or was at least partially disconnected. And yes, we may agree that it is a sliver of shelf that eons ago was cut off from its earlier location by faulting and rifting, and then slid several hundred kilometers along a transform fault to reach its current location with one end near the Siberian shelf. But Dr. Novikov, that is quite different from saying that the Ridge is actually—and for that matter, has always been—a natural prolongation of the Siberian continental shelf, you must admit."

"Also, Dr. Novikov," Li pressed the advantage Lock had opened up for him, "the seabed in the area between the Ridge and the Eurasian continental shelf has features of oceanic crust, or did your studies not make such findings? For one, it is well known that the magnetic profiles on the Eurasian side of the Ridge closely resemble those typical over both the Atlantic and Pacific oceans..."[58]

"The Jokat study..." Novikov tried to reestablish

control of his thoughts and of the presentation. These Sub-commission members were talking circles around him, and he was getting a headache from trying to keep up with the rapid interventions they were throwing at him, followed by the inevitably lagging simultaneous translations.

"Dr. Novikov, I must say," Paolo Kwemba saw that it was his turn to weigh in against the Russians and deliver the *coup de grâ*ce, "the Jokat study is irrelevant to the point in question. All it demonstrates is that the Ridge was a result of tectonic shifting, and that, yes, it may have broken off the Eurasian land mass. But in terms of proving that it is a 'natural prolongation' of the shelf, or a 'submarine elevation that is a natural component of the continental margin'—to paraphrase Article 76 paragraph 6—it does nothing for your case."

Lock could see that Novikov was now getting incensed by these constant interruptions; he had turned red in the face and was breathing heavily. "But as I said yesterday, the International Law Association Committee on the Continental Shelf determined..." Novikov stopped momentarily, as much to catch his breath as to search through his notes for the appropriate reference, but Lock was growing impatient, because he saw that Novikov was now just going to go round and round with the legalese, and he saw his chance to end everybody's pain...Too bad, he had been doing so well, until he was thrown off by the questions and alternative interpretations.

"Dr. Novikov. Let me get to the point. What we need to advance our discussions here is data presented clearly that show that there is no break in the lithologies, nor any magnetic and seismic anomalies that cannot be explained, between the end of the Ridge and the shelf. Evidence that the Ridge is, and always has been, an extension or prolongation of the shelf, not something that broke off and moved to its current position adjacent to the shelf."

Laptov raised his right hand, shoulder high, index finger pointing up, signaling that he wanted to speak. He, too, seemed a little out of sorts with the way the meeting was going.

"I recognize the minister delegate from Russia." Lock gave the polar explorer the floor.

"Mr. Chairman, you and your Sub-commission have the extensive documents Russia has submitted for review. These contain the scientific evidence supporting our claim. If, after your consideration of this material, you have questions or need for additional information, Dr. Novikov and the team will be on standby in the hotel ready to provide this. I myself will be leaving tomorrow, but can be reached by videoconference at any time. I believe we should break now, and allow you to get on with your study of our submission."

"Yes, Minister, I think you are right."

༺༻

In the afternoon, it was Hanne's turn. Dressed in a white blouse and navy blue suit showing off her figure and legs, she was superb in outlining the key data elements that proved beyond any doubt that the Lomonosov Ridge was a natural prolongation of the Greenland / Ellesmere Island continental shelf.

She first focused on the uninterrupted similarity of the geological composition of the sediment and rocks on the Ridge and on the shelf, and then moved to the magnetic data, which confirmed that the Ridge was part of a Precambrian complex that linked to the Canadian Shield. Hanne then wrapped up, suggesting that the team would be ready to come back at a moment's notice to answer questions about the evidence in the submission.

❧❧❧

After the Danes left, Lock took the floor.

"Distinguished delegates, we have had an overview of the structure and content of the submissions. My view is that the Danish—and probably, more than likely, the Canadian—cases are going to be relatively easy ones for us to agree, although we will have to put adjudication over any areas of overlap with known Russian and US claims on hold. The Russian case, though, I believe will be more difficult and as we have seen today, raises several issues. Indeed, we may find that we have to send it back once again due to insufficient appropriate evidence. Nevertheless, I would not want to prejudge it at this point. However, I would propose—and we can put this to a vote—that we start our work by considering the Danish and Canadian submissions first. If you agree with this, please put your hand up."

Lock watched as he saw Li and Guido raise their hands, followed first by Kwemba and then Naitini. That left the Cuban and the Romanian as the naysayers.

"The proposal is carried five to two. We will hear the Canadians first tomorrow morning, and given our vote, after that, please be ready tomorrow to discuss your views on the Danish and Canadian submissions. We will start our work at nine sharp. And be punctual please. Thank you, and have a good evening."

❧❧❧

Lock was the last to leave the room, as he quickly jotted down a few notes. When he closed the door behind him, he saw that Li was just coming out of the nearby men's room. *Oh no, not again!*

"Ah, Professor McTierney! Excellent. You are very good chairman."

"Thank you, Professor Li. You were very cogent this morning yourself."

"Thank you, thank you. We make good team, no?"

Slimy little bugger, Lock thought to himself...

CHAPTER 16

*UN Russian Ambassador's Office, New York City, USA—
Early Evening, Thursday, April 3, same day*

"Gentlemen, thank you for coming." Pavel Laptov sat in a big upholstered armchair in the ambassador's office. Mitkinov had left a few minutes before for some reception, just as Carlos Figueira and Nikolai Contanescu were shown in by the ambassador's secretary. "You have had a long session today, and I am sure you are very tired, but it is important for us to compare notes on the day. I would like to hear how things went from your standpoint as members of the Sub-commission." Laptov stood up and went over to the bar, picking up a tall, sleek bottle of Beluga.

"Vodka?"

"Thank you, Your Excellency," Figueira responded. "Can I offer you a cigar?"

"No, no thank you. But please, please go ahead. I am sure the ambassador won't mind. He smokes your wonderful Havanas too. He has them brought in the diplomatic pouch, so he tells me. Nikolai, Pyotr? Vodka?" As they all nodded, he poured four shots, handed three around and downed the fourth. He ignored the two other men in the room, who, no doubt, were assigned to guard and serve him.

"*Nazdorovya*. Okay, Carlos, tell me, what do you think?"

"Well," Figueira said, stopping to puff vigorously on his cigar as he tried to light it, "I am not sure I like it…"

"What do you mean?"

"For one, and Nikolai can confirm this…Last night we—that is Nikolai and I—were just getting out of the elevator to go to the bar to discuss some points in the Danish submission, and there, right in front of us waiting to get on, was Professor McTierney and that good-looking Danish geologist who heads up their team. Hanne Kristensen, I think, is her name. They were laughing and snuggling…and…seemed very, very friendly with each other."

"Yes, very friendly indeed, just as Carlos says," Contanescu acquiesced. "They were probably coming from a dinner date."

"And it even looked like, well, that they might end up in bed together."

"I checked this morning and McTierney does not even stay at the Alex."

"Not good. Not good," Laptov mused. "I did not think that Western scientists would be so…so decadent. But I should have known better."

"Perhaps, Pavel, we should put a listening device in that Danish whore's room," Novikov suggested. "And McTierney's too. That way, we would know what they are saying."

"Hmm. That is illegal in this country, no? But still, maybe not such a bad idea, Pyotr."

"Sergei, Dmitri." Laptov addressed the two men standing by the door. "I want you to put bugs in their rooms, both of them. The Danish woman and the Australian professor. So we know what they say in bed. How they plot to take the Arctic away from Russia...Go. Now. The sooner the better."

"Yes, you have to move fast," Figueira agreed with the minister. "Already today, in the meeting, McTierney proposed that the Sub-commission give quick consideration to the Danish and Canadian submissions because they would be easy to approve, whereas yours, he considers has a number of problems."

"And did you all agree?"

"He put it to a vote. Carlos and I were the only ones who didn't vote in favor," Contanescu answered.

"Hmm. There is something going on here that I don't fully understand. Besides the Danish woman swaying the chairman with sex..."

"The other thing I did not like..."—this was Dr. Novikov who spoke up—"...was the way that little Chinese runt—Li Zheng or whatever his name is—and McTierney seemed to gang up on me when I was making my presentation. And then that Angolan bastard, Kwemba, came after me too."

"Yes, that was odd. You are right," Figueira agreed. "But the Australians always try to please the Chinese. They are afraid of them. Plus, the Chinese are their best customers."

"And I guess Angola is their client state too," Contanescu added.

"We will have to watch that as well. We know the Chinese do not want Russia to get any more powerful. Or richer."

"In any case, once the microphones are in place, we will know what is going on between that slut and the Australian. We can always use our findings to expose them," Novikov said.

"Not so easy though, because we are doing something illegal by bugging their rooms," Laptov countered.

"Knowing will be important, though. And we will always have that trump card in our hand…"

CHAPTER 17

102 Brownstone, New York City, USA—Night, Thursday, April 3, and Morning, Friday, April 4, the next day

"That was fabulous!" Hanne said, kissing Lock one more time before she rolled over onto the bed beside him from straddling him, gently releasing his still erect penis as she did so.

"Yes. Amazing." Lock could not help but think that this Danish woman was the best lover he ever had. Was he—and he dared not even pose the question to himself—falling in love with her? She was smart, lively, good at everything she did, and, of course, great looking.

"A little more wine?" Lock pulled himself up on the pillows and reached for the half-empty bottle of red still on the table, pouring two glasses.

"Sure. Thanks," Hanne answered. "But now that that's over, you were going to fill me in on what happened today in the Sub-commission meeting. Other than that, my presentation was excellent, which I know already."

"Well, I'm not really supposed to. You know that. But since you are even better in bed than in making a convincing presentation, I guess you deserve to know," Lock answered, adding with a smile: "But the price...What will you do for me?"

"Besides having sex with you several times every

night? What more do you want, you horny bastard? You have the nerve…"

"Well, you could give me a blow job one of these days," Lock said, putting a hand between her thighs.

"You are incorrigible. You should be so lucky." Hanne took a big gulp of the wine, went to kiss him, and spewed it into his mouth. "There, take that for a blow…"

"Puh…Not that kind! No deal then…" Choking on the wine-filled kiss, Lock gasped for air.

"Well, maybe if you reveal all…"

"I have already. I am totally naked." Lock laughed, throwing the sheet off his lower body. "Well then, I'll go first. But just you remember the price…"

"I haven't said yes."

"Anyway, here goes. On spec then. The Russians were a disaster. I do not think they really have the proof to show that the Lomonosov Ridge is an unbroken natural prolongation of the Siberian continental shelf. That Novikov, he keeps referring back to this legalese jargon that the International Law Association Committee on the Continental Shelf determined this and ruled that…Nothing that advances their cause in terms of hard scientific data."

"You mean such as what we presented?"

"Yes. Exactly. That is the proof that is lacking on their side. The composition of the rocks and sediments, the magnetic and seismic data. That's what we need to see. That they are similar and uninterrupted."

"So you're saying their submission will be rejected?"

"Well, not quite yet. Too early to say. But what I did conclude—and I actually put it to vote—was that we should be giving your case, since it seems so watertight, quick consideration now. Only afterwards would we delve into the voluminous material the Russians provided, to see if there is anything there that would be relevant. At the end of that process, we may just have to send it back for insufficient meaningful data again."

"So, did your vote win?"

"Yes, five to two. The Cuban and the Romanian dissented."

"They must be in the Russian camp..."

"Or just wanting to be obstructionist." Lock was distracted for a moment by the thought of how much he loved the soft skin of the inside of a woman's thigh. Especially this one's.

"If you send it back for more study, that means that part of our claim would be held up too..."

"But at least you would have clear jurisdiction over most of what you wanted."

"Yes. I guess you're right. So it does make sense."

"Certainly, I think so."

"Hmm."

"Although we may want you to come back at least one more time before we move it back to the full Commission. I am sure Guido and the other perverted old geezers will want to have another good look at you."

"At least with them, it's just 'look, don't touch'. Not like the horny bastard of a chairman I have to service." Hanne had started to move slowly down Lock's chest, kissing and lightly stroking first his nipples, then his taut stomach muscles, while with her other hand, she was gently working on getting him aroused again.

She was so, so good at this and it did not take long; it was when she finally applied first her tongue and then her lips to his fully erect member that Lock knew it was all worthwhile. The selling out to the Chinese, the surrendering of all scientific objectivity, the breaking of confidentiality...In short, the lapsing into what he knew deep down was questionable behavior, was all worth it to get this woman...At least so he rationalized. He wanted her. He was in love with her.

જ્જ

Hanne relished staying in bed for a few minutes the next morning after Lock closed the door to rush off to his meeting at the UN. With Jens too, back in Copenhagen, she loved these moments alone in the rumpled bed, when she was able to lie back, think about life, or just the day ahead.

It was so good when they were together, she wondered what it was. Ever since that first time up in Warming Land. But she hardly knew this man, what made him tick, what was his philosophy, his politics, his thoughts on family, on the important things. They had great sex, and other than that, mainly talked shop when they got together, usually over expensive, delicious meals. *But relax,* she told herself, *you have only seen him for a few days now...You just need to give yourself more time to get to know him.*

There was one thing that puzzled Hanne though: Lock had earlier been so adamant that the Lomonosov Ridge was an oceanic ridge. Could she have really won him over with the evidence? Was it really that convincing? As a good scientist, she knew that there was always more than one way to interpret data...But he didn't even raise any questions or objections, put forth alternative interpretations...

Could it really have been the loving—was he that much of a pushover? Then that is not a good sign of character either...

A knock on the door derailed her train of thought; she shouted, "Yes?" as she clambered out of the king-sized bed.

"Housekeeping." Hanne heard a muffled but accented male voice through the door.

"Come back in half an hour," she yelled back and made her way naked into the bathroom.

Yes, she was going to have a good long shower, then go back to her hotel for a change of clothes and a hearty breakfast in the dining room before enjoying the beautiful late summer day in New York. She was looking forward to the long walk over to the Dali exhibition at the Met.

Chapter 18

Permanent Mission of the Russian Federation to the United Nations, New York City, USA
--Late Morning, Friday, April 4, same day

"Well, they should be here soon," Pavel Laptov said as he took a bite of the bacon and eggs served up at the conference table in the ambassador's office. "Meanwhile, I will enjoy my breakfast." Mitkinov had gone back to Moscow for consultations, so he had free use of the facilities. "But this is delicious," he muttered to himself, "why can't we have such good bacon in Russia? We certainly have the pigs. Even in politics…" and Laptov smiled at his own little joke.

"It is almost nine," his breakfast companion, Dr. Novikov said, looking at his watch. He had a bowl of muesli in front of him, a dieter's morning meal.

"Ah, there. Finally." Laptov heard the knock on the door, as a tall muscular man dressed in a black short-sleeved shirt and black jeans entered, followed by a smaller but stockier, similarly attired companion. The men came straight over, greeted the two scientists and pulled up chairs.

"Coffee?" Laptov offered, ready to pour.

"Yes. Thank you, Excellency." Sergei, the taller of the two answered.

"Well?"

"Sorry we were late. But we had trouble accessing the room. The girl didn't leave till just twenty minutes ago, and then we had to retrieve the chip."

"So you haven't listened to it yet?"

"No, we haven't had the time."

"Well, get Elena to come in and plug it into the ambassador's computer so we can hear," Laptov said, adding as an afterthought, "but first I want to finish this good breakfast."

⁂

"Disgusting," Laptov commented. "They only have sex on their minds. Especially that Australian. How can he be a professor of Geology?"

"Yes, I wonder…But she must be very good." Dr. Novikov fantasized about being the Australian professor.

"Pyotr," the minister started hesitatingly, "tell me, what is a blow job?"

"Ah, well…" Novikov took great pleasure in explaining the expression in Russian. Sergei used his mouth and hands to demonstrate.

"Enough. They are swine. Capitalist pigs. All of them." He was not a prude—he had had his share, but such blatant corruption…

"Well, anyway it is not good what we are hearing." Novikov tried to be serious.

"Yes. A disaster. Our submission will be turned back, while the Danish and Canadian ones will be approved, just like that. That little slut."

"We could discredit them. And all the work of the Sub-commission."

"You mean release these tapes?"

"Yes. The American press would love it. The public

hates the United Nations. The Australian is obviously influenced by that whore. And he is steering the decision in her direction. Clearly no scientific objectivity. We could destroy the man. And her as well. But she is young and gorgeous, and knows how to use her looks."

"No. We can't do that," Laptov was emphatic. "It would also set us back greatly. We would show ourselves to have done something very illegal. Also, they would just say it is not they. That the tape was doctored…"

"But…"

"…And a newly elected Sub-commission could come to a similar conclusion. We would waste another year, at least. We cannot afford to lose any time."

"Well, we could kidnap her and use her to force that jerk of a professor to rule in Russia's favor," Dmitri suggested.

"Hmm. Possible, but very risky." Laptov was pensive. "It could also backfire."

"You mean, since he seems to have fallen for her, we would threaten to kill her unless he changes his mind?" Novikov tried to understand what Dmitri had suggested.

"Yes. Or even just hurt her in some way." Sergei found the idea downright titillating. "Have some fun with her, you know…"

"No, no. We will not use tactics like that." Laptov put an end to his colleagues' mounting fantasies.

"Well, we can't just do nothing."

"I agree. But I will talk it over with the president. There is too much at stake. He will not allow Russia to lose in the Arctic. While other countries gain additional territory and resources. Now leave me, and send Elena in."

Laptov was left alone to gather his thoughts, as the three men filed out. He knew that the advice he would give to the president was very important for Russia, for the Arctic, and for the world. But he could not hold back. He had to set out the options, and hope that Gusanov would agree with the course of action he thought was the right one.

∽∾∽

"So what you are saying, Pavel, is that our claim will not be agreed by the Commission? That is very disappointing. Very disappointing indeed…"

"I am even more dismayed than you by what is happening here. Yes, that is the likely outcome, but it is not over yet. We put all the evidence we had into that submission. And it was good. But it seems other interests are at play. Yes, in a big way…"

"What do you mean? I thought this Commission would base its approvals on objective scientific grounds."

"So did I. So did I. But the data can be interpreted in different ways. What is worse, though, is that we have an Australian professor who has somehow managed to land the most important position, and he is now the lover of…You won't guess who. That woman who is leading the Danish team."

"Incredible! What about the Americans?"

"On the sidelines, so far. But I am much more worried about the Chinese. They seem to have something going on. And we know they do not want us to gain more resources and a stronger strategic position." Elena had left the coffee pot, so Laptov poured himself another cup.

"So what do you advise?"

"Well, we have several options." Ugh. He did not like cold coffee. Doesn't the ambassador have standards? A thermos, at least?

"What are they?"

"First, we can do nothing and just let things roll out

by themselves. But this is not a good idea. The Danes and the Canadians will definitely end up with a large chunk of the Arctic. Our claim is not likely to be agreed. It seems we just don't have the right kind of evidence to prove our case to a Commission that seems to be biased against us. We will definitely be a loser with this option, especially as we know the Chinese and maybe the Americans are up to something. We have to be proactive."

"Option two?"

"We could put pressure on this amoral Australian to swing the approval of our submission. He just might be able to do it, especially if we also work on some of the other members. It could involve kidnapping and threatening the life of his lover. And, of course, paying him nicely. Some of the other members too. Better than option one, but very risky, and could completely backfire. Also, the outcome is not a sure thing—we would be putting our fate in the hands of the corrupt professor and some of his scientist colleagues."

"So what's left?"

"We can release the tapes we have and try to discredit this woman and the Australian and the entire process, but I doubt that would change the outcome. Just put it off perhaps. Of course, they would deny that the voices in the tapes are theirs. And it would also make us look bad, since we would be shown to have done something illegal. Recording private persons' activities without a warrant is a crime in the United States, I am told."

"That all doesn't sound too good. Any better suggestions, Pavel?"

"Well, there are two other options—more macro scenarios—for you, as president, to choose from, and they are quite the opposites."

"Tell me."

"One would be to withdraw the submission and

renounce all our claims for extension. It would mean putting forward and aggressively promoting a position similar to—and I know you will not like to hear this—the Green Liberation Front..."

"Don't tell me..."

"...For example, I have thought a lot about it and it could be something like this: above 80°N latitude, no extensions of the EEZ of any nation would be permitted. The entire sea area above 80°N latitude falling outside the existing EEZs of those countries that extend beyond this latitude should be declared a world heritage site, a world nature reserve and a nuclear free zone. No exploitation of resources should be allowed in this reserve, and any vessels entering it should need to meet stringent design standards to safeguard the environment. Like what the Canadians have in place for the Northwest Passage. The nations of the Arctic Council—with Russia playing an important role—maybe along with the International Seabed Authority—could be jointly charged with administering this zone for the benefit of all mankind."

There, he had done it. This was his very private vision for the Arctic, one that he had developed over time and nurtured carefully. Based on what that Green Liberation Front group had proposed in that interview...They had it right, he was convinced. But Laptov did not believe that he had dared to lay it out in such detail for the president.

Gusanov did not answer for almost a full minute, and all Laptov could hear was his breathing on the other end. "Pavel, have you lost your mind? You must be joking!"

"Or something along those lines. We have time to refine it, if you choose to go this route..."

"No, I don't like it, Pavel. Not at all. That would completely counter everything we have said and stood for...The Arctic must be Russian. We would be going against our history. We would be giving up what we already have. No, we cannot do that. By the way, Pavel, are you feeling all right?" Gusanov momentarily regretted his decision to name Laptov minister for the Arctic. He seemed to be more fit for the lunatic asylum, the older he got. *Where had all this gobbledygook come from? He must have had a stroke, the old geezer...*

"Yes, thank you, I am perfectly fine. But if we go this route, the Arctic would belong to no one. And be there for everyone. This position would give Russia the moral high ground and win us a lot of favor in the developing world. We could take a leadership role in the Arctic Council to administer the zone. It is something that as a statesman, you should really consider, especially when you think of the possible outcomes of the last option..." Haa, a "statesman!" Laptov couldn't believe he had been so unctuous.

"Fuck it, Pavel!" Gusanov exploded. "I don't want to administer the Arctic. I want to own it. What the hell is your last option? It better be good..."

"Ahem...It would require aggressive action along two axes. And yes, it would make a substantial part of the Arctic Russian. But what kind of an Arctic—I don't know."

"What do you mean?"

"Well, here too, we will need to withdraw our submission, and repudiate the UN Convention on the Law of the Sea. We would no longer recognize it and the authority of this Commission."

"I like it already."

"At the same time, we would lay claim, as the successor state, to the Arctic the Soviet Union appropriated in 1926, based on the sector principle. So right up to the North Pole between—I think it is—32°04'35" East to 168°49'30" West, which is quite a bit more than we are claiming in our current submission, and not subject to all these scientific and legalistic games. As we discussed before you appointed me..." Pavel had hoped that, as minister for the Arctic, this was one proposal he would never again have to discuss with his president.

"I like it." Maybe Laptov was still okay...

"As you pointed out earlier, we could also, at the same time—that is immediately—start to work on Greenland, so that as soon as the Danish claim is formally approved, they unilaterally pronounce total independence from Denmark, and issue a clear statement that they are not part of NATO. We will have to guarantee their independence and offer help with resource extraction. It will mean supporting their demands—possibly with military action—that the US withdraw from Thule."

"Hmm, not bad..." Andrei was liking this better all the time. "Not bad at all."

"But it could mean confrontation with the Americans. It would be a gamble on how far things might escalate. They are weak though, and if Greenland is not part of NATO, then just maybe...Although it could be too close to home for them to just stand back and do nothing. And there is the Thule Air Base issue as well."

"Pavel, this would give us control of well more than half the Arctic, no? And take away substantial marine resources from the Europeans and make them more dependent on us for energy and minerals?"

"I know, your strategy all along, President Gusanov..."

"Brilliant." The old fox of a polar explorer was proving his mettle after all...

"Come to think of it. What an idiot I am!" Laptov stood up, slapping his forehead with his palm. "This must be the game the Chinese are playing...to secure the Greenland resources."

"Well, that clinches it. We cannot have the Chinese in the Arctic."

"But…" And Laptov knew that it was too late to save the Arctic.

CHAPTER 19

Alex Hotel, New York City, USA—Friday, April 4, the same day and Morning, Saturday, April 5, the next day

As she walked across the lobby of the Alex to the elevators, dressed still in her crumpled evening wear, Hanne thought that she should be more embarrassed than she actually felt. But who cared, she told herself—she was sure this happened here all the time. She opened the door to her room, and immediately saw the red message light flashing on the phone.

"Oh God, I forgot to call Jens yesterday! Not very nice of me," she mumbled to herself. She looked at the digital clock by the phone—*hmm, 9:32...3:32 in Copenhagen.* Should be reachable on a Friday, so probably working from home.

Hanne dialed the number she knew by heart and let it ring: eventually, the familiar voice came on the speaker announcing his name and asking the caller to leave a message. Hanne, a little miffed at the situation—more so at herself for not calling earlier, than at Jens—left only a curt message: "Hi. All well here. See you soon. Love, Hanne."

It was only afterwards that she regretted not telling Jens that she would be arriving on Sunday morning.

❦

The Dali exhibition was stupendous: she really liked the surrealists. In many ways they reminded her of the Arctic—the super-real, mixed with the unexpected, the unreal, which is often what the Arctic had in store for those who delved into it. But now, as she was on her way back to the Alex for the second time that day, she was looking forward to changing into her exercise gear and limbering up before the evening.

She was angry at Lock though, because he had told her that morning that he had a dinner at the Australian ambassador's residence and would not be able to see her until after. This, on her last night in New York...Although she would be back in a week or ten days when the recommendations of the Sub-commission were to be voted on by the full Commission. He could have taken her to the dinner, or cancelled. But then she told herself that their relationship, though intense, had been going for just a few days...She needed to pull back, not get so emotionally involved.

When she came back from the exercise room, she saw that the red light was flashing again as she opened the door. *Must be Jens returning the call...Or maybe Lock—his plans changed...*

She was surprised when the voice that came on the speaker was an oily Latin one. Guido, the Argentine, saying: "Ms. Kristensen—Hanne, if I may call you that—I am wondering if you would do me the honor of having dinner with me tonight. Please call at 212-5346129. Look forward to hearing from you. *Adios*."

❦

"Hi. I came as soon as I could get away," Lock said,

as Hanne, lusciously naked under the hotel bathrobe, greeted him. He folded her in his arms with a passionate kiss, and it did not take much effort to peel the robe off her perfect body. Fresh out of the shower, she smelled of lemongrass or lavender, or whatever, he did not really know, but just being near her filled him with pleasure, with excitement. *Why did I spend her last evening in New York with those visiting bores from the Foreign Ministry*, he found himself wondering.

"So what did you end up doing?" He kicked his shoes off as Hanne started to unbutton his shirt.

"Guido called to invite me to dinner."

"The old goat…Did you go? What happened?" Lock tried not to show the surprising feeling of jealousy.

"We had a nice meal, we talked, and then he asked me to go to bed with him. Sort of like you, wanting to use sex to buy his approval for our claim in the Commission."

Lock, now in his boxers, stood back. "How disgusting. You didn't, did you?"

"Don't worry, big boy," Hanne answered, smiling and reaching into his shorts, "I got the creep so drunk on his favorite Malbec that I needed the help of the hotel staff to get him into his room."

"Hmm. I hope it won't hurt your cause…"

"It shouldn't. He will be so embarrassed by the whole thing and he won't want any trouble…" Lock was hard inside his boxers.

"Well…" And the rest of what he was trying to say was smothered by her lips and tongue violating his mouth as Hanne swung him onto the bed, sat on his lap, and gently eased his penis inside her.

༺☙☙☙༻

Lock pulled himself out from under the sheets and

made his way to the counter, uncorked a bottle of wine, and brought it, with two glasses to the bed table. Hanne rolled over on her stomach as he poured.

"You know, I never thought when I agreed to do this for Denmark, that the process would be so…well, how should I put it…decadent. Corrupt, in a way." She had thought about this the whole day, but still, it was difficult to put it in words.

"What do you mean?"

"To put it bluntly, Lock…That all you guys would sell your votes or compromise your positions so easily. For sex, or money, or whatever."

She was certainly hitting too close to home, with the "money or whatever" bit, Lock felt. "You gotta be kidding, Hanne. Our…thing started well before this, in Warming Land. And you know I am passionate about you."

Hanne leaned over to kiss him. "And I am passionate about you. But your view up there in Greenland when we met was very strongly that the Ridge was oceanic."

"So, you convinced me with the data…Your excellent presentations." He hoped he wasn't sounding too defensive.

"You're telling me that the loving did not help?" She playfully reached for and squeezed his testicles.

"The evidence was strong enough." *God, what a hypocrite! And she doesn't even know half of it.* He kissed her, willing himself to get an erection so that they could make love again and put this unpleasant trending conversation behind them. But that was not a hard chore with Hanne…

ෙෂෙ

Late the next morning, Hanne was dressed for travel,

and all packed. Time to say goodbye before going down to check out and catch a cab for the airport.

She nuzzled up to Lock, saying, "Well, this is it for now. It's been great. Thanks for all the dinners. And the great loving, the times together…"

"Yes, but you'll be back soon. For the Commission's meeting, the week after next."

"Yeah. That's my job. Plus, by then I will be dying to see you."

"And I you."

They kissed, and Hanne tore herself away, fighting back the tears. "Gotta go now. Taxi's waiting and I still have to check out."

Chapter 20

Copenhagen, Denmark--Sunday, April 6, the next day

Hanne was sure that Jens would still be in bed as she turned the key in the lock of his apartment. It was early Sunday morning. Saturday nights, they usually went out with his hard-drinking friends and slept late the next day, sometimes getting up only well after noon.

She closed the door quietly behind her, put her luggage to one side, and noticed that the bedroom door was closed. Good, she said to herself, as she tip–toed straight to the guest bathroom, shedding her top and jeans along the way Her plan was to take a quick shower, then surprise Jens by climbing in bed beside him.

Hanne had thought long and hard during the flight, and decided she needed to give Jens another chance. Yes, the sex was great with Lock: it was a fabulous, torrid fling, but her life with Jens was a lot more stable, though less exciting. After seven years, she owed it to herself and to him to try a little bit harder.

And then there was that nagging question about Lock that disturbed her...

Once showered, teeth brushed, Hanne felt a lot better, relishing the surprise ahead as she opened the door. The blind was down, the morning sun kept out, the room in twilight. She tiptoed to the bed, and gently lifted the rumpled sheet to climb in beside her man.

What's this, she remarked to herself, as the lithe and naked, familiar female form she cuddled up against responded with a moan and slowly came to.

"Hanne, what are you doing back?" her best friend asked as she raised a beautiful head of disheveled blond hair, rubbing the sleep out of her eyes.

"Kristi, what are you doing here? In bed with Jens. You…you just got married!"

"Hanne!" Jens, too, was waking, realizing that this could be a difficult situation. "Hanne. It's not like you think…"

"Yes. Henrik left me. He came out," Kristi hurried to tell Hanne the news, sitting up in the bed, pulling the sheet over herself. "He said he loved me, but could not live a lie any more. He moved in with his boyfriend. Just yesterday…Od. Remember, his best man?"

"God, what a mess."

"I came here looking for you. And then…"

"Well, I sort of…filled in," Jens looked at Hanne over Kristi's tanned shoulder. "And things sort of developed…"

Hanne hesitated a moment, thinking they sure did, wanting to feel anger. But then she broke out laughing. "It is fine, you guys. It's all right! Nothing like keeping it in the family." Other than her parents and her nieces, these were the two people she cared most about in all of Denmark.

So, why not?

Yes, and it also helped expiate her guilt to be forgiving, she thought, as she leaned over and gently kissed her friend, relishing the brush of Kristi's firm, shapely breasts against hers.

"You are amazing," Kristi said between avid kisses. Hanne felt Jens' hands gently stroking the inside of her thighs, and, as Kristi started moving down on her, it was his lips that found Hanne's.

Hanne, in making her plans to surprise Jens on her return, had not imagined being welcomed back with anything close to the pleasures she experienced. It was a full forty minutes of blissful love making *á trois*, before Kristi, glancing at the alarm clock, rolled over exhausted.

"I'm sorry to have to break this up. It's been fabulous, guys. But I'm already running late for Sunday lunch with my parents. And I do have to explain to them about Henrik…"

Hanne gave her one last kiss. "Good luck, dear. We'll do this again. Love you…"

"Love you too," Kristi said as she rolled out of bed and made her way into the bathroom. Jens got up too, saying, "I will go make some coffee," while Hanne lay back to try and snooze for a few moments.

This was very different from making love with Lock, but just as wonderful, if not more so, were her last thoughts before she dozed off.

༺༻

"So, how did it go?" Jens asked when Hanne finally came into the kitchen wearing the bathrobe she kept at Jens' that now had Kristi's delicious smell all over it, hair still wet after yet another shower.

"Really, really well. You won't believe it…" Hanne beamed as Jens handed her a mug of steaming coffee.

"Tell me about it."

"Well, it seems that our submission will be approved. That is, it is being recommended to the full Commission for approval. I have to be back there the week after next for that." She sat down on one of the stools at the counter, crossing her legs.

"So you mean, right up to the North Pole? Denmark will own all the underwater resources, and be able to exploit them? What about the Russians? And the Canadians—at least they're not as bad." Hanne could tell from Jens' tone that he was not pleased. "So much for the Arctic…"

"The Russians will probably be sent back to do some more work. But most of our claim to the underwater resources along Greenland's extended continental shelf…Yes, it's being approved."

"Man, that is terrible news."

"What do you mean?" Hanne was stunned: was Jens picking a fight out of guilt? Over the thing with Kristi? But she had just said it was all right…

"How could you be involved in this travesty?"

"But, Jens," she tried to reason with him, "You knew I was working on this. And yes, I did it for Denmark—you don't understand the extent to which this award could make this little kingdom richer and strategically more important."

"God, you are such a sell-out. I never thought this would end up being a major land grab for countries to be able to exploit undersea resources. I thought the United Nations would certainly not condone something as blatantly self-interested as this by a small group of rich countries. And did you ever think of the impact on the environment? It is so pristine and sensitive up there—but you know that. Yet you are still leading this charge! I just don't understand you. I thought we trusted each other. That…that we were in love."

Hanne did not believe what she was hearing.

"But, Jens, the Green Liberation Front position on the Arctic that you spout—that it should be a nature reserve and a world heritage site or whatever—is just so…so naïve. Can you imagine the Russians and the Americans agreeing to that? No way. Better to get something for little old Denmark before the biggies grab it all. At least we Danes will develop it with the environment in mind."

"Sure thing, Hanne…"

"And what the hell does it have to do with *our* love anyway?" She was getting angry at what she considered an irrational outbreak on Jens's part.

"Why wouldn't the Russians and the Americans agree? Has anybody bothered to ask them? Certainly not you or your rotten politician friends…" Jens stormed out of the kitchen, leaving Hanne to empty her mug in silence.

ເຈເ

It took several days for Hanne and Jens, with Kristi's occasional intervention, more or less to reestablish their relationship. They agreed to differ on what their views on the Arctic would be, although Hanne begrudgingly admitted to herself that Jens's position, even if it was somewhat naïve, had the moral high ground.

And what would life be without idealists like Jens, who tried to shape outcomes that were good for the world?

CHAPTER 21

UN Headquarters, New York City, USA—Friday, April 18, several days later

Hanne's flight was late, so she barely had time to make it to the hotel, freshen up and change, and taxi over to the UN to attend the closing reception of the current session of the Commission on the Limits of the Continental Shelf. Even so, she was late when she finally entered the elegant entertainment room at the UN's headquarters, but Guido, the host, must have been keeping an eye on the entrance because he immediately came over to her.

"*Cariña* Hanne, as always, you look superb." He could not keep his eyes on her face as he said this: lasciviously, they slid down to her breasts, which showed amply in the low-cut black strapless cocktail dress she had chosen for the event. "I am so glad you have come back to celebrate your success. Perhaps you will have some time for a great admirer before you leave this wonderful city?"

"Thank you, Professor Guido. Once again, you are too kind." He was relentless, the aging Lothario. Hanne searched for Lock in the crowd but did not see him.

"Ah, my dear Minister. We are pleased you were able to come." Guido's eyes moved up from Hanne's naked shoulders to greet someone who had just entered.

"Thank you, Mr. Chairman. Of course, we are very interested in the results of the work of the Commission." Hanne turned around and saw that it was her adversary, the famous Russian explorer turned minister for the Arctic, whom she was meeting face to face for the first time.

"Ms. Kristensen, permit me to congratulate you on what is a great success for Denmark. If only we would have had someone as beautiful and talented to help make our case…"

"Thank you, you are too kind."

"Ah, the secretary general is arriving…Excuse me, my dear. Minister Laptov, if I may. We'll talk later." Guido scuttled over to greet the entering Sung Chi Park, leaving Hanne alone with the Russian.

"Ms. Kristensen, I am very afraid that these decisions of the Sub-commission mean a dark future for the Arctic we both love. Don't you think?"

"How do you mean?"

"They will lead to conflict and destruction up there. It will be very bad for the Arctic. For the world."

"What would you do?"

"It would be better if we could all agree to stay out. Keep the Arctic for the future, save the environment—make it a natural park for the entire world." This was sounding like Jens; Hanne was astounded. From the top Russian responsible for the Arctic. What a *volte-face*!

"But that is not Russia's position?"

"Ah…"

Just then, Lock, looking fabulous in his well-tailored suit, came over with two glasses of champagne. "Minister, Hanne—how wonderful to see you both." She wanted him to embrace her, but was glad he held back in front of Laptov, who seemed not quite ready to be peeled off by Guido, who was beckoning frantically to him to come over so he could introduce him to the secretary general.

"Hello, Lock. Good to see you too," Hanne said, happy for the brush of fingers as he handed her one of the flutes.

"I've got dinner planned for us after…"

Just then Richard came over with a man Hanne didn't know.

"Hello, Hanne. Lock. I'd like to introduce…"

"Hi, Ron. It's been ages." Lock obviously knew the person.

"Great work as chair, Lock. And this must be the Hanne Kristensen. Ron Hall. I monitor the work of the Commission for the US government. Congratulations. You have made quite a reputation for yourself."

"Thank you." Hanne shook his hand, as Lock moved a couple of paces away to head off the approaching Zheng Li, who was making it obvious that he needed to talk to him.

"And hi, Richard. Great to see you!" Hanne was pleased to see her Canadian colleague.

"By the way, I saw that earlier you were having a serious little exchange with Laptov," Hall said, sipping his whiskey. "I couldn't help notice…"

"Yes, well…He congratulated me too. But he did say something that I thought strange. Coming from him."

"What was that?"

"Well, that we should turn the Arctic into a nature park. Because if we go with these decisions of the Commission, it could lead to conflict and the destruction of the Arctic as we know it."

"What a hypocrite! They are the worst, the Russians." Lock said, coming back to Hanne's side, overhearing part of the conversation.

"Now, now, Mr. Chairman, you need to stay neutral," Hanne chided Lock.

"Hmm. It could be a veiled threat," Richard mused.

"Or just sour grapes." Lock added his comment.

"Or perhaps a diplomatic *démarche*," Hall observed. "Or, just a private opinion. Interesting, though. Very interesting…"

"I haven't really thought about it." Hanne was becoming perplexed by all this.

"So, what are Denmark's next steps?" The American was curious.

"It's not really up to me at this point."

"And Lock, what are you going to do now?" Ron Hall asked, turning to the Australian.

Good question, Ron. I wouldn't mind knowing myself, Hanne thought to herself.

"Have to go back to Beijing to finish the academic year. In fact, we were just coordinating our flights with Li. May as well talk shop on the way…" Lock hoped that his smile was convincing enough.

ඏඏඏ

What Lock was referring to was the brief exchange he had with Li when he stepped away from Hanne, Richard and Ron Hall.

"Hello, Professor McTierney. Just wanted to let you know that the money is already in your account in Singapore."

Lock looked around to make sure no one heard. "Thank you."

"Two million US dollars, as agreed."

"Very good."

"My bosses would also like you fly back with me tomorrow. We will make stop in Nuuk, Greenland."

"Why?"

"To offer deal to Prime Minister Rorsen."

"Ahh..."

"Be ready in hotel lobby at noon. We can go hear secretary general in morning before, then depart." With this, Li turned away, leaving a stunned Lock to return to the small group at the center of which Hanne held forth.

∞∞∞

They ended up just going back to 102 Brownstone after the reception. Hanne was jetlagged, a little tipsy after all the champagne and they were both too eager to make love to sit through a long, though probably delicious dinner.

Afterwards, showered and rejuvenated, they sat on the luxurious king-sized bed, finishing the salad and filet mignon Lock had ordered from room service.

"So, you're leaving to go back to Beijing, I heard you say?" Hanne asked between sips of the Chateau L'Evangile 2000 Pomerol.

"Yeah. I will be leaving with Li tomorrow afternoon. After the secretary general's report."

"So soon? So this is our last night?"

"Yes, my dear. Unfortunately, I have to be back in Beijing to teach. The school year will be starting. And you?"

He reached over and kissed her as he said this. A half-truth, but whatever.

"Yes. I guess I need to go back and start working on what's next..." So as not to let Lock see the welling tears, Hanne got up to put the tray with the empty plates on the desk. "But what about us?" She finally gave voice to the question that had been left hanging all evening.

"Well, Hanne, I was wondering that too. Could we meet up at Christmas somewhere?"

"I don't know. We'll see." Hanne slid back into the

bed beside Lock. She was not sure now about all this. It just did not seem to be leading anywhere. But Lock closed off the conversation with a kiss, shedding his bathrobe and peeling off Hanne's.

CHAPTER 22

UN Headquarters, New York City, USA—Morning, Saturday, April 19, the next day

"…And now I would like to turn to the report on the work of the Commission on the Limits of the Continental Shelf…" This was the part of the secretary general's speech to the General Assembly that Lock and Zheng Li, and for that matter Richard and Hanne, sitting with their respective delegations in the cavernous hall, had been waiting to hear. Although they all knew that there was nothing in the statement that would be a surprise.

"I am very pleased to announce that the Commission has accepted the evidence provided in the submissions by Canada and Denmark in support of an extension of their respective Exclusive Economic Zones along the Lomonosov Ridge. The Commission has nevertheless recommended that with respect to certain areas of overlap between Canada's claim and that of the United States of America, and between both Canada's and Denmark's and Russia's, those areas not be incorporated in the extended EEZ's until the finalization of the claims of all concerned countries, and then if required, only after bilateral negotiations have been successfully concluded…" The head of the UN paused to take a sip of water and a quick glance at his notes before he continued. "With respect to the submission of the Russian Federation, the Commission has not yet been able to complete its work, and has requested that Russia submit additional data for it to be able to do so."

The secretary general's words were drowned out by the noise of Ambassador Mitkinov making a spectacle of standing up, slamming his briefing material shut, and with a huff, walking out of the hall, followed by the rest of the Russian delegation, save one very junior person who moved up from the back row to take the ambassador's seat.

This was the cue for Li to signal to Lock that it was time to go: Lock waited until the Russians had left and then discreetly, as if wanting to go to the bathroom, left by another door.

Li was already waiting in the anteroom, glancing at his watch as Lock approached. "It is time for us to head to the airport, my friend."

They passed the Russians who were lingering just several meters away, gesticulating and speaking in loud voices. "They are not happy. I wonder what they will do now," Lock mused.

"Not my business," the Chinese professor answered as he led the way past them, while Lock tried to mask that he was following Li. Once outside, while Li waved for the waiting limo to approach, Locke vaguely let his mind wander to what Hanne might be up to at that moment.

Chapter 23

Nuuk, Greenland—Early Evening, Saturday, April 19, same day

Although he was tired from the stresses of the past week in New York, and dismayed with the lack of success of their submission, the Russian minister for the Arctic was glad to have the opportunity to visit the capital of Greenland. He had been there, once before as a young man, many years earlier, when it was still just a small fishing village known by its Danish name of Godthaab. Now it was still not a Moscow or New York, but at least the taxi driven by the Inuit driver was travelling on paved, well-marked streets.

Laptov was pleased to be there also because the visit allowed him to be able to put off having to explain to the president why the Russian submission had failed, and gallingly, why the Danish and Canadian ones had been approved. This was the worst possible outcome. The best—when it came right down to it, he told himself—would have been if all three submissions had been rejected, and the UN Commission would have justified this on the basis that they were protecting the Arctic environment. But that would have required a lot of courage on the part of the scientists on the Commission—really, to go beyond their mandate, and make what could have been in fact construed as a political statement…Second best would have been if the Russian case had been agreed and the Danish and Canadian ones rejected. At least then he might have been able to steer matters a little, to protect the environment up there as best he could. But with this, the actual outcome, Laptov felt he had very little room to maneuver.

He still couldn't really understand it all, and was glad that he would at least be able to temper the full exposé to the president on their failure in front of the Commission with a report on what he hoped would be a successful mission in Greenland.

It wasn't just the science he was sure of that. The case they had put together was excellent, though it did leave some room for interpretation. The Danes did have that beautiful little blonde make the presentation—*not our chubby Dr. Novikov*, Laptov smiled to himself...And she did prostitute herself in the most disgusting way with that slimy Australian professor. That would explain why the Danish case was approved so easily, but not really why the Russian was rejected. Although he had known for quite a while now from his sources that the lovely Ms. Kristensen did have that section in there pointing out the weaknesses in the Russian submission. *Clever little tart, she was...*

But maybe Novikov was right, and there was something more behind it all. Something much bigger. The Chinese, they were never to be trusted when their own interests were in play. Could they have gotten to that Australian professor too? Certainly, the way he and that Li two-tagged Novikov. And were they also going to make a play for Greenland? That could be devastating. Best that he got here first...

That was why he had not balked at all when the president asked him to undertake the mission to Nuuk on his way back. To urge this Malik Rorsen—whom he had met once before and who seemed like a decent guy—to move forward Greenland's plans for independence from Denmark. And to assure him that Russia would recognize the new country immediately and guarantee its sovereignty.

But Pavel was actually not too happy with this—philosophically, that is. He did not like meddling in other countries' affairs. It smacked too much of the old Soviet Union, of Stalin, and the bad times he thought were behind them. This Gusanov guy…

ღღღ

"Prime Minister, I am so glad you were able to meet me on my way through. I apologize for the short notice, but I am delighted that you could make the time. And thank you for inviting me to this historic house for a drink…" The taxi driver had told him about Hans Egede House, the oldest western-style building in Greenland, and with its pretty little vegetable garden, originally the home of Godthaab's missionary founder. Now the prime minister used it to receive important guests.

"I am very pleased you have come. Vodka, Scotch? Schnapps perhaps? Akvavit…"

"No, no, thank you. A vodka would be perfect. Chilled, if possible."

"One chilled vodka coming up!"

"Prime Minister, you probably know that I am on my way back home from the United Nations meetings on continental shelf extensions. You must have heard the good news that Denmark's submission has been approved, and Greenland will gain substantial new undersea territory. Full of oil and gas and lots of mineral deposits. I wanted to congratulate you and your country."

"Thank you. Yes, I heard that the submission that was made on our behalf was agreed and that we will gain jurisdiction over additional subsea territory. This is very good news for Greenland indeed."

"Yes, the Danish team was headed by a very professional young lady. Great geologist and glaciologist. Hanne Kristensen. Very pretty too…"

"Thank you. That's good to know."

"Prime Minister, I am aware that you are a keen proponent of Greenland's sovereignty and that you have an agreement with Denmark on a roadmap to independence. I am here at the behest of President Gusanov to let you know that, should you choose a faster road—and wish to declare independence unilaterally, now that you are a wealthy country—Russia would immediately recognize a sovereign Greenland. I am also here to offer you our unconditional guarantee of Greenland's independence…"

"Hmm…That is very generous of Russia."

"The only thing we would ask is that you look upon Russia favorably as a trading partner, as and when you develop your natural resources base. We are happy that you are not part of the European Union, and would, by all means, be willing to step in with whatever capital or goods or technical assistance is required by Greenland going forward. It would be greatly beneficial to our relationship as well, if you were to make a statement when you proclaim your sovereignty that Greenland is not a member of NATO. And, of course, we know that you wish to have Thule back from the Americans…"

"Thank you, Minister. Thank you for your kind offer. You will no doubt understand that I wish to discuss all of this with my cabinet, and you can rest assured that we will be in touch if—and as and when—we get closer to such a unilateral declaration…"

Chapter 24

Permanent Mission of Canada to the United Nations and Alex Hotel, New York City, USA—Early Evening, Saturday, April 19, same day

"Welcome, I welcome you all," Ambassador Denise Laplace lifted her glass, "especially Ambassador Frandsen and our Danish friends, who helped us greatly in the data gathering and paved the way with their excellent defense of their submission. A toast to all of you…"

Richard led the chorus of 'hear, hear's' as he looked over at a beaming Hanne standing beside him, beautiful in a one shoulder navy cocktail dress.

"And, special thanks from the Government of Canada for the great work you all did. Thank you, thank you. For both our nations, strengthening our sovereign claims over the resource rich Arctic has been a key policy goal. It is testimony to your diligence and professionalism, to the ready coordination of our positions and sharing of important data, that we have achieved our mutual objectives. Both our countries have gained access to huge tracts of underwater territory rich in oil and gas and valuable mineral deposits."

Hanne momentarily thought of Jens and his view that this was all wrong, and of Laptov, who had so mysteriously echoed a similar position to his. But why…

And suddenly, she was angry. Damn them, she was going to enjoy being in the limelight for once: it was a great achievement, as the Canadian ambassador said. She didn't need Jens to belittle it with his moral superiority. And what a hypocrite that Laptov was, officially to try to gain more subsea territory for Russia, and then, privately, to express the view that it was all wrong. It didn't necessarily all have to end in destruction and conflict.

And that Lock, too. No moral fiber whatsoever…

Men.

She whisked another glass of champagne—her third—from the tray being proffered by the white-coated waiter, just as the Canadian ambassador came over saying, "Richard, this must be Hanne Kristensen…"

"Yes, Ambassador. Allow me to present…"

"Hanne, let me tell you that Richard—the entire Canadian team—has had nothing but good words to say about you. Your professionalism and intelligence in putting the Danish case forward and thereby bolstering ours were terrific. Fabulous work!"

"Thank you. My Canadian counterparts were great to work with."

"Well, enjoy yourself, Hanne. You certainly deserve it," the ambassador said, as she was pulled away by one of her aides.

So I shall, Hanne, said to herself. *So I shall.*

And why not? The realization that the moment they had all been working towards was now past overcame her: they had achieved what they had wanted to with their submissions. The stress, the tension of especially the last few months of reviewing and updating the papers and preparing for the presentation, were lifted from her shoulders, and a feeling of freedom enveloped her.

Yes, freedom. And success. She was successful, now a free woman, she told herself as she relished yet another sip of the delicious Veuve Clicquot champagne. Time to enjoy this freedom and success.

Richard was beside her, and he looked happy and very handsome, she thought, in his dark, well-tailored suit. "Hanne, let's go have dinner together. We need to celebrate," she was pleased to hear him say.

This sounded like it could be a repeat of Ottawa...But maybe not, now they really had something to fête. That had been a bit of a disaster, for sure.

Why not give Richard another chance? She had been spending quite a bit of time with him over the last year or so and he had grown on her, that was for sure.

Besides, Lock was now gone, and he was so non-committal regarding the future. The bastard! You give these men all—they profess their love and then just flit away with so little care. And, deep down, she could not help being bothered by the ease with which he had given up his position on the Ridge.

Jens too—she went off him at times, and then was keen on him again—could not decide. That threesome thing with Kristi had been kinky and fun and fulfilling, but surely the hedonistic enjoyment would not go far and this weird relationship could not go on forever, even though she liked them both.

"Yes, let's. Anytime you're ready to go," Hanne finally answered after draining the rest of the champagne in her glass.

∽∽∽

"Richard, plans have changed. We're going to my hotel room first, and then dinner after," Hanne said as they exited One Dag Hammarskjöld Plaza onto Second Avenue.

"Okay. Did you want to change into something less

formal?" Richard asked, somewhat puzzled.

"That, too. But what I really want is to show you how Danish women like to make love. No, how I like to make love. Dinner can wait. I can't."

"Yes, well…" Hanne could see that Richard was taken aback. But pleasantly, indeed.

"Forget what happened the last time, Richard. We will start afresh, and go slowly. I will guide you. Okay?"

"You are amazing…"

ఆఈఎ

Needless to say, this time, the loving was great. Richard let Hanne lead, and from the moment that she undressed him until they both finally reached orgasm, he was struck by how adept she was at prolonging and accentuating the pleasures of the sex act. She must have had a lot of practice in life, he thought to himself much later, but so what: now he was the lucky beneficiary of all that, and boy, what an experience.

CHAPTER 25

Nuuk, Greenland—Night, Saturday, April 19 and Morning, Sunday, April 20, the same day and the next day

Finishing the last sip of Rémy Martin Napoléon cognac at the bottom of his snifter, Lock looked out of the window of the Cessna CJ4 business jet—specially rented by the Chinese since it could land on the short strip in Nuuk. Seeing the fading rays of the midnight sun color the land and sea below in hues of pink, violet and mandarin as the orange orb made its way below the horizon, he remembered how much he loved twilight in the Arctic. The pilot announced that the local time was 10:12pm and that passengers needed to fasten their seat belts since they would be landing in less than ten minutes.

Lock had time to reflect on a lot of things under his closed eyelids during the long flight from New York. Despite the tiredness that overwhelmed him with the realization that the Commission's work was done for at least the next six months, he was only able to catnap for less than an hour. Li was in the seat in front, next to the Chinese ambassador to the United Nations, and was fortunately knocked out after the three Laphroaig-16 year-olds he downed early in the flight, so he was in no position to bother him.

Hanne, she was a fabulous woman. Finally, one—the

One—with whom he could think of settling down. They had similar interests, were both well educated, had an international outlook, and the sex was great. And now, he would never have to worry about money ever again. They could travel, live the high life, do whatever they wanted for the rest of their lives.

But the question nagged at him: how would she react to the fact that the money came from the Chinese, whose interests he had served in the Sub-commission? And had contracted to be their advisor.

It would all come out in the end, and she was too smart not to derive the conclusions.

But, of course, not to forget, they were the same interests as Denmark's—and hers, for that matter. And certainly, the evidence she had put forward so brilliantly—that could have convinced him to change his mind.

He would need to act quickly though: once he was able to ease out of the work at Beijing University and plot a course of action as consultant to the Chinese government on resource extraction in Greenland, he would be back in Copenhagen and ask Hanne to marry him, Lock decided. Yes, she was the one he wanted to spend the rest of his life with.

సౌం

Lock was jolted out of his thoughts as the CJ4 did a sharp 180-degree U-turn and flew directly over the little town before coming down onto the tarmac with a thump. The pilot reversed the engines to brake as rapidly as possible on the short landing strip and turned the plane back towards the small gray terminal.

Nuuk is still a mere hamlet in many ways and it took only a few minutes for the taxi ferrying the two Chinese and Lock to arrive at the Hans Egede Hotel, where they were booked for a night of rest before a breakfast meeting with Malik Rorsen, the prime minister of Greenland.

Just as Lock followed the Chinese in through the thick glass front door of the hotel, he was stunned to see the imposing figure he thought was none other than Pavel Laptov step into one of the elevators. *This couldn't be,* he thought to himself.

But then...Why not? Perhaps the Russians were after Greenland's resources too, just like the Chinese. He wouldn't put it past them, especially now that they may have been locked out of getting additional subsea riches through legal means. But still, what a coincidence.

⁕⁕⁕

Fog had settled on the town in the early morning, but the receptionist pointed the way to Hans Egede House, the venue for official government functions. It was only a five-minute walk from the eponymous hotel.

Malik Rorsen, the prime minister himself, opened the door and greeted the foreign guests affably. It was not every day that a person of the stature of the ambassador, who was one of the inner circle in the government of the world's most populous country, set foot in Greenland. And asked for a meeting with the prime minister of a not-yet independent country of less than sixty thousand people.

This, on top of the impromptu meeting he had to take with the Russian minister for the Arctic late yesterday evening—*Greenland certainly was becoming a popular spot for politicians of powerful countries to visit,* Rorsen thought to himself.

When Zheng Li had asked for the meeting several days ago, Rorsen invited the three visitors to come have breakfast at the antique home. He was glad he had organized the two Inuit women, dressed in typical attire, to come and serve traditional favorites such as dried '*ammassat*' or capelin, dried reindeer meat, and whale skin with blubber, called '*mattak*', which was a well-loved delicacy amongst the local population. And, of course, crowberries with yogurt, for something healthy. Rorsen took great pride in showing these guests from far-away China a little bit of native culture.

"Prime Minister, thank you for agreeing to meet with us on such short notice," Wang said as one of the Inuit women pulled out his seat for him to sit down. "And thank you for hosting us to this lovely breakfast."

"We are delighted that you are visiting our country," Rorsen answered. "Please, I hope this traditional meal will be to your taste."

"Thank you, I am sure it will be delicious," Wang said as one of the aboriginal women served him some *mattak*. "Prime Minister, as you can imagine, we are not here as tourists. We have come on a special mission at the behest of General Secretary Wen Shaojing."

Rorsen looked over at Lock—who was just then piling his plate full of the dried reindeer meat, hoping he might be able to avoid the dish of whale blubber—as he answered. "I am greatly honored."

"Allow me to explain the presence of my two companions. You are no doubt aware of the work of the Commission on the Limits of the Continental Shelf in the United Nations, and that your country has just yesterday been awarded jurisdiction over huge off-shore territories with substantial resources."

"Yes, we have been following the proceedings with great interest."

"Professor McTierney chaired the Sub-commission responsible for that award, and Professor Li was the Chinese representative. We are very pleased with the outcome of the decisions of the Commission, and that is what brings us here."

"We, too, are very happy with the result," Rorsen said. He felt some pressure to add: "Thank you, Professor McTierney and Professor Li, for your support. We are beholden to you. Greenland will benefit a great deal from that decision."

"China is aware that Greenland is on the road to independence from Denmark, and that this award ensures its capacity to make this a reality." Wang took a small bite of the whale blubber and set the rest back down on his plate. "We know that your own—and your party's—aim is to fast-track independence. By the way, Prime Minister, the whale is delicious. We should introduce it as a delicacy in China…"

Oh, God no, spare us, Lock thought. Imagine what that would do to species extinction if 1.3 billion Chinese started liking whale blubber. They eat other weird things, so it would not be out of the realm of the possible…

"Yes, independence is one of our core policies."

"We are here to offer Greenland China's full support in that endeavor, and to tell you that China will recognize Greenland immediately and guarantee its independence. I wanted also to let you know—of course, confidentially for now—that the Chinese government has approved a sum of twenty-five billion US dollars to be made available to your country for resource extraction as soon as you declare independence."

"That is very good news. Very good news indeed. Thank you. On behalf of all the people of Greenland."

"Going forward, Professor McTierney will, in conjunction with your officials, work to maximize the benefits from that money, for both Greenland and China."

Rorsen looked over at Lock just as the Australian happened to take the well-chewed remnants of some dried reindeer meat from his mouth and put them on his plate.

"All we ask, Prime Minister, is that we move relatively quickly to make this a reality."

"Yes, of course."

"How much time do you think you would need to be able to make such a unilateral declaration?"

"Sir, we pride ourselves on being a democracy, and therefore I would have to put such a major step to a vote in the *Inatsisartut*—our parliament—or perhaps even hold a referendum. I will need to take advice from my advisors."

"Well, so be it then."

"Thank you. This is a great honor. I will discuss this generous offer with my cabinet, and move as quickly as possible. We will, of course, keep you abreast of how matters are progressing…"

"Excellent. We shall await the announcement of Greenland's independence with great interest."

"Now, may I offer you some Greenland coffee?"

CHAPTER 26

Copenhagen, Denmark—Morning, Sunday, April 20, same day

As the taxi made its way along Fredericiagade, Hanne was at first not sure whether she was hoping to find Jens in bed with Kristi again, so she could just slide in and join them like the last time, or that she wanted to have a serious conversation with him about where their relationship was going as a prelude finally to breaking up. But the more she thought about how delicious it had been to have Kristi make love to her while she was kissing Jens and then vice versa, she knew that that was what she would opt for if given the choice. Serious conversations with Jens always ended up in an unpleasant fight. And that was the last thing she wanted now.

So when she turned the key and saw them sitting at the kitchen counter in bathrobes, sipping steaming coffee from the mugs she had given Jens for his birthday, watching the flat screen television she and Jens had bought together, she felt a tinge of disappointment.

"*Hej*, Jens. *Hej*, Kristi…"

"Shh…Come listen. Gusanov is about to make an important statement," Kristi said. "Great to have you back, love."

"*Hej*, Hanne. Come over here so you can see, quick!"

Jens pulled out a stool and poured her some coffee. "It's something about the Arctic…"

Euronews was showing the Russian president, all bundled up with large wet, spring snowflakes settling on his bear coat and mink hat, standing at a simple, make-shift podium. A big ship was visible in the background. Hanne had missed the introduction, as just then, Andrei Gusanov started straight into a prepared statement.

"My fellow Russians, it is with a sad heart that I announce," the English translated voiceover rushed to keep up, "that once again, as many times in our history, Russia stands alone. And this time, it concerns a matter of the utmost importance to us, a matter that cuts to the core of our very being. I speak of the Arctic. The North has been an essential part of Russian history. It has formed part of our culture, our traditions, our very soul. We have explored it, fought for it, toiled for it, died for it." Gusanov paused for a moment, allowing the camera to pan to both sides to show the similarly fur-clad Laptov and Maslenkov standing beside him, along with a host of other dignitaries.

"Now, the decadent capitalist powers of the West are plotting to take the Arctic away from us with trumped-up legal rhetoric, and blatant and corrupt manipulation of decisions in international forums. But Russia will not stand for this. We are the preeminent power in the North." Another pause as the camera zoomed out to show the cruiser *Pyotr Velikiy*, moored behind Gusanov at the Northern Fleet's base in Murmansk. "It is for this reason that I stand here before you, to tell you that, as of this moment, Russia repudiates the United Nations Convention of the Law of the Sea, and will, as the successor state in the North, exercise its sovereignty over the undersea territory claimed by the Union of Soviet Socialist Republics in 1926 based on the sector principle. This is the entire Arctic, right up to the North Pole extending from the shores of Russia between the meridian 32°04'35" East, and the meridian 168°49'30" West from Greenwich."

"I don't believe it! They are claiming half the bloody Arctic," Jens exclaimed.

"As you know, our brave polar explorer and now minister for the Arctic, Pavel Laptov, who is standing beside me..."—the cameras focused on Pavel, "...and who just returned from a corrupt meeting in the United Nations where Russia's interests were swept aside..."—a window on the screen opened up to show first *Mir 1*'s dive, and then the parachute expedition—"...and his colleagues have visited the North Pole several times, and planted our flag there to ensure that it belongs to us."

"What sore losers!" Hanne could not keep quiet. "I am surprised Laptov is part of this."

"Shh!" From Jens.

"We will commence regular air, as well as intensive surface vessel and submarine patrols of this sector, and any infiltrators that do not have prior approval, will be apprehended by our forces. Moreover, we will expedite the exploitation of the resources of this rich territory, understandably with the utmost regard to the environment and the native peoples of the Arctic."

"There is at least that," Kristi commented.

"Bugger it!" From Jens again.

"Later today, at our revitalized Severemorsk Naval Base, we will be launching the first of the next series of three Yasen class attack submarines, and as well, the first of three new Dolgorukiy class nuclear-powered ballistic missile submarines, to strengthen our Northern Fleet. And, last but not least, in recognition of the importance of his mission, I am hereby promoting Vice-Admiral Maslenkov to full admiral. The Arctic is, and will remain, ours. Thank you, my fellow countrymen, and may God protect Russia."

Disgusted, Jens clicked the remote to turn the television off.

"Shit. I can't believe they are launching more nuclear subs. And laying claim to half the Arctic. But at the minimum it keeps that sector half from those big western oil companies who don't know what the hell they're doing when it comes to offshore drilling. Like those idiots at BP."

"Come on, Jens."

"Well, it's inevitable that the environment will suffer, with all these governments—including our own stupid politicians—clamoring jingoistically to extend their jurisdiction to gain access to more resources for their corporate lackeys to extract."

Hanne could sense that Jens was looking for a fight. "*Hej*, Jens, Kristi, thanks for the coffee. I think I'm going to head out, go back to my place, I'm really tired and I need to go to the office later."

"Don't you want to come back to bed with us?" Kristi asked, giving her a sensual look.

"No. No, not now, Kristi. I'm just exhausted. I'll see you guys later." Hanne picked up her carry-on and left the other bag by the door, she could get that later.

As she headed down the elevator, she knew this was not going to work, this thing with both Jens and Kristi. Or more to the point, even just with Jens…

Chapter 27

Copenhagen, Denmark—Afternoon, Sunday, April 20, same day

"In any case, Hanne, thank you. You did a great job," Lise Frondholm, sitting behind her paper-cluttered desk said. "Our ambassador to the UN has filled us in on everything. Congratulations. I will make sure that you will be appropriately rewarded." The minister of climate and energy had seen that Hanne was in her office, even though it was a Sunday afternoon, and had called her in to express her gratitude.

"Thank you, Lise." Fortunately, Hanne remembered that she was on a first name basis with the minister.

There was a knock on the door, and the minister's male secretary poked his head in. "The prime minister is on line one for you."

"Excuse me, Hanne. I have to take this," Lise said as she reached for the phone.

"Yes, of course."

Hanne watched as the minister's face distorted with obvious stress. "Oh, yes. I heard…cabinet meeting in half an hour? I'll be there," the minister said, glancing at her watch.

Her complexion had turned gray by the time she put the receiver back, and Hanne wondered if the rather heavy-set woman was all right. "Hanne, I have to run."

She stood up, grabbing her jacket from the hook behind her. "As you heard, special cabinet meeting. Okay, in case you don't know: Russia has withdrawn from the UN Convention of the Law of the Sea, and has declared that it will revert to an old Soviet claim of undersea territory based on that outdated sector principle."

"Yes, I heard the news. Terrible."

"By the way, does that affect us? Directly, I mean?"

"Very little, actually. Only some of our newly-won extension. Just the bit that's right at the North Pole. The country that will really be affected is Norway. And of course, the Russians are claiming jurisdiction over huge areas of water that are by rights international."

"Well, we will have to react. Jointly, with other countries. And there is the principle that Russia can't be allowed to opt out of international treaties it doesn't like."

"Yes, of course."

"I have to run now, but tomorrow, Hanne, let's sit down and look at a map together to see what this means for the Arctic."

⁂

Hanne was brought out of her deep jet-lag slumber by the distant ringing of her phone.

"Hanne." The hesitant voice belonged to Jens. "I'm sorry you rushed off. So was Kristi." For once, though, Hanne was glad she had. She had needed the rest, and it was good to have the feedback from the minister.

"I know we don't always agree on the Arctic, but let's put that aside for now. We're all meeting at Bar NASA later. I want to smoke a peace pipe with you, Hanne."

Hanne let herself be talked into joining the group—Jens's friends from the Green Liberation Front, a few hangers on from university, and of course Kristi—who she often thought was the only sane one in the bunch.

※ ※ ※

Hanne was on her third Kir already, and getting more and more fed up, wondering what she was doing there. Kristi was sitting opposite her, looking stunning in the strapless purple dress. As did she, in her favorite low-cut, mid-thigh length red party dress, Hanne proudly told herself, catching a glimpse in the large mirror behind her friend.

Jens and his friends were talking about the recent UN awards of jurisdiction over the seabed and the Russian action in response. The prevailing view in the group was that these were acts of increasing politicization of the Arctic that could lead to no good.

"Guys, we gotta do something to protest. As soon as the weather gets better."

"What do you have in mind?" Sven asked, as he put his Carlsberg down. He was the film director friend of Jens on the Green Liberation Front expedition to Murmansk that had gone awry

"Well, I have talked to Amsterdam and London, and they all agree that we need some coordinated action."

"So what will we do?" Erik asked. He was the club member at NASA, and the son of a rich industrialist. Erik had also been part of the Murmansk protest.

"I suggested that we'll go to Greenland—up in the far north—and disrupt a mine. Those newly opened zinc-lead works at Citronen Fjord, for example."

"Exciting! How do we get there?" Gunnar, the newest recruit to the Green Liberation Front, remarked, after taking a big gulp of his beer.

"We'll fly commercial to Nuuk, and then hire a small plane to get us there. I've checked it out—there is a seasonal airstrip at Citronen Fjord that services the mine. Sometime in late July or early August would be best, when the weather is good."

"Will it just be us?"

"No. We're talking about an internationally coordinated operation. A crew grouped from Norway, Holland and England will go to Longyearbyen and protest the mine at Barentsberg. You know, that Russian coal operation."

"That's a good one." Erik said, somewhat hesitatingly. "But relatively easy."

"We'll also hit a mine in northern Canada and an offshore platform off the coast of Alaska. Oh yes, and a team will try and get to Shtokman. That will be the difficult one. Like when we hit Murmansk…"

"No, not Shtokman!" Sven looked pained.

"What fun," Erik countered his friend.

"Very dangerous," Kristi weighed in, looking somewhat bored. "You guys are crazy." Her relationship with Erik—with whom she had gone out before her failed marriage—was strained. All that she had told Hanne was that he had turned weird on her.

"Yes. That Shtokman's inside their claimed sector. Do you really think the Ruskis will let you get near the field?" Hanne had enough: these boys were just so silly and naïve sometimes.

And when it came right down to it, Jens did not at all seem to be interested in what was happening in her life. Nor even in making peace with her. She stood up, grabbed Kristi's hand, and said, "Come on, Kristi, let's go to the ladies' room." Her friend was glad to oblige.

But Hanne's plan was to go somewhere else, and leave the guys behind to do the planning for their stupid missions.

ಏಲೇ

Another bar and several drinks later, they ended up back at her apartment.

"What would you like?" Hanne asked, as she slipped her dress over her head and threw it on the chair. She unclasped her bra, liberating her breasts, and went over to the kitchen counter. "Something red?"

"Sure that would be great," came Kristi's reply as she also started to undress.

Hanne uncorked a bottle of Grafignana Malbec, grabbed two wine glasses, and put them on the coffee table, just as Kristi threw her bra beside Hanne's clothes. The two girls were close enough to know that it was the time to embrace: still standing, their lips joined in a passionate kiss, their tongues exploring. Nipples rubbed against nipples, and their long, shapely legs wrapped themselves around each other.

The wine was forgotten as Hanne led Kristi into the bedroom, and they shed their panties on the way. They knew from experience how to give each other pleasure, and they took their time, until finally both reached orgasm.

Now this, I will never give up, Hanne thought to herself. *I will always want Kristi.*

Chapter 28

Washington DC, USA—Afternoon, Monday, April 21, next day

It was a gorgeous late summer afternoon, and Ron Hall was looking forward to a long run along Rock Creek Park as his taxi pulled up in front of the Georgetown town house he shared with Susan, his partner of five years. His cell phone rang just as he was working his long legs out of the cab, and quickly glancing at it, he saw that it was the one call he could not refuse to take.

"Hello. Hall here." Silence, as he listened.

"Yes, of course, I will be there in twenty minutes."

Just as well, he thought, *at least the taxi is still here.*

"Change of plans, my man. I'll just run this suitcase in and you can take me over to the White House."

ଏଓଏ

"Hello, Ron. As you can surmise from the short notice, we have a bit of an emergency on our hands," the president said to his deputy national security advisor, as Ron was ushered into the Oval Office, filled with generals and other high-ranking officials. And then to the man who was speaking, Tom Deacon, who was Ron's direct boss: "Tom, please continue."

"Well, as I was describing the situation, it is evolving very rapidly. And it all has to do with the Arctic. The activity seems to have been triggered by the work of the UN Commission on the Limits of the Continental Shelf, which adjudicates on jurisdiction over extensions of a country's Exclusive Economic Zone. Unfortunately, we have not even signed the UN Convention on the Law of the Sea, Mr. President, so we are not really at the table on this one. But, Ron, you were there in New York, why don't you take over?"

"Yes, Mr. President, the UN secretary general made a statement in the General Assembly announcing that, based on the Commission's work, the Russian claims have been sent back for more work, whereas the Canadian and Danish submissions have been approved. The Russian ambassador to the UN walked out with his entire delegation."

"That, Mr. President," the national security advisor took over, "in a nutshell, is the background to Gusanov's statement that Russia withdraws from, and repudiates the UN Convention of the Law of the Sea. And that's why they have now reverted to the sector principle used previously by the Soviet Union in their Arctic claims: it gives them a considerably bigger piece of the pie."

"How much bigger?"

"Well, assuming they were not going to get approval of their claim, we're looking at an area almost the size of Greenland," Ron answered, knowing the other officials would not know the specific details. "Close to two million square kilometers, or eight hundred thousand square miles. And it is in that area where most of the Arctic's resources are concentrated. Much of the extensive hydrocarbon resource base identified by the US Geological Survey in the Arctic is in their sector."

"So, gentlemen, what do we do?"

"Well, Mr. President, we can't just do nothing." This from James Gilchrist, the new secretary of state. "I suggest a strong statement critical of the stance and its implications for international cooperation. Indeed, for the network of international organizations and treaties that makes the system work."

"I recommend we make it clear to Mr. Gusanov that if any of our ships or airplanes are molested in what are essentially international waters, they will have orders to take whatever steps necessary to defend themselves," the head of the joint chiefs of staff enunciated a more bellicose view from his comfortable position on the couch. "Even if that leads to a shoot-out."

"Mr. President, whatever we do, we should coordinate with our allies," the national security advisor added his comment.

"Tom is right, Mr. President," the secretary of state concurred, "I know that the Canadians and the Norwegians are livid—I had their foreign ministers on the phone just before I came in here. Same with the Danes, who are calling for a special session of the United Nations Security Council to condemn Russia, who of course will veto anything there. But we need to support that, as I am sure will all other parties interested in the Arctic. I am sure the Chinese will vote with us too."

Ron Hall felt he had waited long enough to permit the more senior advisors to give their advice. It was his turn now. "Mr. President, if I may, I would suggest that you first issue a statement deploring Russia's withdrawal from, and repudiation of, the UN Convention of the Law of the Sea, just when the US is finally on the verge of signing and ratifying it. And I would try to push this quickly through Congress."

"Hmm, but doesn't this Gusanov move just play into the hands of those in Congress who oppose the

Convention?" The secretary of defense piped up. "Surely, it tells them that Russia is also thinking that it constrains them too much. So then why should we tie our hands by signing and ratifying it?"

"Well, I see your point, sir," Ron Hall jumped back in before anybody else could, "but the problem is that if the Arctic nations don't all move forward together when it comes to divvying up the Arctic, there will be a free-for-all up there, with destruction of the environment and possibly conflict. This Gusanov move, as you call it, is the first step in this direction. Whether we like it or not, the UN Convention of the Law of the Sea is the only legal framework we presently have to keep matters from deteriorating up there. And we're really not even at the table, as Tom said, since we haven't signed and ratified it."

"Gentlemen, I hear you. Ron, I think your arguments are pretty cogent. I must say, I like the approach. It sets us up as an example, as the leaders that we should be in international affairs."

"Bill," and here the president looked at his chief of staff, "will you talk to the leaders of both houses to see how we can move ratification forward quickly?"

"Yes, Mr. President."

"And, Tom, will you prepare a statement for me with Jon? You know the usual: that we deplore Russia's unilateral declaration and withdrawal from the Convention, and that we see this as a very dangerous precedent that could not only lead to destruction of the environment and conflict in the Arctic, but also to cherry-picking by nations of international treaties and their provisions. And then set out, that we, for our part, will work on signing and ratifying the UN Convention expeditiously. Stressing what Ron just said, that this is the only tool or framework we have for maintaining order up there."

"Mr. President, if I may suggest, one more angle to

incorporate in your speech and push forward on the policy front. We need to propose and agree some shipping standards for the Arctic, much as the Canadians have done unilaterally. Only vessels that meet certain standards should be allowed above the Arctic Circle, and registration with the respective authorities should be mandatory. That is, if Russia comes back to the table and plays ball."

"Ron, I hear you, but let's not try and do too much at once. First let's deal with this crisis. We can tackle the shipping issue separately."

CHAPTER 29

Copenhagen, Denmark—Noon, Monday, June 23, several months later

Hanne was sitting at an outside table at the BioM, relishing the last few leaves of her salad, enjoying the warming sun on this, the third day of summer, the break from the routine of work. Her luncheon companion and colleague, Bent, had excused himself to go over to greet the parents of his girlfriend who had just sat down at a table in the far corner.

Sipping her lemonade, Hanne looked idly around at the other customers—mostly office workers, some tourists. Her eyes landed on, and could not help reading the headline on the front page of *Politiken* hiding the face of the man at the next table over.

"Green Liberation Front activist found dead. Viciously garroted."

She felt sick to her stomach, feared the worst. But when she preened to look closer at the accompanying grainy picture, she could tell that it was not Jens. Thank God. She knew them all, though, pretty well every Danish member of the Green Liberation Front. At least those active in Copenhagen...Hanne hurried to finish the drink, and fortunately, saw that Bent was just heading back to her table, so she beckoned the waitress to bring the bill.

On the way back to the office, she picked up *Politiken*

at the news kiosk and perused the article right there on the corner. The short article below the picture read as follows: "Green Liberation Front activist and film director, Sven Erikson…"—oh, God, not quiet, gentle Sven. Hanne, on the verge of tears, forced herself to read on—"…was found dead this morning behind a garbage dumpster in an alley off Gothersgade in Copenhagen. Police confirm that he died of asphyxiation, and suspect that the cause of death was murder by strangulation with a thin metal wire, which left a red mark around the deceased person's neck. Mr. Erikson acquired some fame several years ago with his documentary on the brutal killing of whales by the aboriginal people of Greenland to obtain the animals' blubber which they consider a delicacy, and more recently, with the ill-fated attempt by the Green Liberation Front to film and protest the launch of a Russian submarine. Police are questioning family, friends and colleagues, but have not identified a motive or suspects as of yet. Anyone who has any information that could be useful to help solve this murder is asked to call Inspector Jakobsen at 562-6262."

Hanne was shaken. Although she had been acquainted with Sven for several years, she could not say that she knew him well. He was rather taciturn, and never let loose or really got drunk like the rest of Jens's friends. His only interest, the only thing he got passionate about that she knew of, was the Green Liberation Front and some of the causes he championed with his documentaries as a result of his work. He came across as fundamentally a good man, and she could not imagine who might want to kill him.

On her way up the elevator, she thought about Sven. Yes, he had gone on that Green Liberation Front operation with Jens and Erik to film the submarine launch, and that's where the three had really seemed to bond. Ever since then, Jens had considered Sven his best friend. But she had not really been able to get beyond the outer veneer, and only knew what Jens told her about him.

As soon as she sat down at her desk, she dialed Jens's number. No answer. She did leave a message though, suggesting that she would really like to see him and offer whatever comfort she could. Although she had never lost a good friend, she did understand that this could be a very tough time for him.

જાજા

Jens did call back, and agreed to see her after work that evening at his place.

Over a glass of wine, as Hanne expressed her sympathies, she could not help but feel that he was distracted, remote, almost resentful.

"I guess you guys really became close during that Murmansk operation."

"No, no. We were close before that." Jens seemed to object to her attempt to talk about his relationship with Sven. "But being in a Russian prison with someone does bring you closer."

"Sven spoke Russian, didn't he?" Hanne just recalled that that had been vaguely mentioned at one of the recent Green Liberation Front drinking sessions. "Oh yes, and that's why you were suggesting he should go on the mission you guys were planning to Shtokman."

"You have a good memory, Hanne."

"Have you told the police?"

"The police were at the Front's offices today. We were all interrogated."

Hanne sensed that Jens was annoyed with her questioning, but persisted.

"Have they found any leads yet?"

"Give me a break, Hanne! I don't know. Ask the goddamn police, will you?"

"Sorry I asked." Boy, Jens was ill tempered. But, perhaps understandably so, after losing his best friend.

"Anyway, I need to go and see Sven's parents. They are devastated."

"Do you want me to come with you?"

"No. No. I will do it alone. Better so."

CHAPTER 30

Copenhagen, Denmark—Early Evening, Wednesday, June 25, a couple of days later

Hanne had just stepped into her flat, stormed into her bedroom, and started to take her work clothes off, when she heard the knock on the door.

"Shit! Who could that be?" She was irritable; it had been a frustrating day at work, the heat had gotten to her, and on the way home she had been bothered by the thought that her personal life was not going anywhere. She desperately wanted a cooling shower, to change into her cutoffs and halter top, and then go up to the rooftop terrace of her building. Along with the half empty bottle of Torrontes she knew was still in the fridge, with plans to finish the thriller, *Twisted Reasons,* she was so enjoying on the recommendation of Kristi. Instead, she now had to pull her skirt back on—"…but dammit, the halter top will just have to do!"

"Who is it?" Hanne asked through the closed door.

"Ms. Kristensen? Inspector Jakobsen." The man at the door flashed a police badge in front of her eyes.

"Sorry?"

"I am in charge of investigating the Sven Erikson case. Could I just ask you a few questions, please?"

Hanne opened the door hesitatingly and said, "Of

course, Inspector. Would you like to come in?"

"Ms. Kristensen, I know this is irregular, but alternatively, I'd have to request that you come down to the station."

"No, no, please ask your questions here. Come in, Inspector."

She closed the door behind the police officer, and beelined for the fridge, needing that drink now even more than before. "I was just about to have a glass of white wine. Would you care to join me?" She looked over at Jakobsen, noting that he was fit and handsome. Not bad. In his late thirties, perhaps early forties, she thought. "Please, please, do sit down, Inspector."

"No, thank you, not while I am on duty. But may I begin? I do not want to take much of your time."

"Of course, Inspector. Please, go ahead."

"Ms. Kristensen, how well did you know Sven Erikson?"

"He is…was a good friend of my boyfriend, Jens Andersen. He was often part of a group of us that went out together, but I can't really say I knew him well."

"What do you know of his recent activities, Ms. Kristensen?"

"As you know, he was active with the Green Liberation Front. And there was some talk of him going on a mission to Russia. To the Shtokman gas fields, I think it was. But Jens would know more about that."

"When was that going to be?"

"I don't really know the details, but the Green Liberation Front was planning several coordinated missions when the weather got better. Anytime now I guess. No, end of July or early August."

"Some of his film friends mentioned a project he had started to work on: a documentary on the impact of the Russian oil and gas industry on the Nenets indigenous people. Do you know anything about that, Ms. Kristensen?"

"No, this is the first I've heard of it. I only knew of the possible mission to Shtokman. But it does sound like something Sven would do."

"Do you have an idea of who might want to kill him, Ms. Kristensen?"

"No, Inspector. No. He was such a nice man..." Hanne thought a bit longer while she sipped her wine. "Other than the Russians maybe, if they didn't want him to do that film. Or they found out about the Green Liberation Front's plans regarding Shtokman and wanted to stop them. But why kill him? Inspector, I am not the one to ask about such things."

"Ms. Kristensen, how close was your boyfriend to Sven Erikson?"

"Very close, I think. Jens considered Sven his best friend. But I must admit, I didn't really get any sense for that closeness."

"Hmm. I see what you mean."

"They were in prison in Russia for almost two weeks, I think, after that failed mission they ran for the Front to film and disrupt the launch of a Russian nuclear submarine in Murmansk."

"Yes, I know."

"I think that's when they really bonded. Jens, Sven, Erik—the three Danes on that mission. After that, they became inseparable."

"Erik?"

"Erik Olafson."

"Oh, yes. He is active with the Green Liberation Front as well. We have questioned him already. Interesting man..."

"Yes. Like Jens's other friends, I don't really feel I know him."

"Ms. Kristensen, thank you for taking the time."

"Of course."

"Maybe the next time, I can buy you a drink. I, too, love the Torrontes grape. I would like to go to Argentina one day."

"Well, thank you, Inspector Jakobsen."

And, as she closed the door behind the police officer, Hanne remarked that besides being good-looking, the man was really quite pleasant and charming.

CHAPTER 31

Copenhagen, Denmark—Early Evening, Friday, July 25, same day

Hanne had just two minutes left to go: she was pleased, the calorie counter was showing three seventy-three already, so she was sure she would exceed the four hundred she liked to burn off as a minimum in the half hour or so workout on the elliptical. The vigorous exercise helped take her mind off the day at work, where she was trying to finalize a proposal on how to move forward with an assessment of the resources gained by Denmark in the new UN award.

Just then Kristi, who was over by the weights, caught her attention, vigorously pointing at the TV screen high on the wall in front of her. Hanne put on the earphones and listened to the breaking news on the Danish government-owned television channel, TV2.

"This just in from Nuuk in Greenland." The anchor was standing in front of Hans Egede House with the statue of the missionary up on the hill in the background. "Prime Minister Malik Rorsen has issued a unilateral declaration of Greenland's independence from Denmark…"

"Holy shit!" Hanne said, stopping dead in her tracks, even though the counter only showed three ninety-one. "Un-fucking believable!" She hardly ever swore, but this was one of those rare occasions when she pulled out a phrase she had picked up as an exchange student in Boston.

৶৩৶

Hanne had the news blaring on the TV in the living room and the door to her bedroom open as she unzipped the light summer dress and slipped it over her head, changing into jeans cutoffs and a bikini top. The still hot, late afternoon sun streaming in through the open sliding glass doors felt good if you were appropriately dressed.

"Prime Minister Malik Rorsen's surprise unilateral declaration of Greenland's independence earlier today has thrown capitals around the world into complete disarray. This, coming so soon after Russia's huge undersea land grab and repudiation of the UN Convention of the Law of the Sea..." The Euronews reporter's voice droned robotically. "Brussels has issued a statement saying that the European Commission is examining the implications, but the people of Greenland had, already in a 1982 referendum, voted to opt out of the European Union, which they formally did in 1985. Nevertheless, it is clear that the unilateral declaration was motivated by the recent award to Greenland of jurisdiction over substantial seabed resources by a UN Commission. Denmark, a member of the EU, will undoubtedly be affected by the loss of its richest territories. It is still unsure at this point to what extent Greenland will live up to the 2009 agreement granting it partial autonomy, which called for an equal split between Denmark and Greenland of any profits from natural resources after the first Danish Kroner seventy-five million, which is to stay in Greenland. Another question the declaration brings into focus is the status of the self-proclaimed new country under NATO."

Hanne puttered over to the kitchen counter in her bare feet even as she used the remote to change the channel to TV2. As she uncorked a bottle of Malbec and poured herself a large glass, she listened to the panel of talking heads rage over Rorsen's action.

"The government should certainly consider sending a bill to Greenland for the three billion kroner in annual subsidies we have been sending their way since 2009. And all the support before—"

"How would we collect if they don't want to pay, pray tell? And any of the profits going forward that are due us according to the agreement?"

"Seize their assets, here and internationally—"

"But those assets are already ours."

"We could corral ships carrying Greenland minerals and tankers carrying oil from there—"

"They are not exporting much yet other than fish. And when they do, it is more than likely going to be vessels of countries like China and India that you are talking about. Would we really want to aggravate those relationships?"

"Well, we could send troops to occupy the country...the dependency, I mean. Until they pay up."

Hanne found this discussion silly and switched to CNN. For once, the breaking news there was more of interest to her: "...The Chinese Ministry of Foreign Affairs has just announced that it recognizes the sovereign state of Greenland. This comes less than twenty-four hours after the unilateral declaration of independence by the prime minister of Greenland, and within minutes of the statement by the Russian foreign minister earlier doing the same, and calling Greenland's step '...the final, long-overdue nail in the coffin of imperialism...' Both countries have also said that they will stand behind Greenland's sovereignty and act as its guarantor. This is a serious slap in the face for Denmark and the EU, even though Greenland was not part of the union. It has also been mooted that India, Brazil and, indeed, most emerging nation governments will be announcing their recognition shortly…Possibly Canada too. The big question is how the White House will react."

Just then, Hanne's phone rang. Jens? Probably not—he'd be busy scheming how to get to Rorsen with the Green Liberation Front agenda. He usually calls on the cell anyway. Lock—unlikely, it would be the middle of the night in Beijing. Kristi—well, maybe? Hmm. It could be nice to spend the evening with her, even though she was quite tired after a heavy few days and her vigorous work out.

It was Richard. They hadn't talked for a couple of weeks as he had gone off to New Brunswick on a fishing trip with some of his buddies.

"Hanne, amazing, all this news, isn't it? I go away for a few days and the whole world has changed."

"Yes. What's Canada going to do? People here are pretty irate."

"I don't know, but I was worried about you, since you worked so hard for Denmark. And now Greenland gets it all."

"Well, we were one and the same until recently…"

"Anyway, it was really just an excuse to tell you how much I miss you."

Just then her cell phone rang.

"Richard, I have to go. The other line is ringing. Bye." She added as an afterthought, "I miss you too, Richard". And she was surprised that she really meant it this time. "I'll call you back." But she was not sure whether he heard.

The caller was Kristi. She was wondering whether Hanne was angry with her, because she had bolted so quickly from the gym.

"No, of course not my dear. Just concerned about this announcement. You know, Greenland's independence…"

"Well, honey, so what? You can't let a thing like that get to you!" That was vintage Kristi. "Why don't we go out and have a drink, and a bite to eat. Charlie's bar?"

"No…no. I'm not up for it. We might bump into Jens and the gang there."

"So? What's with you and Jens these days?"

"Kristi, I'd rather not talk about it." Hanne was thinking. "I'd love to see you, but why don't you rather come here. I'll open a bottle of wine, and we'll order in. How's that?"

೧౩೧

Kristi came. Hanne opened a bottle of Torrontes, and they ordered sushi.

And they had an un-fucking believable night. She rather liked that adjectival phrase, now that she had rediscovered it. Even though it wasn't truly descriptive of how they spent their time in bed.

Chapter 32

Washington DC, USA—Evening, Friday, July 25, same day

Ron Hall was dressed in gym shorts and tee shirt, just mixing his second vodka tonic. He was ready to start the barbecue in the little square patio behind the townhouse on Olive Street in Georgetown he owned jointly with Susan, when the call came.

"Oh, shit," he said to himself, as he saw who was calling. And into the phone: "Hello. Yes, of course, I'll be there."

Never mind that it was Friday night and he had promised to grill T-bone steaks for Susan's tennis foursome and partners. Never mind that he had promised Susan that he would be there for her this evening for sure, absolutely positive, having had to miss her birthday, Valentine's Day, and the anniversary of their having met. *Oh well, this was the lot of a White House slave,* he told himself…

"Susan!" He yelled to be heard above the Eric Clapton music she was playing as he went to look for her in the kitchen. At least he knew she was in a good mood, because that's what she put on when she was up. She looked great preparing the salad, in one of his old dress shirts with the sleeves torn off, and cutoffs, with flip-flops on her feet.

"You won't believe it, my dear. Your friend, David's

secretary, just called, demanding my presence. Right now. So, my love, you'll have to do the barbecue on your own tonight. Sorry…"

"Oh shit, Ron, not again! Don't do this to me."

Instead of words, he just hugged her. "Come on, girl. You know I love you. And you know this is part of the deal. At least for now…"

"Fuck it anyway, Ron. I was counting on you." He saw the tears come into her eyes.

"Look, I'm sure you can ask Jim to cook the meat. And I'll be back to help you eat it…"

Susan just reached into his shorts. "I'm going to cook your meat before you go…" as she kissed him, long and deep. "And then I'll eat it when you come back."

This is the girl I love, Ron thought to himself, as he took delight in making the president wait.

೧೨೧

It was standing room only when the president's secretary, June Stewart, ushered Ron into the Oval Office. *Just too many advisors, all wanting to make a point to show off,* Ron thought to himself.

"Mr. President, we must remember that the beginnings of our country were similar." This from the majority leader of the House. "Our founding fathers declared the independence of our mother country the same way. Casting off the yoke of imperialism—"

"We do have to consider that Denmark is a member of NATO." Ron heard the secretary of state say. "And of course, it brings into question whether Greenland should be considered as such, now that it has broken away."

"Of course, the fact that it took a separate path from Denmark on the EU makes that an even more poignant question," Ron's boss, Tom Deacon, added.

"Damn it, gentlemen, why don't we have a better grasp of the situation?" This president did not swear often, so when he did, it was clear to everyone that he was not pleased.

"Mr. President, if I might..." Ron started in his usual humble way, having let the more senior advisors have their say. "You may wish to call Mr. Rorsen to congratulate him on Greenland's independence."

"No, no, no. We can't do that," Gilchrist said. "That would upset our allies in Europe."

"With all due respect, Mr. President, our allies in Europe will be angry anyway. I would be more concerned that Rorsen may be playing to the Russians or the Chinese. It is difficult to imagine that he would make a unilateral declaration of independence without some assurance of support from a major power. Diplomatic, financial, and possibly military. And unless I am not aware of something, I don't think we gave such guarantees. Iceland certainly would not count."

"So you think the Russians or the Chinese..."

"Mr. President, just look at Russia's recent repudiation of the UN Convention on the Law of the Sea. Cozying up to Greenland could be the next step in their plan to control the resources of the Arctic. Or just to keep them out of the hands of the Europeans. I think what Gusanov wants above all else is to make Europe beholden to Russia for energy."

"So, Ron, if you are right, what should we do?"

"Mr. President, this is a big moment for the prime minister of a newly independent Greenland, a country of less than sixty thousand people. You, the leader of the most powerful nation in the world, should call to congratulate him. If nothing else, it will make him feel good, and maybe we'll learn something."

෴

"The president of the United States of America is on the phone, sir. Can I put him through?"

"Of course, of course," Rorsen heard himself mutter, hurrying to finish the bite of the boiled cod his wife had served him. Lucky that he had gotten the phone—now that he was prime minister of an independent country, he may even have to have permanent secretarial service. This sure was a surprise, though. Even more so then the earlier calls of congratulations from Gusanov and Shaojing.

"Prime Minister? I am honored to have you on the line."

"The honor is all mine, Mr. President."

"Why don't you just call me David. And may I call you Malik?"

"Of course, Mr.…David."

"I wanted to congratulate you and your people on this fine moment in your history. We, of course, feel a lot of empathy since, as you know, we threw off the chains of imperialism in a similar fashion."

In the Oval Office, the secretary of state cringed when he heard the president say this. But there was nothing he could do. Ron, of course, was loving it.

"Thank you, Mr. President, for those kind words. We certainly appreciate your support."

"Well, we will have to arrange a face-to-face soon, Malik."

"Ahem…Mr. President, there is one small matter that I was going to call you about anyway in the next few days. But now that I have you on the line, it may be the appropriate time to mention it."

"Of course, Prime Minister."

"Mr. President, an independent Greenland can no

longer tolerate the presence of foreign troops on its soil. We would therefore like the United States of America to withdraw all its men and *matérièl* from the Air Base at Thule, and hand it back to us, its rightful owners. You can rest assured, Mr. President, we will not be making claims in the International Court of Justice for environmental and other damages…"

Chapter 32

Copenhagen, Denmark—Morning, Saturday, July 26, the next day

It starts to get light early in the Danish summer, and the rays of the sun somehow always manage to find their way into a room, even through or around curtains. The sun's progress in the sky meant that the entering rays finally lit up and warmed Hanne's face, and it was this that started to bring her back to consciousness. Yes, it was late Saturday morning, and how delightful it was to have Kristi there beside her. She snuggled up from behind, started kissing her neck and gently kneading her nipples.

It was just as Kristi started to moan that the phone on the night table started to ring.

"Oh, no, I'm not going to get it."

It would not be Jens: he would still be asleep, as would Richard. Maybe Lock. And then she remembered that she had received two calls on weekends from the minister in charge of her department, and with Greenland's declaration of independence, it could very well be she.

"Damn," she said as she reached for the receiver across Kristi, lying spread-eagled on her stomach now, still smelling deliciously of last night's sex.

"*Hej*? Hanne Kristensen."

"Hello. This is the prime minister's office." Hanne sat

bolt upright, letting the sheet fall away from her torso. What the…Why would she be calling her? "I'll put you through."

A click and a few seconds later, a man's voice came on the line. "Hello. Is this Hanne Kristensen?"

"Yes, hello." Hanne was puzzled. The Danish prime minister was a woman. "Who is this?"

"I am so sorry. Of course…Malik Rorsen, from Greenland."

"Oh!" Hanne was relieved, but still befuddled. She recognized the name, but had not met the man. "Hello. Prime Minister, sir." *Why would he be calling her?*

"Congratulations…Independence is a great step for Greenland," she muttered hurriedly, even though she was not sure how she really felt about it.

"Thank you. But Ms. Kristensen—Hanne, if I may— I will keep the call short. To get to the point: I am wondering if you would agree to serve as my minister for natural resources. And as head of the newly created Geological Survey of Greenland. You come highly recommended. All my advisors came up with your name. Plus, you have some high profile international supporters."

Hanne was speechless. She could not accept…But, then, why not?

"This is too great an honor, sir. Will you permit me to think about it?"

"Of course, Hanne. But you must realize that I do not have much time. I have to put together a first-class team in this field very quickly. One that stands up internationally. I need your help."

"Yes, Prime Minister. I will get you an answer…"

"Tomorrow, please. My secretary will call at the same time. I do hope you will decide in Greenland's favor. Of course, we will pay you very well, and there is a lot of interesting work to do here. We will come to an arrangement so you can become a Greenland national as well, but do not have to live here full-time. We can be flexible. Now, goodbye, Hanne."

"Thank you."

Wow!" Hanne said, climbing over Kristi to get to the washroom. Her need was urgent. "You'll never guess who that was."

"Your wild Australian lover?"

"No, no. Of course not. He's a shit," Hanne answered through the open door. "It was the prime minister of Greenland. The man we saw on TV announcing their independence."

"What did he want?"

"My dear, he asked your lover to be the minister for natural resources of Greenland. Isn't that something?"

"Well, whoopee do! Does he want to have sex with you like every man you ever met?"

"Are you jealous, my little lover?" Hanne, coming back into the bedroom, jumped on her and straddled her.

"Seriously. Does that mean that you would leave Copenhagen? Leave me?"

"No, my dear. Certainly not." Hanne gave her a full kiss on the mouth and stretched out beside her. "I would spend some time in Greenland, but I would probably not be away any more than now. He said 'we can come to an arrangement.' "

"Then you must take it, Hanne."

"That's what I was thinking."

" 'Madam Minister'. It sounds great!"

"Yeah. Thanks."

"Just imagine…little old me, the lover of a cabinet minister. Wow, I could certainly create some scandals by telling all."

"You wouldn't dare…"

"Or else what? You would stop fucking me? Haa!"

"Never. You're too delicious."

ა⁄ა⁄ა

When Kristi left, Hanne took her mug of coffee and the papers back into bed. But once the coffee was drained, she chucked the papers on the floor and lay back again. Hanne loved to lie in late, stretch and luxuriate between her own high thread-count cotton sheets. Whether with someone or alone…

She had so much she needed to think through, so many decisions to weigh. Real life-decisions.

That offer from Rorsen. To be minister of natural resources, for all of Greenland, a newly independent state, with huge hydrocarbon and mineral resources. What a great opportunity! She would be silly not to take the job. But would it be viewed as treacherous in Denmark? Probably, yes, by small-minded people. People like her parents. And Jens, of course, would condemn her for helping to exploit the riches of the earth. Although her defense would be that she would implement very rigorous environmental protection laws and standards.

To hell with them. Damn Jens.

She had her own life to live.

Next, her love life. It definitely needed housecleaning, structure, coherence. She could not go on like this.

Well, what to do?

When faced by multi-faceted choice, Hanne usually resorted to one of her favorite pastimes.

Rating.

She loved to rate the different foods, restaurants, books, movies, people, friends. Now it was time to rate lovers. The best time, because she was still lying in bed, naked, all by herself, and it would not be hard to conjure each one up.

There were four. Four that made the cut to be rated.

Jens, the long-time boyfriend. Definitely not number one now, Hanne told herself. On the way out. Self-absorbed, judgmental, a bit boring, and only truly exciting in combination with Kristi. No, definitely low in the ratings. In fact, there was nothing there between them anymore. Time to break up with him, she realized. Say goodbye. Finally.

Kristi, her oldest friend, her first sex partner. She would always love her, probably never give her up. But she was a special case, not one for a permanent relationship. *I am bisexual, not lesbian,* Hanne told herself. I like men, and I want to have children. Gets a special prize in the ratings though.

Lock. He was a real conundrum for Hanne. She found him so, so exciting to be with. Physically, sexually. Bright, cultured, similar interests, great in bed, international, the right mix of giving and taking—all the best ingredients. But there was something that was not right. There was something slippery about Lock. She just could not put her finger on it.

That left Richard. Yes, he was definitely a comer. The comer, she told herself, relishing her own little dirty joke. She had virtually ignored him since that untoward episode in Ottawa where she had given him a try...But he had made a real comeback (another little inward smile). Richard had hung in there, just been himself with her all along, not tried to force himself on her as many men would have. They had that great evening in New York...And *voilá*, he was now number one!

As she thought about this trinity plus one, she did not refrain from exciting herself under the sheets, and, turning over onto her front, with her Mound of Venus still in her palm, she reached orgasm within seconds.

Chapter 33

Copenhagen, Denmark—Early Afternoon, Saturday, July 26, same day

By the time she got out of bed, took her shower and had another mug of coffee, Hanne had decided to take matters in hand. She called Jens, asking him to meet her at the BioM for a late lunch.

Unusually, she was there first, and, to summon her courage, ordered a bottle of the café's house white, a decent Languedoc. Jens arrived, and she let him kiss her cheek, holding onto her glass to prevent anything more intimate.

"So, we've both been pretty busy," Jens said. "Sorry, I haven't called."

"Have you been seeing Kristi?" Hanne asked pointedly, just to put him on the defensive, but knowing that he hadn't.

"No. But isn't she great? You two are fabulous together!"

"Yes, I know."

"Hanne, I am quite excited…"

"I am sure you are, Jens."

"Stop it. Seriously. You know those plans we talked about? To go up north in Greenland to protest at that lead-zinc mine—Citronen it's called…"

"Umm…"

"Well, they've come together quite nicely. Coordinated with other protest actions the Green Liberation Front will be carrying out elsewhere. Too bad about Sven though. He would have loved all this. Poor guy…"

"Yes, poor Sven."

"…But Erik, Gunnar and I will be leaving for Nuuk the Monday after next, and then up to Citronen from there."

"Well, fancy that," Hanne said, getting angrier by the moment with Jens's smugness. "I will be on my way to Nuuk right around then too."

"Oh, yeah? What for?"

"I've been asked to be Greenland's minister for natural resources. And head of their Geological Survey."

"You gotta be kidding!"

"And that brings me to why I wanted to have lunch with you today."

"What's that?"

Just then the waiter came to take their order. She asked for a mushroom quiche, he, a smoked salmon plate.

"Jens. We're no good together any more. It's time we broke up. Especially with you going off to Citronen, and me spending time now in Nuuk. It just is not working…"

Jens poured himself some wine and took a big gulp. He certainly had not expected this.

"So, Madam Minister," Jens finally spoke again, but his tone was sarcastic, evil. "I'm not good enough for you anymore?"

"No, Jens. It's not that—"

"Well, a minister can't hang around with a mere activist from the Green Liberation Front movement. That certainly would not do." Jens was getting warmed up. "Hanne, you're a total fucking sellout. You have just so gotten into your own self-importance—that you single-handedly won Denmark great riches. And now, haa, it ends up being for Greenland—all that undersea territory. And of course, now you must go and see how you can despoil the pristine environment up there by helping Greenland build all those polluting extractive industries."

"No. No, Jens. Stop it…"

"What are they paying you, Hanne? It must be a huge amount—or come to think of it, maybe not, since you are such a cheap whore. A bisexual cunt, ready to sell yourself to anyone—"

That was it for Hanne. She stood up, refilled glass in hand, and said, "Well, Jens, if that's the way you feel about me, then here's to my leaving you. Best decision I ever made." She calmly drained the glass, picked up her purse, voiced an audible "Good riddance, asshole," and left her boyfriend of seven years to stew while he finished his plate of smoked salmon and paid for both lunches.

Chapter 34

Skodsborg, Denmark—Early Afternoon, Sunday, July 27, next day

Hanne was in the garden with the girls, her beautiful blond nieces, Alise, aged nine, and Madja, seven, playing 'Mother May I' and loving it. She was certainly glad to be with them and away from the adults, and not just because she had exempted herself from helping with the dishes.

Her sister, Beatha, had called in the morning, asking her to a family Sunday lunch. She would also invite their parents, whom Hanne recalled she hadn't seen for three weeks. She was happy to accept: she always loved to go out to Skodsborg, a quaint little port and seaside community north of Copenhagen. Beatha's and Karel's house was right on the beach, so the air was good, and there was always a cooling breeze.

It might be a good venue to tell the family about her news, too, she thought. At least the news that she had been asked to be the minister for natural resources of Greenland, because she was not quite ready to talk about the breakup with Jens. And, of course, she was happy that she would see the girls, whom she loved as if they were her very own. She really did need to get on with starting a family, but now it seemed more out of reach than ever.

Hanne picked her time over dessert to pluck up enough courage to broach the topic.

"Mama and Papa, I have some news..."

"Well, I am so happy for you!" Hanne's mother beamed. "It's about time."

"I wanted to tell you all that I have been asked to be the minister for natural resources by the prime minister..."

"Wow!" Karel whistled. "That's fan—"

"...of Greenland."

Silence. Broken only by the coughing of her father choking on the apple cake.

"So you will read that big book in church in Greenland?" little Madja finally asked when she finished her slice of the dessert.

"No, no. Not that kind of minister," Hanne answered, laughing, glad for the distraction. But she stopped when she saw that her mother was crying.

"Hanne, how could you!" Her father spoke, gasping air at the same time, having struggled the apple cake finally down the right tube. "We always fought for Denmark. You come from a line of soldiers..." Yes, she knew this: it was a sore point for her father that his wife had given him two daughters and no son. And thus far there were no grandsons. No male heir who could give his life for little old Denmark.

"And here I was thinking you were going to tell us that you and Jens were finally engaged," her mother got her only thought out between sobs. "And you would have babies!"

When Beatha and Karel sided with her parents as well and made critical and pointed remarks—"How could you, Hanne? They have stolen our future, all our assets. Without Greenland, Denmark has nothing," and, "You're not really going to work for that traitorous half-breed!"—she decided it was time to take her dishes out to the kitchen.

While there, she made sure she clattered a few plates as she put them in the dishwasher to make her absence in the other room that much more noticeable, and when she finally came back into the dining room, she said to the girls, "Who wants to come and play 'Mother May I' with Auntie Hanne?" knowing that they would jump up from the table and follow her outside.

"Hanne," she heard her father say as she slid the glass patio door shut behind her.

She was glad she was going to spend more time in Greenland, so she wouldn't have to put up with this small-minded bullshit.

༄༅༄

Madja was 'Mother' and she had just told Hanne to take two baby steps backwards when Hanne's phone rang. She hesitated, but decided to take it: the girls could continue playing without her.

"*Hej*," she said, wondering who was calling.

"Hello, Hanne." It was Richard. "How are things?"

"Hi, Richard. Thanks. I'm glad somebody cares."

"What do you mean?"

"Never mind. What to start with? Well, just the other day I got a call from Malik Rorsen—you know, the prime minister of Greenland"—she paused a moment before the big news—"asking me to be his minister for natural resources. And to head up the Geological Survey of Greenland."

"Fantastic! You accepted, of course."

"He will be calling shortly for my answer."

"You must take it. What a great job! Huge potential. And you, Hanne, are perfect for it." She found his enthusiasm and positive response refreshing after what she had just been through inside the house.

"Thanks. And, Richard, I do miss you too. Just in case you didn't hear me say yesterday."

"I'll see if I can work something out to come and see you. To celebrate, Madam Minister!"

"That would be great. I could use some moral support."

ᛒᚱᛒ

Once back in her apartment, Hanne luxuriated in a bath, washed her hair, and more or less put the unpleasant family scene behind her. She was at her laptop reading a sexually charged email that had just come in from Lock when the phone rang.

"Hello, Ms. Kristensen?"

"Yes? *Hej*." Her mind was still chewing on Lock's cheeky erotic double entendre. *The bastard!*

"I am calling from Prime Minister Rorsen's office."

"Oh, yes. Hello. Thank you."

"I would like to be able to tell the prime minister that you will accept the positions he offered you. minister of natural resources and director of the Geological Survey of Greenland."

"I am greatly honored, and I do accept."

"Excellent. The prime minister is currently traveling, but should be back early next week. Could you come to Nuuk then? Say, Tuesday?"

"Yes, I think that should be possible."

"Should I make the arrangements for you?"

"That would be kind."

"I will send your itinerary and the tickets by email."

"Thank you."

"We will see you then, Madam Minister."

Even though she knew that Rorsen's secretary was playing with her ego, she loved the way that sounded.

Yes, I will definitely enjoy my new persona, Hanne told herself.

Madam Minister!

Chapter 35

Copenhagen, Denmark—Evening, Friday, August 1, a few days later

Hanne knew Kristi was almost there, so she let her phone keep ringing. Her lover finally moaned with delight, as Hanne scrambled on top of her, lunging playfully for the cell phone on the night table.

"*Hej*. Hello, Richard," Hanne panted into the phone, still relishing the taste of Kristi.

"Hi, Hanne. Am I disturbing you? Were you exercising?"

"Well, sort of…What's up?" Hanne rolled off Kristi, but kept her left hand between her thighs.

"I thought you'd like to know…" Hanne thought she sensed some hesitation in Richard's retort.

"What?"

"Hanne, turn the TV on. Look at the breaking news. The Chinese have just announced a big deal with Greenland. Twenty-five billion dollars for resource extraction. US. That will give you a huge budget to work with, but also, no doubt, an enormous headache in your new position."

"God, yeah…"

"And can you guess who's the main man in all this?"

"Who?" Kristi put a hand across her waist.

"Your friend, Lock. Professor McTierney, from

Beijing University."

"You must be kidding!" Hanne's heart sank as the implications started crowding into her mind. "It can't be true."

"Oh yes, my dear."

"What's wrong, love?" Kristi whispered, sensing the upset in Hanne's voice.

"Okay. Thanks for letting me know. I'll call you soon, Richard. Bye." And added, for Kristi's benefit as she pressed the red button on the mobile and jumped out of bed, "I'll go get some wine."

೧೩೧

"Shit," she said to herself, pushing the power on the remote for the TV in the kitchen. It can't be true.

Indeed, what she saw on the screen just made her even angrier. There was Lock, and that little prick, Li, standing behind Wen Shaojing, the secretary general of the Communist Party of China, who was holding the press conference to announce the deal.

The CNN voiceover went on to say that Lock McTierney, the Australian professor of geology at Beijing University, and expert in Arctic mineralization, would act as consultant to the Chinese government, and guide how this money was to be spent over the next few years. He would be their advisor on the development of mines, as well as oil and gas fields in and around Greenland, and the building of the necessary infrastructure to exploit these resources.

Presumably, all for the benefit of the Chinese. Oh, yes, and maybe a little bit for Greenland. Just enough so they would not miss those subsidies from good old Denmark.

That bastard, Hanne thought to herself. The Chinese must have had him in their power all along. They must have offered him this position…Yes, probably right after he was elected to the Commission. This must have been their plan right from the start, to get control of Greenland's resources by throwing huge amounts of money at it. And buying whomever they needed along the way. Including the key person in the Commission.

Or, shit, maybe they bought Lock even before, and helped him get elected—God, this was monstrous!

Well, they would have her to contend with…

Damn them, and damn Lock.

Maybe Jens was right, and they should just not allow anyone to exploit the resources of the Arctic…

Damn, damn, damn!

Chapter 36

Kremlin, Moscow, Russia—Morning, Saturday, August 2, the next day

"So. That Shaojing has totally outsmarted us once again." Andrei was livid. "Why didn't any of you clever dickheads recommend that we offer Greenland what the Chinese did? Money! Pretty obvious isn't it?" The president looked around the table at the faces of his closest advisors. He had called them to an emergency meeting of his Inner Cabinet, to discuss the Chinese initiative.

"Andrei, as you know, we have other budgetary priorities." Dmitri Mendeleev, the prime minister, took the first stab at pacifying the boss. "Even if we just talk about the Arctic, we need to develop our own resources and to strengthen our armed forces there. That all costs a lot of money…"

"Yes, yes, Dmitri. I know all that…" And I am not paying you to tell me the obvious, you little schmuck, he thought to himself. "But it is unacceptable that when it comes to the north—our birthright—we keep getting outplayed, first by the Danes and the Canadians, and then by the Chinese…Who are not even supposed to be in the game up there!"

"If I may…" Pavel felt that as the minister responsible for the Arctic, he was on the hook here. "Indeed, I agree with you that the Chinese have outmaneuvered us in this instance. In fact, what happened is that they manipulated the decisions in the UN Commission to go against us. That Australian professor standing behind Shaojing in the press conference—who is now their consultant on developing Greenland's resources—was the chairman of the Sub-commission dealing with both our and the Danish and Canadian submissions on extensions to our continental shelves. Clearly, the man was bought by the Chinese. They had this planned all along. Plus, I am quite sure he was bedding the sexy and clever little lady who led the Danish team."

"Well, why didn't we bribe the guy? Provide him as many whores as he wanted..." Gusanov asked, knowing the answer. It was simply not Laptov's style. Yes, it was his own fault: he had been so confident in the polar explorer's capabilities and renown that he had not thought it would come to that...

"We..." Laptov started, but decided that silence was better at this point than excuses.

"Evgeny, can we get rid of this Australian?"

"Yes, of course," Evgeny Botnikov, the head of the FSB responded. "I will get on it." And he punched an *aide-mémoire* into his iPhone.

"All right, gentlemen. I will back off," Gusanov decided to try a different approach. "But I need ideas on how we can remedy the situation. Besides killing that meddling professor..."

"Well, for one," the soft-spoken Arkady Serdyov, minister of defense, spoke up, "we could send an expeditionary force up to Northern Greenland. Somewhere where there is a mine or an oil field being developed. One that the Chinese would prioritize in the development plans they are going to pay for. You know, as a show of strength. Say, six or eight submarines. Just to demonstrate to them who is boss. After all, we did offer Greenland that we would guarantee their independence…"

"Hmm…That's good, Arkady. I like it. It would certainly up the ante. The Chinese may throw money at Greenland to develop their resources, but we show the world that we are in control up in the Arctic."

"Yes, it could be very bad for us if they got a foothold there," Boris Lebedev, the long-time minister for foreign affairs said.

"As it happens," Botnikov interrupted, clearing his throat, "an operative we placed within that pesky Green Liberation Front has recently informed us of the actions they will be taking to protest the dividing up of the Arctic. They plan to disrupt a newly opened lead-zinc mine in Northern Greenland. Very soon, in fact. Citronen, I think it is called. The mine is high on the agenda for Greenland to develop."

"Pavel, you know the Arctic," Gusanov asked the famous polar explorer, "have you heard of this mine?"

"Yes. It is located on the Citronen Fjord," Laptov answered. And then added, against his better judgment: "Which is deep enough for submarines to get in."

"Well, that is excellent," Botnikov said, standing up, and exchanging looks with the minister of defense. "We could instruct our operative to make sure that serious damage is caused to the mine, and, at the same time, have the submarines land a force to occupy the site. To show the world who is boss in the Arctic, as you said, Andrei."

"I must caution you,"—Laptov was clearly agitated—"such a move, in my view, would be very counter-productive. It would antagonize Greenland and it could lead to conflict with not just the Chinese, but also the Europeans and the Americans. And likely the devastation of the entire north…"

"But…" Serdyov interrupted.

"You must remember…"—Laptov bulldozed right over the minister of defense, who was more senior, but he didn't care—"…that the Americans have their base up there at Thule. They would view an armed landing on the northern shore of Greenland as a major threat. And, depending how they see the status of an independent Greenland, possibly as an attack on a fellow NATO country."

"In fact, that is just it," Serdyov was able to capture the floor from the minister for the Arctic who had finally run out of breath. "That's the beauty of it. We can just say our landing is in support of Greenland's demand that the Americans leave Thule and hand it back to them. We know this has been a sore point with the local peoples there for a long time."

"Arkady, that is brilliant! At the very least, what you propose could allow us to get rid of Thule. The American military has been spying on us from there since the Second World War, and it has been a thorn in the side of every one of our administrations since then. Brilliant."

"Thank you." Serdyov was very pleased with the way this meeting was turning out.

Laptov, on the other hand, was not at all happy. He felt he was losing control, but hoped that, in spite of this, he might still be able to steer matters in a positive direction for the Arctic at a later time. He had the impression that he was the only obstacle now standing between the Arctic and its total plundering by his uncaring colleagues. Amongst others.

"Well, there you have it, gentlemen. Are we all in agreement then?"

All six of the ministers, other than the minister for the Arctic, voiced loud support for the proposed invasion of Northern Greenland. Laptov looked forlornly out the window, and hoped that Gusanov would not put him on the spot. That would be his end...

"Well, gentlemen. Then I shall authorize—no, order—Arkady to send a force of six submarines to this Citronen Fjord in Northern Greenland. Arkady, I would like you to add to the orders for the commander of this little fleet that if they encounter resistance or attack from any quarter, they are to release a cruise missile to take out the Thule radar. At least we should get that benefit from having to protect our new ally in Greenland! And Evgeny, you give instructions to that operative you planted within the crazy Green Liberation Front to destroy that citrus fruit mine." Gusanov stood up, laughing at his own little joke.

"But—" Pavel started to speak.

"What is it, Pavel?"

"No, nothing." Laptov backed down, knowing there was no way he would win this.

Chapter 37

Copenhagen, Denmark—Evening, Saturday, August 2, same day

She heard the *Turkish March* play in the bedroom.
"Kristi, can you get the cell, please?" Hanne yelled from the bathroom. "It's on the night table by the bed. I'm on the loo."

"Okay," Kristi shouted back, and through the crack in the door Hanne could see her lithe dancer's body, wearing only panties, bend over as she reached for the mobile. God, she is a fabulous woman, Hanne thought to herself.

"Hanne Kristensen's phone," she heard Kristi answer in Danish. Then a long pause while Kristi listened to the caller, before she said, "Just a second please."

She came into the bathroom, addressing Hanne: "It's for you, my dear."

"Who is it then?"

"Some guy." Kristi reached the phone towards Hanne, who was still sitting on the toilet. "He said his name is something like Lock Mac-something."

"Shit, Kristi. I don't want to talk to him. Hang up quickly."

Kristi did as she was told and pushed the red button. "Isn't he your sexy Australian lover? The one you have been raving about?"

"Not any more. There's nothing between us now,"

Hanne said, standing up to flush. She was stark naked.

"Well, maybe then I should have talked to him," Kristi threw this in, just to tease Hanne.

"Not on your life. He's a duplicitous son of a bitch. I hate his guts...And you're not going anywhere near him."

The *Turkish March* sounded yet again. This time, Kristi handed the cell straight to Hanne, saying, "Well, do what you want. He's your problem."

Seeing the Australian area code, Hanne cut the music off, and threw the phone on the bed. "I refuse to talk to that amoral monster."

A moment later, there was a bleep, indicating that a text message had come through. Hanne hesitated, but decided she was too intrigued by what the bastard wanted. And it was pretty innocuous just to open an SMS...

"Booked ticket. Arriving tomorrow. So look forward to seeing you."

Hanne was incensed. "The balls the guy has. To think that he can just show up and I will be waiting for him with open arms..."

"And legs no doubt. Well, if not, my dear, maybe you can send him over to my place. I can always use a good lay."

"Stop it, you tease. Are you not satisfied with what you have here, bitch?"

"I meant with a man...It is different, you know," Kristi said, chuckling.

"I'm going to get you," Hanne said, jumping on the bed to try and catch Kristi. But her lover was too quick for her and ran into the bathroom, closing the door behind her.

"Come out, you little slut, or I will leave you forever," Hanne shouted, as she quickly used her two thumbs on the mobile to write a message. "Am traveling." Yes, that was enough to tell the bastard that it was not worth his while to come to Copenhagen. She was not there for him, now, and never will be.

"Okay, I'm leaving now…" To Kristi.

A few seconds later, she heard the bathroom door being unlocked, and opened until it was slightly ajar.

"No, you're not, Madam Minister," Hanne heard Kristi say in her sexiest voice. Her words were drowned out by the shower. And Hanne knew what Kristi had in mind.

***

Much later, as they were lying side by side, still in bed but with a bowl of grapes they were idly munching on between them, Hanne said, "You know, Kristi, I'm so glad we have each other. Seriously. Things with you are just so uncomplicated, our friendship is so strong and the sex so good."

"Yeah. But we've talked about this before, and we always come to the same conclusion, don't we? We both still want the man thing as well. It is different, as we said earlier. And we do both want babies."

"It's too bad that Lock turned out to be such a pig. He seemed so ideal at first. But he was really so wicked. So…so amoral."

"And Jens?"

"He's just boring. And self-absorbed. You know, I didn't tell you yet, but I finally broke up with him."

"I saw that coming."

"Never mind. Pity it didn't work out for you with Henrik, though…"

"Yeah, he was so right at first too, but there was that entire other side of him I did not know about."

"And you had that fling with Erik for a while, didn't you?"

"Yees..."

"Now Kristi, you never really told me what happened there. Except that he turned weird on you." Hanne had been keen to learn the truth for some time.

"He sure did. Ugh, I still have nightmares about it. It makes my skin crawl just to think of it now..."

"Come on, love, you can tell me. It's been several years." And Hanne stroked her friend's face.

"Okay. Here goes." Kristi took a deep breath before continuing. "The first two times I went home with him, things were fine—the sex was okay, not fabulous, but good enough. He was smart, and pretty good-looking, although I didn't much like his piercings and tattoos, I must say. But the third time, after one of those sessions at Bar NASA—I remember you were off somewhere—we went back to his place early, and things were going well...Even the sex was good.

"We were just lying there afterwards, naked and sipping some wine—actually talking about you and Jens—when all of a sudden, the creep pulled up a rope tied to one of the bars at the head of his iron bed, grabbed my wrists and tied them so tight that I couldn't move my arms. I struggled and kicked him as hard as I could, calling him names and screaming, asking what the fuck he was doing. But he pinned me down hard, and then reached down under the bed again and brought out this thing...a rod of some sort. And when he pressed a button on it, it made a pinging, throbbing sort of electrical noise. He laughed a crazy laugh, and tried to pry my legs apart, but I gave him a big kick and screamed at the top of my lungs..."

"God, Kristi, you never told me...You poor thing."

"Well, fortunately, Sven—who, you remember, shared the apartment with Erik then—came home at that very moment, and hearing my screams, broke into the room. He punched Erik, wrestled the gizmo from his hands, and asked him whether he had lost his mind. Then he untied me, made sure I was all right—and…and I remember, I cried on his shoulder…"

"Boy, you were lucky!"

"It was when I came out of the bathroom, all dressed but still shaking, and Sven had his arm on Erik's shoulder, that he told me I should not judge Erik too harshly. That was one of the things the Russian secret police had used to torture them when they were in prison. You know after that Murmansk fiasco…"

"Whew! I never knew."

"It was scary…"

"What was it?"

"Sven said something they use on cows…"

"A cattle-prod. God! He could have killed you!"

"Now you know why I hardly ever speak to Erik. He is demented, but you have to feel pity for him. For them all, I guess."

"Well, Kristi, with these flawed and crazy men around, I am really glad we have each other." Hanne stroked the inside of Kristi's thigh. "But I know we will both find the right guy eventually. In the meantime, though, we may as well enjoy being together."

"You're telling me," Kristi said, pulling Hanne's face to hers and giving her a deep kiss.

Hanne was aroused by the sensation of Kristi's soft tongue probing the inside of her mouth. She moved the bowl of grapes onto the night table, and then wrapped her legs around her friend and lover and things just progressed naturally from there.

Chapter 38

Murmansk, Russia—Morning, Sunday, August 3, next day

Admiral Maslenkov was glad that it was a warm summer day as he watched the Russia State Transport Company's Ilyushin jet pull up in front of him on the tarmac. It had actually been a rare pleasure for him to stand for the fifteen or so minutes in the baking sun, waiting for the plane carrying not one, but two ministers to arrive.

"Welcome, welcome," Maslenkov first grabbed Serdyov's right with both his hands before he kissed him, then turned to Laptov and did the same. He was good friends with the minister for the Arctic, but the minister of defense was his boss and technically the more senior of the two VIP visitors.

Why in God's name would Gusanov send two of his Inner Cabinet to see him—it must be something very important. He did not like the president and most of his coterie, the *siloviki*, all former KGB...Particularly since they had implemented those ridiculous reforms that put the armed forces firmly under the control of the minister of defense, the slimiest of the former intelligence agents now in power. No professional soldier liked or respected him.

"Yevgeni, so good to see you," Laptov was earnest in his greeting. "We would not have both come, but the president wanted to be certain that the orders were properly understood by you." *And I wanted to make sure to hold that bastard Serdyov back however I could*, he finished the thought silently, hoping his friend would understand his meaning.

※※※

The Zil drove them the short distance to the admiral's office, and once seated around the little coffee table with cups of tea in front of them, Laptov let Serdyov deliver the president's orders to the commander of the Northern Fleet.

"Admiral, yesterday we took a decision at a meeting of the Inner Cabinet to send a fleet of six submarines—three Yasens and three Dolgorukiys, armed with their ballistic missiles—to Northern Greenland."

"I am sure the decision was not taken lightly."

"With Greenland's declaration of independence, Yevgeni," Laptov took over, "there are some strong indications that the Chinese want to meddle up there. And the Inner Cabinet felt that the arrival of a small submarine force would show them and the rest of the world who really controls the Arctic."

"Where exactly did the Inner Cabinet have in mind for the fleet to go to?"

"The decision was to send the submarines to land a force at the Citronen Mine—a newly opened lead-zinc operation in the north that we think the Chinese will have their eyes on. Also, we think the fjord there is deep and it should be easy for our submarines to penetrate right to the mine."

Maslenkov fetched his laptop from the desk and

brought up Google Earth, typing in Citronen Mine. Even the Russian military relied on a western search engine sometimes.

"Yeah, it's at about 83°North by 30°West," Laptov continued, "but it's pretty ice-free now all the way. A few floes here and there, but that should not bother our experienced sub commanders."

"Good. And what do the boats and the men do when they get there?" Maslenkov asked. Typically, he was sure that the politicians had not considered the important details.

"Flex their muscles," the defense minister answered. "Land a force, send any Chinese packing, and stick around for a few days. Just so you know, an FSB operative planted inside the Green Liberation Front has been instructed to make sure that maximal damage is caused to the mine. So the international news channels will be making a big thing out of this, for sure."

"Well, the US and Europe will certainly protest. As will the Chinese."

"Fuck them. That's why we're going there." This from Serdyov.

"What if they take action against the fleet?"

"You are to give the commander orders that if any of our vessels or men are attacked, they are to release a missile to take out the Thule radar." Laptov winced as Serdyov took pleasure in communicating this part of the orders. "The president sees that as one of the side benefits coming from this mission. That we finally get rid of that meddling American spy post. Do you get my drift, Admiral?"

"Clearly. We don't want to start a war though, Yevgeni," Laptov added.

"Yes, of course. I do understand."

But the politicians sure didn't, Maslenkov thought to

himself. Bombing Thule will certainly elicit an armed response from the US.

And then what?

CHAPTER 39

Hotel Hans Egede, Nuuk, Greenland—Evening, Monday, August 4, the next day

Hanne was lost deep in slumber when the incessant beep-beep from her phone brought her back to consciousness. She had only intended to take a brief nap after her arrival at the Hans Egede, but had set the alarm for 7pm just in case. Her body had needed the rest, but she knew this was not the best way to combat any jet lag, even though the time difference was only two hours between Copenhagen and Nuuk. She had wanted a little snooze, just so she would be ready the next day to start into her new job as minister for natural resources.

The prime minister had left an envelope at the reception with a welcome note for her and an invitation to a breakfast meeting with him. This was to be followed by the official swearing-in ceremony where she would meet her new cabinet colleagues.

Hanne took her time in the shower, and then dressed casually in a simple wrap-around skirt and an open-necked blouse to go up to the restaurant for dinner. She was planning to have only a glass of wine and a quick bite before coming back down to her room.

Her plan was to go through some reading she had brought from Copenhagen on the mineral deposits, and oil and gas reserves in and around Greenland. She had started to look at this material on the flight over, but had barely made a dent. Oh well, she was well rested now, and the whole night was ahead of her.

⁓⁓⁓

Hanne took the elevator to the fifth floor where the Skyline bar and the Hereford Beefstouw restaurant she had cased out earlier were to be found. Yes, why not check out the scene in the bar?

As she stepped into the Skyline, she saw a familiar figure wave at her from across the room: standing at the long black bar with his Green Liberation Front buddies, Erik and Gunnar, was Jens, holding a pint in one hand, the other up in the air eagerly beckoning her over.

She could not very well slink away, she thought, and it would be rather odd for her to have a drink all by herself at the bar with some of her Danish friends there. *Oh well, maybe I'll let the asshole buy me a drink. For old times' sake. Even though he had been such a jerk the last time we met.* And Kristi's story had turned her quite off Erik…

She and Jens did the double-cheeked thing a little stiffly—it had habitually been more passionate and fully on the mouth for the last seven years. So it seemed odd—plus, he held onto her hand for an embarrassingly long while before Hanne could extricate it.

Jens ordered her a glass of a decent Sauvignon Blanc from Chile, as he recounted that they finally managed to arrange the hire of a plane to fly them up to Citronen Fjord.

"You're not seriously going to try and disrupt their operations up there, are you now?" Hanne asked. "That would be pretty stupid."

"Just a little protest. Nothing major. No harm will be done."

"You know, now that I am a minister in the government, I may have to have you arrested. Just don't do anything stupid."

"Not if we buy you dinner, you won't, Hanne," Jens answered, laughing. "You are alone, aren't you? Would you care to join us?"

Hanne thought quickly: there was all that work upstairs, and it could be seen as compromising for the new minister for natural resources to be treated to dinner by a bunch of Green Liberation Front activists. But what the heck, she was alone, and it was her ex-beau, and eating by herself with her three old friends at another nearby table would amount to a ludicrous situation...

"Sure, thanks. I'll join you. But don't count on me to save your ass if you do something illegal up at Citronen."

ცოც

Maybe it was that they were finishing their third bottle of wine at the table, or that they were far away from Copenhagen, but Hanne was glad that she had agreed to have dinner with the Front guys. Jens was in his element playing the role of anti-hero, recounting tales of earlier exploits.

She experienced a tinge of regret that she should not have precipitated the break-up. But there was no looking back: it didn't feel right then, and, if it didn't feel right, it wasn't right, she told herself. And he had been such a jerk the last time. You have to move on in life.

It was dessert time, and the men all asked for Greenland Coffees. Jens ordered one for Hanne as well—when she asked if it was alcoholic, they all laughed. She said she had consumed too much wine already and still had work to do, but they guffawed again and said she simply had to have one. The waiter eventually brought the four drinks—a brownish concoction of whisky, Kahlua and coffee, topped with whipped cream and flaming Grand Marnier as she later found out. They all dug right into the drinks amidst further merrymaking.

"If you don't finish it, Hanne, you'll be insulting your new country. This is their national tipple. Not to speak of your hosts. You'll just have to pick up the bill if you don't drink all of one, I'm sorry," Jens said between sips.

"Hello, Hanne," she heard a familiar accent behind her break through Jens's chortling, just as she was lifting her face back out of the whipped cream with a white moustache on her upper lip, the strong taste of the drink searing her throat. "Fancy meeting you here…"

She turned around, and the features matched the voice: Lock. He loomed large behind her, both hands on her chair, three Chinese lingering further away.

"Lock!" Her first reaction was…well…almost pleasant surprise. But then the anger, the venom kicked in. "Get the hell away from here. I don't want you near me," and, on an impulse, she poured her entire Greenland coffee into his face as she stood up and took satisfaction in watching the sticky white and brown drink drip down, soil his suit jacket and shirt and tie.

Jens and his friends jumped to their feet, the Chinese moved menacingly in behind Lock, and several waiters rushed to the scene.

"Is this jerk bothering you?" Jens asked, rolling his hands into fists.

"Gentlemen, ladies. Let us all calm down," *the Maître d'*—who, Hanne remarked in passing, was rather stern looking, and somewhat gay—pleaded, pushing himself between Lock and Hanne.

"Okay, Hanne," Lock said in his Aussie drawl,

between wipes of his face with Hanne's napkin, "if that's the way you want it. At least for now, it's okay…" And he turned and beckoned to his Chinese lackeys to follow, giving her one last icy look.

∽∾∽

"Who was that?" Jens asked, Hanne sensing some jealousy.

"A real creep," Hanne answered, as she grabbed Gunnar's unfinished goblet of Greenland coffee and drained it. "The guy who adjudicated on the submissions to the UN Commission. But I know he was bribed by the Chinese. That's why he's hanging out with them."

"Hanne, you're not making much sense," Jens was perplexed. "The bottom line is: did you sleep with him?" And he let out another drunken guffaw.

"You stupid pig, Jens. It's none of your business." Hanne was livid. She stood up, struggled to get into the small pocket on her tight skirt to pull out some cash, and threw several bills on the table. "Here, that should cover my share. Thanks for the company. Such as it was, you asshole. Good night."

And she stormed out of the dining room.

Men.

Chapter 40

Hotel Hans Egede, Nuuk, Greenland—Night, Monday, August 4, same day

Still angry, and now regretting that she had agreed to join Jens and his buddies for a meal instead of coming back to the room to work—not least because she certainly shouldn't have chugged Gunnar's Greenland Coffee in her anger and was feeling its effects—Hanne inserted the key card into the slot. Nothing happened at first, so she pulled the plastic card back out, turned it over and reinserted it. This time, she heard the click and pushed the handle down to open the door.

As she stepped into the dark room, she was startled by two muscular arms that wrapped around her from behind, grabbing her breasts, strong knees and chest shoving her inside.

"What the—" Hanne muttered, struggling, hearing the door slam shut behind her. Eerie light seeping in through the window from the outside illuminated the dark shapes of the furniture in the small room.

"Hanne, it's me." She recognized the voice, as Lock spun her around still holding her tight, pinning her against the wall with his body.

"You bastard, let me—" Hanne started to yell, but her words were smothered by Lock planting his mouth on hers, wanting to kiss her. She turned her face away, but he grabbed it with one hand, his fingers digging into her cheeks as he forced her lips toward his.

"Hanne, I love you. I want to marry you," her assailant said when he came up for air, sliding her further in the room and slamming the inner door between the little hall and the bedroom shut behind them.

Hanne spat the forced kiss back at him and struggled to free herself. Lock responded by slapping her hard, and when she reeled and almost fell over, grabbed her by the blouse, ripping it off her.

Crazed with lust and anger, he yanked her back towards him, then bent over her now-naked shoulder to be able to see to unclasp her bra. The side of his head was next to her face and she saw her chance, biting into his left ear, pressing her jaws together with as much force as she could muster.

"You bitch!" Lock yelped in pain, grabbing for his wounded ear. She turned and almost got away, but bleeding profusely, he lunged after her, tackling her by the legs. Her fall was broken by the bed and she felt his hands grope up her thighs inside her skirt. "You're going to regret that, you stupid little cunt."

Lock stood up, and straddling her legs, lifted her with two hands by the back of her skirt and threw her onto the bed, popping the button and tearing the garment off her body. Knees on her buttocks, he deftly unbuttoned and took off his shirt. Next, he unzipped his pants, then, as Hanne tried to struggle, bent her right arm back until bones almost snapped, and when she felt the tears of pain gathering, with his left, he pulled his pants and boxers off, throwing them in the corner. Naked, he laughed as he tugged her panties off, and when she tried to kick him, grabbed her foot and twisted it until her knee almost dislocated.

Lock straddled Hanne, her face in the pillows. She

looked sideways, only to see him reach for the tube of body lotion she had left on the night table. The next thing she sensed was the shock of his two fingers pushing the cold cream up into her bottom…

"Okay, baby, now we're going to have some fun," she heard him say, as he dabbed some lotion on his erect member. She cried out from the pressure and pain she felt as he shoved it into her rectum.

"No, no, please…" Hanne sobbed, but Lock moved inside her with a rhythmical motion that, as she struggled, seemed to her as if someone was sawing her in two. Indeed, she felt that body and soul would never be one again. And then, after what seemed an eternity of pain and humiliation, his sudden release, his fluid spewing way up inside her…Thank God, the sawing stopped and the pressure and pain eased.

A few moments passed, punctuated only by Hanne's sobs and Lock's still heavy breathing.

"I hope you enjoyed that as much as I did, my dear," Lock spoke condescendingly, seemingly from far away as he sat on her legs. "I've now done what I call the holy trinity with you—fucked you in all your orifices, bitch. It's something I like to do with all my women." He got up, slapping her on her firm buttock, and muttering, "So I'm a happy customer," as he went to the bathroom to clean himself up.

Hanne lay there on the bed, whimpering, lower insides still hurting, the outside world far away. Slowly, she turned over, just starting to think about standing up to try and get away when Lock came back into the room.

"Well, well, doesn't the ravaged damsel look lovely? Are you ready for some more action, my dear?" the Australian posed the rhetorical question. Viciously, he grabbed her by the ankles and yanked her over to the edge of the bed, forcing her legs apart, kneeling down between them. Before Hanne knew what was happening, his face was in her pubic area, his lips on her labia, his tongue attacking her clitoris. She struggled for a moment, still trying to escape, then forced her mind to leave her body while Lock continued to violate her nether parts with his tongue and lips…

And then, once he himself had hardened again, he moved up on her, hands groping everywhere, and leading with his tongue that licked her body all over, until it reached her mouth, which it penetrated the same time his penis entered her vagina.

All over again Hanne thought she would die as the sawing motion resumed in another orifice, punctuated by the loud rasping crescendo of Lock's breathing. But this too, came to an end, as the brute she had once thought she loved shuddered to a second orgasm on top of her.

As she lay there, violated—Lock completely cold on top of her—Hanne mustered the strength to shove him from her with disgust, and turning away, said: "You bastard, Lock. You rotten son of a bitch. Get the hell out of here, you pervert. Before I call the police."

"Okay, Hanne. If that's what you want," Lock answered as he stood up and started to get dressed. "But this was so you would never forget me as a lover."

And Hanne knew that she always would remember him. But with hate, not love. Still sobbing, she was glad when he closed the door behind himself and left her in peace.

No, in turmoil.

CHAPTER 41

Nuuk, Greenland—Tuesday, August 5, next day

Hanne was dragged out of deep slumber by the phone ringing on the night table. For a moment, she thought she was back in Copenhagen and reached out beside her to poke Jens into action to get it. But the ringing continued, and as she moved her battered body across the bed, the events of the night before came streaming back into her brain: all of it, the shock, the trauma, the pain, the confusion and the humiliation. She shuddered as she remembered, momentarily reliving the unreal terror in her mind.

It was the wake-up call she had asked for the evening before, and Hanne realized she had to hurry now to make herself presentable for her first meeting with the prime minister and his cabinet, and the official swearing in session.

She dragged herself out of bed and took her time to inspect her face in front of the mirror and then her body in the shower: a few scrapes and bruises from all the violence the night before, but otherwise, no apparent great damage, at least physically. Nothing that the hot shower and some body lotion—*God, that had been a lifesaver,* she thought to herself, without that it could have been really much more painful—would not make feel better.

Once dressed in her signature red suit and white

blouse, with a bit more make-up on than usual to hide the bruises, Hanne looked out her window across the frontier capital city, out to the inlet, and saw that it was a beautiful northern summer morning, the kind she loved, so she decided to walk the short distance to Hans Egede House.

Prime Minister Malik Rorsen had invited her for breakfast, and, as she descended on the elevator, she realized that she was particularly glad not to have to face the hotel's restaurant where she might run into Jens and his crowd. Or worse still, Lock.

What should she do about Lock? She considered going to the police to have him arrested for what he had done to her last night, but...but she knew it was not that easy. They had, after all, up until very recently, carried on a torrid love affair, and he would surely dredge that up—and possibly all of her active sex life—to show that she was a willing participant. He would no doubt insinuate that she was a whore, and the press would love that, she was sure. The Danish media back home especially would revel in the filth with *Schadenfreude*...And that was not something she wanted at the best of times, but now, with her appointment as a Greenland cabinet minister, the timing could not have been worse.

No, she could not go to the police, not now. She would have to get her revenge some other way. She would have to swallow her pride and her hurt and work with Lock in his capacity as advisor to the Chinese, but she would get back at him somehow, she vowed to herself. She would not let the bastard get away with it.

⁕⁕⁕

"Hanne, you don't know how pleased I am that you accepted my offer," the prime minister said, once they were sitting at the dining table. "Coffee?"

"Thank you, sir. It is I who am honored and pleased to be here."

"You will certainly have your task cut out for you. As you may have heard in the news, the Chinese have made a remarkable proposal to spend twenty-five billion US dollars to help build our extractive industries. It is with this, more than anything else, Hanne, that I will need your help."

"Yes, Prime Minister, I am aware of the offer."

"We have to make sure that this is all done without despoiling our environment. And that enough revenue is produced to provide for Greenland's current and future needs. Like Norway has done, but with even more care and more money put aside. Another pancake, Hanne?"

"No, thank you. I understand the concerns."

"You will need to develop a resource development plan. To cover, say, the next five years. For that, you and your team will have to undertake a thorough survey of all our natural resources. As you know from your previous job, we have something in place, but it needs to be updated and expanded."

"Of course, Prime Minister."

"The Chinese will no doubt want to have their say since they are providing the money. Not too much interference though. We must keep control of our destiny."

"Definitely."

"Hanne, do you know this advisor of theirs? This Australian professor? I met him briefly, as I told you, when the Chinese delegation came to see me."

"Lock McTierney? Yes, he was the chairman of the Sub-commission that gave us the award," Hanne said, hoping not to betray any emotion.

"Of course. Well, I certainly hope you can handle him, Hanne."

"Yes, sir," Hanne said, putting the last bite of the

pancake doused with blueberry syrup in her mouth. *Yes,* she thought, *the brute may have gotten the better of her last night by raping her, but there was no way he would best her professionally.*

౸౸

They walked the short distance to the Landstingssalen, the parliament of Greenland, and then next door to where the cabinet ministers and the chief justice were already assembled for Hanne's swearing-in ceremony in the center of the round council chamber. Prime Minister Rorsen introduced Hanne individually to the chief justice and to each of her eight other new colleagues. The four female cabinet members were all dressed in colorful native ceremonial costume while the four men had on the male ministerial uniform, the same crisp white sweat shirt and black trousers the prime minister wore.

They were beguiling, and Hanne immediately took a liking to all of them, and they to her. The chief justice, too, was charming, and it did not take them long to get through the ceremony. This, too, Hanne thoroughly enjoyed: standing on the massive polar bear rug in the center of the chamber, surrounded by the large tapestries on the wall telling of daily life in Greenland, she repeated the words of the oath as best she could in the Inuit language.

The chief justice had explained to her beforehand that this would be a promise to act in the interests not only of all the peoples of Greenland, but also of all the animals on the land, the birds in the air, the fish in the sea, the plants in the soil, the rocks in the ground, the ice on top—in short all of nature. This she was proud and pleased to swear.

After the ceremony, Prime Minister Rorsen laughingly told Hanne that out of respect for her, they were passing on the traditional toast with seal blood, which was meant to fortify both the body and the spirit. Instead, he welcomed her to his team with a local beer called Eric the Red, brewed with two thousand year old ice harvested from Greenland's glaciers.

ఞఞఞ

Prime Minister Rorsen accompanied Hanne to her very first meeting as minister for natural resources in an adjacent conference room. When they entered, on one side of a table Hanne saw three Greenlanders, while on the other sat three Chinese and Lock. She took pleasure in seeing the surprise on Lock's face when she threw him a glance.

The Prime Minister quickly introduced the locals—one more Danish than Inuit, the other two the other way around—to her as her new colleagues, and then, going over to the stunned Lock, addressed him: "You must be Professor McTierney. I believe we met a few months ago."

"Yes, sir. Very nice to see you again." And turning toward Hanne, "Hanne—"

"This is Hanne Kristensen, the new minister for natural resources for Greenland. But you do know each other, I believe."

"Yes, sir. Ms. Kristensen and I are well acquainted." Lock jumped in as Hanne refused to say anything. She finally squeezed out a distant "Good day, Professor," before moving to the first Chinese standing patiently beside Lock.

After the introductions, Rorsen left, and Hanne took charge of the meeting.

"Thank you for coming," she said looking at the

Chinese scientists, but avoiding Lock's eyes. "We are particularly grateful for the offer your government made to help us build our extractive industries. Over the next few months, we will be completing a resource survey of Greenland and the offshore subsea territories under our jurisdiction, including those recently awarded to us. With your input, we will then develop a five year development plan that will meet the objectives of both Greenland and China."

"Excellent," Lock answered, having recovered enough from the surprise that Hanne was now the minister he would have to deal with, to take charge of the Chinese side. "There is one area where we believe we could move relatively quickly. We are aware that a lead-zinc mine has recently started operating on the shores of Citronen Fjord in Northern Greenland. We believe that development of this mine could be speeded up and radically expanded. It would be in both Greenland's and China's interests to showcase how our cooperation is working early on."

Hmmm, that was where Jens and the Green Liberation Front boys were headed. The mine they wanted to protest at.

"We propose that we go to the mine site to examine the possibility of such an expansion. We have at our disposal a plane that could take us there as early as tomorrow, if that works for you, Madam Minister." Hanne did not like the rush, nor the facetious tone in Lock's voice.

Nevertheless, she did agree to go, but only the next day. She hoped if she called Richard right after the meeting he would be able to get to Nuuk in time to join her on the trip. He did say he would work something out to come and see her. And she needed someone she could trust at her side.

⌘⌘

After the meeting, Hanne caught up to Lock in the corridor, tapping him on the shoulder.

"Can we speak for a moment?"

"Of course, my dear, any time." They moved away from the chatting Chinese and Inuit. His condescending tone infuriated Hanne.

"Listen, Lock. You were a real bastard last night, and normally I would never have anything to do with you again. Except in court. Unfortunately, my job and the interests of Greenland demand that for the time being, I work with you, and I am reluctantly willing to do that. But, if you ever so much as touch me again, I will go to the police and expose you for the fraudulent and corrupt son-of-a-bitch sodomist and rapist that you are. Or better still, I will kill you myself. Is that understood?"

Hanne did not wait for an answer, but turned around and stormed down the hall after the three members of her new team.

⌘⌘

"Hello, Richard." Back in the hotel, Hanne was sitting on the bed in her panties.

"Hanne, great to hear from you..." She had caught Richard still in his office, finishing up for the day.

"Richard, could you come? To Nuuk. As soon as possible. In fact, can you get here by tomorrow night?"

"What's the rush?"

"The minister for natural resources needs you. Her trusted advisor," she said in her sexiest voice. "I need you, Richard. Friend, partner. Lover."

"Well, if that's the way you put it!"

"You know, that Australian is here. The chairman of

our Sub-commission. He is now advising the Chinese. I don't trust him. I need your help."

"Hmm…"

"Richard, please? Please! Come. Tomorrow…"

CHAPTER 42

Nuuk, Greenland—Morning, Wednesday, August 6, the next day

"Okay, Kayi," Hanne said to the pretty young aboriginal petroleum geologist sitting across the desk in her new office. "I want you to get quotes from three exploration firms that can work with you to help update the oil and gas survey."

A knock on the door and Hanne's secretary, Aniuk, poked her head in.

"A call for you. From Washington. A Mr. Ron Hall. He says it's urgent."

"I better take it. Excuse me, Kayi. Please put it through, Aniuk."

⁂

"Hello, Ron. What a pleasant surprise…"

"Hello, Hanne. Yes, indeed. But I am afraid what I am calling about is not all that pleasant. Other than to congratulate you on your appointment. That was well deserved, I'm sure."

"What is it then, Ron?"

"Hanne, I've just been informed by Naval Intelligence that our radar has picked up a squadron of six Russian submarines approaching the northern coast of Greenland."

"God! Do you know what's going on?"

"We have no idea. They are still a ways from entering Greenland's waters, and may not, but we've put Thule on alert. We thought that your government should be made aware ASAP. And, since we haven't yet officially recognized an independent Greenland and you are now in the cabinet, after consulting with the president, we thought this...informal channel between us would be the best way to let your government know."

"I better inform the prime minister."

"Yeah. But no need to panic. Not yet, anyway. You know what, Hanne—maybe try and get in touch with your friend in Russia, the minister for the Arctic over there. That guy Laptov. See what gives..."

"Hardly my friend. But good idea...If he'll talk to me."

"This is all highly unusual, but you know, we're concerned that it could be a ploy by the Russians to counter the Chinese offer of money to help Greenland with resource extraction. The Russians certainly won't want them in the Arctic game. It seems that they want to control not just the half of the Arctic they recently annexed unilaterally, but...well, as much of it as they can in whatever way works."

"Hmm. You may be right."

"Yeah. We clearly don't like this kind of show of force. Anyway, find out what you can, if you don't mind..."

"Okay, Ron."

"And let me know if you learn anything."

"You, too, keep me posted on their movements up there, please. In fact, Ron, I am planning to be up in that area—at the Citronen Fjord—tomorrow afternoon. My secretary will be able to patch a call through if need be."

"Good, Hanne. Best of luck to you. Bye for now."

"Good bye, Ron. And thanks."

※

"Prime Minister," Aniuk had made the call and put it through for Hanne. "I just had a talk with a highly placed friend in Washington. He was putting us on alert unofficially that their naval radar has picked up six Russian submarines nearing our waters in Northern Greenland."

"What?"

"The Americans are concerned that it could be a counter to the Chinese helping us with our resources. According to them, the Russians will not want the Chinese in the Arctic."

"Well, let's see how this plays out…"

"Sir, you or I could call Pavel Laptov, their minister for the Arctic. You told me that he came to see you, and I know him from the UN Commission. Maybe he could throw some light on what their intentions are."

"Good idea, Hanne. Hmm, perhaps it might seem less…how should I put it, panicked…if you called."

"Of course, Prime Minister. I would be glad to give it a try. I'm sure he'll remember me."

"I don't doubt that for a moment. Let me know what he says."

"Sure, Prime Minister."

"Thanks, Hanne. And you know what: let's drop the titles. Just call me Malik."

※

Hanne kept Kayi waiting for another few moments while she had Aniuk place the call to Moscow, to the number she had for Pavel Laptov. But the secretary came back after a few moments to report that the minister was not available, and the person she had talked to was not authorized to give out his private numbers.

Hanne did leave a message though, that Greenland's minister for natural resources had called.

Chapter 43

Hotel Hans Egede, Nuuk, Greenland—Afternoon and Evening, Wednesday, August 6, same day

As soon as she entered her room, Hanne kicked her shoes off, threw her briefcase on the bed, and, as was her habit, clicked the remote to turn the TV on. She was climbing out of her pants when her attention was attracted to the screen by mention of "...the Citronen lead-zinc mine..."

With her turtleneck already over her head, she started focusing. The young Inuit news reporter was standing outside the local offices of Goldenrod Mining Corporation, just down the street in Nuuk.

"In a remarkable statement today, Goldenrod Chief Operating Officer Derek Tate announced that a team of activists from the Green Liberation Front have blown up the entrance and the access road to the Citronen Mine, and that, as a result, further operations have been suspended indefinitely. Shares of Goldenrod and Ironlode—the other owner—lost twenty-four and twenty-one per cent respectively in today's trading on the Vancouver exchange. The three criminals—and these were the COO's own words—have been apprehended by mine officials at the site, and Goldenrod and Ironlode are considering legal action against the Green Liberation Front and the individual perpetrators..."

"Oh God, Jens! What an idiot," Hanne muttered to herself, unclasping her bra as she headed into the bathroom to run a steaming hot bath. "I should have stopped you."

Through the open door, she heard the newscaster drone on: "The attack in Northern Greenland was part of concerted protest activity launched against several sites by the Green Liberation Front in response to a recent ruling by the UN Commission on the Limits of the Continental Shelf parceling out jurisdiction over resources in the Arctic. "It is reprehensible that the United Nations is condoning, and in fact leading, the doling out of large chunks of the pristine Arctic for exploitation by a small coterie of rich nations. Natural resource extraction in this sensitive environment should be forbidden, and the entire Arctic zone should be turned into a world nature reserve and a world heritage site," commented the head of Green Liberation Front International, Paul Fichte.

"Additionally, the usual concerted Front protests have been reported at the coal mine at Barentsburg on Svalbard, at BP's Liberty offshore oil drilling site in Prudhoe Bay, Alaska, and at the Polaris lead-zinc mine off Little Cornwallis Island in the northern archipelago of Nunavut, Canada. Russian authorities today also reported the arrest of five Green Liberation Front activists who were caught just as they were preparing to drop depth charges in an attempt to break the gas line connecting the newly opened Shtokman gas field in the Barents Sea to mainland Siberia. Sources in Moscow claim that the police may have been tipped off. Nevertheless, it is clear that the action in Northern Greenland was by far the most destructive of the series, and indeed quite atypical of the Green Liberation Front in the extent of damage and economic loss it has caused for the companies involved. And, of course, for Greenland as well…"

Hanne dunked her head underwater to drown out the remainder of the newscast. She had too much else to think about, and did not have the mental energy to devote to the actions of Jens and the Green Liberation Front.

☙❧

The phone rang. Hanne was many miles away, still lingering in the bath, which by now had become lukewarm, so it was time to climb out anyway. She had just been lazily indulging herself after a tough day at the office, thinking not of the very flawed men that surrounded her, but of Kristi. But she did hope it was Laptov calling back, as she grabbed a towel to wrap around her dripping body on her way to answer.

"Hello, Hanne." It was Richard.

"Hi. Am I glad you're here." At least he was less flawed than all the others.

"I just got in. I'm in room 303. Give me half an hour and we can meet for a drink. Upstairs…is it, the bar? Dinner too, I hope?"

"Of course. I'm all yours."

And that, certainly, was more than Richard had hoped.

☙❧

He was already there, she saw, at a far corner table drinking a beer, when she entered through the door. Hanne had dressed up in her sexy black cocktail dress and pearl necklace and earrings—perhaps a little over the top, just for dinner in Nuuk, Greenland, she told herself when she saw her image in the mirror on the way up in the elevator…

She knew she was stunning, because all eyes at the long bar turned towards her. It was mainly men—Nuuk still had the aura of a frontier town, now full of oil men, geologists and mining engineers—and she could tell with glee that every single one of these lonely beings was lusting after her. It did occur to her—a little late maybe—that perhaps it was the wrong message to portray after the abuse she had suffered the other night, but she could just not help making herself look good.

They hugged at the table, and when she sat down, Hanne was pleased that Richard, too, could not stop feasting his eyes on her. She asked for the Chilean Sauvignon Blanc before Richard posed the question that he had pondered all the way over on the long flight.

"So, Hanne, what was the rush? Other than that you could not wait to see me, I hope."

"Certainly that, Richard. But I desperately need someone with a clear head around me now. And someone I can trust. You're it, my friend. Other than my girl friend in Copenhagen, but she would hardly be appropriate."

"Okay, so I'm here. Tell me what's going on."

Over drinks and dinner, she told him everything that had happened and everything that was being planned, except what Lock had done to her. That, she kept to herself until the very end of the evening. The moment when Richard obviously wanted to come into her room, after an altogether unsatisfying good night kiss in front of her door.

"Richard, come in," Hanne said, opening the door, and stepping in first. "But not for what I know you want." She closed the door behind Richard and went over to the mini-bar. "There's one more thing I need to tell you. But only if you pour us both a cognac first." She had already had a lot to drink, but yearned for the sensation of the brandy burning inside her. To burn the memory of that bastard Lock away once and for all…

When he had poured the drinks, and she had taken a

solid gulp, she sat him down beside her on the bed and said, "Richard, I have to tell you this so you understand where I am coming from. I was brutally raped two nights ago. Sodomized. Here in this very room…" She fought to keep the tears back.

"What the—Hanne, who? No, no…You poor thing…" Richard was stunned; he could not fathom what Hanne was telling him.

"Never mind all that. I have put it behind me, and eventually, I will get over it. That is why I desperately wanted you here, so that I could feel secure. I need someone around whom I can trust and turn to…Someone who can protect me, if need be."

"I understand, Hanne." Richard put his arm around her and she laid her head on his shoulder.

"…And Richard, I wanted you to know this now, so you understand. Well, that I am just not ready for sex. With time, I'm sure I will be, and I will let you know when, believe you me."

"God, did you report it to the police?"

"No. But I have my reasons."

"Is there anything I can do? Tell me who did it, and I will kill the bastard!"

"No, Richard," Hanne stroked his chin, "No. You will not do anything of the kind. I have it all under control. But thank you." Hanne stood up before continuing. "Now, I want you to go and get some rest. I know you are tired. We leave early tomorrow for Citronen, and I will need you to have your wits about you there."

"But…"

"No, Richard, there are no buts. And Richard, just so you know, I love you. But please go now."

And she ushered him out the door with only a quick kiss.

Chapter 44

Greenland—Morning, Thursday, August 7, the next day

Hanne was surprised by the large contingent of Chinese assembled early the next morning at the small terminal facilities of Nuuk Airport. She recognized the three from the meeting two days before, plus there were another two: these, though, were huge men—Mongolians, not Han Chinese, she told herself—most likely some kind of security guards. Together with Lock, the Chinese team made up six of the nine passengers, with Hanne and Richard and one of Hanne's trusted colleagues, Kristian Oreson, the geologist she had brought in as deputy head of the Geological Survey of Greenland, filling out the balance. Oh well, the Chinese were paying for the flight, so she could certainly not argue.

Lock must have read what was on her mind, because he came over and said: "Hanne, good morning. You must have heard the news that some activists from the Green Liberation Front have destroyed the entrance to the mine up there."

"*Ja*," Hanne said, looking away, trying to limit her interaction.

"Some Danes, they say. Friends of yours?" Lock asked, laughing.

Little did he know how close to the truth he was.

"Well, that'll make our job that much harder," he continued when he again got no meaningful response. "I brought along a few extra hands in case they mean trouble. But I think the mining company officials have taken them into custody. And we'll bring them back here for trial."

Hanne pointedly ignored him.

※※※

The flight was uneventful and Hanne slept a little, but for most of the trip, concentrated on the background reading she had wanted to do already two nights earlier. Mostly she was happy that despite the tight quarters, she could ignore Lock.

Fortunately, the landing strip at Citronen had been extended at the beginning of the summer to allow for increased use now that the mine was supposed to be fully operational. Even so, the CJ4 needed the full length, and pulled up right at the edge of the drop off to the fjord. Hanne was glad to deplane, and, as she went down the steps, marveled at the beauty of the inlet, now dotted with mini-icebergs, at the end of which she could see the snow-white glacier flowing into the azure blue water.

A tall, thin man stood at the bottom of the stairs, greeting everybody.

"Hi, I'm Derek Tate. COO of Goldenrod."

"Hanne. Kristensen."

"Yes, Ms. Kristensen. I am so pleased to meet you. I have heard so much about you. And it is a real honor for us that you have chosen Citronen for your first visit as minister."

"Well, Mr. Tate, our friends from China have some interesting ideas that we would like to discuss with you."

"So I understand. But first, let's go and have a bite of

lunch. You must be hungry." Tate led the way toward the three makeshift buildings a few hundred meters away. "Oh, by the way. That's the entrance up there," he said, pointing halfway up the bluff, "To the mine. Or what's left of it after those Green Liberation Front thugs detonated that bomb there two days ago."

"Perhaps afterwards we can take a look?"

"Yes, of course. We've opened it up a bit, and built a make-shift access ladder…"

&ᴏ&ᴏ

It was after lunch, and Tate showed Hanne to his room, which he said he was glad to offer to her for the overnight. He would sleep with the men in the miners' bunkhouse. Since the explosion, the mining operations had come to a virtual standstill and many of the workers had gone south for R&R, so there was ample space to house everyone.

As Tate went to open the door, Hanne was surprised when from behind the hut, Jens and his two friends appeared in handcuffs, being roughly pushed along by what must have been some of Tate's men, aided by two of the Chinese. They looked like they had been roughed up a bit.

"Excuse me," she said to Tate, and then shouted, "Jens!" running after the small troop. The honor guard slowed down the pace, allowing her to catch up.

"Jens, you are an idiot. But never mind, I'm glad you're alive."

"Hanne…"

"I don't know where they're taking you, but I'll get you out. I'll get the prime minister to give you a pardon." She said this, even though she remembered that she had warned him that she would not intervene. For the moment, though, she was glad she did not have to deal with her former boyfriend: she already had enough on her mind.

Chapter 45

Citronen Fjord, Greenland—Afternoon, Thursday, August 7, the same day

"Come on, Hanne," Lock said, "Let's go and look at the mine entrance. Derek says that it's just a short walk over, and it should be an easy climb up the access ladder for someone as fit as you."

"You sure you don't mind if I don't come with you?" Tate asked. "I can get one of the guys to take you up there…"

"Naw. You and your men have got a lot on your hands. Besides, it would be good if our engineers got to know each other before we get down to work. And, as you say, we can't really get into any trouble up there."

"You're right…"

"Where's Richard? I'd like him to come along," Hanne said, looking around and noting the sour look on Lock's face.

"He's in the ops room with my men. I'll send him along. Kristian is an old friend, and there are a couple of things I'd like to discuss with him, if you don't mind."

"By all means."

ఇఇఇ

It took the three of them around fifteen minutes to

walk to where the ladder started up the bluff. As they got closer, Hanne saw that the damage caused by the bomb had, in fact, been a lot more serious than she had thought.

The last twenty-five meters of the narrow road that meandered up the side of the bluff had been blown away at the crest, making access by road impossible. The only way to the mouth of the mine was straight up the steel ladder, which, at the top, had been replaced by a makeshift wooden one after the explosion. Plus, the mine entrance was a mess of rock and debris, over which, once they got up there, they would have to clamber.

No wonder the company officials had been livid, Hanne thought to herself. This work stoppage will cost them the rest of the season's output, wiping out any hope of profits and putting them significantly in the red. The newscaster had been right: this was way more disruption than typically the Green Liberation Front wanted to cause. Something must have gone wrong…Stupid, stupid Jens.

Richard launched himself into the ascent first, followed by Hanne, with Lock bringing up the rear. It took them a good ten minutes of climbing straight up with a few stops to catch their breath before Richard crawled over the rim, coming to the big boulders and rubble strewn across the entrance by the bombing.

"Phew, that was a tough climb," Hanne said as she straightened her fleece, feeling the sticky discomfort of perspiration inside her turtleneck.

"Boy, they've sure made a mess of this," Lock observed.

"Yeah," Richard concurred, picking his way over and around the rocks and debris.

"Nothing that can't be quickly remedied with Chinese ingenuity and money," Lock said, surveying the scene as he moved into the mouth of the mine. "I'll get Shen Wong, the chief mining engineer, up here with a couple of his guys, and he'll have a plan in no time. It's not as drastic as it looks."

"What about the access road?" Hanne asked.

"I'm sure they'll devise a solution. A mini-rail system would probably make more sense anyway. It would be cheaper in the long run, less costly to build, and they have lots of experience in using them in their mines in China. But I'll leave it to them—they're the experts. They'll come up with the best solution."

Hmm, Lock was good. Very good, Hanne thought to herself. Too bad he was such an amoral bastard.

"We'll come up here with the gang later today and tomorrow, generate some ideas, cost them out and make a proposal to you, Madam Minister, and to Goldenrod and Ironlode. And once you all agree, we'll get going on it. It's as simple as that."

ღადღ

But, my life will be simpler and safer, if you fall down the cliff, just as I have planned, my dear, Lock thought to himself, as he watched Hanne's lithe body scramble over the rocks in the mine entrance. *I simply cannot have you hanging out there, with the prospect of exposing me at any moment, and putting my whole life in jeopardy. You gotta go, my dear, I'm sorry, even though we did have a good thing for a while...And maybe I sort of even loved you. Too bad, but you just have too much on me...*

"I think we've seen enough for now. As I say, I'll be back up later with the team."

"Yeah, I think there's nothing more we can do up here," Richard agreed, heading toward the top of the ladder to start the descent, and looking out over the fjord. "But the view sure is magnificent." And then he grasped the bit of steel railing left embedded in the rock after the bomb explosion and started the climb down.

"Don't crowd him. Give him some space," Hanne heard Lock say behind her, as Richard's head disappeared over the rim.

A moment later: "Now. It's probably okay now…"

Hanne approached the edge.

She felt the impact of Lock's shoulder in the middle of her back, and she would have gone over the lip, if she had not grabbed the twisted steel rod left in the rock just at that very moment. Instead, it was Lock who hurtled down the cliff, tripping over Hanne's outstretched leg as she fell to the side.

"Holy shit!" Hanne heard Richard from over the edge. "What was that?"

"Richard, please…" Hanne whimpered, shaken, not daring to look down.

Richard's head appeared back above the verge.

"I can't believe it." He looked back down the cliff. "Did Lock just fall?" But he saw the mess at the bottom.

"No, Richard. He tried to shove me over the side. But it was he who went over…"—she was sobbing now, so Richard sat down behind her and put his arms around her—"…hoist by his own petard." She surprised herself with this Shakespearean quote at this difficult moment.

And then, after a pause, wiping her eyes with the sleeve of her fleece: "The bastard. He deserved it. I didn't tell you, but he was the one from the other night…"

߷

They sat there for a good twenty minutes, Richard holding the still trembling Hanne, who was not ready for the tough climb down the ladder after what had taken place. She had wanted to get revenge on her former lover, but she never imagined it would be like this.

"It's beautiful up here, Hanne. The view. You should look." Richard tried to distract her.

But Hanne could not get her mind off Lock flying over the edge, and could not help wondering what would greet them down below.

So, for another few minutes, they sat there admiring the beautiful grays and browns and blues and whites of the landscape, with the fjord as its majestic centerpiece.

And they watched breathlessly as six black metal sharks surfaced, one after the other in succession.

"Incredible!" Richard said, standing up. "Those are submarines. Only the Russians have that many up here."

"That's them then. The ones Ron Hall told me about. Let's get down there."

The spell had been broken, and Hanne was all activity again.

Chapter 46

Citronen Fjord, Greenland—Afternoon, Thursday, August 7, same day

By the time Richard and Hanne reached the bottom of the ladder, they had observed that from every submarine two Zephyr rubber dinghies had been launched, with what Richard counted on the way down as eight or ten armed men in each. It was truly impressive: within less than twenty minutes from the time the subs surfaced, a force of over a hundred Russian soldiers had landed.

Hanne hurried past Lock's broken remains, looking the other way, leaving Richard to ascertain that he was truly dead. When they finally arrived at the mine buildings, armed men were swarming everywhere. They nodded at the groups of soldiers as they passed them, and Hanne led the way to the main office, where, as she entered, she saw that Tate was standing in discussion with three officers.

"Ms. Kristensen. I'm so glad you're here. This is Captain Zaitsov of the Fourth Submarine Brigade of the Russian Northern Fleet. Captain, this is Hanne Kristensen, Minister for Natural Resources in the government of Greenland."

"Pleased to meet you, Captain," Hanne said, as the handsome naval officer clicked his heels together, took her proffered hand and nodded his head in a little bow, saying in beautiful English: "The pleasure is all mine, Ms. Kristensen."

"What, may I ask, is the purpose of your mission, Captain? You are no doubt aware that an unauthorized landing such as this constitutes an invasion of Greenland's sovereign territory." Yes, she was rapidly growing into this role of being a government minister, Hanne thought to herself, proudly.

"Madam...Minister,"—boy, this guy was good—"We are here in support of Greenland's independence. Not in violation of it. We are taking protective custody of the mine until the international community can be assured that it is being operated in accordance with Greenland's interests. We have rounded up and taken prisoners five Chinese, some of whom have already revealed to my men that they are working for Chinese intelligence..."

"Hmm..." Under duress no doubt, Hanne thought.

"...As well as a group of three men who claim they are with the Green Liberation Front, but who are probably also paid Chinese agents."

"Captain Zaitsov, the Chinese are here as guests of Greenland, and I ask you to release them immediately." Hanne showed appropriate anger. "Also, those men from the Green Liberation Front. They are definitely not Chinese agents. I can vouch for them."

Zaitsov did not acknowledge her intervention but continued. "Moreover, we are here to put pressure on the United States of America to honor your government's legitimate request that the Thule base be returned to Greenland."

"And how long do you intend to be here, Captain?"

"My orders are to stay until the Chinese have left the area and we are certain that the mine is secure and operating normally. And we see signs that Greenland's sovereignty, which Russia has guaranteed, is being honored by all parties."

"That could be a long time, Captain. I don't think you are aware, but a few days ago, there was a bomb placed at the mine's entrance which has effectively closed it down. Now, unless your men are trained mining engineers and prepared to work with us to get the mine up and running as quickly as possible, you better release those Chinese technicians and let us get on with the job. Clearly, I can't order you to leave, so I will put up with you and your men, provided you don't get in my way."

"All right, Madame Minister. We will release the Chinese, but keep a watch on them day and night."

"By the way, Captain…And Mr. Tate. A man…Lock McTierney…fell to his death at the mine entrance a few minutes ago."—Hanne had managed to squash her guilty thoughts of Lock's 'accident' while she dealt with the crisis of the Russian landing—"…You better send some men to collect his body."

"What? How?" This from Tate.

"He tripped and fell. The access is unfortunately not as safe as you were led to believe," was all Hanne said as an answer.

"Of course, Minister…" Hanne liked this Russian more and more. Perhaps she might even be able to use him—and his troops—to fix the mine access. He will no doubt be glad to give his men a task while they're waiting around for the US to hand back Thule. Which could be a long time, maybe never, she told herself.

"Mr. Tate, I need to make a call or two on this radio phone, but I would like to do this in privacy, once everyone leaves."

"Yes, Ms. Kristensen."

"Richard, can you go with Captain Zaitsov to make sure the Chinese are released and Lock is…well…taken care of? And then can you and Kristian go back up to the mine entrance with the Chinese engineers and some of Mr. Tate's men…"—Hanne turned to the Captain—"…and if you, Captain Zaitsov, have some engineers on board your submarines, we would welcome their participation. To help start the preliminary assessment of what needs to be done to reopen the mine."

"Of course, Hanne." This from Richard.

"Yes, Minister…"

"Great idea, Ms. Kristensen…"

Yes, she was really getting into this role of Ms. Minister. Especially when she saw grown men jump to her orders like these three were doing.

൪ൠ൪

When everyone had left the office, Hanne dialed the prime minister's number.

"Hanne, how is it going up there?"

"Well, Prime Minister –sorry, Malik—the Russians have landed. They are here, just as we thought, to counter the Chinese influence, and to try and get the Americans out of Thule. So far, they are not causing trouble."

"Good, Hanne. We certainly could do nothing about it if they did. So the best way to get them to leave is diplomatically. And I know you are very good at that."

"Thank you. I will try my best."

Hanne liked working with this man.

She made one more call, and that was to the number Ron Hall had given her. But the mobile was turned off, and there was no answer.

Chapter 47

Washington DC, USA—Afternoon, Thursday, August 7,

"It is in flagrant violation of Greenland's sovereignty," Secretary of State Gilchrist said.

"Which, by the way, we still haven't recognized…" Tom Deacon, as always, was extremely frustrated by how slow the State Department was to adapt to new realities.

"Well, we are simply not going to hand over Thule," Admiral Moore, the head of the joint chiefs of staff made his views known, "not under any circumstances."

"Tom, would you please read the press release again for me," the president asked, addressing his national security advisor.

"Yes, Mr. President."

The announcement was fresh from Andrei Gusanov's office, issued to the press corps in Moscow just twenty-five minutes earlier. It read as follows:

"Just a little over an hour ago, a fleet of six submarines from the Fourth Division of the valiant Russian Northern Fleet landed one hundred and twenty two men on the shores of Citronen Fjord in Northern Greenland, in an exercise consistent with Russia's commitment to guarantee Greenland's sovereignty.

"A large crew of Chinese intelligence agents, some of whom were masquerading as activists of the Green

Liberation Front, had earlier blown up the access to the important Citronen lead-zinc mine, bringing its operations to a halt. The force has orders to remain in place until this situation is remedied, and until there are signs that the United States of America ends its illegal occupation of Greenland's territory with its base at Thule in Northern Greenland, as has been demanded by the newly independent government of Greenland. It is intolerable that the two largest economies of the world are joining forces to exploit and steal the resources of a sovereign country for the benefit of their military-industrial machines. Russia will not stand by and let this happen."

"That sounds pretty aggressive to me," the president said. "And brazen, coming from Russia. By the way, James, have we ever clarified the status of an independent Greenland under NATO?"

"Well, Mr. President, I can't say that there is a clear answer..."

"James, that's not what I wanted to hear."

"Mr. President, it does not seem to matter to Russia that Denmark did not have a mutual defense treaty with them," Tom Deacon said.

"Yeah, we need to drop a few anti-submarine torpedoes there to make it uncomfortable for those bastards." Admiral Moore weighed in. He was interrupted by a knock on the door, as June Stewart, the president's secretary came in and handed Barlow a note, saying: "Mr. President, this just came in from Beijing."

President Barlow glanced at the piece of paper, frowned and handed it to Gilchrist, kicking his chair back and swiveling to look out the window toward the Washington Monument. "Here, James, you read it out. Press release from our friend Wen Shaojing."

"The Government of the People's Republic of China condemns the invasion and illegal occupation of Greenland by armed units of the Federation of Russia. Earlier today, we learned that a force of six submarines from Russia's Northern Fleet landed troops to occupy the Citronen Mine in Northern Greenland, arresting innocent Chinese nationals, there on a mission to advise the government of Greenland, and brutally murdering a contractor retained by the Chinese government. Pursuant to its guarantee of the sovereignty of the Republic of Greenland, the government of the People's Republic of China demands that Russia withdraw its occupation force, release the Chinese nationals illegally held and pay appropriate compensation to both Greenland and China for any environmental, economic and human damages caused during, or as a result of, its occupation. Should we not have a favorable response from President Gusanov within twenty-four hours, China will take the necessary actions to comply with its commitment to the government of the Republic of Greenland."

"The plot thickens…" the president mumbled. "Now the damn Chinese are getting involved. These assholes are going to start a war right on our doorstep!"

"Plus, the Russians want to use this pretext to drive us out of Thule," Deacon observed.

"We cannot let the Russians dictate to us, sir," the head of the joint chiefs of staff took another stab at getting his view across. "We have to evict them from that fjord. By force if necessary."

"Mr. President," Ron Hall piped up from the rear of the Oval Office, "One idea might be for you to give Prime Minister Rorsen a call. After all, sir, the Russians may very well have been invited in by the government of Greenland. They did commit to guarantee Greenland's sovereignty. As have the Chinese. So we don't really have a good fix on what's going on there. And Greenland has pointedly asked us to hand Thule back to them. This is, in my view, a very delicate situation, and one I think that requires diplomacy. Before we jump to any military measures…"

The president looked around the room, and before anybody else could come up with some contrary advice, said: "You're right, Ron. Tell June to get Rorsen on the line."

⁂

Hall stepped out of the Oval Office, and came back a few minutes later with the president's secretary.

"Mr. President, the prime minister's office is trying to find him, and he will call as soon as they get to him."

"Thank you, June."

"Mr. President," Ron interrupted while he thought he still had the initiative, "I know the new minister for natural resources in Greenland. She, in fact, happens to be up there in Citronen, where the Russian submarines landed. Perhaps I can get through to her, and we can get a closer reading of the situation that way."

"Good idea, Ron. Why don't you go with June and give it a try…"

⁂

"Okay, gentlemen, then we have decided," the president was just summing up what had been agreed by the crisis committee while Ron Hall was out trying several times to reach Hanne. Without success.

"I authorize overflight of the Russian submarine force in Northern Greenland and the dropping of several depth charges, with the objective of driving away and, if necessary, maiming, but not outright destroying, one or more of the subs. Loss of life is to be limited, and for any further action you are to come back to me, Admiral. Thank you everyone."

Heaven help us, Hall thought to himself, as he filed out of the Oval Office behind a beaming chairman of the joint chiefs of staff.

CHAPTER 48

Citronen Fjord, Greenland—Morning, Friday, August 8, next day

Hanne dreaded the moment when she would come to the spot below the cliff where Lock's once magnificent body had lain, broken and oozing blood. She was sorry that she had not gone up close to see his shattered remains; now all that was left there to mark his fall was the blood stained, snow patched earth.

And the rest, where was it now, where had Richard buried it? She made a mental note to ask him later.

The fall that she had helped by stretching her leg out…Yes, she had killed him. But it was in self-defense, she told herself. And the bastard deserved it, after what he had done to her. The law of the jungle was sometimes better than man's version, which would have taken years of wrangling, and which would probably have let him go free and besmirched her reputation, ruined her life. Yes, it was right that he died, but all the same, she did feel pangs of guilt.

She and Richard were bringing up the rear, following the small troop led by Kristian, consisting of the Chinese geologists and mining engineers, a few Goldenrod and Ironlode professionals as well as four of Zaitsov's men, who, he claimed, were naval engineers and scientists. She was sure though, that they were there mainly to keep an eye on the Chinese and to report back to the captain at the end of the day.

Hanne was almost all the way up the steel ladder when she first heard the sonic boom of the jets, and by the time she struggled over the edge, and, out of breath, turned around, the three planes had come in view from behind the bluff. Richard and the two Russians, who were just clambering over the boulders and into the mine, also looked up to the sky.

The airplanes flew over the fjord in tight linear formation, sweeping low: within seconds of their appearance, Hanne saw them drop several slender objects into the water with a splash as they raced away. They were almost directly overhead again when she heard the muffled booms one after the other and saw huge geysers of white water erupt around the submarines, the bow of one of which popped completely out of the fjord with the force of the explosion right in front of it.

"Holy shit!" she heard Richard exclaim, as the two Russians exchanged heated words that she didn't understand, before rushing to climb back down the ladder.

And in the next moment, there was a high-pitched swooshing noise, as something sped through the air overhead like a comet in pursuit of the planes, released from the submarine furthest away from shore.

"That's a bloody cruise missile," she heard Richard say, pointing. "The Russians must be fucking bombing Thule!"

"God!" was all Hanne could mutter.

CHAPTER 49

US Base at Thule, Greenland—Morning, Friday, August 8, same day

"Holy Mother of Christ!" Private First Class Jessie O'Reilly, brought up as a devout Catholic in South Boston, mumbled to himself out on the tarmac as he saw what he knew was a cruise missile streak down from the sky toward him. And then, a few seconds later, a loud and sinful "Fucking hell!" as the missile made a direct hit on the radar building up on the hill above the base.

O'Reilly watched in horror as what had been the strange looking ten-story structure with the high-tech radar on top disappeared in a ball of fire. Later, he remembered somehow sensing, rather than directly seeing or hearing the activity around him: within moments, planes were scrambled to seek out the enemy, and fire trucks screamed in the direction of the explosion.

Making his way as fast as he could to the Command Center, he thanked the Lord that he had not been on duty up at the radar at that very moment, but then felt a pang of guilt as he realized that a number of his friends would have been annihilated by the bombing. He said a quick prayer under his breath that death would have come quickly to them and they would not have suffered.

Later, he remembered also praying in his daze that

there would only be one single cruise missile, and thanking the Good Lord and his patron saint, James the Lesser, as well, that the one that had arrived had not been nuclear tipped.

༺༻

Inside the big room that served as Thule's Command Center, it was all activity. Blind without its own formidable eye on the sky, Thule was relying on its communications lines with NORAD command center inside Cheyenne Mountain in far away Colorado.

Jessie went over to where his buddy Hank Lorimer was sitting with earphones on his head, and tapped him on the shoulder.

"Hank, what the fuck's going on?"

"Bloody cruise missile. Russian. Those subs we've been watching up in Citronen. The radar blown to smithereens. Twelve or thirteen dead up there in the tower, we think…"

And Hank reeled off the names: his best friend, Les, and…Jessie knew all the others well, too; he had trouble fighting back the tears. Lorimer confirmed that it was a single rogue cruise missile, released after three of the anti-sub fighter bombers had gone from the base to overfly and warn off the Russian submarines on the orders of the president—what, less than an hour earlier. Cheyenne had confirmed that the submarines dived immediately and went silent. All except for one, which limped to shore, wounded in the waters of Citronen, knocked out by a depth charge dropped by one of the anti-subs.

The planes at the base had not had time to take off in time; the ultra-modern radar had picked up the signal, and the command had just been given…But the distance from Citronen was just too short for a proper response.

So it was tit-for-tat. A radar installation for a wounded nuclear sub. Twelve, maybe thirteen men, his buddies, for…How many Russians? They didn't have a count.

And what would come next?

For this, Hank did not have an answer.

Chapter 50

White House, Washington DC, USA—Morning, Friday, August 8, same day

"Mr. President, we're in the Situation Room," David Barlow heard his national security advisor say over the phone. "Thule has been hit."

"Thule? What, those Russian subs in Northern Greenland?"

"Yeah…"

"You gotta be kidding, Tom."

"No, Mr. President."

"The bastards. Any loss of life?"

"Twelve, Mr. President. The count so far…"

"Collateral damage?"

"The radar was destroyed. Completely…"

"Hold your post. I'll be right down."

℘℘℘

It took the president a couple of minutes before he was down in the Situation Room in the basement of the White House, and just as he entered, Bill Connelly, the secretary of defense, mooted that it was pretty sure that the order must have come from Gusanov himself.

Settling into the chair at the head of the table, Barlow asked, "Why do you say that, Bill?"

"Well, Mr. President, it seems that our friend Gusanov has taken a personal interest in the Arctic. Plus, it fits in with the fact that he is a control freak, and we certainly know that he wants to make Europe dependent on Russia for energy and minerals. And he definitively wants us out of Thule."

"All makes sense…"

"Moreover, he has made it very clear that he will keep the Chinese out of the Arctic at any cost," Tom Deacon added. "The press releases certainly reflected that they are gearing up for something up there. As a matter of fact, it is very convenient for them both that Thule is gone."

"So, gentlemen, where do we go from here?"

"Mr. President, we cannot take this lying down," the chairman of the joint chiefs of staff was not shy to make his opinion known. "I recommend that, as a next step, we bomb the Russian naval base at Severemorsk, Murmansk."

"Admiral, isn't that a bit heavy-handed? Next thing we know, they will be bombing New York." *God, this guy is too much of a hawk,* Barlow thought to himself. *He's got to be replaced soon.*

"But, Mr. President, we have to teach these bastards a lesson…"

"Come on, Bob, I'm not going to bomb Murmansk into the Stone Age. That's a large city with lots of civilians."

"Mr. President, we have to retaliate somehow. And that would be the next level of escalation."

"Listen, Bob, I don't give a damn what the next level of escalation called for by your military doctrine is. I want a sensible solution with a minimal, or better still, absolutely no loss of life. Ours or theirs. I am not going be the president who starts World War Three."

"Well, Mr. President..." The admiral, feelings seemingly hurt, shrank back in his chair.

"Have we called in the Russian ambassador?" Barlow asked, looking at Gilchrist.

"He's back in Moscow on consultations. His chargé is meeting my deputy even as we speak. We are, of course, expressing our dismay in the usual language appropriate in such circumstances."

"Okay, all you well-paid, smart guys. What other options do we have?"

"Mr. President, may I?" From the back row, Ron broke the silence that had descended on the more senior occupants of the chairs around the long table.

"Of course, Ron. Your counsel is always wise."

"As I mentioned yesterday, I am friendly with Greenland's new minister for natural resources. Some time ago, she told me about an exchange she had with Pavel Laptov, Russia's minister for the Arctic, before she was appointed to her post..."

"Yes? Do go on."

"Mind you, it was at a social function, at a reception at the United Nations, but it has stuck with me as possibly being relevant at some point. Laptov apparently made the surprising statement to her, that he believed that the decisions being made by the UN Commission on the Limits of the Continental Shelf were...well...if not arbitrary...but certainly very divisive and potentially destructive. He expressed the view that the Arctic should become some sort of world nature reserve or something. Basically, a zone free of resource extraction and nuclear and other arms..."

"Interesting, Ron, but what's the point?" James Gilchrist, the secretary of state, asked. "That's certainly not consistent with what Gusanov said. And whatever they are doing up there now with those submarines."

"I guess, sir, my view is that we could use this opinion expressed by a senior Russian government official—someone we know Gusanov listens to on Arctic issues—to explore whether we could engineer just such a result. We could let it be known to Laptov that we would support such an outcome—that is, a resource extraction and nuclear-free Arctic—and he might just be able to get Gusanov and his colleagues to agree and back down from this crazy situation we are finding ourselves in. And it would benefit us—and in fact the whole world—in many other ways not to have to pursue an arms race in the Arctic."

"Hmm…What about the Chinese?"

"If we can get the Russians and Greenland on side, I think the Chinese will have to agree. They will have no leg to stand on. Of course, we will need Canada's support, and they have not always seen eye-to eye with us on Arctic issues, but such a peaceful solution might suit everybody. It just might work, sir, if we put our weight behind it. It might defuse the current situation."

"Mr. President," Admiral Moore interrupted. "I disagree with Mr. Hall. There is no way the Russians will buy in." And, turning to Ron, he continued: "What about Thule, my friend?"

"For the time being we could draw the line at 80°North. Thule falls just outside," Ron improvised. "But as part of the deal, we could agree to a time-frame to de-arm the site and withdraw, provided that the Russians also make a concession regarding arms somewhere further south as well…Say, Kaliningrad. The details could be worked out, but at least this would be a start. And some kind of a framework would be in place."

"What if Bob is right and they don't agree?" This from the secretary of state.

"Then we can still bomb Severemorsk." *And start World War Three,* a frustrated Ron thought to himself. "But at least, Mr. President, you will have tried to avoid hostilities without showing weakness."

The president had been listening to Hall and the other advisors, and he knew that it was the moment for a decision to be taken. Possibly, the most important decision of his presidency.

"How long would you need to explore this option?" he asked Hall.

"The more time, the more chance of success…"

"Mr. President, you will also have pressure from congress, the media and the American people to take decisive action," Gilchrist reminded the president.

Barlow was silent for a moment, then stood up, leaning forward on the table.

"Gentlemen, I'm going to give the Russians an ultimatum to withdraw from Northern Greenland within forty-eight hours, or they will face reprisals for their savage bombing of a US base and the killing of American citizens. James and Tom, I want you to stay behind and draft something along those lines. Ron, you get off your ass and see what you can do through your friend to bring about the resolution you suggest. I am prepared to take the political heat in the meantime."

"Yes, Mr. President." And Ron was halfway to the door when he heard Barlow mutter more to himself than to the assembled advisors: "Hmm. I like that. The Arctic, a world nature reserve. Could be a nice legacy…"

CHAPTER 51

Citronen Fjord, Greenland—Afternoon and Evening, Friday, August 8, same day

"Hanne, I'm so glad to reach you." It seemed it had taken Hanne's secretary a very long time to patch the call through to Goldenrod's operations at the Citronen Mine, and it had taken Tate, who had answered the radiophone several minutes to haul Hanne out of the meeting with the mining engineers.

"Ron, I tried to call you…"

"And I, you. But I'm happy we're talking now and that you're okay."

"Ron, what's going on?"

"The Russians sent a cruise missile to Thule. Destroyed the radar and killed twelve."

"Yes, I saw it being fired after you guys blew one of their submarines out of the water."

"Hanne, listen. That is what I am calling about. There is a very small window and an even tinier chance for us to stop this lunacy from escalating. The guys back here want to bomb one of the big Russian bases in retaliation. And possibly Murmansk in the process."

"God help us!"

"Yes. It will be World War Three before we know it. But I managed to convince the president to hold off for forty-eight hours. I remembered what you told me…You know, about that conversation you had with Laptov at that UN reception. That dividing the Arctic was madness and would end up…Just as we are seeing now."

"Yes. Exactly."

"Didn't he also add that his view was that the Arctic should be a zone free of nuclear weapons? With no resource extraction allowed…A world nature reserve or something like that?"

"Yes…"

"Well, if we could get to him…If *you* could get to him, that is, and suggest that the USA would support such a stance if he could engineer it with his government, then that might allow us to defuse this situation."

"What exactly do you have in mind?'

"We haven't worked out all the details. I thought you could help. But for a start, something along the lines that, say, above 80°N latitude, no extensions of EEZs would be permitted."

"*Ja.* Hmm…"

"…And that the entire sea area above 80°North falling outside EEZs—you know, like in the case of Greenland—would be declared a world heritage site, a world nature reserve and a nuclear free zone. And, of course, as Laptov himself proposed, no exploitation of resources will be permitted in this area."

"That would mean that Greenland and Canada would have to give up on the recent awards…"

"Well, yes. But we could also add something the Canadians will like. That any vessels entering it will need to meet stringent design standards to maximally protect the environment."

"Hmm. That is quite radical. Isn't that…the package, I mean, something like what the Green Liberation Front has been proposing?"

"I don't know, Hanne, but it picks up on what Laptov

said to you, I think. The situation is...rather fluid. Tell him that if he agrees the principle, we would be happy to negotiate the details. Including some phased withdrawal from Thule. You can give him my private number and tell him that I am authorized by the president to discuss this with him. But I need you to make the first call for me, since he knows you personally, and you might be able to get through. We have to use these back door channels because we cannot get mired down in the bureaucracy. Time is of essence, and all this crap at our front doors needs to be defused."

"Okay, Ron, I'll call Laptov right away. But it's late there…"

"Try anyway. We don't have much time. And he needs to get to Gusanov as soon as possible."

꽃꽃꽃

"Minister Laptov? I am so happy to have caught you." Hanne had called his office number, and was surprised and glad to have found Laptov there, even though in Moscow it was getting on to midnight. "But you are working late."

"Yes, yes. The times are difficult. Listen, Hanne—if I may call you that—now that we are ministerial colleagues, we should use first names. I never did like all that formality."

"Thank you, Pavel. I'm the same way."

"But, Hanne, what is so urgent that you call this late?"

"Well, Pavel…"

"Yes, yes, I know, you don't like that our submarines are up there in Northern Greenland and that we have sent a cruise missile to bomb the radar at Thule. I tried to stop it."

"That's just it, Pavel. We must put a halt to this.

Otherwise we will have World War Three on our hands and the Arctic will be destroyed. And that's exactly what I'm calling about."

"Good. But what do you have in mind?"

"I just talked to someone I know in Washington who is an advisor to President Barlow. I had told him about the discussion we had—remember, at the reception back at the UN—when you said that all this dividing up of the Arctic will not end well, and that we should rather turn it into a world nature reserve and not allow resource extraction there?"

"Yes, that is still my personal view. Although…"

"Well, Pavel, my friend assures me that the highest echelons of the US government see that avenue as a possible way of getting out of this mess. Avoid World War Three and save the Arctic too. If Russia and the US could agree that, for example, above 80°N latitude, there would be no extensions of EEZs, and that all the rest of the ocean up there that falls outside the EEZs beyond this latitude would be declared a world heritage site, a world natural reserve and a nuclear free zone, we think that we can swing Canada and Norway. And Greenland will support such a stance, even though we lose the new awards. Not that we count for much. But that would be all the relevant countries. The other Arctic Council members and the observers will no doubt be happy. Except for China maybe. We could also all agree that no exploitation of resources will be allowed in this zone, and any ships entering it will need to meet stringent design standards and register with national authorities. The rest of the details we could negotiate later."

"Sounds ideal. What did they say about Thule? You know that is a sore point for Russia."

"For Greenland, too, as you are aware. But my friend did say that some kind of phased withdrawal and handover to Greenland could be possible. We would certainly press for that."

"Hanne, I doubt that I can get our politicians…how do you say…on side. Although I know Admiral Maslenkov, who is in charge of the Northern Fleet where those submarines belong, would agree."

"Pavel, this is our only chance. Otherwise the Americans will escalate…"

"Hmm. Hanne, thank you. Thank you for your efforts. I will try my best."

"Good. And thank you. Call me when you have something. On 004540711395. Day and night. I am flying back to Nuuk in half an hour, and after that you can reach me again in four or five hours. And, Pavel, here is my friend's number in Washington. In case you can't reach me or want to check out that what I am saying is true. His name is Ron Hall. 202 874 9321. Good luck."

"You'll hear from me."

∽∽∽

Hanne was exhausted after the conversation with Laptov, but mustered enough energy to place a call to Hall to report that she had reached the Russian minister for the Arctic. And that he promised to do his best. She also told him that she would leave immediately for Nuuk, and that she would contact him again when she arrived at the hotel.

Hanne knew she had to make one more phone call though, before she could leave: to Rorsen, her boss, to inform him of the latest developments, including the proposal to create an Arctic Nature Reserve. Although this would mean that Greenland would have to yield much of the newly won subsea territory, she was sure she could cast it in a positive light.

After all, if this would result in the withdrawal of the Russians from Citronen Fjord and the return of Thule by the Americans, it was a price worth paying, she reasoned. Greenland was rich enough in minerals and fossil fuels to spend all the Chinese money developing the resources currently under its jurisdiction several times over, without touching the hard-to-get-at underwater deposits further north in the newly awarded subsea territories.

Hanne was glad that Rorsen was receptive and agreed to think it over. As a good politician, he seemed to understand that what seemed to be on offer was a worthwhile compromise.

CHAPTER 52

Citronen Fjord, Greenland—Evening, Friday, August 8, same day

Hanne hurried over to the building that served as the canteen for the miners working at Citronen, thinking that the mess would be the best place to find the pilot of the Cessna. While she was talking to Hall and Laptov, she had made up her mind to go back to Nuuk as soon as possible. She would be able to achieve more from there, she told herself. With events happening so rapidly around her, she needed to be where communications were better than they were at the remote mine.

Hanne bee-lined for Rolf, the pilot, who was sitting talking to his counterpart who worked for Goldenrod, and told him that her position in the cabinet made it necessary for her to fly back to the capital immediately. Rolf stood up and excused himself to go and make the preparations for the flight, while Hanne went over to where Richard, Kristian and Tate were sitting and talking over a six-pack of Musk Ox ice beer that the Goldenrod COO had broken out.

"Hi, Hanne," Richard greeted her as she approached. "Come and have a brewski with the guys!"

"*Hej*. I'm sorry, but I'm going to have to pass. I have to go back to Nuuk immediately. I've just asked Rolf to make the plane ready."

"What's up?" Tate asked.

"Oh, just the usual ministerial stuff. Richard, will you come back with me?"

"Of course, Hanne. With this crisis in the making, I need to get back to Ottawa myself as soon as possible."

"Would you please inform Captain Zaitsov that we are leaving on the jet—just so they don't shoot us down. Then bring Jens—those three Green Liberation Front activists along. That is, with your permission, Derek. I will take responsibility for them."

"Of course. As a minister of the state, I can't very well stand in your way."

"Thank you. And, Derek, thanks for your hospitality. Kristian, will you stay behind and coordinate the Chinese team? Tell them we're taking the plane now, but we'll send it back for them tomorrow. Greenland will cover any extra cost."

"Ja. Of course, Hanne."

છ৩છ

Once the CJ4 was at cruising altitude, Hanne briefed Richard on the calls to Hall, Laptov and Rorsen.

"You know, Richard, if we go this route, as I told my prime minister, Canada and Greenland will have to give up the jurisdiction over the extended EEZs that we fought so hard to win. I think I can swing it in our case, because Greenland has so much untapped wealth and even undiscovered resources that we could easily spend the Chinese money and generate enough surplus for a nice little sovereign fund for the future. And in any case, as you well know, much of the new subsea territory awarded to us would be difficult and expensive to exploit even with the latest technologies."

"Well! If the proposal is that the reserve includes

everything outside the traditional definition of continental shelves and EEZs—although I'd have to look at a map—I think Canada would potentially have the most to give up. Other than Russia, of course, which has unilaterally claimed half the Arctic."

"Hmm..."

"But, as you say, that is difficult territory to exploit up there. And thinking about it, Canada would gain a great deal, especially if the principle of vessel registration and monitoring is accepted by all Arctic countries. This is a huge issue for Canada, and one that threatens its control over its existing territories and northern waterways."

"Yes, I know."

"But this whole concept should also work further south...Perhaps one idea to incorporate in your proposal would be that countries can extend the principle of an internationally recognized world nature reserve within their own territorial waters to...say...as far south as the Arctic Circle."

"Good point, Richard. I think Greenland would like that option as well."

"This would give Canada the monitoring rights it has been seeking over ship traffic in the several variants of the Northwest Passage."

"How do you think we should proceed with your country?"

"Leave that to me, Hanne. I will fly back to Ottawa and brief the minister for foreign affairs personally. And all the other relevant officials. Just before leaving, I had the deputy minister on Tate's line saying Ottawa is very concerned about these developments."

"Of course, you could be next..."

They were served drinks by one of the crew, and Hanne took hers and went to sit in an empty seat in the back beside Jens.

"You have to admit, Jens—that was pretty stupid what you did up there. Very destructive. And totally unnecessary."

"Not so, Hanne. In fact, it was very important."

"It will cost Greenland and the two companies significant lost revenue."

"But the mine is causing pollution and destruction of the Arctic environment. Besides, the point was to demonstrate against the politicization of the Arctic. And its willy-nilly parceling up—"

"Look, Jens, you know very well that the Green Liberation Front already has a bad reputation in Greenland, because of its stance on seal hunting. Which, as you know, is the lifeblood of the aboriginals. And the whales. You have managed to turn yourselves into demons among the native people."

"But I know they also don't like these dirty mines."

"Okay, Jens. I will make a deal with you. I will ask Prime Minister Rorsen to give you and your colleagues amnesty, provided you are willing to go on Nuuk Television to make a statement that you regret the damage you caused at the Citronen mine. And that your Green Liberation Front will cease its unilateral disruption of any type of corporate operation in Greenland. Instead, you will work with native communities, the government, and companies operating in Greenland to ensure that environmental concerns are maximally taken into account."

"Hanne, that's just a lot of bullshit and you know it."

"Hear me out, Jens. Part of the deal that I am offering is that I, and some well-placed powerful people—who shall remain nameless for the time being—are working on convincing the five countries with Arctic Ocean coastlines to create a world nature reserve above 80°North. Along the lines you were always proposing to me. And we are making good progress."

"Cool..."

"Let me finish. Of course, this is all confidential for now, and if you breathe any of it to anybody, I will make sure you rot in prison and never speak to you again. Part of the outcome I hope for is that the Green Liberation Front can work with the Arctic Council as a whistle-blower if forbidden activity, such as resource extraction or nuclear weaponry of any kind is observed in the proposed reserve. But for that, you guys have to start working more *with* government authorities as opposed to always against them."

"Hanne, this is becoming more interesting. Let me discuss this with the Green Liberation Front International folks..."

"First, you think about it, Jens, and write out a little statement along the lines I suggested and let me see it. Then I will talk to the prime minister and we'll go from there."

"Hanne, thanks," Jens said, as Hanne stood up to go back to her seat. "I still love you, you know..."

But if she heard, Hanne did not respond.

CHAPTER 53

Kremlin, Moscow, Russia—Morning, Saturday, August 9, next day

"Thank you for agreeing to see me first thing on such short notice," Laptov said, as he approached the large desk behind which sat the diminutive figure of Gusanov. Selfishly, he was pleased that Andrei was such a workaholic, and that he had found him at his desk at 6am on a Saturday morning, because he knew he did not have much time.

"Is it about the ultimatum, Pavel?" Gusanov grumbled.

"Well, yes, but not exactly…"

"What then?" Unfortunately for the minister, the president was not in the best of moods.

"Through my sources, I am led to believe that the Americans will bomb Severemorsk—no doubt, also not sparing Murmansk—if we do not withdraw the submarines from Citronen Fjord."

"Out of the question. Until they leave Thule. Or at least give us a tight plan of withdrawal that we can watch them carry out."

"If I may…There could be a way around this mess. A way where everybody wins. But it needs a little compromise from everyone, including us."

"What the hell are you talking about, Pavel? Get to the point, man!"

"Based on my information," Laptov had thought through what he was going to say, so he was unruffled by the president's ire as he continued. "I believe the Americans would agree to a situation whereby a world heritage site and a world nature reserve are created above latitude 80°North, within which no resource extraction is allowed and no nuclear activity…"

"Pavel, you have lost your fucking mind. The cold has addled your brains up there at the North Pole. You talked to me about something like this once before…I don't give a shit about a world heritage site, nor a world nature reserve. I will never agree to give up our half of the Arctic. It is our birthright, and you, of all people, know that."

And what a half that will be, Pavel thought to himself, *if we, the Americans and the Chinese are firing cruise missiles and dropping nuclear bombs all over.*

"What about Thule?" The president continued when Laptov remained silent. "What do your goddam sources say about Thule? They still have a huge air base there, even though we took out the radar…"

"They said that they would negotiate a phased withdrawal."

"For sure only if we give up one of our bases in the north. Or our new radar at Kaliningrad. Yes, that will be it certainly." Gusanov stood up and looked out the window. "Fuck that, Pavel. The answer is no. I am not buying this crazy scheme."

Laptov knew he had lost, and knew he would now have to go to Plan B. To save the Arctic, to prevent a Third World War, as Hanne had said.

But Gusanov was not finished. He came back to the desk, sat down, took up his pen and started signing papers. After a few moments' silence, he said, "By the way, Pavel. I want your resignation on my desk within twenty-four hours. And get the hell out of here before I have you arrested for treason, you old fool."

༄༅༄

Lying awake in his bed before the early morning meeting, Pavel had rehearsed the entire scenario. It had gone exactly as he had predicted. He prided himself on knowing his colleagues well, and Andrei Gusanov had not disappointed him.

No, he had known all along that this would not work.

But he had to go through the motions, to legitimize what he would do next.

Plan B.

And that is why, as he approached Gusanov's desk, he had switched on a mini camcorder in a special button given to him by Sergei in New York he had sewn on his jacket. He had captured the entire exchange, and the old Arctic fox knew that this could be his launch pad.

But he would have to move fast with Plan B. Surprise was important, and fortunately, he had laid a lot of the groundwork well in advance.

CHAPTER 54

Hotel Hans Egede, Nuuk, Greenland—Morning, Saturday, August 9, same day

When the telephone rang at a few minutes after three-thirty, Hanne was still awake, not having slept at all.

She had been glad at first that she had gone straight to bed after they arrived at the hotel. On the way in from Nuuk airport, she had hesitated for a moment whether she should ask Richard up to the room, but decided against it, even though he looked longingly after her as they said their "Good nights" and went the opposite way at the elevator. She was just not ready for a man again emotionally, after the attack five days ago.

The one Hanne really wanted beside her, as she lay there in bed with insomnia, was Kristi. Gorgeous, sexy, uncomplicated Kristi. She was the best lover of them all, knew best how to turn her on. Or just to hold her, or talk to her, when that was what she needed. Only a woman could know what another woman really wanted. Hanne missed her, and resolved to call her in the morning.

And then, as she was running the crazy international political situation, she was getting involved in through her head over and over again in the dark, the phone rang. Reaching across the bed, she fumbled before she held the mobile firmly enough to press the green button.

It was Laptov.

"Hanne, good morning. It is early there, I know, but you did say to call at any time."

"Hello, Pavel. Yes, that's fine. What's up?"

"Well. Not good news. I talked to President Gusanov about our plan. He kicked me out of his office, and told me to resign."

"That's terrible. So much for that, then. Goodbye, Arctic, hello, World War Three…But what about you, Pavel?"

"Not so fast. I am not giving up yet. I just got off the plane in Murmansk and am in a car on my way to discuss Plan B with Admiral Maslenkov…"

"Pavel…"

"Don't worry, Hanne. The driver does not speak English. I know Maslenkov will not want to see his men killed in some futile war we are certain to lose. And I know he does not want to see the Arctic destroyed. We have talked about this many times, and he and I agree."

"Pavel, what is Plan B?"

"It is simple, my dear. The admiral orders the submarines back from Greenland and together we appeal to the Russian people to support us in saving the Arctic and avoiding war. Just like you appealed to me…"

"You mean…You mean…A putsch?"

"Well, if that's what you want to call it."

"Pavel, isn't that treason?"

"Hanne, I don't care what it's called. I have had it with these *siloviki*. These corrupt former secret policemen who run Russia only for their own good. I am an old man who loves this country and the Arctic, and these criminal thugs are ready to destroy both. I am prepared to stick my neck out, as you say, and try and save Russia and the north."

"Fabulous, Pavel. You are a brave man. Will the armed forces support you?"

"I will find out. But based on previous conversations with Maslenkov, there are other good men in the top brass who do not want to see this country destroyed."

"What can I do to help?"

"There are maybe three things, I think, that would help. One, if you were able to get the American president to announce that he supports your world nature reserve proposal as a way of resolving the political stand-off in the Arctic."

"It was originally your idea."

"Never mind. And that he will push for it in the Arctic Council and the United Nations."

"I'll get on it right away, Pavel."

"And two, Hanne, work out the exact proposal that makes sense and send a written version to me by email. And by fax, just in case. You have my card. As soon as possible."

"No problem."

"Lastly, Hanne: I sent you an email with an attached video clip before leaving home. Showing my conversation with our president. It will help the cause if we can get it out to the media. On that You Tube, or whatever. After I have talked to Maslenkov, in say…one hour."

"Pavel, you are amazing!"

"You too, Hanne."

"Be careful. And good luck."

"We will need it."

⁂

Hanne had too much adrenaline pumping in her veins after that conversation with the Russian minister for the Arctic to go to sleep, and she knew that the next step in any case would be for her to try to reach Ron Hall. He would no doubt want to know, even though the clock on her cell said that it was just 3:55am. 1:55am Washington time.

"Hello." A sleepy woman's voice answered after the persistent twelve rings. "What is it?"

"Is this Ron Hall's residence? Sorry for disturbing, but this is urgent."

There was silence as Hanne assumed the woman was passing the phone.

"Ron Hall speaking."

"Ron. Hanne. I talked to Laptov…"

"And?" Ron was waking up fast.

"Gusanov did not agree. Threw him out of his office and wanted his resignation. But Pavel is on his way to speak to the admiral who heads up the Northern Fleet. Maslenkov or something. He is sure he will side with him. In fact, Laptov is talking about some kind of putsch."

"That is big news!"

"His plan, I think, is to get the support of the armed forces and then appeal to the people."

"Interesting. Not likely to succeed. And very dangerous. The *siloviki* are well entrenched everywhere."

"I told him, but he is determined. He said it would help if we could get your president to make a statement in support. You know, the usual…Including a broad outline of the proposal. Oh yes, I will work on fleshing out the details to establish the Arctic Nature Reserve…or whatever we'll call it. And I'll send it to you for your comments before I send it off to him."

"Great. I will brief the president and get him to make a statement."

"He also sent a video clip of his meeting with Gusanov. Asked me to post it on You Tube in an hour or so. I haven't looked at it yet, but he said it could help."

After she hung up, Hanne took out her laptop and opened the email from Laptov. Yes, the attached video was good, but perhaps not as devastating as she had hoped. But it would definitely help the cause. She would post it on You Tube in now less than an hour, she told herself, looking at her watch.

Hanne clicked on the remote, knowing that sleep was a lost cause by now. She would have the news on in the background while she turned to the task of starting to write down all the tenets of what she thought the new Arctic Treaty to set up the Arctic Nature Reserve should look like. She was not a lawyer, but had enough to do with international law in the context of her work on the continental shelf extensions that she could even start to write the proposal as a draft treaty, she told herself.

But the half-hourly news summary on Euronews kept her glued to the TV. The report she tuned into took the viewer from capital to capital around the world as the cities woke, capturing the concern in the halls of officialdom as well as the turmoil in the streets over the possibility of international conflict.

Asian markets had crashed, and the prospects for the European ones and Wall Street were dire. Gold and other precious metals, the Swiss franc, and the US dollar had been the big winners.

What really drove the perilous state of the global situation home for Hanne were the pictures Euronews showed of panic buying of food and other household goods, the emptied shelves in the stores in cities throughout Asia and Europe where stores had already opened for the day. Riots and looting in some places. And she was devastated at the thought that this would soon spread to Copenhagen and envelop her parents, her sister, her little nieces, her friends. In short, her entire world. But she was already at the center of the storm…

Just as the half hour report came to an end at 5:00am, Hanne finally turned to her computer to post the video, and then started working on a map showing the Arctic Nature Reserve as she now called it, to serve as an annex to the treaty. She then worked on the draft, before sending it to Ron Hall for his input both on substance and form. And, of course, to Richard, to get the Canadian stance—among the countries that bordered on the Arctic Ocean, that would only leave the Norwegians, and they were not immediately affected and would therefore surely support the concept. Jens too—what a good idea—he would no doubt be able to make it watertight from an environmental standpoint. It would also be an olive branch of sorts—although it was more he who needed to send one her way.

When this was all done, she glanced at the bedside clock: 6:34am. Haven't slept yet, she thought to herself, but these were demanding times. And, as she was more hungry than tired, she picked up the phone and dialed room service. Some coffee, fruit, yogurt and toast to start the day.

Chapter 55

Severemorsk Naval Base, Murmansk, Russia—Late Morning, Saturday, August 9, same day

"Yevgeni, thanks for seeing me on such short notice."

"Pavel, you know I am always ready to make time for you. You are one of my great heroes. Also of my sons and their friends. One of the few true Russians left, men of the North…"

"Thank you, Yevgeni. And that is why I have come to you. Another true Russian."

"How so?"

"We are in a very grave situation. The future of the Arctic, of Russia—indeed the world—is at stake."

"What do you mean, Pavel? Because of Greenland?"

"The last time I came, just a few days ago, was to relay an order from the president to send six submarines to Northern Greenland. As you know, Yevgeni, that order has resulted in bringing us close to open war with the Americans."

"Not good…"

"We lost one submarine and a number of your men were killed. We have destroyed the radar at Thule and killed several American soldiers. You saw the ultimatum from the president of the United States for us to withdraw the force from Northern Greenland. Or else they will escalate."

"Yes, we are preparing our defenses for that…"

"So you should. My sources tell me that the likely target for bombing will be Severemorsk. And then Murmansk won't escape. There will be huge loss of life. And World War Three will be upon us, Yevgeni."

"Yes. Lamentably…"

"We will be at war with not just the Americans, but all of NATO, as well as the Chinese. You saw their ultimatum too. Just think of that!"

"We cannot win such a war. But our forces can cause maximum destruction."

"And they to us. Sadly too, to the Arctic, where this war will all play out."

"Yes. I know."

"Yevgeni, I came here because the Americans have made an informal *démarche* via my contacts. A suggestion that they would like to defuse this dangerous scenario by agreeing to turn the Arctic into some kind of a world nature reserve where no weapons and no resource extraction would be permitted. In short, a preserved area that our children and their children would be able to enjoy."

"Yes, you and I have talked about that kind of a utopian solution to save the Arctic."

"They would start negotiating this—and I will receive the exact proposal shortly—as soon as we withdraw our forces from Citronen."

"Could we get the president to agree?"

"Yevgeni, I have already approached him."

"Oh?"

"I came directly from seeing him to talk to you. Gusanov would not listen to reason. He ordered my resignation, threw me out of his office. And probably already has his FSB friends on their way here to arrest me."

"No way…"

"You will see. I made a recording of my meeting which is quite damning."

"What?"

"Yevgeni, I have thought about it long and hard. The only way this will have a chance to happen is if we appeal directly to the Russian people. Especially the young. Like the Arab spring all across the Middle East and North Africa. But I cannot do that alone—for that to work, I need you and the armed forces behind me."

"Pavel, you are proposing treason. A putsch…"

"Well, yes. But putsches, as you call them, have changed the course of Russian history many times. Most recently, as you know, our drunken friend Boris Yeltsin put us on the path towards democracy when some hardliners attempted such a putsch. Sort of, on the way, anyway…"

"I don't like this coterie of former KGB smartasses who are stealing Russia blind any more than you do. And if this proposal of yours will save the Arctic and prevent World War Three, I am behind it. I think I can get most of my senior colleagues to join our cause. Certainly, the men will be keen. Not one of us wants to fight a war against the US, Europe, and the Chinese all at the same time, that's for sure."

"We have to act fast, Yevgeni. In fact, on the way up here, I drafted this statement, and I have asked Russia 1, Channel One Russia, NTV and some of the other channels as well as the main international networks—CNN, BBC, Euronews, France 24—to be here at noon for some important news regarding the Arctic. We will also have to get the message out via cell phones, the internet, and all these new media that I don't understand—like that You Tube and Twitter and Facebook…"

"Pavel, let me make a few phone calls to my colleagues. But first, I will send the order to Captain Zaitsov to stand down and withdraw from Citronen. And then I will get some of my young technology savvy soldiers to help us get the message out."

"Thank you, Yevgeni. I knew I could count on you, old friend."

Chapter 56

Kremlin, Moscow, Russia—Late Morning, Saturday, August 9, same day

President Gusanov's private iPhone, lying right by the inkstand he indirectly inherited from the last Tsar, started playing his favorite piece of music from Borodin's *Palovtsian Dances*.

"Andrei, can I come to see you? Now? It is rather urgent."

"Yes, of course, Aleksey."

Aleksey Botnikov, a close confidante who joined the KGB the same time he did, now the head of the FSB, did not often call his cell number, let alone to say that he wanted an appointment urgently, so Andrei knew that this was important. In fact, Botnikov must have been already nearby when he made the call, because Gusanov's secretary showed him in within seven minutes.

જીજી

"Aleksey. Please, please sit," Gusanov said, looking up from his papers. "Coffee? Or tea? Or a shot of vodka?"

"Perhaps the latter, given the circumstances."

"Well, I'm sure you wouldn't be here if it was not something urgent." Gusanov took out a bottle of Moskovskaya and two iced glasses from the fridge in the mini-bar behind his desk and poured the clear liquid.

"I wanted to see you because I received some troubling material regarding one of our colleagues."

"Who is that, Aleksey?" Andrei downed his shot without looking at Botnikov.

"Pavel. Laptov."

"What, then?"

"One of the drivers in our pay up in Murmansk whom we use—you know—to keep a check on Admiral Maslenkov…"

"Yes, that is wise of you. Just like in the old times. They cannot be counted on, the military."

"This driver reported to the station head that the admiral asked him on short notice to fetch the minister for the Arctic at the airport this morning."

"Hmm, the old fox was here earlier. Supposedly to relay a ludicrous proposal that came via some sources he claims to have. Something about the Americans wanting to turn the Arctic into some kind of nature preserve. Saying that otherwise they will bomb Murmansk."

"A nature preserve?"

"Yes. Ridiculous. He's become senile, the old fart. Useless. No, dangerous. I asked him to hand in his resignation within twenty-four hours."

"Well, he has now gone to talk to his friend Maslenkov. Those two seem to have become really chummy. And what's more, the driver reported that Laptov had a discussion over the phone in English with some woman—and although he couldn't really understand very well, they talked about some kind of Plan B and appealing to the Russian people."

"Goddamit! Could he be plotting some kind of a putsch? With Maslenkov?"

"That's sort of what I was thinking…"

"Well, get on it, Aleksey. Get your men to arrest the

cocksucker for treason. Maslenkov too. I never did like the little prick. And that woman—she must be that meddling Danish tart who is now Greenland's minister for natural resources, no? Can we get rid of her? She is one fucking dangerous whore."

"Done."

"Good man, Aleksey. Keep me posted."

ఎఇఎ

Ten minutes later, Andrei's iPhone beeped. A text message had come in.

Distractedly, Gusanov picked up the phone, clicked on the message icon and opened the latest missive.

"We appeal to all Russians who love their country, to join us to prevent an unjust war with the rest of the world over control of the Arctic. Such a war would not only destroy the north, but leave our country devastated, with many dead. We support the peaceful solution proposed by the international community, to turn the Arctic into a world heritage site and world nature reserve. If you agree with us, join us in the streets today at six pm."

"What the fuck…"

Gusanov picked up the remote and turned on the large screen TV on the opposite wall. Just in time, to catch the tail end of an interview on NTV with Maslenkov.

"…we were asking for trouble when we landed a force in Greenland. We invaded a sovereign country that posed no threat to us. It was totally unjustified, and I disagreed with it at the time. Clearly, our political masters were in the wrong to order it. It has brought us to the brink of war with the rest of the world, and it is time to step down. Especially when such a neutral, in fact beneficial solution is on offer…"

"What do you mean, Admiral?"

"Under the proposal on the table, Russia will not lose jurisdiction over any of its existing undersea territory. That is, what is currently recognized by the global community according to international law as belonging to Russia. But neither we, nor any other country, will gain new subsea territory. In fact, the recent awards by the UN to other countries that triggered this entire situation will be reversed. Much of the Arctic will be turned into a preserve for humanity, so that our children, and our children's children, can enjoy it."

"Admiral, you are expressing views which we know are not shared by the present government. Some would say your words amount to treason."

"The armed forces of Russia support Minister Laptov in his sensible appeal to the people of Russia. An appeal for peace and rational behavior. It is not in the interests of Russia to fight a war that we are sure to lose against the rest of the world."

ରାର

"Fucking traitor! You defeatist prick, I will have you pilloried." And then he shouted at the top of his voice, "Irena, get me Botnikov. Now, immediately. And Serdyov. General Morozov, too. And of course Dmitri." As Gusanov said this, he picked up the remote, and in his fury started switching around the channels. His finger stopped, momentarily paralyzed, when on CNN, he saw a grainy image of himself spitting words at his minister for the Arctic:

"…Pavel, you have lost your fucking mind. The cold has addled your brains, up there at the North Pole. You talked to me about something like this once before…I don't give a shit about a world heritage site, nor a world nature reserve. I will never agree to give up our half of the Arctic. It is our birthright and you know that…"

The president went ballistic, and tore out of his office, yelling at his secretary, "Where the fuck are they? Why does it take them all day to get here?"

Going back inside and slumping down in his seat, he reflected that at least it wasn't all that bad. At least he came across sticking up for Russia in that tape that shithead Laptov had illegally made and was now circulating.

But then on the TV screen, CNN had switched to a reporter commenting that "…in fact the future of the Arctic has caused a rift in the Russian government, and it seems from interviews of highly placed officials that the armed forces are backing Pavel Laptov, the minister for the Arctic, who was the protagonist in the video we just aired. We have also learned that Laptov and the high-ranking officers behind this action—what in fact could be described as a putsch—have called on the people of Russia to show their support by demonstrating in the streets all across the country today at six pm Moscow time. That will be a critical moment for the future of not just the Gusanov government, but also of Russia and the world. We will keep you abreast of the moment-by-moment developments right here on CNN…"

CHAPTER 57

Hotel Hans Egede, Nuuk, Greenland—Morning, Saturday, August 9, same day

"Who is it?" Hanne shouted, approaching the door of her hotel room in her bathrobe, hair still wet, comb in her hand.

She found the TV remote and pushed the mute button just in time to hear the familiar voice faintly through the thin door.

"Jens. It's Jens. Just bringing the comments on your draft. And that little speech you wanted me to write." Hanne opened the latch to let her glum looking former boyfriend in, and was pleased that he did not try even the two-cheeked kiss.

"Thanks. You must have worked all night on them."

Jens was unusually pale and somewhat agitated.

"Not a problem. I couldn't sleep anyway."

"Sorry. Why?"

He was in no mood to answer that question.

"Here. They're both on this stick. You may want to just load them on your computer and we can talk about them later."

As Hanne reached out with one hand to take the proffered memory stick from Jens, her bathrobe came slightly undone, revealing most of her shapely right breast. Hanne noticed that Jens's eyes did not fail to delight in the revealed flesh: she quickly pulled the belt tighter—she certainly didn't want him to start anything—and moved toward the desk where her laptop was in sleep mode. She leaned over to flip it open, got it revved up again and inserted the stick into a USB portal.

Jens admired the arch of her back, the curve of her buttocks, the body that for so many years he had taken his pleasure of, and he felt a tinge of regret at what he would have to do next…

But he knew this was his chance, the one that he had planned and thought about all night once he had finally gone to bed after his midnight drink with Erik, so he quickly took a step to move in close behind Hanne. And, with one rapid motion, he pulled out the thin metal wire he had positioned to hang from his belt behind his back, slipped it around her neck and pulled it as taut as he could.

"What the…" Hanne grabbed at her throat, gasping for air.

Jens pulled the garroting wire tighter and tighter, but his own being was now spooning the body that he had held naked this way so many times before…Hanne's belt came loose again, her bathrobe flipped open, and he was surprised that he was getting aroused. Did this happen to all murderers? Did they get an erection in the very instant of the crime, he found himself wondering. Or just to him, with the woman he still hopelessly loved?

Hanne was turning blue, no longer able to breathe, on the verge of passing out…

And then…all of a sudden, her air pipes opened again with a gasp, and life-giving oxygen flooded into her lungs.

Jens released his grip on the wire, whimpering, "I can't, I just can't…I cannot do this. Not to you." He turned away, and for the first time in their more than seven-year off-and-on relationship, Hanne heard him cry.

"Jesus, Jens. What the hell was that all about?" Hanne didn't know whether to be angry with, or sorry, for her whimpering ex-boyfriend. Whether to call the police, or to go over to the bed, where he sat with his face buried in his hands, and comfort him. The feelings merged into some kind of strange hatred.

"You bastard, Jens. You just tried to kill me!"

"I'm sorry, Hanne. I didn't really want to…"

"What in God's name does that mean?"

"I am sorry, Hanne."

"It's not something you can brush off by just saying you're sorry."

And then, wiping his face on the sheet, Jens looked up at Hanne. "Look, Hanne…" he started, pausing momentarily to muster some courage for what he was about to say. "Hanne…Listen to me. I have a confession to make."

"It better be good, because I'm about to call the police."

"I have been working for the FSB—you know, the Russian secret police—for a number of years. Ever since I was in jail in Murmansk. They recruited me after that protest against the submarine launch."

"You gotta be kidding! You stupid idiot, Jens."

"They needed plants in the West. Inside the Green Liberation Front. They threatened to kill me and harm you and my parents if I didn't agree. And my nephews and nieces. Plus, they have been giving me money too. Paying me a lot. How else do you think I could afford…"

"Now I am calling the police. I've had enough of this crazy bullshit."

"It was they who ordered me to kill you."

"*Ja*. That would be it." Hanne paused, and then added, as if an afterthought, "But didn't you just say you were cooperating with Russian intelligence so they wouldn't harm me?"

"I still love you, Hanne."

"Boy, you are really messed up!" Hanne shook her head and dialed the front desk to ask them to get the police.

※※※

Hanne saw on the muted screen that the CNN cameras were flashing to street scenes in Moscow and St. Petersburg, and as she put the receiver down and picked up the remote to turn the volume up, the correspondent's voice-over excitedly reported on what she was seeing.

"We have not witnessed anything like this here in Russia since the fall of Communism. These scenes, with millions of people pouring into the streets of the largest cities, eclipse even the demonstrations that brought former President Yeltsin to power in 1991 and put this country on the path toward democracy. It is clear that the people and the military have united with one voice to tell their government that they will not fight an unjust war and that they want another solution to the Arctic than the one vigorously being pursued by President Gusanov. The support is monumental for the respected minister for the Arctic, Pavel Laptov.

"The big question now is whether Gusanov will be forced out and a new government will emerge in this country. Gusanov's remaining power base seems to be the *siloviki*—the former secret service officials he has brought into government and to head up some of the biggest companies in Russia—but it is doubtful that this will be enough to stare down the combined might of the armed forces and the people..."

"Fantastic," Hanne said more to herself than to the still-whimpering Jens. "Good job, Pavel. You wily old fox, you..."

‌‌‌‌‌‌‌‌‌‌‌‌‌‌‌‌ఎఇఎ

A knock, accompanied by someone from the corridor shouting, "Police." Hanne turned the volume down again and opened the door.

"Are you all right, Ms....Minister?" The two aboriginal officers entered, and seeing a broken Jens sitting on the bed and Hanne still in her bathrobe, asked, "What happened here?"

"This...friend...Sort of lost it. Became violent and attacked me."

"Will you be pressing charges?" The more senior of the two police officers asked, as he roughly grabbed Jens's arms to put handcuffs around his wrists.

"Gently, please. This man needs serious psychiatric help. He has to be sent to a clinic in Denmark, but for the time being, take him to a facility here and keep an eye on him. He did try to kill me..."

"Yes, Minister."

"I will talk to Prime Minister Rorsen about his case."

"Of course."

And they carted Jens away as he mumbled in a hoarse voice, "Hanne, I love you. I love you," between sobs.

ఎఇఎ

"Richard?" Hanne was glad to hear a friendly voice over the phone. "You won't believe what just happened..." She told him about Jens's attack, and then asked whether he had any comments on the draft treaty she had sent over in the early morning.

"No, Hanne. Excellent piece of work."

"Good enough for you to discuss with your minister?"

"Yep. And thanks."

"Well, then good luck with him."

"Yeah, and let's hope Laptov wins out in Russia."

"Actually, Richard, I was starting to think beyond that. Assuming that things go our way, and settle down there quickly. I will propose to Rorsen and to Ron Hall that we start thinking about a venue to sign this treaty, and put this messy situation behind us."

"Good idea, Hanne."

"It should probably be the Arctic Council, no?"

"Yes. That's right. And since in Canada we will be the most impacted by it—along with you in Greenland, of course—it would look good if we hosted it, don't you think?"

"Great idea, Richard. Well, that solves that."

"I will see what I can do and let you know, Hanne."

"Terrific."

"Hanne," Richard started hesitatingly, "can I come by for a quick kiss before I go off to the airport?"

"Well, just one little peck. I thought you'd never ask."

※※※

It was only after she closed the door behind Richard, went back into the bathroom, and took off the hand towel she had wrapped around her neck, revealing the thin red mark in the mirror and running her fingertips gently over the throbbing welt, that the monstrous thought hit her.

"Jesus Christ! Wasn't Jens's friend Sven Erikson killed just like this? Garroted with a wire?" She asked her reflection in the mirror. "Jens? Could Jens be Sven's murderer?"

Hanne rushed back into the bedroom, looked around for the instrument of death. She found the thin metal strand on the floor underneath the desk, where it must have fallen after Jens released the tension. As she picked it up, Hanne thought to herself, God, if Jens really was

Sven's killer, the implications were too horrendous. She did not have the time or energy to think them through now. At least he was in custody, and could do no more damage.

But she needed to get in touch with that policeman in charge of Sven's murder. Yes, and take this wire to him…What was his name? Inspector Jakobsen or something like that…And she would need to arrange for the police here to accompany Jens and hand him over to Jakobsen. No, let the Inspector arrange it all…

సౌ

Fortunately, Hanne did find Jakobsen's card.

"Ms. Kristensen. Yes, I do remember. But I never thought I would hear from you again. Is it about that glass of Torrontes I promised to buy you?"

"No, Inspector…"

"Please. Please call me Anders. May I call you Hanne?"

"Of course."

"As a matter of fact, Anders…I am calling from Nuuk in Greenland and I think there is something your investigation may be interested in."

"What do you mean, Hanne?"

"Well, my former boyfriend, Jens Andersen—remember, the best friend of Sven Erikson—just tried to kill me with a garroting wire. The same way Sven was killed."

"You must be kidding. Are you okay? Did you go to the police?"

"Jens is in police custody here. I will speak to the prime minister here…"

"Yes, I heard that you were appointed to the cabinet. Congratulations!"

"…to have him sent to Copenhagen. But you will need

to make the arrangements with the police here."

"Thank you, Hanne. Thank you. And...When you're back, I will definitely buy you not just a glass, but an entire bottle of Torrontes."

Chapter 58

White House, Washington DC, USA—Noon, Saturday, August 9, same day

Ron Hall felt pride swell in his breast as the president of the United States walked up to the podium in the Press Room. After all, he had been instrumental in moving him in this non-bellicose direction, and in fact, in drafting the statement Barlow was about to make.

"Your Excellencies, esteemed representatives of the press, my fellow Americans: I am sure you have been following the rapidly unfolding events in Greenland, and some of you are no doubt aware of the repercussions these are having internally within Russia. As you know, yesterday I issued an ultimatum to President Gusanov to withdraw the Russian submarine fleet that is illegally occupying a position in Northern Greenland and threatening the security of our country. It was this flotilla that was so egregiously ordered by the highest authorities in Russia to bomb our radar base in Thule with serious loss of life and damage to material. The United States has held back from avenging this unprovoked act of aggression pending the response of President Gusanov to the ultimatum. I want you to know that I also sent a message via special channels to the Russian government telling them that if they withdraw this occupying force, the United

States would be prepared to negotiate an agreement with all concerned governments and institutions, within the context of the United Nations, to create a world nature reserve and world heritage site in the Arctic, free of resource extraction and nuclear and other weapons and for the benefit of all mankind. Such a reserve would serve as a fitting memorial to the men and women who gave their lives at Thule recently and elsewhere in the Arctic over the many years. The clock is ticking, and we await Russia's answer. Meanwhile, we are contacting the other member countries of the Arctic Council to be able to move forward with this proposal at the earliest possible moment. Should Russia, however, not respond favorably to our reasonable requests, the United States of America will take all necessary actions to protect its interests and those of its friends and allies. God Bless America."

Ron's pride turned into fleeting gratitude that the phone on his desk hadn't rung until after the president was finished. And then curiosity, when it did.

"Ron, the Situation Room." It was Gilchrist, his boss. "In five minutes."

෴෴

It was the usual mix of military personnel, politicians, spooks and advisors that was already assembled in the room in the basement of the White House, when Ron Hall entered. The president was just sitting down as the screen on the wall showed a large map of the North Atlantic and Arctic Oceans with five small red rectangles off the coast of Greenland and one stuck in a little wedge that must have been Citronen Fjord.

"There." This was rear Admiral John Peters, the vice chief of naval operations, speaking. "They are just about to decamp from Greenland's territorial waters. I wonder what they'll do with the injured sub…"

Several of the eighteen people packed into the small room joined in a loud "hip-hip-hurrah".

"Congratulations, Mr. President," Tom Deacon said from the corner where he was standing, tie loosened, shirtsleeves rolled up, one foot against the wall. "You stared him down. Gusanov, that little prick."

"A far cry from that predecessor of yours who looked into the Russian president's soul through the window of his eyes and saw a God-fearing man he could trust and work with…" Gilchrist said laughing.

"Now, now, guys," the president joined in the laughter, "Let's not get carried away."

A knock at the door; the marine manning it opened it a crack and a piece of paper was handed to him which he immediately took over to Lawrence Richardson, the tall, thin, taciturn man who was the respected head of the CIA.

"Mr. President. Could we turn the TV on?" Richardson asked after reading the message. "Probably CNN, but we may also want to surf the Russian and European channels. This could be big. Really big."

"What is it, Larry?"

"Demonstrations all over Russia."

And then the CNN voiceover kicked in as all eighteen officials in the room glued their eyes to the screen, which showed the main square in St. Petersburg packed with protesters.

"…St. Petersburg, Moscow, Ekaterinenburg, Novosibirsk, Perm, Murmansk…No matter what city you go to, it is all the same here today. This afternoon, the people of Russia spilled into the streets across the entire country in response to a call by Pavel Laptov, the minister for the Arctic, to support the breakaway faction in the government demanding that Russia join negotiations to turn the

Arctic into a world nature reserve and avoid what could develop into a Third World War over the region.

"In Moscow and elsewhere..."The cameras switched to Red Square, which was completely packed with protesters carrying placards and chanting something that none of the eighteen men in the room except for Richardson could understand—"...the demonstrators are calling for the resignations of Andrei Gusanov and the so-called *siloviki*, his powerful friends from the secret service who have been in control of modern day Russian politics and much of the economy. The armed forces have come out in support of Laptov. And, of course, the people of Russia are making their views known. Discreetly, in the streets leading off the square and behind it, we are seeing the appearance of some tanks. Earlier, I witnessed a force of six tanks and several truckloads of soldiers moving down Mokhovaya ulitsa. The big question is: will it come to open fighting, or will Gusanov and his gang resign peacefully?"

"Ron," the president addressed Hall, "anything to add?"

"No, Mr. President. Except, we may just want to check out the video clip of the exchange between Gusanov and Laptov that was posted on You Tube. According to my sources, it comes directly from the minister for the Arctic himself."

"Yeah, we know that they made a wide appeal to the people using the internet and cell phones as well as the more traditional media," Richardson added. "Very clever. Not even Gusanov and his gang could control those networks. No wonder there are so many people in the streets..."

CHAPTER 59

Nuuk, Greenland—Afternoon, Saturday, August 9, same day

"Prime Minister…Sorry, Malik…I still can't get used to calling the leader of an independent country by his first name," Hanne started, with a little laugh, after the usual greetings. "Thank you for seeing me on such short notice. But, as you see, events are moving very fast. Events that—as you well know—could have a huge impact on Greenland's future. I need your help with a few matters…"

"Tell me, Hanne. What's on your mind?"

"Well, I talked to Laptov. As we agreed."

"Good. And?"

"You may have seen on the news that he is now leading a putsch against Gusanov with the support of the Russian armed forces. Quite amazing…"

"Is this your doing, Hanne?"

"No. No. It is all Pavel. He's a brave man. And by the way, the submarines have withdrawn from Citronen. All except one that was damaged."

"Excellent!"

"But the price for all this…And I think it is a very positive outcome all around in fact…could be the creation of a world nature reserve in the Arctic."

"That sounds interesting."

"It would mean giving up our newly won jurisdiction over the extended continental shelf."

"Hmm..."

"My view though, is that, with the melting of the ice-cap, Greenland will have more than enough resources to develop without any additional ones that would now fall into the reserve. It will not be a problem to spend the Chinese money. And even much, much more..."

"I see your point."

"Plus, for Greenland, it would be a great outcome to have a world nature reserve and world heritage site immediately to its north. It would ensure that the High Arctic will be kept pristine for generations to come. And there will be regulations in place to control ship traffic, so that accidents like the one a few years ago with that cruise liner—the *Akademik Kurchatov*—would not happen."

"Yes, it seems like a wise trade-off to agree to, don't you think?"

"That's really my point. I have taken the liberty of starting to draft a treaty proposal to create the geographic and legal foundations for such a nature reserve," Hanne said, taking a file from her briefcase.

"My, you're a busy lady!"

"An Arctic Nature Reserve. Laptov asked for just such a proposal."

"Is this it?"

"Yes. And I am wondering whether you would be willing to go on air today to make a statement that you are sending a draft treaty proposal to all Arctic Council members—not just the eight permanent participants but also all the observers—which by the way will include China—and as well, the indigenous peoples and the various concerned international bodies—to establish such a nature reserve in the Arctic. And that you are calling for a conference in the very near future to discuss this proposal and sign the treaty."

"Good, Hanne. Should we host this meeting here in Greenland?"

"Well, it might be better to get another country, for example, Canada or Norway, to do it rather. Norway is less directly involved, but if we can get Canada behind it, it would make sense, because they would be most impacted by the proposal. Along with us. In fact, I already have my Canadian friend working on it."

"My, you are efficient!"

"Should I talk to Prime Minister Prudhomme? That might help move things along."

"Yes, that would be helpful. To have you put your weight behind it. We also need to think about how we present this to China. If we don't do it right, they could get difficult."

"Perhaps, Hanne, you should go to Beijing and personally explain the situation. We can't have the Chinese messing this up. And we can't afford to lose their twenty-five billion."

"Hmm. I was going to go to Copenhagen where there are a few things I need to attend to…including organizing the transfer of some files from the Danish Geological Survey, now that we have separated."

"You are amazing, Hanne. Hmmm…Maybe you could continue on from Copenhagen and meanwhile I will call Wang Xu, their ambassador to the UN who came to see me and who is a close confidante of Wen Shaojing. To get you a meeting. And I will read your draft and arrange a press conference."

"Thank you."

"Good, Hanne. Anything else?"

"Yes…Malik…There is one more thing. Something…a bit more personal."

"What is it, Hanne?"

"You know, those three Danes from the Green Liberation Front who caused all the damage at the Citronen mine?"

"Yes, aren't they being held by Goldenrod officials until charges can be brought against them?"

"I know all three quite well, and actually brought them back to Nuuk with me yesterday on the plane. I made a deal with them that I would talk to you about amnesty in Greenland, provided they made a formal apology and promised to work with your officials in the future to further the environment. Clearly, all that will need to be worked out in detail."

"Sounds reasonable to me. That is, if you can get Goldenrod to agree to drop any charges."

"One of these men needs serious psychiatric attention, and was taken this morning to the Queen Ingrid Hospital's psychiatric ward pending your agreement that he be sent to a facility back in Denmark. In fact, there is an ongoing police investigation in Copenhagen that could be interested in him."

"Our officers should be able to arrange for him to be handed over to the Danish police."

"Thank you, Malik. I will ask Derek Tate to drop the charges."

"Go on, then, so I can read your draft treaty."

"Bye, I will call you from Copenhagen."

"You are one hell of a woman, Hanne!"

சுசு

Back at the hotel, Hanne placed a call to Ron Hall to update him and to see if the Americans had any views on the draft treaty she had sent earlier. Of course they did, but nothing substantial, so she asked him to send the amended draft to her and to Rorsen. Given that she had done all the work on it, it was only right that the prime minister of her new country should get the kudos for tabling the final version.

After Hanne put the phone down, she turned the TV on to catch the news. BBC had nothing interesting, but Euronews, on the other hand, showed the developing situation in Novosibirsk.

"It is unclear who is fighting whom, or if indeed anybody is fighting anybody," a journalist reported, as he stood in front of a picture of two lines of tanks facing each other. "But there seems to be a tense stand-off here in the central square after a unit of seven tanks from the local Third Armored Battalion cleared the square earlier of demonstrators. They came to mop up an angry mob that, in a gruesome act, had lynched several men accused of being former KGB officials—members of the *siloviki*..." The camera panned to show an avenue lined with trees from some of which corpses were hanging. "...These pictures, horrific as they are, are reminiscent of the Hungarian Revolution in 1956 when the outraged public took their revenge on the secret police who had oppressed and tortured them for so long. The seven tanks in the square..."—the cameras moved back to the open space—"...have, however, now been surrounded by a force of twelve tanks that arrived just less than fifteen minutes ago. We will keep you posted as the situation develops here and we learn more of what is happening in this city..."

Switching to CNN, Hanne saw a window of the same picture in the corner, while the anchor in the studio commented that "...it seems that a breakaway group within the Third Battalion, apparently loyal to Gusanov, was able to clear the streets of demonstrators, some of whom had turned violent, but a larger tank force from outside the city, clearly siding with Admiral Maslenkov and Minister for the Arctic Laptov, has forced them to stand down and surrender..."

And then CNN brought in a feed from Moscow showing General Morozov making a statement which the voiceover translated as follows: "I have ordered the different branches of the armed forces of Russia to support the people in their clearly expressed wish to solve the current international crisis through peaceful means. Any rogue units that disobey this order will be apprehended and tried for insubordination and treason..." The anchor came in over the voiceover and the feed saying "...that although it is still early days in this tense state of affairs in Russia, it is apparent that President Gusanov is losing his control over key elements of the country..."

"Go to it, Pavel," Hanne could not help rooting aloud for her friend, "we're almost there!"

Chapter 60

Kremlin, Moscow, Russia—Evening, Saturday, August 9, same day

"Have we heard from Morozov?" Gusanov shouted into the intercom so that not only his secretary but anyone else out in the atrium would hear.

"No, sir," his secretary poked her head in, answering meekly. "No news yet."

"What the fuck is wrong with the man?" Gusanov asked rhetorically as he slammed the door behind him.

"I will try him on his personal cell phone again," the defense minister, who along with the head of the FSB and the prime minister, had trickled into Gusanov's office over the last half hour, piped up.

"You do that, Arkady. Tell him we want him here half an hour ago, and that his fucking job is on the line."

"We should declare a national emergency." This from Dmitri. "That will allow us to take all necessary measures to stop this rebellion."

"Look! There is that renegade Laptov." Botnikov drew their attention to the muted TV screen. "And he's with General Morozov and Admiral Maslenkov."

"So that's why we couldn't reach the bastard," Gusanov said, as he finally found the remote under some papers and turned up the volume. "He, too, is a traitor.

But why is state TV showing this crap? Why haven't we blocked it?"

"...indeed, extraordinary times. The minister for the Arctic, Pavel Laptov, is entering the legislature accompanied by the head of the joint chiefs of staff of the Russian armed forces, General Morozov, and the officer in charge of the Russian Northern Fleet, Admiral Maslenkov. Laptov is heading for the speaker's podium, and there is total silence among the assembled deputies, no doubt all eager to hear what he has to say."

The camera focused on Laptov, who seemed relaxed and in control. "Ladies and Gentlemen, fellow deputies, honorable members of the government, respected officers of the military, citizens of Russia. Today, the motherland stands at what is probably the most important crossroads in its history. One path leads to a terrible war which has all but started with much of the rest of the world—a war which our military experts say we cannot win, a war which will cause the death of millions of our young and old, the devastation of much of our country and the destruction of the Arctic. This is the desperate road that Andrei Gusanov and his fellow *siloviki* want to take us on. The other path leads to peace, democracy, and over time, the flowering of Russia within a friendly global community, with an unexploited, pristine Arctic preserved for our children, and our children's children.

"This is the path the people of Russia want, as you can see right outside the doors of the White House, our legislature, and in all the centers of population throughout Russia. This is also the path the wise leaders of our armed forces, who are here with me, are telling us is the right direction to follow. Earlier today, Admiral Maslenkov undid the orders of Andrei Gusanov, commanding the submarine force that had been sent to invade Northern Greenland to withdraw and come home. Had he not taken this brave step, it is almost certain that the United States of America would have bombed Murmansk, in response to the launch of a cruise missile from one of our submarines against their radar base at Thule. General Morozov informed me just before I entered these hallowed halls to talk to you, that from the Eastern Military District, Colonel General Selyokov has reported signs of the commencement of mobilization of the Chinese armed forces on our borders.

"Ladies and Gentlemen, we were standing on the very brink of World War Three, and had not our military leaders taken the initiative to opt for peace and explore the solution to this crisis being offered by the international community, disaster would have struck us and the entire world. I stand here before you to defend this course of action and to attest that the government of Mr. Gusanov has lost its credibility, the confidence of the Russian people, and its right to govern. I hereby call for its resignation. Thus, even though we know the constitution grants the president the right to declare emergency rule, we are asking you, my fellow members of the Duma, to take this power upon yourselves. I have discussed this with General Morozov, and he is prepared to issue a command to the military to maintain order throughout Russia during such an emergency state of affairs. We propose that this extraordinary régime be in place for a period of up to two weeks during which you, the representatives of the people, will select an interim government to take control until such a time as nationwide elections can be called in a more orderly manner. Now, if we can proceed to a vote…"

Laptov's comments were greeted by thunderous applause, although several legislators were seen to get up and slink away as unobtrusively as they could.

"I will have them all executed! The bastards...Botnikov, have them all arrested as they come out of the White House."

"They don't have the right to do this. The constitution explicitly gives you the right to call emergency measures in place," the prime minister said. "And even if Laptov and his renegades win a no-confidence motion, it is not binding. Damn them..."

"My men cannot even get near the White House," Botnikov knew that the president would not like this. "And they would be lynched if they moved against any of these traitors. Perhaps better to lay low for now..."

On screen, when the applause died down, Laptov continued.

"Mr. Gusanov, we know you are listening! The people want you and your government to step down. I am asking you in the name of all of Russia to hand in your resignation to General Morozov within the next twenty-four hours, as I will be doing as a member of your government. If you do so, you will be allowed to go in peace; if not, you will be treated as a traitor to Russia. The Duma will start selecting a new interim government to replace yours tomorrow."

Again, applause.

"Shoot the fucker!" Gusanov was red in the face, arteries on his temple close to bursting. "Someone, string the prick up by the balls. Botnikov, for fuck's sake do something. Or has the FSB become totally useless under your command?"

"It seems that the options for President Gusanov and the members of his government are limited," the newscaster commented, as the cameras switched to the scene outside the gates of the Kremlin. "We understand that the president is holed up in his office in the Kremlin, with some of his top advisors, including Prime Minister

Mendeleev, Defense Minister Serdyov and the head of the FSB, Aleksey Botnikov. As you can see, the Kremlin is now surrounded by tanks from the famous Fourth Tank Division, as well as men and artillery from the Thirty-fourth Artillery Division and, of course, thousands of civilians. It is only a matter of hours now, because, as we heard, if the men inside do not hand in their resignation, Morozov's men will enter and arrest them as traitors to Russia. It is astounding how quickly the tables have turned here, and it is all because the people and the armed forces have found common ground in their resistance to an unjust war over the Arctic. Who would have imagined this outcome a month ago…"

And the viewers could see the newscaster shaking his head, genuinely dumbfounded by the course of events. As were they.

Chapter 61

Copenhagen, Denmark—Night, Sunday, August 10, and Morning, Monday, August 11, a couple of days later

Even though it was night—almost ten pm, she saw on her cell phone when she checked for messages—and she was tired, Hanne was glad to be back in Copenhagen, as she followed Jens and the Inuit police officer through the customs zone in the beautiful modern glass Terminal 3 of Copenhagen Airport designed by Vilhelm Lauritzen. She had sat several rows behind Jens on the Air Greenland flight and had tried to catch some sleep, and it was only now that she took a good look at him and saw what a mess he really was. Bags under his eyes, hair greasy, needing a shave and change of clothes, he was obviously suffering from stress.

On the contrary, when she passed through the opaque sliding doors, and caught sight of Kristi, she was bowled over by the freshness and beauty of her girlfriend. She rushed up to her, and they embraced unabashedly, kissing deeply like love-starved partners and holding each other tight for a couple of minutes. Glancing over at them and seeing this, Jens looked even more forlorn.

The two girls only untangled their bodies when they heard a man's voice. "Ahem…Ms. Kristensen. Hanne…" and Hanne felt a gentle tap on her shoulder.

It was Inspector Jakobsen. Overwhelmed by the

pleasure of seeing Kristi, she had totally forgotten that he would be there, in the Arrivals Lounge, to meet Jens and take him into custody. Fortunately, she did remember his first name.

"Why, hello, Anders. How nice to see you!"

"And you..." Jakobsen devoured not just Hanne, but also Kristi, with hungry eyes.

"This is my friend, Kristi. Kristi Olafson. Inspector Anders Jakobsen."

"Pleased to meet you."

"You did find Jens, did you, Anders?"

"Yes, thank you. We met up. But I wanted to arrange to meet with you sometime...Tomorrow, if that's possible."

"To buy me that bottle of Torrontes?" Hanne asked, giving Jakobsen an impish look.

"Well, yes, that...But also to ask you a few more questions. Regarding what happened in Nuuk. And about Sven Erikson."

"Sven Erikson?" Kristi piped up. "I knew him too..." And then turning to Hanne: "What happened in Nuuk?"

"I'll tell you later, Kristi. Anders, I have a lot to do tomorrow. But I could see you around three pm. Does that work?"

"Perfect. And Ms. Olafson...May I call you Kristi? Could you please come too? Since you knew Mr. Erikson as well."

"...and she knows Jens too. Good idea, Anders."

"Fabulous," Kristi gave the inspector one of her seductive looks.

"At three then? See you." The Danish police officer seemed pleased with himself as he said goodbye and made his way over to take charge of his prisoner from the colleague from Greenland.

"He's fantastic!" Kristi said looking after him.

"Yeah. I've been saving him for you. But first, I want you for myself."

"Is that what you meant when you said you had a lot to do?"

"How did you guess? That, my dear, is the most pressing of many things…"

"Let's go!"

༄༅༄

They went back to Hanne's.

It was when Kristi was helping Hanne undress to take their shower together that she ran her index finger along the red welt around her friend's neck.

"That must hurt. It's pretty deep."

"Yeah…A little. It stings more when water gets into it."

"Poor you! I just can't believe that Jens did that." Kristi gave Hanne a deep kiss.

"Well, he did," Hanne said when she surfaced. "The bastard. He tried to kill me. I was completely shocked. And then he confessed that he was working for the Russian secret police!"

"God, how could he?" Kristi slipped out of her panties.

"And you know, I think he may have killed Sven. Although, that is also hard to fathom. They were best friends. Sven was strangled too, with a thin piece of wire. Oh, shit, I forgot to give it to the inspector." They were now both naked.

"What?" Kristi opened the shower door.

"The wire Jens tried to kill me with…" Hanne's voice was drowned out by the water gushing from the showerhead and Kristi's tongue penetrating her slightly open mouth.

It was only in the morning, as she was rushing to get ready to meet with Lise Frondholm, her former boss, the minister of climate and energy, and they had the TV on low in the kitchen, that she learned of events in Russia.

The BBC news report showed pictures, obviously from the night before, of Red Square in Moscow full of people, some sitting on the treads of tanks next to soldiers with flowers in their helmets, and bottles of Nazdrovie and other cheap imitation bubblies being handed around.

"Holy shit! What's going on?" Kristi—hair disheveled, still unshowered after the night of love-making, and sitting on one of the stools at the counter in the bathrobe Hanne kept for visitors—was vaguely watching the screen as she sipped her black coffee.

"Shh! Listen..." Hanne turned the volume up, the better to hear the newscaster.

"There is euphoria all over the country. No one would have predicted this extraordinary turn of events even just a few days ago..."

The cameras switched to a scene inside the Kremlin, where soldiers, including some high-ranking officers were leading Gusanov, Mendeleev and several other officials out of the president's office.

"...As we reported previously, at six pm sharp yesterday, General Morozov and his men entered the Kremlin unopposed, as guards from the crack regiment charged with protecting the president and the Kremlin stood by and saluted them. They made their way to Gusanov's office, where, we are told, the president and three of his closest aides were assembled. All four of these men apparently had signed and witnessed letters of resignation at the ready, and handed these to General Morozov, who, as we see in the picture, led the officials away to an unknown destination."

The camera showed a defiant Gusanov and a glum-looking Mendeleev climb into a black limousine that then sped away surrounded by a number of heavily armed vehicles.

"In a further surprising development, the Federal Assembly—the joint session of the Duma or Lower House and the Federation Council or Upper House—met throughout the night to elect a provisional government to rule the country until orderly elections can be organized across Russia in the six months to one year time frame. We learned this morning that the voting among representatives has resulted in a troika of Pavel Laptov, the minister for the Arctic in the previous government who triggered this crisis, General Morozov, the chairman of the joint chiefs of staff, and Oleg Kasyanov, the widely respected economist and finance technocrat, being chosen to head up the government. What is indeed remarkable is that in a country with as violent and autocratic a political history as Russia, the people came out into the streets and said no to an unjust war, speaking out to bring about a peaceful change of leadership…"

"That is indeed unbelievable," Kristi remarked.

"Yes. Good work, Pavel!"

Chapter 62

Copenhagen, Denmark—Morning, Monday, August 11, same day

"Thank you for seeing me, Lise. Especially under the circumstances."

"Well, we can't blame you for what happened. Denmark will just have to put this behind her, and see Greenland as its friend. And hopefully, a good one at that, given all the common history." The Danish minister of climate and energy flashed a smile at her guest before continuing. "Meanwhile, some accommodation will have to be made by both sides on some matters."

"Thank you for that, Lise. Indeed, that is why I am here, in my capacity as Greenland's minister for natural resources."

"Yes, I thought that this would be more than just a courtesy call."

"Lise, from when I worked here, I know that your ministry and the Geological Survey have an incredible amount of valuable material on Greenland's geology, geophysics and glaciology. We would love to be able to get our hands on all that, of course—especially since now it has little value to Denmark and a great deal to us. Or copies of whatever you won't part with. We would be prepared to pay, of course."

"What amount did you have in mind?"

"How does twenty million Danish Kroner sound?"

The Danish minister let out a low whistle and did a quick calculation in her mind. It was more than her budget for an entire year. "I could live with that. But, Hanne, how did you come up with that figure?"

"I guesstimated how much it might have cost over the years to send all those teams out to the field and do the research, and doubled that figure. Greenland can afford to be generous."

"Thank you, Hanne. I will assign your former colleagues Bent Pedersen and Andreas Hansen to work with you to gather the material. And good luck to you in your new job. You know that whenever you want to come back, we will always have a place for you here. Although not necessarily as minister." Another little grin from Hanne's former boss.

"Thank you, Lise. I am already learning how difficult it is to be one. Goodbye."

෴

Hanne called from the lobby of the ministry of climate and energy.

"*Dobruj Djen.*" She was surprised to get Pavel right away on his private cell number. "Laptov."

"Pavel...This is Hanne. Congratulations! You have done marvelously!"

"Well, thank you. But remember, none of this would have happened without you."

"Pavel, we have a final version of the draft treaty. You know, to set up the Arctic Nature Reserve. I will send it to you today unofficially."

"Excellent!"

"And we want to arrange a signing. Soon. Probably in Ottawa. When could you make yourself free, do you think?"

"Hanne, it is impossible to say. You know, things here are still very hectic, and there is so much to do. But this is very important, so I could make it over to Ottawa for a day sometime…Give me two more weeks, and then it will be easier, I am sure."

"Thank you, Pavel. You will receive an invitation in the next couple of days. And an official version of the draft treaty."

"Terrific!"

Hanne wondered for a moment whether she should tell the newly elected provisional president of Russia about the attack on her by a confessed operative of the Russian secret police who was working within the Green Liberation Front. But she decided against it: this was not the right time—Laptov had much bigger things to worry about, and if there was a spy ring to be mopped up, she needed more facts. Better to do it later.

"Good luck, Pavel."

"To you too, Hanne."

Chapter 63

Copenhagen, Denmark—Afternoon, Monday, August 11, same day

They were crowded into Anders's small office at police headquarters, all sipping bad coffee from the machine. Hanne recounted everything that had happened two mornings before in her hotel room and handed over the offending piece of wire.

"Thanks, Hanne. I am very sorry you had to be put through all this again. Lucky, though, that Andersen let up on the wire when he did."

"*Ja*. I would be dead if he hadn't."

"Okay, I need your help with something."

"Sure."

"Do either of you recognize this voice?" the inspector asked, as he fiddled with a cell phone—which he must have taken from Jens—and turned the speaker on.

"Come by. You gotta do it. I have what you need," a muffled voice said rapidly in Danish.

"Hmm…" Hanne looked at Kristi.

"Play it again," Kristi moved closer to the desk where the mobile was resting.

Jakobsen pressed a few buttons. "Here goes."

"Why that's Erik," Kristi piped up as soon as the voice finished. "I'm absolutely positive."

"Of course! You're right." Hanne joined in. "And that

all makes sense, then…" It was all dawning on her, what might have happened. "He's telling Jens to kill me, and that he should come and collect the weapon—the metal wire. The bastard. So Erik must have been behind it!"

"Erik…Larsen?"

"Yes," Hanne answered. "Jens's friend. He was the third Danish Green Liberation Front representative—along with Jens and Sven—you know, on that mission to protest the launching of a Russian submarine several years ago. The one I told you about, where they were arrested. And Erik was with Jens up at the Citronen Mine."

"It sounds though that they were in this together. And maybe it was this Larsen who killed your friend Sven Erikson. Especially since Jens adamantly protests that he didn't do it."

"That would make more sense to me," Hanne said.

"Yes, he's more of a killer type," Kristi agreed. "Erik wears metal and chains and that kind of stuff. Ugh…"

"Kristi…" Hanne thought for a moment that her friend was going to tell the inspector about her terrifying experience with Erik. But she backed off.

"Would you be willing to join me for the rest of the questioning?" Anders asked. "The two of you. I have a sense that we may get more of the truth out of Andersen. After all, you did tell me that he said he was in love with you…" He gave Hanne a pointed look, punctuated with a smile. "But let me first give the police in Greenland a call to pull this Erik Larsen in for questioning as soon as possible."

"Sure. I wouldn't mind seeing how Jens is doing."

೧೩೮೧

"Okay, Mr. Andersen, some friends have come by to visit you."

Jens looked up from where he was sitting, blond mop sticking out from arms folded on the table. Hanne saw that he was a shadow of himself, a broken ghost of a man. And so he should be, she thought to herself, after he tried to kill me. But she could not help feeling pity for him.

There was another man in the room, and in response to Hanne's questioning look, Jakobsen introduced him.

"Morten Espersen. State Security. Since you told me that Mr. Andersen had claimed to be working for the FSB."

"No lawyer?" Suddenly it seemed to Hanne that this was not entirely how things should be proceeding.

"Under the circumstances, Ms...." it was Espersen who answered.

"Kristensen." Anders filled in, a bit embarrassed.

"No. At least not at this stage."

"Hmm..."

"Mr. Andersen," the inspector started, not wanting his interrogation to be derailed. "I am going to continue our questioning. For one, the ladies have confirmed to me who that voice on your phone belongs to—remember, the one that you said was just a friend..." Jakobsen paused as Jens raised his head a few inches. "...Erik Larsen. Yes?"

Jens looked like he was about to cry, but just nodded in agreement.

"So he carried the murder weapon—this wire..."—and the inspector pulled out from a cloth bag the metal loop Hanne had turned over to him—"...and gave it to you with instructions to kill Ms. Kristensen. Is that correct?"

Jens, ashen faced, just sat there staring straight ahead.

"Did he also kill Sven Erikson?"

The prisoner did not answer.

"You told Ms. Kristensen you were working for the

Russian secret police. Did Mr. Larsen also work for them? In fact, could it be, Mr. Andersen, that you were recruited together when you were incarcerated in Russia several years ago? Was Sven Erikson also working for them, but there was somehow a falling out?"

Jens kept mum.

But Hanne piped up. "Look, Jens. You are being even more of an idiot, now. For God's sake, tell Mr. Jakobsen the truth, otherwise you will die in some rotten jail. They will level all kinds of spying charges against you and you will just disappear. They will pin Sven's murder on you, and that will be aggravated with the crazed attempt you made to kill me. Why did you do that? Did the secret police order it?"

"I told you, Hanne." He was prepared to answer his former lover. Or maybe finally it was the threat of rotting in jail, of disappearing. "Yes, they wanted you killed. You were getting in their way...In the way of their efforts to wrest the Arctic away from these capitalist pigs." And he gave Espersen a piercing look.

"What about Sven? He worked for them too? You all worked together, didn't you?"

And then Jens finally broke. "Sven? He was no different. Yes, we all agreed to work for them, of course we did, after what they did to us. Hanne, we became one and the same, with just one goal in our pitiful lives: to survive, to have the torturers stop the pain. You can't imagine what they put us through in jail, Hanne, during that week. You can't...No one can."

"I'm sure, Jens, and I feel sorry for you."

"Yes, goddamit. We all came back and worked for the Russians. They wanted to place operatives within the Green Liberation Front. Someone high in the FSB had the brilliant idea to turn it into one of their tools. With agents in the right place, any Front mission to protest a

Western oil platform or mine or industrial site could be turned into one that took it totally out of operation or even completely destroyed it. Things could just go wrong slightly, and poof, the mine can't produce iron for the next year, or there is a major oil spill, or even a nuclear meltdown. That's not what the Green Liberation Front may have had in mind...But oh, well, that's just too bad. It was economic warfare, pure and simple. And with any missions against Russia and its allies, their operatives within the Green Liberation Front—that is, we—would warn the authorities in time so they could stymie the action before it was carried out. Or work to be a spoiler in some other manner. A brilliant strategy, no?"

"So that was going to be Sven's role on the Shtokman mission..."

"Yeah, to let the Russian authorities know exactly when and where the operation was going to take place. But he balked, the idiot, and told Erik and me that if he was going to do that, he would also tell the Danish authorities about Citronen. Out of fair play, he said. But we were well beyond fair play, we were. He wanted us to go back to doing things the way we used to, no matter what the consequences, he said. But the Russians had made it quite clear to us that if any one of us backed out, we would all die. Erik panicked, and killed Sven...And then it was he who warned them about Shtokman."

"Boy, crazy. You guys are real whacko."

"Not if you had to go through what we did, Hanne. You cannot judge us, you...you bitch. You cannot judge us!" He collapsed onto his lap, sobbing. "You whoring bitch...And I loved you so much."

"At Citronen, you and Erik placed a much bigger charge than intended—that's why the huge explosion and all the damage? Because the Russians told you to?" Hanne did not stop probing.

A "yes" was audible in between the sobs.

"God."

"Was Erik the leader of your cell?" Anders asked.

"Yes. You might say." Jens lifted his face up, trying to rally, and looked at the inspector. "The Russians communicated through him. He and Sven both spoke Russian."

"Mr. Andersen, the police in Greenland told me when I was just now asking questions about your friend Erik that there was another death at Citronen when you—and I guess this Erik—were up there. An Australian geologist fell over a cliff. They say they have no leads at all, but are investigating it as possibly the result of foul play. Did you or Mr. Larsen have anything to do with that?"

Hanne felt a weakness in her legs when she heard this and had to sit down. She was desperately trying to decide whether to interrupt and tell the inspector the truth about Lock, but fortunately, just then, a police officer burst into the interrogation room.

"Oh, excuse me..." The policeman looked around, but continued straightaway. "Anders, we just got word from Nuuk that Larsen is already on a plane. Supposed to arrive in Copenhagen just before nine pm. Should we pick him up?"

"Of course. Make the arrangements, and I'll join you."

"Erik?" Hanne recovered enough to ask. "Boy, that was quick!"

"We'll have these bastards in jail by tonight," Anders said as he glanced first at his watch, then at his prisoner.

"The answer to your question, Inspector," Jens returned to the question posed to him, "is no. I had nothing to do with the death of an Australian professor. I have never murdered anyone."

"Thank you, Mr. Andersen." The inspector stood up, and came over to where Hanne and Kristi were sitting side by side opposite Jens. "And thank you, ladies. We have quite a bit more work to do here, and I have to discuss matters with Mr. Espersen before he has to go."

"Yes, of course, Inspector," the smooth man finally said something as he adjusted the crease on his pants.

"You have been very helpful and we don't need to take up more of your time. And I would still like to invite you both for a bottle of Torrontes," Anders continued, looking pointedly at Kristi. "But it may have to be put off again."

༺༻

Outside the police station, while Hanne waited for Kristi to visit the ladies' room, Hanne had a fleeting pang of guilt again about not owning up to the truth on Lock's death. But, damn it, she told herself, there's no need to: justice has been done, the bastard is dead, and there is no necessity to dredge all that up. It would only bring back all the pain and unpleasantness, just as the questioning in there had brought back all the suffering for Jens.

The difference, though was, that justice still needed to be carried out for the wrongs Jens and Erik had done.

༺༻

Hanne was glad to get an early night, in her own bed—the last few days had been exhausting, and she still had the long flight to Beijing to look forward to the next day. Despite her earlier plans, she had even said no to Kristi, and was about to take a sleeping pill when her cell phone rang.

"Jakobsen speaking. Hello, Hanne…"

"Why, Inspector. Hello, Anders."

"Sorry for the late call, but I just wanted to let you know that Mr. Larsen was not on that flight."

"What do you mean?"

"Apparently, the Greenland police think he may have had a passport in another name as well, and bought two sets of tickets. He must have boarded another plane in Reykjavik where he was changing—not the one for Copenhagen."

"Unbelievable!"

"All we know is that he was on that flight out of Nuuk. We are now checking passengers on all the other flights out of Reykjavik. But if you should hear from him…Or if your friend should—"

"Of course, Anders, I'll let you know. But I'm off to Beijing early tomorrow, so why don't I give you Kristi's number and you call her directly."

"Fine by me. Delighted…"

Hanne was happy to oblige, because she thought Kristi and the inspector would be well suited for each other. But for a moment, she had a pang of jealousy over sharing Kristi with yet another person.

Chapter 64

Beijing, China—Afternoon, Tuesday, August 12, next day

Hanne felt out of her element as she was ushered along the cavernous halls of the Huairentang. Lock's friend, Zheng Li, was a step in front of her, a soldier from the crack Central Guard leading the way. But she had not been her usual confident self ever since she landed in Beijing airport, was met by Li at the gate, ushered through VIP passport control and chauffeured straight to the Forbidden City. She thought back to her days up in Warming Land, last time exactly three years ago, how much she had enjoyed that. Maybe it wasn't so fulfilling to be a minister after all. She could not help but be impressed though: Rorsen had clearly prepared the way well for her to trigger such a smooth reception.

The guard knocked on the large door, pushed it open and showed Hanne and her companion inside. Li bowed deeply; the distinguished looking man behind the desk said something rapidly in Chinese to the fawning geologist and then stood up and came forward to greet Hanne.

"Ms. Kristensen, your reputation precedes you. I am very pleased to meet such a talented and beautiful woman." So this was Wen Shaojing, the general secretary of the Communist Party of China, who ruled over the most populous empire in the world ever. Li translated, surprisingly fluently.

"Thank you, Mr. General Secretary, I am honored that you were willing to receive me on such short notice." Indeed, now as a representative of Greenland, one of the least populous and newest countries on earth, Hanne thought.

"We understand that you have a proposal to make to us. One, which Comrade Li was concerned would alter the terms of our pact for us to participate in the development of your resources. Is this true, Ms. Kristensen?"

"On the contrary, sir, what Prime Minister Rorsen has asked me to discuss with you is something that builds on our existing agreement and places it in a globally peaceful context. I am not in any doubt that a statesman of your stature will see it as a positive development."

"Perhaps you can elucidate further, Ms. Kristensen."

"As you are aware, up until yesterday, the world stood in very grave danger of a fragile situation in the Arctic escalating into a world war. This was brought about by the bellicose stance of the régime in Russia, which has fortunately since then been deposed by a government that wants peace and an Arctic that is preserved for the benefit of all mankind, and not just for the five littoral states."

"Yes, Ms. Kristensen, China is watching these developments with great interest."

"This is a position also being advanced by the United States in the pursuit of peace, and Prime Minister Rorsen is taking the initiative to try to generate agreement among members of the Arctic Council around a draft treaty that would turn the high Arctic into a world nature reserve and a world heritage site. I have brought a copy of this treaty…" Hanne paused to open her briefcase and pull a file out, "…and China, as an observer in the Arctic Council, will very soon receive an invitation to a meeting where this document will be discussed and hopefully signed."

"But Ms. Kristensen, my question is: does this mean that Greenland will not fulfill its agreement with China to allow us to participate in the development of your resources? We put a great amount of effort into ensuring that Greenland was awarded jurisdiction over vast tracts of additional undersea territory. Mr. Li here, and your friend Professor McTierney—who, by the way, I understand perished under uncertain circumstances—played a significant part in helping Greenland gain those resources." Wen gave Hanne a pointed look as he said this.

Yes, you bastard, it was your underhanded meddling and their conniving that started this entire crisis, Hanne thought to herself. But instead, what came out of her mouth was, "We are very grateful for China's assistance."

Hanne, though, found that she could not go as far as to bring herself to thank Li and Lock in front of their master for their deceitful role. "...Yes, Professor McTierney died in an unfortunate accident."

"Our men claim that he may have died at the hands of some Russian agents who were posing as activists from that Green Liberation movement."

"Mr. General Secretary, I was there when it happened, and I can assure you, that was not the case," Hanne said emphatically before continuing, "But, if I may answer your concerns, Greenland intends to fully live up to its accord with China to cooperate in the development of its resource base with Chinese help and financial assistance. We do not believe that creating this Arctic Nature Reserve above latitude 80°North would impact on our ability to perform under our agreement. In fact, any resources in the newly awarded subsea territories would have been substantially more difficult and expensive to exploit than those found further south on the mainland or within the existing EEZ of Greenland. The money your government so generously committed to make available for the development of our resource base will, I can assure you, be more productively spent in these areas. As the first tangible example of our cooperation, your engineers and scientists are currently working with ours and the relevant companies to expand a new lead and zinc mine in Northern Greenland."

"I am delighted to hear that."

"And in terms of the international perspective, if I may add, this new Arctic Nature Reserve would not just impact Greenland, but would have a potentially much more significant effect on Russia's maritime territorial aims. By signing this treaty, they would agree to give up their current claim on almost half the Arctic based on the sector principle—which, though illegal, if it were to stay in place, could only be contested through major international confrontation. Moreover, they would also be prevented from winning jurisdiction in the future over additional subsea territory there through legal means. This new Arctic Treaty would not only turn the area above latitude 80°North and not within countries' EEZs before the recent UN awards into a world nature reserve and a word heritage site, but it would also supersede the UN Convention on the Law of the Sea as it relates to the Arctic."

"A very cogent argument, Ms. Kristensen." Hanne could see that she was winning.

"And the treaty would restrict all five Arctic littoral states from extending their EEZs in this manner above 80°North altitude in the future." Hanne saw in Wen Shaojing's eyes that this was indeed the *coup de grâce* as far as he was concerned: yes, this clearly meant that only China would have benefitted directly from this entire round of gamesmanship in the Arctic. And, of course, Greenland. China would walk away with access to

Greenland's resources and Greenland with its independence and twenty-five billion dollars of Chinese money. The rest of the world would have to settle for a nature reserve in the Arctic.

"Thank you, Ms. Kristensen. You can take the message to your prime minister that the treaty will have China's full support."

"Thank you, Mr. General Secretary." Hanne could tell that the meeting was over, as Li started his bowing and Wen said something in Chinese to him that he didn't translate.

But she was happy: mission accomplished!

CHAPTER 65

Copenhagen, Denmark—Evening, Thursday, August 14, two days later

She spotted them sitting there, snuggling at a corner table when she came into noisy Charlie's Bar. Knowing that Hanne would want to have a good rest after her long flight to Beijing and back for the short meeting with Wen Shaojing, plus all the stressful events she had been through in Greenland before, Kristi had sent a text message that Hanne only read when she woke from her sleeping pill enhanced Snow White sleep late in the afternoon.

"Anders needs to speak to you. And I want to see you. Charlie's, at seven."

"*Hej*, Kristi. *Hej* Anders," Hanne said, stooping to exchange kisses before she sat down next to Kristi.

"Hanne, I am so glad you're back. I missed you so..." Kristi hugged her friend.

"Hanne, thanks for coming. A glass of Torrontes—we've got a bottle going. Or something else?"

"Thanks."

Anders poured, and then raised his glass. "Hope your mission was successful. But that's really not why I wanted to see you..."

"It's about Erik." Kristi could not wait. "I told Anders."

"Well it's not that." Blushing, he took a sip of the wine

before he continued. "We are quite sure now that he killed Sven Erikson. But you know that we lost track of Larsen after he boarded a plane in Nuuk."

"Yes."

"He's wanted for murder. Possibly compromising state security. And now your story too, Kristi…"

"So…"

"Well, we have confirmed that a man resembling Larsen travelled with a Russian passport in the name of Mikael Resnikov and transferred to a flight bound for Minsk. You know, in Belarus. I am afraid he is out of our reach there."

"Why Minsk?"

"Well, that's the question we and State Security are asking as well. The only answer I can come up with, Hanne, is that Belarus is a rogue state. And even Interpol can't get to him there."

"So you'll never catch him."

"Certainly not any time soon." The waitress came over and Anders asked for another bottle of Torrontes.

"What about Jens? How is he?"

"We took him today to the Mental Health Center. The one at Bispjeberg."

"He did not look good, poor guy," Kristi added.

"Maybe I should go see him tomorrow."

"Can't. He's not allowed visitors. Plus, we are watching him closely in case there is any contact from Larsen."

"Hanne, why don't you just relax tomorrow," Kristi interrupted. "You deserve a break. You've been working really hard the last while."

"Hmm, not a bad idea."

"Let's you and I spend the day together. Shopping and stuff…"

But Hanne knew what her friend had in mind for at least a part of that day.

CHAPTER 66

Ottawa, Canada—Morning, Monday, September 21, five weeks or so later

Hanne was pleased. The Canadians had worked effectively and had pulled this high-level meeting of the Arctic Council together remarkably quickly, Hanne thought to herself, as, at twenty minutes before ten, she crossed Rideau Street from the Chateau Laurier to the Government Conference Centre. Richard had kept his promise.

She relished the notion of spending a few days after the conference with this humble and capable man whom she had grown to like a lot. Yes, even love, she dared to admit to herself. Really love. He had suggested last night over dinner at his favorite Thai restaurant that when this was all over they make a long weekend out of it, and go up to the cottage on the Gatineau River that had been his family's vacation home for generations. To de-stress, to chill out, he said. To make love, take long walks, enjoy the fresh air, she hoped, she knew. Hanne wished that the radiant Indian summer Ottawa was experiencing would stay long enough to warm the days and color the leaves for their country sojourn as well.

The meeting had already been in the calendar, but as simply a regular biannual Senior Officials Meeting of the Arctic Council. The Canadians had turned it into an extraordinary ministerial one—indeed a conference attended by several heads of government—to sign what, at first glance, seemed to be just an innocuous agreement to create another world nature reserve and world heritage site, but in fact, was a major peace treaty establishing a new world order.

They had managed to convene it with very little notice, getting the leaders of some, if not all, of the Member States and high-ranking ministers or officials from the Observer States and Observing Organizations to attend. The most difficult ones to get to agree, Richard had told her, had been the representatives of the so-called Permanent Participants of the Arctic Council, the six Arctic aboriginal communities that by right took part in the meetings but did not have a formal vote on any issue.

The Arctic Athabaskan Council was the last one to yield to the persuasion of the Minister for Northern and Indian Affairs. They agreed only when it was made clear to them that all the ancient rights of the indigenous peoples of the Arctic—to hunt, to fish, the freedom to roam—would be grandfathered and protected in the treaty, and that the document's purpose was in fact to ensure that there would be no encroachment by development or military entities above latitude 80°North.

What at first loomed as a very difficult issue—the status of Greenland in the Council—needed to be resolved before any meeting could take place. Denmark was the official member, and represented the so-called dependencies of Greenland and the Faroe Islands. But now that Greenland was independent, and in fact the one and only true polar littoral state in the constituency, it needed to have its own seat. So Richard and his friends in the Canadian Department of Foreign Affairs and International Trade engineered the obvious compromise solution: first getting Denmark to agree to separating out Greenland as a member in its own right, then obtaining, one by one, the consent of all the other Member States to add a ninth member. Formal ratification of Greenland's membership as an independent state by the Council was the first item on the morning's agenda.

The venue for the meeting was the magnificent former railway station built in 1912 by the Grand Trunk Railway Company, which had also owned the Chateau Laurier across the street. The Government of Canada had restored the Beaux Arts style building to its full grandeur and now used it for conferences such as this one.

Richard had given Hanne a tour the afternoon before, showing how they had converted the former departures hall—which had been sumptuously modeled on the Great Hall of the Baths of Caracalla in Rome—into a perfect setting for the gathering. He pointed out to her, how throughout the meeting, the map she had drafted of the Arctic showing the proposed nature reserve, would be projected on huge screens along the walls of the huge space.

જીજીજી

The meeting inside went off without a glitch. All the heads of government, cabinet ministers and officials attending were relieved that such an elegant solution had been found to defuse a potentially very dangerous international conflict, indeed one that might well have developed into a Third World War. And some, though not all, attendees were happy to see that the Arctic would be maintained in a pristine, environmentally safeguarded state.

Particularly happy were President Barlow and ruling troika member Laptov—who met for the first time at the meeting and were scheduled to have bilateral discussions right after. And of course, both Prime Ministers Prudhomme and Rorsen thanked their officials who had played a key role in bringing about this favorable outcome.

The treaty was duly signed by all parties, although a few small changes and additions to the draft Hanne had originally prepared had been negotiated during the intervening month or so and included in the final version. As a token of Hanne's contribution, immediately after the signing, Minister Laptov walked over to where she was sitting behind Prime Minister Rorsen and gave her the Mont Blanc fountain pen he had used to sign his name on the document. Although Hanne knew, that if anybody, it was Laptov who deserved to be congratulated, since it was he who had implanted the thought in her subconscious that this outcome was possible, and it was he who had masterminded and executed the dangerous Plan B, to lead a putsch against Gusanov and his gang of *siloviki* thugs in an attempt to save the Arctic and prevent World War Three. Hanne did something she had never done before: she gave the aging polar explorer a warm hug, whispering in his ear, "It was you who did it, you old fox, you who deserve the credit!"

But they left it at that, as Prime Minister Prudhomme came over to add his congratulations, having learned from Richard that these two were the key architects of this peaceful outcome.

CHAPTER 67

Ottawa, Canada—Afternoon, Monday, September 21, same day

Meanwhile, outside the Government Conference Centre, where this very congenial meeting of the leaders of the world to bring about such a peaceful solution for the crisis in the Arctic was taking place, the world was falling back into turmoil.

Hanne and Richard only found out about these terrifying new developments when, after several glasses of celebratory champagne at the post-signing reception, they decided not to drive the hour or so to Richard's cottage and rather went back to his cozy apartment. There, sitting on Richard's comfortable couch, snuggling close, they turned on his big-screen TV to watch the newscasts on the gathering of the Arctic Council they had just attended before deciding whether to go out for dinner or to order in.

But the lead report was not on what they had just experienced that day, nor on the always-turbulent Middle East. Rather, it was on a very troubling and unexpected consequence of the path that had led directly to the signing.

The CBC News anchor was, to say the least, excited in his comments: "Less than an hour ago, Euronews picked up this rather distressing feed from Belarus TV."

At the mention of Belarus, Hanne disengaged herself from Richard, who had his arm around her and was nibbling on her ear.

"That's where Erik went!" she blurted out.

The camera switched to a grainy picture showing three hooded men sitting at a table, with the central figure making a statement in Russian. The voiceover in English translated:

"We are prominent members of the Russian *siloviki*, now in a secure hiding place outside the country. We support the illegally deposed Andrei Gusanov, who himself is in voluntary exile, as president of Russia. We demand that the criminal régime of that American puppet Pavel Laptov step down and hand the reins of government back to Andrei Gusanov, the democratically elected president of our great country. We demand that the signing of the new Arctic Treaty by the usurper Laptov be voided and Russia's rightful claim to its half of the Arctic on the basis of the sector principle be honored by all nations. Russia will be restored to its former glory and we will not let anything stand in the way…"

"God, they are mad!" Richard blurted out.

"Shh! There is more."

"…We, the *siloviki* in exile, are in possession of enough nuclear material that we have set aside from several of the former Soviet nuclear sites, to devastate London, Paris, New York and Beijing. We warn the despot Laptov and his western henchmen that if we do not see progress towards the meeting of our demands within what we judge to be a reasonable time frame, one of these cities will suffer a nuclear catastrophe. And some time later, another, and then, if still nothing has happened, the third, and the fourth. Similarly, if there are attempts to capture us, or President Gusanov, or if there are further round-ups of our colleagues within Russia, we will order our operatives to carry out these attacks. Long live Russia!"

"Man! So what's next? It never ends…" Richard was stunned.

"Shocking."

"How can we prevent a catastrophe? We don't even know how much time we have!"

"Richard…" Hanne decided it was time for her to take charge. "Put it out of your mind for now."

"I can't."

"Yes, you can, my dear…"—and she stood, pulling him up by his hand—"…Now we go make love. We worry about all that another day."

Hanne gave Richard a deep kiss and led him into the bedroom.

EPILOGUE

Arctic Treaty – Hanne's Draft

THE ARCTIC TREATY

The Governments of Canada, the Kingdom of Denmark, the Republic of Finland, Greenland, Iceland, the Kingdom of Norway, the Russian Federation, the Kingdom of Sweden, and the United States of America, hereinafter referred to as "Contracting Parties",

And

The Governments of the Democratic People's Republic of China, the Republic of France, the Federal Republic of Germany, the Republic of Italy, Japan, the Kingdom of the Netherlands, the Republic of Poland, the Kingdom of Spain, the Republic of South Korea, and the United Kingdom, as well as the European Union, hereinafter referred to as "Associated Parties",

Taking into account the relevant provisions of the 1982 United Nations Convention on the Law of the Sea ("UNCLOS"),

Recalling the 1996 Ottawa Declaration on the Establishment of the Arctic Council,

Recognizing that it is in the interest of all mankind that the Arctic shall continue forever to be used exclusively for peaceful purposes and shall not become the scene or object of international discord;

Recognizing also that it is in the present and future interests of all mankind to preserve the Arctic environment and to create a zone free from resource extraction, industry and unlimited maritime traffic;

Convinced that the establishment of a firm foundation for the continuation and development of international co-operation within the context of the Arctic Council will promote these objectives and the progress of all mankind and further the goals and principles embodied in the Charter of the United Nations;

Have agreed as follows:

Article I

All sea, ice or land territories in the Arctic above 80°North latitude falling outside the Exclusive Economic Zones ("EEZ") of those Contracting Parties that extend beyond this latitude (See Annex 1 Map) will be declared a World Heritage Site and a World Nature Reserve (the "Arctic Nature Reserve" or the "Reserve").

Above 80°N latitude, no extensions of EEZs pursuant to UNCLOS will be permitted. In this respect, this Treaty supersedes the provisions (paragraph 76) of UNCLOS that permit such extensions provided certain conditions are met. Extensions agreed during the course of the year of the signature of this Treaty pursuant to UNCLOS will be rescinded.

Any Contracting Party may unilaterally extend the Reserve to include land, sea or ice-covered territories within its jurisdiction or EEZ as far south as the Arctic Circle, with appropriate notification to the Arctic Council. The provisions of this Treaty will apply to such extensions of the Reserve. Such extensions may be unilaterally revoked by the original proposing Contracting Party or its jurisdictional successor with a one year period of notification to the Arctic Council.

Article II

The Reserve shall be used for peaceful purposes only. There shall be prohibited, inter alia, any measures of a military nature, such as the establishment of military bases and fortifications, the carrying out of military maneuvers, as well as the testing of any types of weapons.

Under no circumstances will nuclear weapons be permitted in the Reserve. Nuclear explosions in, under or above the Reserve and the disposal there of radioactive waste material shall be prohibited.

The present Treaty shall not prevent the use of military personnel or equipment for scientific research, monitoring of compliance with the provisions of this Treaty pursuant to Article VII or for any other peaceful purpose.

Article III

No exploitation of resources shall be permitted in the Reserve. Specifically, there will be no mining or extraction of fossil fuel resources, commercial fishing or hunting permitted in the Reserve.

Notwithstanding the provisions of paragraph 1 of this Article, the historic rights of indigenous peoples to hunt and fish for their livelihood will be grandfathered within the

Reserve, unless the Contracting Parties, in consultation with the Permanent Participants of the Arctic Council, determine that a particular species is endangered.

Article IV

Any ships over 300 tonnes entering the Reserve will need to register with the Arctic Council and provide information on its

- flag
- purpose
- destination
- ice class
- cargo
- the amount of oil or other fuel it is carrying
- passengers and staff

Only ships meeting stringent design standards to maximally protect the environment will be permitted in the Reserve. The minimum design criteria are set out as Annex 2 to this Treaty.

Ships carrying hazardous material will be prohibited entry into the Reserve.

Article V

Freedom of scientific investigation in the Arctic, and cooperation toward that end, shall continue, subject to the provisions of the Treaty and notification to the Arctic Council.

In order to promote international co-operation in scientific investigation within the Reserve, the Contracting Parties agree that, to the greatest extent feasible and practicable:

information regarding plans for scientific programs in the Reserve shall be exchanged to permit maximum economy and efficiency of operations;

where practicable, scientific personnel shall be exchanged for expeditions and research within the Reserve; scientific observations and results from the Reserve shall be exchanged and made freely available.

In implementing this Article, every encouragement shall be given to the establishment of co-operative working relations with those Specialized Agencies of the United Nations and other international organizations having a scientific or technical interest in the Reserve.

Article VI

Each Contracting Party shall contribute the sum of USD 10 million within one month of ratification of the Treaty to finance the costs of carrying out the provisions of this Treaty.

Each Associate Party shall contribute the sum of USD 2 million within one month of ratification of the Treaty to assist in the financing of the costs of carrying out the provisions of this Treaty.

The Arctic Council shall, on an annual basis, assess the adequacy of the funding, and, if necessary, call upon both Contracting and Associate Parties to provide additional funding on a pro rata basis.

Article VII

A permanent Arctic Council Secretariat will be created to carry out the provisions of this Treaty. It will be the task of the Secretariat to carry out the provisions of this Treaty and to ensure compliance with it within the Reserve.

Each Contracting Party shall make available at its own cost a minimum of five and a maximum of ten of its nationals to serve on the Arctic Council Secretariat. The particular expertise of the individuals provided will be determined between the Director of the Secretariat and the Contracting Party.

Associate Parties may, at their discretion and cost, provide up to two individuals to work with the Secretariat. The particular expertise of the individuals provided will be determined between the Director of the Secretariat and the Contracting Party.

Notwithstanding the provisions of this Article, and with notification to the Arctic Council, aerial or maritime monitoring may be carried out at any time over any or all areas of the Reserve by any of the Contracting Parties.

Each Contracting Party shall inform the Arctic Council, the responsibility of which will be to notify all other Parties, of

a) all expeditions to and within the Reserve, on the part of its ships or nationals, and all expeditions to the Reserve, organized in or proceeding from its territory;

b) all stations within the Reserve occupied by its nationals and

c) any military personnel or equipment intended to be introduced by it into the Reserve subject to the conditions prescribed in paragraph 3 of Article II of the present Treaty.

Article VIII

In order to facilitate the exercise of their functions under the present Treaty, and without prejudice to the respective positions of the Contracting and Associate Parties (together the "Parties") relating to jurisdiction over all other persons in the Reserve, personnel of the Secretariat provided by Parties shall be subject only to the jurisdiction of the Party of which they are nationals in respect of all acts or omissions occurring while they are in the Reserve for the purpose of exercising their functions.

The Parties concerned in any case of dispute with regard to the exercise of jurisdiction in the Reserve shall immediately consult together with a view to reaching a mutually acceptable solution.

Article IX

Any or all of the rights established in the present Treaty may be exercised as from the date of entry into force of the Treaty whether or not any measures facilitating the exercise of such rights have been proposed, considered or approved as provided in this Article.

Article X

Each of the Parties undertakes to exert appropriate efforts consistent with the Charter of the United Nations, to the end that no one engages in any activity in the Reserve contrary to the principles or purposes of the present Treaty.

Article XI

If any dispute arises between two or more of the Parties concerning the interpretation or application of the present Treaty, those Parties shall consult among themselves with a view to having the dispute resolved by negotiation, inquiry, mediation, conciliation, arbitration, judicial settlement or other peaceful means of their own choice.

Any dispute of this character not so resolved shall, with the consent, in each case, of all Parties to the dispute, be referred to the International Court of Justice for settlement; but failure to reach agreement or reference to the International Court shall not absolve Parties to the dispute from the responsibility of continuing to seek to resolve it by any of the various peaceful means referred to in paragraph 1 of this Article.

Article XII

The present Treaty may be modified or amended at any time by unanimous agreement of the Contracting Parties. Any such modification or amendment shall enter into force when the depositary Government has received notice from all such Contracting Parties that they have ratified it.

Article XIII

The present Treaty shall be subject to ratification by the signatory States. It shall be open for accession as an Associated Party by any State which is a Member of the United Nations, or by any other State which may be invited to accede to the Treaty with the consent of all the Contracting Parties.

Ratification of or accession to the present Treaty shall be effected by each State in accordance with its constitutional processes.

Instruments of ratification and instruments of accession shall be deposited with the Government of Canada, hereby designated as the depositary Government.

The depositary Government shall inform all signatory and acceding States of the date of each deposit of an instrument of ratification or accession, and the date of entry into force of the Treaty and of any modification or amendment thereto.

Upon the deposit of instruments of ratification by all the signatory States, the present Treaty shall enter into force for these States and for States which have deposited instruments of accession. Thereafter the Treaty shall enter into force for any acceding State upon the deposit of its instruments of accession.

The present Treaty shall be registered by the depositary Government pursuant to Article 102 of the Charter of the United Nations.

Article XIV

The present Treaty, executed in the English and Russian languages, each version being equally authentic, shall be deposited in the archives of the Government of Canada, which shall transmit duly certified copies thereof to the Governments of the signatory and acceding States.

In Witness Whereof, the undersigned Plenipotentiaries, duly authorized, have signed the present Treaty.

Done at Ottawa this twenty-first day of September, two thousand and

Annex 1
Hanne's Map of the Arctic Nature Reserve

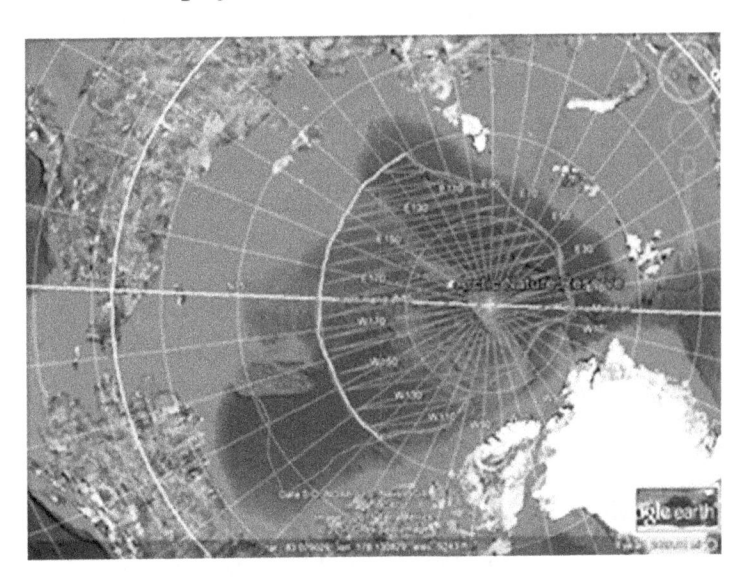

The Arctic Nature Reserve proposed in Hanne's Draft Arctic Treaty is the area cross-hatched in brown, bounded by Latitude 80N, except where the EEZ of a country protrudes above this Latitude, in which case the EEZ becomes the boundary.

The magenta line shows the EEZ boundaries, the green the relevant section of Latitude 80N that serves as the Reserve's boundary.

Distances are not exact.

[1] This and the following are adapted from "Last of the Firsts: Diving to the Real North Pole"–Flag #2 Report on the Arktika 2007 Expedition, Mike McDowell and Peter Bratson

[2] "Cold War Goes North," Alexander Gabuev, Kommer-sant, August 4, 2007

[3] "Trying to Head off an Arctic Gold Rush," Paul Reynolds, BBC News / Special Reports, May 29, 2008

[4] "Russia expands its Arctic ambitions," Neave Barker, Al Jazeera, May 12, 2009

[5] "Denmark joins race to claim North Pole", Ben Leapman, Sunday Telegraph, London, 12 August 2007.

[6] "Lomonosov Ridge, Mendeleyev elevation part of Rus-sia's shelf - report," Interfax Moscow, September 20, 2007

[7] "Cold War Goes North," Alexander Gabuev, Kommer-sant, August 4, 2007

[8] "National Security Presidential Directive 66 and Home-land Security Presidential Directive 25," January 9, 2009, The White House

[9] "Cannon slams Russian plan to drop paratroopers in Arctic," The Canadian Press, April 6, 2010

[10] "Admiral Urges Government to Stake Claim In the Arctic," South China Morning Post, March 6, 2010.

[11] "Great Game Moves to the Arctic," Robert Sibley, Ot-tawa Citizen, October 29, 2011

[12] Chinese billionaire plans massive Iceland resort," Brendan Coffey, Forbes, September 29, 2011

[13] "Riches at the North Pole–Russia Unveils Aggressive Arctic Plans," Matthias Schepp and Gerald Traufetter, Spiegel On-line International, January 29, 2009

[14] "After the Ice," Alun Andersen, Smithsonian Books, 2009, pages 106-108

[15] "Solving the Ridges Enigma of Article 76 of the United Nations Convention on the Law of the Sea," George Taft

[16] Re the Alpha-Mendeleev Ridge see CLCS 01.2001.LOS/USA UN Document, "United States of America: Notification regarding submission made by the Russian Federation to the Commission on the Limits of the Continental Shelf", March 18, 2002.

[17] "Canada Makes a Claim to the North Pole, https://www.livescience.com/65659-canada-claims-north-pole.html, June 7, 2019

[18] On thin ice: water rights and resource disputes in the Arctic Ocean, Andrew Wellington Cordier, Journal of International Affairs, March 22, 2008

[19] "After the Ice" by Alun Andersen, Smithsonian Books, 2009, pages 110-111

[20] "Russia presses ahead with Arctic research," The Voice of Russia, April 16, 2010

[21] "Russia scores scientific point in quest for extended continental shelf," by Levon Sevunts, The Barents Observer, April 5, 2019

[22] "Russia's Lawful Land Grab," Lawfare, August 11, 2016

[23] "Greenland and Denmark present claims relating to the Continental Shelf to the United Nations in New York," Ministry of Foreign Affairs of Denmark, Au-gust 18, 2016

[24] "Defining Canada's Extended Continental Shelf," Foreign Affairs & International Trade Canada, July 31, 2009

[25] "Canadian, Danish scientists set to map Arctic Ocean," Randy Boswell, CanWest News Service, October 19, 2009

[26] "Cannon slams Russian plan to drop Russian para-

troopers in Arctic," The Canadian Press, April 6, 2010

[27] "Sovereignty and UNCLOS," Fisheries and Oceans Canada, August 18, 2018

[28] "Canada files submission to establish continental shelf outer limits in Arctic Ocean," by Radio Canada Inter-national. The Barents Observer, May 27, 2019

[29] "Canada to submit its Arctic continental shelf claim in 2018," Radio Canada International, May 3, 2016

[30] "A Cold War in the Arctic Circle," Paula J. Dobriansky, WSJ Opinion, January 12, 2018

[31] UCLOS, Annex II, Article 8

[32] Huw Llewellyn, "The Commission on the Limits of the Continental Shelf: Joint Submission by France, Ire-land, Spain, and the United Kingdom," 56 INT'L & COMP. L.Q. 677, 680 (2007), quoted in "An Evaluation of Russia's Impending Claim for Continental Shelf Expansion: Why Rule 5 Will Shelve Russia's Submission," Brian Spielman, Emory International Law Review, Vol. 23, 2009, pg. 3177

[33] "The Future History of the Arctic," Charles Emmerson, Public Affairs, 2010, pg. 86

[34] Ibid, pg. 86

[35] Ibid, pg. 85

[36] Ibid, pg. 88

[37] "The Scramble for the Arctic," Richard Sale, Francis Lincoln Limited, 2009, p.138

[38] Ilulissat Declaration, May 28, 2008

[39] "Putin Calls for Arctic Cooperation at Arctic Conference in Moscow," The Arctic–The World Affairs Blog Network, Monday, September 27, 2010,

[40] "Riches at the North Pole–Russia Unveils Aggressive

Arctic Plans," Matthias Schepp and Gerald Traufetter, Spiegel On-line International, January 29, 2009

[41] Canada, Russia Build Arctic Forces," by David Pugliese and Gerard O'Dwyer, Defense News, April 6, 2009, quoting Yevgeni Patrushev, who wrote in the March 30 issue of the Rossiiskaya Gazeta newspaper.

[42] "Here's What Russia's Military Build-Up in the Arctic Looks Like," Robbie Gramer, Foreign Policy, January 25, 2017

[43] "A Cold War in the Arctic Circle," Paula J. Dobriansky, WSJ Opinion, January 12, 2018

[44] Russia begins its largest ever military exercise with 300,000 soldiers, The Guardian, September 11, 2018

[45] "Nato holds biggest exercises since Cold War to counter Russia's growing presence around the Arctic," Alec Luhn, The Telegraph, October 25, 2018

[46] "Greenland and Denmark present claims relating to the Continental Shelf to the United Nations in New York," Ministry of Foreign Affairs of Denmark, Au-gust 18, 2016

[47] This argument is based on some of the response to Canada's announcement of its new maritime registration rules for the Arctic as of July 1, 2010. See for example "New Canadian Shipping Rules May Contravene International Law" by Mia Bennett, July 9, 2010 on the Foreign Policy Association's blog site

[48] For example in "Russia's Arctic Strategy: Ambitions and Constraints" by Katarzyna Zysk, ndupress.ndu.edu, Issue 57, 2nd quarter 2010, pg. 103-110

[49] Although the USGS studies do show substantial natural gas resources in the Arctic, the 25% figure for oil and gas was a misstatement by a Christian Science Monitor journalist that was widely quoted thereafter and would probably have been picked up by Russian officials. See discussion in "Peak Oil– True or False," by Stephen Lendman, on www.rense.com or "An oil and gas Shangri-la in the Arctic?" by David Cohen, in Energy Bulletin, October 10, 2007

[50] Based on discussion in, for example, "Cold Wars: Russia Claims Arctic Land," by Carolyn Gramling, Geotimes, August 1, 2007

[51] Appears, for example, in a discussion skeptical of both Russian and Canadian / Danish claims in "Sea-floor Sunday #73: Territorial Disputes in the Arctic Ocean" by Brian Romans, September 19, 2010 in Wired Science Blogs / Classic Detritus on www.wired.com

[52] See for example "Magnetic Data on the Structure of the Central Arctic Region," by Elizabeth R. King, Isidore Zietz and Leroy R. Alldredge in The Bulletin of the Geological Society of America, January 21, 1965

[53] Some license is being taken here, since normally submissions are taken in order of receipt by the Commission and there is, as stated, already a formidable queue. As Elizabeth Riddell-Dixon points out in her excellent paper "Meeting the Deadline: Canada's Arctic Submission to the Commission on the Limits of the Continental Shelf" (available on the http://www.cpsa-acsp.ca website), in 2009, it was estimated that the Cuban submission - the 51st to be received - would not be re-viewed until 2030. However, given the

explosive nature of the Arctic controversy, and the players and potential resources involved, it is not out of the question that these submissions would be moved up in the Commission's agenda.

[54] Most of this and the following discussion is based on material found in, for example, "Russia's Claim in the Arctic And the Vexing Issue of Ridges in UNCLOS," by Marc Benitah, American Society of International Law Insights, November 8, 2007, Volume 11, Issue 27 and elsewhere.

[55] "Cold wars: Russia claims arctic land," by Carolyn Gramling, in Geotimes, August 1, 2007

[56] Here I have the fictitious Dr. Novikov refer to studies by the eminent German Marine Geophysicist, Wilfried Jokat, who with his colleagues did a lot of seminal re-search on the geophysics of the Arctic Ocean.

[57] See for example, "Physiographic provinces of the Arctic Ocean seafloor," by Martin Jakobsson, Arthur Grantz, Yngve Kristoffersen and Ron Mcnab in the Bulletin of The Geological Society of America, 23 February 2003

[58] "Magnetic Data on the Structure of the Central Arctic Region" by Elizabeth R. King, Isidore Zietz and Leroy R. Alldredge in the Bulletin of The Geological Society of America, January 21, 1965

ABOUT THE AUTHOR

Born in Budapest, Hungary, Geza Tatrallyay escaped with his family in 1956, immigrating to Canada. He has a BA in Human Ecology from Harvard University, and, as a Rhodes Scholar, attended Oxford University, obtaining a BA/MA in Human Sciences followed by an MSc in Economics from London School of Economics and Politics. Geza represented Canada as an épée fencer in the 1976 Olympic Games in Montreal. His professional experience has included stints in government, international organizations, finance and environmental entrepreneurship. He has thirteen published books—five thrillers, three memoirs, four poetry collections, and a children's picture storybook. His fascination with the Arctic and environment goes back to his student days when he spent two summers there working for the Geological Survey of Canada.